Pulling Power

CHERYL MILDENHALL

BLACK
lace

Black Lace novels are sexual fantasies.
In real life, make sure you practise safe sex.

First published in 1997 by
Black Lace
332 Ladbroke Grove
London W10 5AH

Typeset by CentraCet, Cambridge
Printed and bound by Mackays of Chatham PLC

ISBN 0 352 33139 9

Chapter One

The sun was strong for early June, its reflection dazzling as it bounced off the car in front. Its glare forced Amber to avert her gaze for just a moment. Despite the tinted visor on her racing helmet she was finding the bright light difficult to cope with. And this drive was so important. It was her final test run of the morning and, if she stuck rigidly to the racing line as she intended, probably her fastest lap time ever.

Porsche racing was her life. Her first and probably only true love, she reflected wryly, depressing the clutch pedal and thrusting the gearstick into third as she approached Luffield. It was the penultimate corner of the Silverstone Club circuit and in a moment she would be flashing past Carla in the pits. Glancing up and to her left as she rounded Woodcote Corner she saw her best friend and chief mechanic.

Carla's blonde hair was ruffled by a slight breeze as she hung over the pit wall. And in her hands was a board which showed Amber her average speed – 79.82 mph.

Seeing this, Amber gunned the accelerator and embarked on another circuit with grim determination. All this practice and she still wasn't fast enough!

Grinding her teeth as she set out on this, her final lap

before lunch, Amber vowed that this one would be it. She had to break into the low eighties come hell or high water. As she rounded Maggots Curve and floored the accelerator to take the fast Club Straight, she glanced briefly at the wing mirror.

A sleek blood-red Alfa Romeo was coming up behind her at such a rate she felt her stomach clench with envy. Looking at her speedo she realised that, as she was doing 140 mph, the Alfa had to be approaching 170. By rights she should move out of the way and let the quicker car streak past her. But Amber was Amber and therefore extremely determined. Sod it, she *was* going to stick to her racing line, let the Alfa driver fend for himself.

The vehicle bridge that spanned the track loomed in front of her, the Alfa Romeo almost touching her rear bumper. If she was going to move, now was the time. Staring resolutely ahead, mentally preparing for a quick gear change as she went into Brooklands, Amber missed the actual moment the Alfa Romeo left the track. The next time she saw it was a split-second later as it spun in the gravel beside her. She gave a mental shrug – oh well, too bad.

Still not satisfied with her overall speed, Amber did one last final lap before pulling off the track and into the pits where Carla and the rest of the crew were waiting for her. Their expressions and body language were ecstatic. Her last lap speed had been an impressive 81.49 mph – a good morning's work by anyone's estimation.

Expecting Carla or one of the male mechanics to open the door for her, Amber was startled when a bronzed young man with flashing dark eyes flung it open and dragged her bodily from the car. Holding her tightly by the collar of her emerald green racing overalls, he thrust his face close to her visor and began to yell in rapid and, as far as Amber could tell, abusive Italian. Despite her amazement, Amber couldn't help noticing how good-looking he was for an angry young man.

Also dressed in racing overalls – though his were red and white – he had stripped down the top and tied it around his waist to reveal an enviably muscular torso. Perspiration glistened on his olive skin as he continued to rant and rave. Then he pulled his free arm back. In the split second that Amber realised he intended to strike her, several mechanics rushed forward to restrain him.

With adrenalin already coursing through her at the speed of light – as it always did when she was in racing mode – Amber found herself shaking. Reaching up she pulled the helmet from her head, then removed the fireproof balaclava she wore underneath. With undisguised amusement she watched the changing expression on the struggling man's face. It turned from anger to incredulity as she shook out her shoulder-length curls, which were the same shade as her name.

'Hi,' she said, holding out her hand with deliberately casual aplomb, 'I'm Amber Barclay and it looks to me as though we have some sort of problem to sort out.' She smiled broadly, her deep blue eyes twinkling as she added, 'You'll have to forgive me, though. I don't speak a word of Italian.'

'OK. OK, *scusi*. I didn't realise she's a *lady*.' The Italian glanced at the mechanics who were still holding him, though more lightly since he had stopped struggling.

At Amber's nod of assent the men released him. Nevertheless, they hovered in the background as the Italian reached out and took Amber's outstretched hand. Glancing down, she noticed how pale her skin looked in comparison to his. To her delight he raised her hand to his lips and kissed it, his lips soft as velvet. Now the adrenalin coursing through her was for a different reason. Only one thing affected Amber as deeply as racing or money, and that was sex. And this man reeked of it.

Even as she accepted his offer of lunch in the VIP restaurant she cursed herself for succumbing to the cliché of Latin charm. But why shouldn't she? she reasoned. Carla had warned her that the car would not be ready for testing again before three o'clock at the earliest. Which left her with plenty of time to pursue her carnal inclinations.

Over a delicious meal of poached salmon and asparagus, washed down with lime-flavoured mineral water, Amber discovered that the Italian driver's name was Eduardo Santanini. Furthermore, he was testing his Alfa Romeo prior to entering the British Touring Car Championship.

'I'm already the top name in *Supertourismo*,' he explained, in decadently dark accented tones that liquidised Amber's insides. 'To win the *Inglese* Championship always has been my fate. I feel it deep in here.' He punched the left side of his ribcage lightly.

The warmth Amber was feeling now had nothing to do with the temperate weather. Or the double layer of her racing overalls and fireproof underwear. It had everything to do with the embarrassment she felt for having forced him off the track, however, and the way his uncompromising gaze made her feel as though her clothing was made of cling wrap.

'*No importa*,' he assured her, after she apologised for the third time for sticking to the racing line, 'I understand.'

She smiled. He had a slightly faltering way of pronouncing words which she found incredibly attractive. And that was if she closed her eyes momentarily, or glanced away from him. If she allowed herself to look at him, for her gaze to take in his unruly dark wavy hair and the soft, boyish features which bore testimony to his youthful 21 years, Amber found herself losing a battle she had not wanted to fight in the first place.

By the time they had waved away the dessert menu and opted for cups of strong dark espresso instead, Amber was in no doubt that they were going to indulge the physical attraction that existed between them. The only question was, where?

Silverstone, she mused, as she dropped two lumps of demerara sugar into her coffee, was not renowned for providing comfortable locations for lovemaking. At best, its facilities only slightly exceeded the merely functional.

'I – that is – we, the team, have a motor home,' Eduardo offered, as though he could read her salacious thoughts.

Amber chuckled to herself. Of course he could read her thoughts. Hadn't she gone out of her way to exploit every one of her seduction tricks? Licking her lips, playing with her hair, deliberately stroking her own body and constantly reaching out to touch the back of his hand – these were all part of her repertoire.

She nodded and by unspoken agreement they stood up. Apologies had been made and accepted long before, now a deal had been struck. All that was left for either of them to do was deliver the goods.

Sunlight streamed through the slatted blinds that obscured the windows of the huge Iveco motor home, marking golden trails across their naked bodies. They lay side by side, discovering each other properly by sight and touch.

Amber saw no reason to tell Eduardo that she was 28. There was nothing about her slight, angular body to give away her real age. And her official press pack stated that she was a mere 23. For racing purposes it suited Amber to be younger. The older a driver got the less competitive they were assumed to be, which didn't go down too well with potential sponsors.

More important was that she kept her true identity as separate from her racing persona as possible. Even if that meant assuming a false name, wearing a wig and lopping five years off her real age.

'Cara, cara, so beautiful.' Eduardo's voice was as seductive as his caress as his hand skimmed her breasts.

Amber sighed and stretched luxuriously, arching her back so that the small, pointed mounds seated high on her ribcage were thrust into more prominence. Her nipples hardened as he bent his head to suck them, sharp darts of desire racing down her body to pierce her womb.

She allowed her thighs to drop open, drawing in her breath as the warm breeze wafted over her naked sex to dry the moisture that gathered so copiously there.

Reaching out, she stroked his thick hair away from his forehead and gave a long sigh of satisfaction.

His dark eyebrows beetled as he glanced up at her face. 'You are happy?' he asked, an uncertain smile tweaking the corners of his full-lipped mouth.

'Very,' Amber murmured. 'What's the time?'

As he held up a darkly tanned wrist, bearing an outrageously expensive metal-strapped watch, she saw that it was only a quarter to two. There was a lot to be said for a quick, passionate fuck, she mused, remembering the way they had fallen on each other the moment the door to the motor home had closed behind them. But foreplay was her real heart's desire. As she eyed his strong fingers and sulky mouth she had the distinct impression that he would prove very good at it, given a little encouragement.

Raising her hips from the motor home's one double bed, she rotated them lewdly and reached down to stroke her own sex.

'We've got a lot of time left,' she murmured suggestively as she splayed her fingers across her hairless mound. 'Now what do you suppose we could do next?'

'This,' Eduardo said, seizing on her blatant hint, 'is the Club Straight.'

Amber held her breath as his fingertips danced lightly down her torso. She sighed. 'Mm-hm.'

His smile increased, lust glittering in his dark eyes. 'Here,' he continued as his fingers swirled around her navel, 'is the tight Brooklands corner, going around to Luffield. And now – ' he paused, his touch becoming so tantalising that Amber groaned loudly ' – we drive past the grandstands – hurrah, hurrah, three cheers for the champion! – and into the pits.'

So saying, his fingers negotiated her hand, which still lay protectively over her pubis, and dived straight into the waiting wetness of her vagina.

6

Amber gasped. She couldn't help herself. His voice was as mesmerising as his touch; his words as playful as his final action was insolent. She felt his fingers probing inside her, stroking the sensitive, fleshy walls of her most secret domain as he slithered down the bed to view her sex at close quarters.

His hair, like spun silk, stroked her belly and the tops of her thighs as he moved his head. She could no longer see his face, just the back of his head. Snatching her hand away, she gave herself up to the delectable sensation of his soft lips brushing the pale, fleshy purse of her vulva.

Being naturally dark, Amber had spent weeks agonising over the possible ways she could conceal her true colouring. It was easy to cover her real hair with wigs and to bleach her finely arched brows and shade them with eyebrow pencil. But her pubic hair was a different matter altogether. She didn't dare attempt to bleach it. Nor could she pretend to be a blonde, or a redhead, or whatever, when her bush was naturally thick and black. The only solution had been to shave it all off. It was a nuisance but better than being caught out. If there was one thing Amber dreaded more than anything, it was the possibility of discovery before her mission was successfully completed.

'This is so unusual,' Eduardo murmured, raising his head from between her legs for a moment. 'I like.'

Amber assumed he was talking about her shaven sex. Funny, she thought, a lot of men seemed to find it a real turn-on.

'I like,' she said, wriggling her hips by way of encouragement. 'I like feeling your mouth there, don't stop.'

I *like*. She almost laughed aloud. Like it? She loved it. Oral sex, either giving or receiving – but mostly receiving – was fabulous. Men who didn't indulge were given short shrift by her. No excuses accepted. At this stage in her life she was way beyond sublimating her own needs for the sake of her partner's feelings. She'd done that with Greg and look where it had got her.

Not only had her former lover left her feeling frustrated and inadequate, he had also talked her into going into business with him. Even though Eduardo was doing magical things to her, she could not help recollecting the hurt that Greg had caused her – it was still so acute.

His contribution to their joint venture had entailed spending long hours attending important and horrendously expensive lunch meetings with potential clients, while she was left to manage their finances singlehanded. Finally, when they had reached their overdraft limit, Greg's solution had been to run off, leaving her with a stack of debts and creditors banging on the door of her South London flat day and night.

Her beloved Porsche – safely hidden in a barn at the farm belonging to Carla's brother, Frank, when it wasn't being raced – was the only good thing to have come out of her relationship with Greg. An alliance which, for want of a stronger description, had turned out to be a complete disaster.

Anyone attempting to take her car from her would do so over her dead body. Not only was racing her overriding passion, she also stood a very real chance of winning the Xtreme Oil Challenge Cup and the fifty thousand pound prize that went along with it. If she were to succeed, all her problems would be over.

Annoyed with herself for allowing her thoughts to intrude on this unexpected interlude with Eduardo, Amber forced her mind to clear of everything except the eroticism of his touch.

His fingers were still inside her, stroking, scissoring, plunging in and out. And his mouth was everywhere else, sucking the soft lips of her blossoming sex, his tongue stroking the delicate folds of her inner labia and swirling tantalisingly around her clitoris. The teasing lightness of his touch was sheer torture but, she had to admit, as she ground her sensitive flesh unashamedly against his lips, it was torture of the most exquisite kind.

Forcing herself not to give in to the erotic lure of instant orgasm, she hung on, willing her body and her mind to continue slowly along the ascending path of pleasure. It was difficult to hold back. His caresses were unbelievably experienced for such a young man. She liked the way he paid attention to detail, seeking out and finding her G-spot and alternating the movements of his lips and tongue.

She opened her eyes a fraction and gazed thoughtfully at his back. Long, lean and toasted brown, it tapered from broad, quite muscular shoulders to a neatly rounded bottom. She liked men's bums, and considered herself quite an aficionado. Round, tight ones like Eduardo's were the best kind, she always thought, especially when clad in denim. Lazily, she allowed her gaze to travel up his spine again. The definition of the musculature on his upper body did not surprise her. Racing drivers had to have strong arms and shoulders to cope with the demands of the cars they drove.

She herself had quite a well toned figure. Not because Porsche racing was particularly arduous but because she preferred to look her best. If she had one fault it was a tendency towards perfectionism, which was one reason why finishing anything less than top in her chosen sport would not do. Not by a long shot.

She reached out and ran her fingertips lightly down the side of Eduardo's body and over the curve of his buttocks. From where she lay she could touch both of them and delighted in stroking a single fingertip down the cleft between, before moving her hand under them to cup his balls. Covered with thick, black curly hair, so reminiscent of her own lost thatch, they felt warm and weighty. She could almost feel the virility surging inside them, and pictured the young driver producing a clutch of sloe eyed, glossy haired bambinos.

Damn! Her mind raced suddenly. She was out of condoms, but did Eduardo have a packet secreted about the motor home? Earlier, even in the heat of the moment, she had remembered to fumble for the emergency condom she kept in her purse. But that was it. If he wanted to make love to her again, he would have to produce some of his own.

Though he showed no indication that he was tiring of his oral efforts, Amber realised time must be moving on. Now she could indulge herself in the orgasm she craved so desperately. Closing her eyes again and moving her hands to her breasts, she stroked herself mindlessly as she concentrated on the sensation of her approaching climax.

Outside the motor home she could hear the muffled roar of engines firing up and the vague mélange of instructions being shouted across the pits. Inside, all seemed peaceful save for the soft, liquid sound of Eduardo's fingers moving in and out of her and her own breath, faster and harsher than his.

A moment later she heard a soft whimpering which she realised was her own. Her thighs trembled. She felt so hot down there, between her legs. Eduardo's lips were both soothing and exciting; balm and stimulant. She moaned as his fingers slid out of her, and a wet trail trickled from her body. Her vagina felt bereft, wide open and aching for something else to fill it. She imagined it grasping at thin air, wanting to cling to something, convulsing powerfully.

A fraction higher, she felt her clitoris pulsing between his lips. He moved his mouth away and she sensed the tiny bud straining, needing to be touched. All at once his tongue flickered across it, back and forth, around and around. She clutched at her breasts, her short rounded nails digging into the soft flesh. Her whole body was on fire now, careering down a dark tunnel towards the ultimate pleasure. Waves of it engulfed her, slick and warm, desire bursting from every pore as she thrashed and groaned on the hard foam mattress.

'Shh! Everyone will hear you,' Eduardo warned as she gave full vent to her ecstasy. He glanced over his shoulder at her but, despite his urgent entreaty, his expression was not of panic but of undisguised desire.

Feeling the onslaught of pleasure finally recede, Amber lay spent, her shuddering body glistening with the sheen of perspiration.

'I don't care,' she whispered hoarsely, attempting a shaky smile.

She noticed his smile increased. It curved up to touch the corners of his eyes as she scrambled on to her knees and pushed him back against the bed. She licked her lips, making it obvious to him what she intended to do next.

'You crazy woman,' Eduardo said as she lowered her head. 'I love you.'

No, Eduardo, you don't, Amber thought as she flicked out her tongue and stroked it along the length of his stiffening shaft, but you won't forget me in a hurry, either.

As it turned out the motor home was equipped, not just with one box of condoms but a whole drawer full. Essential items for any self-respecting motor racing team, Amber mused, as she ripped one of the foil packets open with her teeth. It made her smile to think of the procession of pit groupies who must have passed through the hallowed portals of the Italian team's Iveco.

Contrary to popular belief not all racing drivers were automatically attractive. But somehow that did not stop the powerful chemical allure of grease, sweat, excitement and power from breaking down the reserves of even the sanest female spectator.

Shame it didn't appear to work both ways, Amber reflected wryly. While the male contingent of drivers seemed to have women climbing all over them, the elite band of female racers to which she belonged was placed on a pedestal and worshipped from afar. Fan mail was one thing, fanciable males chasing after female drivers quite another.

She smiled down at Eduardo as she positioned herself over him. His cock was large and the condom a snug fit. The first time they had screwed had been passionate, desperate and over in a flash. This time she intended to make the most of it.

As she slid down over his cock, Amber fancied her vagina gave a sigh of relief. It felt good to have him

11

inside her, she liked the powerful sensation of her body encompassing something so hard and virile. Liked it – who was she kidding? She loved it. And most of all she enjoyed being on top.

Lying down, Eduardo appeared younger somehow, his expression at once questioning and blissful. She let out a soft moan as his hands came up and cupped her breasts. And, as she started to rise and fall, he held them, his gaze seemingly transfixed.

'Bellissima,' he kept murmuring as Amber rode him. 'Bellissima, bellissima!'

As far as Amber was concerned his compliments were as good as talking dirty. She felt her body thrill to the tone of his voice and the obvious pleasure he exhibited.

His fingers were gripping her breasts now, his efforts concentrated on her nipples. He held them between the thumb and forefinger of each hand, squeezing the tender buds until she cried out. The pain was exquisite. Almost acidic in its intensity, it left her with a rapidly spreading warmth that enveloped both her breasts. When the sensation faded he pinched them again, as though he could tell when it was the right moment to do so.

She reached behind her and felt for his balls again. This time they no longer felt huge and soft but rock hard. They were drawn up against the base of his cock like chestnuts clinging to a sturdy branch. And trickling down them was the creamy fluid of her own arousal. Capturing some on her fingertip, she raised it to her lips and deliberately caught his gaze before she sucked.

He groaned. He called her a witch – a *tentatrice*.

Amber smiled wickedly and did it again. The third time she held her fingertip to his lips and watched him relish the taste of her.

The provocation seemed to do something to him. All at once he took her by surprise, suddenly rolling her over on to her back, his cock momentarily slipping out before being thrust back in. He was in control now, his actions assured her. And he began to pound into her with such intensity that it left her gasping.

12

The crashing waves of her orgasm precipitated his. She smiled inwardly as she felt her climax recede and watched him lose himself in his own private moment of pleasure. A man in control of her? That would be the day.

Loud banging on the window at the rear of the motor home broke them both apart eventually. Scrambling into his boxer shorts, Eduardo rushed to the window and knelt on the padded banquette that ran underneath it. He raised the bottom edge of the blind and peered out. Then he glanced over his shoulder at Amber.

'I think it is for you,' he said, dropping the blind abruptly.

Muttering curses, Amber glanced around for something to cover herself with. When she couldn't find anything she pulled her fireproof vest over her head and went to see who was at the window.

It was Carla, looking red faced and more than a little annoyed.

'Come on, you dozy cow, I've been looking everywhere for you,' she shouted through the pane of glass.

'Problem?' Amber asked, raising an eyebrow. Carla, she noticed, looked as though she were about to burst a gasket. Realising it wouldn't do to upset her, she smiled and added quickly, 'OK. Don't worry, I'll be right out.'

Dropping the edge of the blind, Amber stood up, stretched, then began to gather up her clothing. She sat down again and pulled on first her fireproof leggings – which looked like old men's long johns – followed by a pair of fireproof socks. As she glanced up she noticed that Eduardo, still undressed save for his boxer shorts, was watching her intently as he reclined on the bed.

'So sexy in those clothes,' he murmured, grinning at her as he gave her a cheeky wink. 'Look what you do to me, *cara*.' He pulled down the front of his boxer shorts to reveal a brand new erection. 'My body does not lie.'

Tempted though she was by the sight of his stiff cock, Amber was forced to resist. 'Sorry, Eduardo,' she said.

'Much as I'd like to stay here with you I've got to go. According to my crew chief there's a problem with the car.'

'That young girl, she's your crew chief?' Eduardo asked with a look of amazement.

Amber gave him a wry look as she pulled on her racing overalls. 'Cut the macho bullshit, Eduardo. Carla's the best mechanic I've ever come across.'

She noticed he looked doubtful and felt a flicker of real annoyance. Typical bloody man, she though. He probably believes in women being barefoot and pregnant.

'Well,' she added airily, tucking her gloves in one pocket and her purse in the other, 'thanks for lunch and everything. It's been nice.'

She knew the word 'nice' didn't do justice to their interlude but she felt like punishing him just a little bit for his remark about Carla. Love me, love my crew chief, was her motto. She slipped her feet into dark green racing boots and bent down to tie the laces. In the next instant she was surprised to feel a pair of arms encircle her waist. Something long and hard was nudging her buttocks insistently.

'Please, Amber, don't go yet,' Eduardo murmured in her ear.

Sighing, she wriggled out of his grasp. 'I have to,' she said, pleasantly but firmly. 'One thing you would do well to learn about me, Eduardo, is that my car always comes first.'

The first thing Amber noticed when she walked into her garage in the pits was that the bonnet was still up on the Porsche. Carla, along with Brett and Gary – two male mechanics who were friends of Frank – were standing around the car looking glum.

'What's up?' Amber asked as she walked past the car and glanced under the bonnet.

'Heater hose,' Carla said shortly. 'We'd just finished prepping the car when I noticed a water leak.

Amber shrugged. 'So? It won't take a minute to change, will it?'

'Not if we had a new one to put on it wouldn't,' Carla replied, glancing at Amber sheepishly under her pale blonde lashes.

Amber looked askance at her, fuming inwardly. Of all the . . .! Spare engines and gearboxes were a bit thin on the ground, but to forget something as simple and inexpensive as a spare hose was unbelievable.

'I know what you're thinking,' Carla said quickly, 'and if you want to blame anyone, blame me. I should have checked the spares box last night but I didn't.'

'You went out last night,' Amber pointed out evenly. She was anxious not to let the extent of her annoyance show. 'And for the first time in ages, I might add. I can't really blame you for not concentrating on the car for once. That guy – whatshisname? – was gorgeous.'

'Rory,' Carla supplied for her, a smile touching the corners of her thin, pink-lipped mouth. 'Yes, he was rather horny. I didn't get back until gone three, as you probably noticed.'

'Not me,' Amber lied, 'I was dead to the world by ten thirty.' She turned to glance at the car again. 'Have you tried begging, borrowing or stealing from one of the other teams?'

Carla glanced down and scuffed the toe of her Doc Marten along the dust covered floor. 'Not really. I just asked the boys next door and I tried Ted's crew but neither could help.'

'So tough and yet so shy,' Amber teased her friend. 'OK, give me a minute. I'll do the rounds of the other teams and see what I can come up with.'

Carla brightened. 'Any hose'll do,' she said. 'As long as it's a good nine inches we can cut it to fit.'

'Right.' Amber threw down her gloves and purse on the work bench that ran the length of the wall behind her and stuck her hands in her pockets instead. 'Won't be long.'

* * *

Strolling along the pits, enjoying the sunshine, Amber glanced automatically into each garage. Today being a test day there was a bewildering variety of cars of all makes and classes. Hesitating for just a moment outside Eduardo's garage, she admired the sleek bodylines of his Alfa Romeo before moving on.

In the next garage was a red Porsche 968 which belonged to fellow racer Darren Standish. Like Amber, he, too, had dropped out of the more prestigious Pirelli Production Championship, believing he stood a better chance of winning the less competitive Xtreme Oil Challenge. As things stood at the moment, he was lying in a respectable second place behind Amber's top position in the points championship.

Amber immediately spotted the familiar, sandy haired figure of Darren. He was dressed in white overalls which were covered with the badges of about twenty minor sponsors. Some people had all the luck, she reflected, remembering how she had practically had to sell her soul to the devil to get each one of her five sponsors. And the only reason she had a major sponsor was because she worked freelance for SmartTech computers, the company in question, as a saleswoman.

'Amber, hello, what can I do you for?' Darren loped toward her, wiping his hands on a greasy rag.

'I'm looking for a bit of hose,' Amber said. 'About nine inches,'.

Dropping the rag, Darren stuck his hands in his pockets and rocked back and forth on his heels. He glanced over his shoulder at his team of four mechanics.

All strapping boys, Amber thought as she cast them a winning smile – with only half a brain between the lot of them.

'Here lads, Amber's looking for someone to slip her a length,' Darren called out to them. 'She says about nine inches will do. Can any of you oblige?'

'Mine's twelve inches but I don't use it as a rule,' one of them quipped unoriginally as he stepped forward and leered at Amber. Glancing over his shoulder he grinned at Darren and the rest of the crew, who all laughed and called out lewd comments.

Eyeing his shaven head and crooked nose with distaste, Amber resisted the immediate urge to respond with something sarcastic. Instead, she clenched her teeth and forced herself to smile back at him.

'It's my heater hose,' she explained, 'it's blown and I haven't got a spare. If you could just – '

'I'll tell you what, darlin',' the bullet headed mechanic interrupted. Leaning forward as he spoke, he covered Amber with beer fumes. 'You do me a little favour and I'll do you one.'

'No thank you,' Amber said, forcing herself to stand her ground and not grimace. 'If you don't have a hose I can buy off you, I'll go and find someone who does.'

To her relief Darren put a protective arm around her shoulders. 'All right, Stomper, leave it out,' he said, adding, 'Of course we've got a hose you can have, Amber. Take no notice of him.' He cast Stomper a withering glance. 'Tell you what, love, you go back to your garage and I'll sort one out and bring it along in a minute.'

Amber gave him a genuine smile. 'Thanks, Darren, you're a mate.'

He winked. 'Don't mention it, just let me take the win at Zandvoort. I've got a regular fan club going over there. It's sort of like I'm their hero or something.'

Amber grinned, and looked at him with raised eyebrows.

'OK, OK,' he protested, laughing and holding his hands up in self-defence. 'I'm only joking.'

Later, on the drive back to London in Carla's Metro – having waved her beloved Porsche safely on its way back to Frank's farm until the following weekend, when she would be racing at Zandvoort – Amber took off her wig and ruffled her fingers through her short black hair.

'God, that thing makes my head itch,' she grumbled, rubbing furiously at her scalp.

Carla turned her head to smile at her friend. 'Well, you won't need to bother with it for another week.'

Amber flipped down the sun visor and glanced up at her reflection in the mirror on the back. Large blue eyes and a generous mouth, which were encapsulated by a delicate, heart shaped face, smiled back at her.

'Welcome back, all is forgiven,' she murmured to the more familiar view of herself.

Although she didn't realise it her tone had resumed its natural soft Scots burr. She was no longer the up-front, take no bullshit Amber Barclay, simply by removing the wig she was back to being plain old Marie Gifford for another week.

Chapter Two

'Marie, you're crazy, you can't possibly keep this up.' Carla's voice was a low hiss as she stood with her back pressed against the bedroom door, her arms folded. Cocking her head in the direction of the wall which separated Marie's bedroom from the living room of the tiny flat they shared, she said, 'He's not to know what you look like normally. Why go to all the bother?'

'He might, or he might not. I'm not taking any chances,' Marie whispered back forcefully, as she jammed a long, straight chestnut haired wig on her head. 'I know it sounds as though I'm being paranoid but I keep getting the distinct impression I'm being followed these days.'

As she glanced at her reflection in the round mirror in front of her and rubbed hastily at her eyebrows to dull the colour, she caught the sceptical expression on her friend's face. She swivelled round on the stool in front of her small, white painted dressing table and stood up.

'Look at me now. You wouldn't know me from Adam, would you?' she said, stretching out her arms either side of her. 'Let's see, who shall I be? Why not Dottie O'Shay from Ballytringle?' This was said in a soft, lilting Irish accent. 'Or how about hippie Jane just back from Nepal? I've got a pair of psychedelic flares somewhere.' She noticed Carla did not return her smile.

19

'Just decide on something and get your arse out there,' Carla grumbled. 'He's starting to get tetchy and I can't keep pouring tea down his throat.'

Marie stared gloomily after her friend as she slammed out of the room. Bloody banks. Bloody finance houses. Bloody everyone. If I ever get a hold of Greg again, she vowed silently, I'll have his balls for paperweights.

Searching through a chest of drawers for the psychedelic flares, she came across a cropped purple skinny rib sweater. The sweater, she decided, would match the trousers perfectly. As she got changed hurriedly she could hear voices coming from the living room. As far as she could make out, Carla was starting to sound desperate. She paused to drape a few long strands of glass beads around her neck and slip her feet into a pair of flat, thong sandals before making her entrance 'on stage'.

On entering the living room she waved a careless hand at her visitor. 'Hi, man, what's happenin'?' she drawled.

Shunning the lumpy brown tweed sofa, 'Jane' flopped down into an empty armchair and sprawled, one leg dangling carelessly over the arm. Somehow she managed to keep a straight face as she saw Carla suck in her cheeks hard and make a dash for the door.

The nondescript little man perched on the edge of the armchair opposite her, tugged down the front of his shiny grey jacket and offered her an official-looking buff envelope.

'Marie Gifford?'

Smiling as she resolutely ignored the envelope, Marie shook her head. 'No way man, never heard of her.'

'That's what your friend said – more or less,' the man said, looking somewhat bewildered. 'However,' he continued in a monotone, 'we, that is Scratchwood & Sons Commercial Credit, acting on behalf of our client – ' his tapping finger pointed to the name of one of the big four banks, which was printed on the envelope in his hand, ' – have every reason to believe that Miss Gifford resides at this address.'

Marie grinned inwardly as she twirled her beads and stared blankly back at him.

'Well, sorry,' she insisted with a shrug, 'but you've got your facts wrong.'

Ten minutes later she poked her head around Carla's bedroom door and grinned for real. 'You're OK, he's gone now,' she said. 'Probably scuttled back to the little rock he lives under.'

Carla glanced up from the magazine she was reading. 'Well, thank Christ for that,' she said with real feeling. Looking at Marie askance, she added, 'So who is it you're supposed to be again?'

'Hippy Jane.' Marie executed her own version of a clog dance, making her flares flap around her ankles. 'Fancy going out to boogie, man?' she asked. She waved her arms around in the air in a way which, she thought, was very reminiscent of the opening sequence of *Tales of the Unexpected*. The idea made her chuckle.

'As it happens,' Carla said, trying to look as serious as she possibly could in the face of Marie's irrepressible spirit, 'it's rave night down at the Plaza. You look just the part.'

Marie nodded happily. 'Yeah? OK, I'll just – ' The sound of her mobile phone ringing stopped her mid sentence. 'Sorry about this, Carla,' she muttered, looking sheepish all of a sudden, 'I'll take it in my own room.'

'Sure.' Carla shrugged. 'Far be it from me to eavesdrop on your pervy conversations.'

Doing her best not to feel too guilty, Marie left Carla with an apologetic smile and crossed the hallway to her own bedroom. Flopping on to the unmade bed, which was strewn with discarded clothes, she reached out to the bedside table and picked up her black Motorola.

She flipped open the mouthpiece. 'Yes?'

'Portia, it's Chantal,' said the voice at the other end.

Marie felt her pulse quicken. Whenever Chantal phoned it always meant excitement of a very special kind.

'Hi, Chantal, are you calling to tell me we're on for tonight?' she asked.

'Absolutely,' Chantal confirmed. 'Wendel's coming over and he's bringing a couple of friends. I called Fay and she said she'll be here in about half an hour.'

'It'll take me a bit longer than that,' Marie said. 'I'll have to get changed first. Any ideas what I should wear?'

She heard Chantal's distinctive, husky laugh. It sounded very lascivious. 'Anything, or nothing, it's up to you. Oh, I know, what about that rubber catsuit thing you wore the time before last – the one with the zips?'

'Just what I was thinking,' Marie replied, glancing over to her wardrobe where the door hung open. 'Do you need me to bring anything else?'

'No,' Chantal said, 'just yourself. Oh, and a lot of energy. I think it's going to be a long night.'

Chuckling softly, Marie disconnected the call by flipping the mouthpiece shut again. Then she stood up and stretched. Carla was going to be a bit put out by this, she mused wryly as she started to dispose of Hippy Jane, but she would understand. Like the very best of best friends, she always did.

Half an hour later, Marie emerged from her bedroom looking totally transformed. Gone was the long brown wig and in its place was a waist-length black ponytail which she had pinned to the crown of her natural hair. Moving her head from side to side, she delighted in the weight of the hank of hair as it swung back and forth. She glanced down, noticing with satisfaction the smooth glossy lines of her black rubber clad torso and legs. On her feet she wore a pair of impossibly high heeled ankle boots in fake black snakeskin and leather, the cuffs of which were strapped and buckled.

'You're Portia again, I see,' Carla commented dryly when Marie stalked into her room with her back straight and her head proudly erect. 'Can I take it our night's raving is off?'

Marie looked apologetic. 'Sorry, Carla,' she said, 'do you mind?'

'Doesn't really matter either way, does it?' Carla shrugged and reclined back on her bed, eyeing Marie critically. 'How on earth do you manage to get that rubber thing on?'

'With a lot of effort and half a ton of talcum powder,' Marie said with a grin. She sat down on the end of the bed looking contrite. 'Oh, Carla, I am sorry. If I'd known Chantal was going to ring – '

Carla put up her hand to silence her. 'Never mind, I'm feeling a bit tired anyway to tell you the truth.' She smiled. 'I can't pretend to understand some of your odd little quirks, Marie, but it doesn't stop me loving you all the same.'

Despite being immersed in her strong Portia persona, which she had created originally to outwit someone who was chasing her for money, Marie felt moved by Carla's typical selfless generosity.

Although she had promised Chantal she would be at her place as quickly as she could, Marie did not feel inclined to simply dash off and leave Carla in the lurch. Instead, she lolled on her flatmate's bed and allowed her gaze to travel around the room.

Unlike her own bedroom, her friend's was neat and nicely decorated. Carla had stowed the unwanted cheap and nasty furniture which had previously occupied the room in their garage downstairs, and spent her own money on a range of second-hand furniture in honey coloured pine. Her bed was a four poster, draped in red, blue and cream Liberty print fabric. The curtains were of the same material, which in turn matched the frieze running around the cranberry painted walls.

The stylish elegance of the décor was in direct contrast to the shelves of motor racing books, mechanics' manuals and Revell model cars which took up a whole wall. Even her make-up brush holder, which took pride of place on her dressing table, was a defunct piston. Tons of chrome polish and elbow grease had made it look brand new.

'I love this room,' Marie sighed enviously. 'When I finally get myself straight I'm going decorate mine like this.'

Carla snorted with laughter. 'It doesn't matter how wonderful it looks, you'll never keep it tidy.'

About to deny her friend's claim, Marie suddenly realised she was absolutely right. 'It's a fair cop,' she said sitting up and raising her hands, palms up, in a gesture of defeat. 'You put me to shame, Carla, you really do.'

'Oh, get away with you.' Carla leaned forward and punched Marie lightly on the shoulder. 'There's no need to knock yourself out with flattery and cupboard love. I told you, I don't mind about you going out tonight. Go on, have a good time doing whatever it is you weirdos do.'

'Oh, thanks a lot.' Marie pretended to look affronted but the sparkle in her eyes gave her real feelings away. 'OK, I'll be off then. I don't know what time I'll be back.'

Carla rolled her eyes. 'I'm not your mother,' she said, 'I wasn't planning to wait up. See you later, love.'

Marie stood up. 'Yeah, see you, Carla.' Just as she reached the doorway she paused, glanced over her shoulder and added with feeling, 'You know you're the best friend a girl could have, don't you?'

Laughing, Carla picked up her discarded magazine and threw it at her. 'Get out! I can't take any more. If you keep on with this hearts and flowers stuff, I swear I'll throw up.'

During the taxi ride which took her across the river to Chantal's house in central London, Marie found herself forgetting all about Carla and concentrating instead on settling into her Portia character.

She had realised some time ago that she had chameleon tendencies and this was a typical case in point. Whereas Marie was down to earth and quite normal, she supposed, and Amber was fiery and competitive, Portia was altogether different. Which was just as well, she mused, as she gazed idly out of the window at the familiar city streets, because Portia's activities were not exactly what one would call everyday.

Meeting Chantal six months ago had been quite by chance. It had happened shortly after Marie's newly acquired Portia character had managed to give a major creditor the run around. Still clad in the black leather jeans, bustier and black ponytail hairpiece she'd chosen to wear, and high on the adrenalin which her successes always seemed to produce, Marie had gone out alone to a new club. Though she hadn't realised it before she went, the club was holding a fetish evening. In her leather outfit, Marie had no difficulty getting in.

Chantal, a statuesque, auburn haired woman in her forties, had wasted no time in introducing herself while Marie was still at the bar buying her first drink. She had been dressed only in a scarlet leather corset and matching fishnet stockings which, though outrageous in Marie's view, hardly drew a second glance from the other club goers.

As Portia, Marie had been quite happy to sit and chat with Chantal. Despite being considerably older than herself, Marie thought the other woman had a charismatic air about her that was intriguing – even more so than the sight of her pierced nipples, which swelled through peepholes in her corset, or her unashamedly displayed shaven pubis. And now Marie recollected how the fortuitous encounter had ended up turning her life around and revealing a side of her that she had never realised existed.

Almost straight away Chantal had asked 'Portia' if she was dominant or submissive. With an inward smile, Marie recalled how she had given Chantal a blank look for a moment and then, deciding that the word dominant most suited her current personality, had blithely given her answer.

Chantal had nodded. 'I thought so, you don't seem too fazed by the fact that you're here on your own.'

'Well, why should I?' Marie replied with a careless flick of her ponytail. 'I can take care of myself.'

'Oh, absolutely,' Chantal said, casting her a thoughtful look. After a moment, during which they sipped their drinks and glanced vaguely around, she added, 'I don't suppose you'd like to come back to my place to play?'

Marie's casual nod of agreement, which totally belied the surge of excitement inside her, had transformed her life. What she had not realised – and did not discover until half an hour later when they arrived at Chantal's place – was that her new friend organised private, very exclusive parties for devotees of sadomasochism.

Entering Chantal's world – a three storey end of terrace house in Kensington – was like stepping into another dimension. The house looked expensive from the outside and was tastefully decorated inside. But, Marie's sixth sense told her, that was where its similarity with its neighbours ended. Gazing around, her heart thumping behind her ribs, she rapidly came to the conclusion that some intriguing secrets lay behind the closed panelled doors which led off from the granite floored entrance hall. She was not wrong.

The first two floors, she discovered when Chantal offered her a guided tour, were divided into four rooms that each had their own particular theme: a school room, a stable, a gloriously tented 'harem' room – in which the only furniture was a huge, round, red satin covered bed – and a hospital 'ward'.

'These cater to most people's fantasies,' Chantal explained, allowing Marie a peep into each one. 'I occupy the top floor and downstairs in the cellar is where I keep my dungeon.'

Jangling an impressive set of brass keys, which Marie assumed were supposed to add to the general authenticity of the place, Chantal led the way through the scullery and down a narrow wooden staircase to the dimly lit cellar. The sight that met Marie's eyes there took her breath away.

Walled in bare brick, with a lowered ceiling of black

trellis, the cellar had every conceivable trapping of Marie's vague idea of a proper 'dungeon' – even an oddly thrilling atmosphere of close confinement.

Wandering around, she discovered there were three rooms in all. Two – the cells, as Chantal described them – were small and narrow. One contained a black wooden rack and a leather sling that hung from chains attached to the ceiling. The other featured a low, padded bench covered in red leather. Barred 'windows' about three feet long and a foot high afforded the occupants of one cell a view of the next. In addition, each room, and the narrow passageway that linked them, had black metal piping running around the walls just below ceiling height. From the piping were hung numerous sets of studded leather cuffs and collars and pairs of iron manacles.

The first thing that Marie noticed, when she set foot in the largest room, was a set of stocks with padded arm and neck rests. Along the wall to her right, which was covered with a grid of studded metal, hung a row of whips, canes and other implements. Against the far wall stood two solid wooden contraptions painted in black; one in the shape of a cross and the other a capital 'X'.

'As you can see, there's plenty of scope here,' Chantal said as she idly sliced the air with a thin whippy cane. She seemed oblivious to the fact that Marie didn't 'see' at all.

However, thanks to Chantal, Marie soon got to grips with the whole business of sadomasochism. The older woman's initial tutorial was very thorough. And Marie had left her house the following morning with both a bruised bottom and an aching right arm.

At Chantal's insistence, and with the help of a couple of the older woman's friends, one male and one female, Marie had tried being both submissive and dominant. She soon found that her original assumption had been right. According to Chantal she was a natural dominant. All she needed was a bit of training and then she would be ready to join The Inner Sanctum, a group well known among exclusive circles, as a fully fledged dominatrix.

Early on in their odd relationship, Marie had admitted to Chantal that her real name was not Portia after all. But the other woman had waved away her explanations.

'Your assumed character is perfect,' she had insisted. 'Sometimes it doesn't pay to allow your everyday existence to encroach on your fantasy life. Do you honestly think my real name is Chantal?'

Her question had been accompanied by the slight raising of her perfectly plucked auburn brows and the merest ghost of a smile.

Summoning the memory, Marie also recalled, with a shiver, how the other woman's green eyes had glittered like emeralds in the candlelight that flickered from niches set into the dungeon walls.

Now here she was six months later with a new set of friends, most of whom were fairly wealthy. Although no money ever exchanged hands, Marie was not above networking. She happily accepted introductions by her new acquaintances to any associate of theirs who was planning to purchase a computer system. Consequently, her increased sales helped to pay her living expenses and cover some of the debts left to her by Greg. This still left her with a good chunk of income to put towards the most important thing in her life: her Porsche.

She knew Carla did not understand what she called Marie's 'dark side'. And Marie had long since given up trying to explain the pleasure of pain and the erotic charge she got from her visits to Chantal. In some ways she was still unable to get to grips with it herself. But, like Porsche racing, it was an element of her life that she could not imagine doing without for one moment.

When Marie arrived at Chantal's house she was greeted by Susan, one of Chantal's live-in slaves. As always, when it was a party night, Susan – whose real name was Barry – was wearing a traditional maid's costume.

'Chantal is waiting for you in the dungeon,' Susan said in a cracked, husky voice as she helped Marie shrug off her ankle length mac. 'Fay's down there, too, but the others haven't arrived yet.'

Marie smiled. 'Good,' she said, 'that means we'll have a chance to discuss tonight's agenda.'

Leaving Susan to await the arrival of the other guests, Marie made her way through the scullery and down the stairs to the dungeon. She found Chantal and Fay sitting on a red leather-covered sofa, chatting. They both looked up as she appeared.

'Hi, there, Portia,' Chantal said, getting to her feet. 'Fay and I were just discussing who's going to do what to whom.'

'I thought as much,' Marie replied. 'Sorry I couldn't get here any quicker.'

Throwing one black rubber-clad leg over the whipping bench, she sat down astride it and glanced firstly at Chantal and then Fay.

Chantal was wearing very little, as usual, Marie noticed with a wry smile. Her outfit for tonight involved little more than a complicated arrangement of black leather straps and silver chains, while Fay looked amazing in a white leather corset, matching G-string and thigh-high boots, the colour a stunning contrast to her dark skin.

Half Egyptian and half Tibetan, Fay was a sight to behold under any circumstances. Her tall, willowy figure gave away the fact that she was a model by day, though still struggling to make a name for herself. And her face was exquisite: finely boned with slanting, almond shaped eyes above high cheekbones and a wide, usually upward curving mouth. Marie couldn't help likening the young woman to a Persian cat. Even her long, silky black hair seemed to cry out to be stroked.

Tentatively, Marie reached out and did just that. She received an answering feline smile from Fay which set her erotic senses aflame. Marie was achingly aware of her bisexual yearnings. Though she hadn't actually indulged in anything sexual with another woman yet, she knew it was only a matter of time before she did.

And if there was one woman she would like to make love to first it was this enigmatic beauty.

She was brought out of her lascivious reverie by Chantal, who pointedly cleared her throat.

'Sorry if I'm interrupting something – ' the older woman said, smiling at both Fay and Marie. Her smile broadened as Marie snatched her hand away from Fay's hair in embarrassment. 'Hark,' she went on theatrically, putting a hand to her ear, 'I think I hear footsteps.'

The three women glanced up just in time to see six pairs of legs descending the staircase. Chantal stepped forward, her hands outstretched to the first of the three men to appear.

'Wendel, darling,' she enthused, kissing the visitor on both cheeks.

'Lovely to see you again,' Wendel said. He smiled warmly at Chantal before casting an approving glance in the direction of Marie and Fay. 'And you too, Portia,' he added, 'but I don't believe I've had the pleasure – ' He broke off and stepped forward to take Fay's hand.

Marie smothered a grin as she watched him raise Fay's slender hand to his mouth and press his lips to the palm. Wendel was one of her favourite people. Tall, well dressed and steely haired, he was every inch a gentleman. Knowing he was a leading figure in the country's banking system made it all the more inconceivable to Marie that in a short while he would be grovelling naked at her feet.

She turned her head as he introduced his two friends. Martin was a good six inches shorter than Wendel. Also grey haired, he too wore a smart business suit that strained ever so slightly over a distinct paunch.

The other man was much younger than either Wendel or Martin.

If Wendel was to be believed, this third visitor to Chantal's dungeon was an Arab prince whose name was so difficult to pronounce that he preferred to be known simply as Jay. Naturally, Jay was dark, with dead straight hair that fell to just below collar length. And his features were almost as exotic as Fay's, though instead of having a perfectly straight, fine-boned nose like Fay's, his was quite broad and slightly hooked.

'Gentlemen,' Chantal said, handing each of them a tall flute glass almost brimming over with champagne, 'perhaps you would like to drink this while we discuss your preferences. Then afterwards we can get down to some serious fun.'

An hour later the air was alive to the sounds of the crack of leather and bamboo on naked flesh, interspersed with ecstatic groans. Like a symphony, the sounds formed their own harmony, echoing off the bare stone walls of the cavernous dungeon.

Marie paused to wipe a hand across her brow. The temperature of the dimly lit room seemed to have increased a hundredfold since her arrival and now she felt anxious to strip off the layer of rubber that clung to her like a second skin. But not before time, she reminded herself, my discomfort is Wendel's pleasure and vice versa. She glanced sideways at him. Naked and spread-eagled, secured by leather wrist and ankle restraints to the wooden X, he panted loudly.

'Mistress, please – ' he gasped.

Marie smiled to herself, wondering if he even knew what he was pleading for – release from his bonds, or perhaps more pain? Then again, she mused, glancing at the rigidity of his cock, perhaps he was seeking release of a different kind.

She squatted down beside him and ran her fingers lightly along his shaft. The expression on her face was one of thoughtfulness, tinged with amusement. His moans caught Marie's ears, delighting her and at the same time encouraging her to run her fingertips over the bulbous head of his glans. The soft pads of her fingers streaked the taut purple flesh with the viscous fluid that emerged drop by drop from its little slit.

'Are you feeling desperate, my darling?' she crooned to Wendel. 'Would you like Mistress Portia to take your naughty little organ in her mouth?' She deliberately stressed the word 'little', seeking as always to humiliate him in every way possible.

'Please,' he groaned, 'please let me come on your breasts.'

She stood up abruptly and grasped his hair, yanking his head back so that she could gaze into his eyes. Her eyes narrowed and with her left hand she gripped his cock hard.

'Bad boy,' she hissed between her teeth. 'I say when and where you come, remember? I say.'

He tried to nod, despite the fact that she was still clutching his hair.

Marie watched the prominence of his Adam's apple moving along his throat as he swallowed deeply. She thrilled inside to the sight of it – of him. Glancing down, she saw that his buttocks, pale skinned and quivering, still bore thin red stripes where she had caned him. Even though her clothes were tight, she felt the hardening of her nipples and the telltale wetness of her own arousal seeping from her. Her vagina itched and tingled unmercifully. She needed physical release every bit as much as Wendel.

'I'm going to let you touch me,' she announced magnanimously.

Letting go of Wendel's hair she reached down and tugged at the zipper between her legs. As she did so the rubber parted to reveal the pink slit between her labia. For a moment she ran her fingertips along the length of her crease, gently stimulating her own desperate flesh. It felt hot and sticky. Their flow impeded by the tightness of her catsuit, her creamy juices clung to her flesh instead.

She turned back to Wendel and began to unfasten the restraints around his wrists. As he stood, rubbing his recently released flesh, she squatted down and unbuckled the leather ankle restraints. Spreading her legs made the slit in the rubber part more and now she felt her sex flesh oozing through the gap.

She glanced down between her legs, noticing how lewdly her swollen vulva pouted through the slit. The contrast between her pink, shaven sex and the black rubber surrounding it made her aesthetic senses cry out with delight. An invisible coil of musk rose up to tickle each of her nostrils. Oh, God, she thought, almost dizzy with sensation, I have to get some satisfaction soon!

'Turn around,' she ordered Wendel as soon as she had released his ankles. It was an effort to control the tremor in her voice. She stood up and watched him as she shuffled around to face her. 'That's better. Now,' – her excitement was so great she had to pause to catch her breath ' – kneel down and lick me.'

Gripping the wooden X, using one hand to support herself, she opened her legs wide. She trembled precariously on the high heels of her boots as the first touch of Wendel's tongue on her throbbing clitoris sent spasms of pleasure through her entire body.

'Touch me as well,' she gasped. 'Finger-fuck me. Three fingers. Go nice and deep. Yes, that's it. Oh, you good boy. That's so good . . .'

The weight of her lust forced her to close her eyes as she felt his fingers slide inside her gaping vagina. He stroked her expertly. It was not the first time he had pleasured her and she was gratified that he remembered exactly how she liked to be touched. There was no doubt she would reward him for this, she decided, feeling the first indisputable flame of her impending orgasm. He was, as she had said, a very good boy.

When she opened her eyes after the final waves of her orgasm subsided it was to see Fay standing a couple of feet away. Through slanted, catlike eyes she was watching Marie and Wendel intently. Although she had just come, Marie felt a fresh wave of desire that almost drowned her senses. Then, remembering that Wendel still knelt patiently at her feet, she ordered him to stand up.

'Would you like to watch Fay and I caress each other?' she offered him, amazed at her own daring.

Glancing at the other woman, she was pleased to receive a nod of confirmation. She felt her heart miss a beat as Fay crossed the room to stand beside her, the heels of her thigh high white leather boots clicking on the stone flagged floor.

'What about Jay?' Marie asked her.

Fay smiled. 'Don't worry about him. I left him hanging,' she said, 'in more ways than one.'

Marie recollected that Fay had taken Jay into the farthest cell, which contained the leather harness. Chantal, meanwhile, had taken Martin to the second cell. Through the gap in the wall she could see the older woman flexing her right arm, a black leather tawse dangling from her hand.

'Looks as though you've got a very bad boy here,' Fay continued, flashing a contemptuous glance at Wendel.

'Very,' Marie agreed. 'Look at that cock.' She reached down and flicked it disdainfully with her fingertips.

Cupping his testicles in both hands, shoulders hunched, Wendel gave an anguished groan. He glanced from Marie to Fay, his lips moving although no words came out. As he looked back at Marie his expression became pleading.

'OK,' Marie said, taking a deep breath for courage, 'Fay and I are going to entertain you, Wendel but,' she added sternly, 'although I'm going to let you touch yourself you must not come until I give you permission. Is that understood?'

She smiled thinly as Wendel gave a meek nod. Right, Marie thought, this is it. As she reached her arms out to Fay she felt a sharp electrical jolt, desire coursing through her with more intensity than she could ever have thought possible. When their lips met, she thought she would faint from ecstasy. Fay's kiss was so different, softer and sweeter than those she was used to. Her mouth tasted of a heady mixture of the most succulent fruits: strawberry, blackberry, peach and apricot. When she finally disengaged her lips from Fay's, she gave in to the urge to lick them.

As they kissed again she felt Fay's hands stroking the back of her neck. Marie's own fingers slid along the silky length of the young woman's hair then dived into it, tangling in the glorious mass. She felt suffused by sensation: the satin texture of Fay's skin, the softness of her hair and lips, the sweet patchouli perfume she wore and the urgent pulsating sensation between her own legs. She felt her sex blossoming out from the gap in the rubber and the bittersweet agony of her tingling flesh.

She gasped as long, gentle fingers slid questioningly over her moist sex flesh, the nails scraping ever so slightly. It was exquisitely pleasurable and Marie found herself thrusting her pelvis forward, lewdly encouraging Fay to explore her body more thoroughly without actually saying a word. From the corner of her eye she noticed Wendel.

His face was flushed and his eyes glazed as he stroked his own throbbing member.

'Don't come,' she reminded him in a harsh, broken whisper.

He shook his head, his expression one of acute desire. 'No, Mistress,' he gasped, the movement of his hand slowing.

Fay laughed lightly in Marie's ear, her warm breath tickling the delicate membranes there. 'You can come, though,' she whispered tantalisingly as her fingertips stroked Marie's swollen clitoris, 'any time you want to, my love. This little honey's just crying out for it.'

The words were so suggestive, so liberating, and Fay's caresses were so knowing that Marie found herself arching her back and rubbing her sex shamelessly against the other woman's hand as she felt a hot wave of lust sweep over her.

'Oh – oh, God!' she cried, almost weeping with arousal. 'Come, yes, come!'

It was only as she felt the hot spasming of her sex and allowed her head to loll slightly that she realized Wendel had obviously misinterpreted her. While wave after wave of delicious sensation poured over her, she watched through heavy lidded eyes as Wendel rubbed his penis so fast his hand almost became a blur.

A moment later his pleasure jetted from him, the fountain of semen spattering both Marie and Fay and leaving blobs of creamy fluid on the rough stone floor.

Chapter Three

*A*s Wendel had disgraced himself, Marie decided to punish him by ordering him to clean up his own mess.

'Lick that up,' she said. She spoke scathingly, making sure he felt well and truly ashamed of what he had done.

While he busied himself on his hands and knees, looking suitably penitent, Marie sat down next to Fay on the red leather sofa and poured them both a glass of champagne.

'I feel as though I should be celebrating,' she murmured to Fay. 'That was my first experience with another woman.' She noticed how the young woman's eyes mirrored the flickering candlelight, making her dark irises appear as though they were aflame.

'I did wonder,' Fay admitted, 'but don't think for one moment it's over yet. I also have certain needs.' She smiled as she spoke the words, reassuring Marie and also letting her know that, as far as she was concerned, their erotic alliance had only just begun.

As Fay rose gracefully to her feet Marie gazed at the seemingly endless length of her slender legs. She felt her breath catch as the young woman wriggled out of her leather G-string. Her coffee hued buttocks were firm and silky skinned, with just a faint covering of dusky down at the base of her spine. And, when Fay bent forward to pick up the G-string from the floor, Marie couldn't help gazing at the dark valley between those globes where the puckered, even darker eye of her anus winked beguilingly at her.

Reaching out, Marie stroked her fingertips wonderingly over the taut bottom in front of her. As Fay shuffled her legs a little wider apart, Marie allowed her questing fingers to slide lower. They lightly traced the contours of the young woman's buttocks and skimmed down the back of one thigh and up the other. Still bending forward from the waist – her legs straight and shoulder width apart, the ends of her long dark hair brushing the floor – Fay balanced herself by pressing her fingertips upon the flagstones.

Marie gazed in wonder at Fay's body as her fingers stroked the dark flesh in front of her. She was trying to pluck up the courage to explore further. The plum coloured purse of the young woman's sex pouted enticingly between her thighs, the wrinkled flesh of her inner labia protruding slightly. Around the rim of her vagina silvery threads glistened, proving how aroused she was obviously feeling.

All at once, Marie felt herself gripped by an equal measure of compassion and desire for the other woman. Anxious to give Fay the same kind of pleasure she had recieved, Marie allowed her fingers to slide between the woman's legs. For a single, heart-stopping moment she cupped Fay's sex, feeling the crisp texture of her pubic hair and the moist warmth of her flesh. Fay's body seemed to be throbbing gently, she noticed, and the heat her sex generated seemed to set Marie's hand aglow, the warmth travelling up her arm and suffusing her whole body.

With a groan of arousal, Marie stroked her fingers along Fay's slit, widening her sex lips and gently rubbing the hard, swollen bud of her clitoris. With the fingers of her other hand she explored the outer rim of Fay's vagina, circling her fingertips around the slick edge for a moment before daring to plunge a couple of fingers into the enchanting depths of the other woman's body.

It thrilled Marie to hear Fay's whimpers and to explore ever deeper the pulpy interior of her vagina. She stroked the inner walls searchingly, delighting to their velvety texture, feeling every ridge, every bump, while all the time the young woman thrust her elegant bottom in the air provocatively and ground herself against Marie's hand.

Lost in the blissful realm of discovery, Marie was startled when Wendel interrupted her.

'Mistress, I – ' he began. He stood in front of her, nervously wringing his hands, his expression sheepish.

She snapped her head up and fixed him with a firm gaze which was tinged by softness. 'Have you finished cleaning up after yourself?' she asked.

Dumbly, Wendel nodded and Marie sighed inwardly. She was enjoying herself so much with Fay she resented the intrusion. But, she scolded herself, she shouldn't forget her slave's pleasure. For one thing, Chantal would never forgive her and for another it simply wasn't fair on Wendel.

'Sit,' she ordered, pointing to the empty space next to her on the sofa. 'Watch my fingers. See how delectably they glide in and out of Fay's body. Notice how wet she is, how smooth and creamy her juices.'

She felt her breath catch in her lungs even as she spoke. Her own words, she realised, were arousing her as much as they were obviously affecting Wendel. She could see he had become erect again already and that his expression was rapt as he concentrated on what she was doing to Fay. Slowly, she slid her fingers out of Fay's vagina and held them in front of the older man. Flexing her wrist, she turned her hand this way and that, noticing how the ivory film coating her fingertips took on a spectral translucency in the flickering candlelight. In a low voice Marie ordered Wendel to lick her fingers clean.

As she spoke she heard Fay whimper. Her legs were

trembling, Marie noticed, and it was with a slight feeling of regret that she felt compelled to suggest she stand up again. As she did so, Marie smacked the young woman smartly on the bottom, enjoying the thrill the small but nevertheless stimulating gesture provoked in her.

'I'm sure we could make good use of one of the rooms upstairs,' she suggested to Fay. 'Why don't you go and release Jay so that we can continue the party in more comfortable surroundings?'

'Sure, baby, anything you say,' Fay murmured, treating Marie to another of her catlike smiles. 'Won't be a moment.'

Fay walked away, her neat hips undulating in a way that made Marie's mouth go dry with desire. As soon as the young woman was no longer in view Marie turned to Wendel, a slight smile playing about her lips.

'Are you OK?' she asked. She wondered why the question was necessary when she could see, just by the expression in his eyes, that he was enjoying every minute.

'Oh, absolutely, Mistress,' he said, daring to stroke a reverent hand along her rubber-clad thigh, 'but I know we're both capable of a lot more pleasure.' His hand slid over the taut mound of her thigh muscle, deliberately allowing his fingertips to brush her sex where it swelled pinkly through the slit in the crotch of her catsuit.

Marie felt herself quiver. Arousal for her was instant and demanded immediate release. One thing she had never learnt was patience. Life was too short, she often told herself, followed by another favourite adage: there's no time like the present.

'You may touch me while we wait,' she said, with a sigh that was a mixture of feigned passivity and pleasurable anticipation. Opening her legs wider, she sighed again as Wendel's hand slipped between her quivering thighs.

'Come on, you two, stop that!'

Marie, who had closed her eyes to concentrate on the blissful sensations Wendel was creating, smiled as she heard Fay's command. She opened her eyes and looked at Fay, arching her eyebrows and giving her a quirky grin.

'Yes, Mistress,' she said drily. As she pushed Wendel's hand away and got slowly to her feet, she noticed that Fay was leading Jay by a lead attached to a studded leather collar. She waited until Wendel stood up before prodding him between the shoulder blades with her index finger. 'Move,' she ordered crisply. 'Upstairs. The bedouin tent.'

Smoke rose up in thin, swirling plumes from the cluster of joss sticks which burnt in a little brass vase standing on the low table beside Marie. Their scent was powerful, making her feel light-headed and almost apart from herself as she lay naked on the wide, satin covered bed. She fancied she could see herself from above, her flesh pale and ethereal against the scarlet backdrop; her heavily made-up eyes like two dark pits in the ghostly canvas of her face.

All at once the image changed as Fay flicked a switch on the wall beside them and the whole room became suffused in a rosy glow. The young woman's skin, Marie noticed, seemed to gleam as it took on the colour of Morello cherries. She, too, was naked now, her leather corset and boots long since abandoned.

Fay crawled on hands and knees across the wide bed with the feline grace and appearance of a black panther. Her neat behind swayed tantalisingly as she headed for Jay, who stood rooted to the spot at the foot of the bed.

'Come,' Fay said, crooking a finger at Jay, 'attend to Mistress Portia.'

Marie felt her breath catch as the Arab prince almost fell on top of her in his eagerness to do Fay's bidding. His skin tone was a blend of her own and Fay's, she noticed. It was darker than merely tanned yet not as dusky as that of his mistress. Reaching out to him, Marie felt the slickness of his skin where a thin film of perspiration lay on top of the body oil Fay had anointed him

41

with. Her nostrils quivered as they were filled by the oil's rich scent: rose and almond overlaid with musk.

Jay moved to lay full length beside Marie, his stiff penis pressing hard against her hip, one hand lazily stroking her breasts and torso. Marie noticed as she glanced down how her nipples hardened instantly, two ripe firm buds of flesh longing to be sucked and nibbled. As though he could read her mind, Jah lowered his head and began to lathe her desperate nipples with his tongue.

With a groan of satisfaction, Marie reached out to Fay who in turn grasped Wendel's hand and pulled him on to the bed with her. He fell – conveniently, Marie thought, with a wry smile – face forward between the young woman's outspread thighs. She heard Fay moan, the sound transmitting a fresh surge of desire which surged through Marie's body with the power of an electrical charge. She felt aflame with lust yet again. Her sense of touch embraced the texture of the satin coverlet beneath her; the soft brush of Jay's hair as it skimmed over her torso; the sensuous sweep of his tongue across her flesh, and Fay's warm breast, which her hand now cupped.

The young woman's breasts were a delightful surprise to Marie. When released from the tight confines of the white leather corset they had spilled out in abundance, large and pendulous yet still firm to the touch. They were tipped by large, dark areolae, with nipples as huge and juicy as blackberries. Good enough to eat, Marie had mused when she first set eyes on them. Now she wasted no time in assuaging her desires.

Fay twisted the top half of her body around, and allowed Marie to stroke both her breasts while their lips met for a long, sensuous kiss.

Suffused in the wonder of their kiss, Marie could still hear the soft lapping sounds the two men made as they pleasured her and Fay. Even as she ground her hips against Jay's mouth and felt the slow, inexorable rise to paradise she did not release the young woman's lips or breasts. Her fingers roamed over Fay's torso, capturing her breasts in two delicious handfuls, her fingertips tweaking at the nipples until they stood out proud and firm.

Moving as if to a choreographed sequence, she and Fay turned and rose to their hands and knees. Lips pressed together once more, they sighed into each other's mouth as the men entered them. Their tongues danced and parried, imitating the erotic movements of the hard members inside them.

For Marie it was a night of discovery and sublime pleasure . . . one which she half hoped would never end.

Just two days later, Marie's interlude with Fay had been confined to her storehouse of erotic memories. All she could think about now was the coming weekend.

It was Saturday and five-thirty in the morning. With a red sun rising from the flat horizon to illuminate their surroundings, Marie was quick to realise that the Dutch countryside was every bit as featureless in the daylight as it was at night. She and Carla had been driving for hours. Since their ferry docked at Calais the small car had been eating up miles of flat road. Steadily, they made their way up from France, through Belgium and deeper into the heart of the Netherlands.

Zandvoort was their destination. The famous Dutch race track was the location for round five of the Xtreme Oil Challenge. Marie knew the Porsche would be waiting for them when they arrived. Frank and his friends had phoned the night before to confirm that the van and trailer were loaded up and just about to set out on the same route Marie and Carla were taking now.

Towing a trailer involved driving at a much slower speed and Marie had not envied them their journey. She did, however, feel overwhelmingly grateful for their dedication. Success, when it came – and she felt certain it would by the end of the season – would not be hers alone but something they would all share. As the driver, Marie's place was perhaps the most important on the team. But without a loyal, highly proficient crew, her driving skills would count for nothing.

'Not much farther now,' Carla said, breaking through Marie's thoughts. 'Do you fancy taking over for the rest of the drive? I could do with a bit of a kip.'

'Sure, pull over in the next layby and we'll swap places,' Marie agreed.

Until now she had done very little of the driving. Carla had insisted that Marie should arrive at the track fresh and alert, ready for the first practise session at ten o'clock. But now Marie could see with a sideways glance the tiredness her friend must be feeling; it showed so clearly on her face. And by this time she felt too hyped up to sleep anyway. The prospect of getting back behind the wheel of her beloved car and putting in a few good lap times was too exciting to contemplate relaxation.

As field after field and windmill after windmill flashed past the car window, Marie started to feel frustrated. She couldn't help wondering if they would ever arrive at their destination. Glancing in the rear view mirror, she saw her friend curled up on the back seat. Dressed in bleached-out blue jeans and a white cotton top, with her blonde hair all tousled, Carla slept with her mouth open, emitting gentle snores.

Eventually, after it felt as though she had been driving for hours, Marie caught a glimpse of the coastline away in the distance to her left. A few minutes later she was relieved to see the first signpost to Zandvoort.

For the next few miles the car seemed to fly along the road and Marie felt like cheering as she finally drove through the main entrance gate to the track. Having collected track passes for herself and Carla and a paddock pass which she stuck to the windscreen of the car, Marie was directed by a dour official in blue overalls to the paddock area.

Once she had parked up in the entrants' car park, she reached out to Carla and shook her gently by the shoulder.

'Come on, sleepyhead,' she said gently. 'Wake up, we're here.'

'Wha – Where?' Carla sat up suddenly and glanced around with a bewildered expression on her face.

'We're at the track. Remember – Zandvoort?' Marie said with a trace of laughter in her voice.

'Oh, yeah,' Carla mumbled rubbing her tired eyes with her fists. 'God, I wish I hadn't bothered to go to sleep, I feel like death warmed up now.'

'No time for self-pity,' Marie responded firmly as she opened the car door and started to climb out. 'We've got to get out there and put in some good times.' Now she was totally fired up with enthusiasm.

She grabbed a holdall from the boot of the car, and walked smartly over to the line of garages, quickly finding the one where her car sat unattended. She marched straight through the garage and out the back to a concrete area where the silver Mercedes van was parked. Thankfully, she found Frank had left it unlocked. He and the crew had obviously gone off somewhere in search of an early breakfast, but she had no time to think about food, she had to transform herself into Amber as quickly as possible before she bumped into someone she knew.

Fifteen minutes later she slid open the van's side door and emerged dressed in her racing overalls, carrying her helmet under her arm. Just as she stepped down from the van she bumped into Darren Standish.

'Hi, Amber,' he said cheerfully. 'Nice day for it, eh?' He glanced up at the sky which stretched above them in a cloudless blue canopy.

Feeling in love with the world, Marie smiled at him. 'I'll say,' she said. 'How was your journey?'

'Oh, the usual.' He paused and grinned at her and by unspoken agreement they started walking towards the rear of the garages. 'The hard men spent the whole crossing groaning about feeling seasick,' he added drily. 'The hard men' was a commonly held nickname among the Porsche racing fraternity for Darren's crew. The two stopped outside Marie's garage. 'Mind you,' he went on, 'it doesn't seem to have done them any lasting damage. I just left them all tucking into bacon and eggs.'

Marie pulled a face. 'Yuk! How could they?'

'It's called rapid recovery,' he said with a further grin. Then he lowered his voice to a conspiratorial tone to add, 'Have you noticed *he's* here?'

Marie didn't need to ask who Darren was referring to. At the Brand's Hatch race earlier in the season a new car had appeared on the scene. It had been driven by someone who obviously knew what he was doing behind the wheel of a Porsche but preferred to remain an enigma. After the race was over and the new driver had taken second place he had resolutely kept his helmet on during the prize-giving ceremony and then disappeared into a long American motor home immediately afterwards. All the other racers knew about him was that his name was Lawrie Samson.

It had been inconceivable to Marie that someone could hope to do well in a championship which was already half over, but Lawrie Samson's skill and driving time had stunned everyone. So, too, had the number of sponsor's logos which the brand new purple and white car had sported.

'I hope he doesn't think he can come over here and take my win away from me,' Darren said with a mite too much arrogance for Marie's liking.

'*My* win, you mean,' she said pointedly.

He gave a nonchalant shrug. 'Whatever. Anyway, Amber, I can't stand around here chatting all day.'

'No,' she murmured, 'neither can I.' From the corner of her eye she could see Carla drumming her fingers impatiently on the roof of the car. 'See you out on the track, Darren,' she added, throwing him a confident smile, 'and may the best woman win.'

Before he had a chance to come up with a suitable retort Marie turned on her heel and sauntered nonchalantly into her garage.

'The car's ready to roll,' Carla said as Marie strolled

up to her. 'What did laughing boy want?' She cocked her head in the direction of Darren's retreating figure.

'We were talking about that new guy,' Marie replied, stroking a loving hand absently over the wing of her Porsche. 'You know, the one who miraculously appeared and took second place at Brand's.'

'As if I could forget.' Carla rolled her eyes meaningfully. 'Mr Mystery Man.'

'Mr Rich Mystery Man, you mean,' Marie said, taking her racing gloves from her pocket and pulling them on her hands. 'Anyone who can afford to take out a brand new car halfway through the season must have more money than sense. Not only that, but did you notice how much sponsorship he's got? Obviously, there are a lot of people out there with a hell of a lot of faith in him.'

'Probably just a five-minute wonder,' Carla responded dismissively. 'I wouldn't worry about it.'

'I wasn't,' Marie lied as she opened the car door and slid into the driver's seat.

As she wrapped her fingers around the steering wheel, she experienced an equal mixture of relief and excitement. She always felt like this just before a race. Sitting in her car made her feel like a whole person again. And taking it out on to the track in competition gave her such a surge of adrenalin she felt as though she could conquer the world. Nevertheless, she couldn't ignore the slight feeling of disquiet that the newcomer's presence gave her.

During the warm-up laps at Brand's Hatch she hadn't been able to ignore Lawrie Samson's driving skill. He drove like no one she had ever seen before. And his car was far more competitive than hers. Even though he was well down in the points championship it would only take a few wins to put him in serious competition with her. And if there was one thing she couldn't afford it was to lose the Championship. If she lost that, she would lose everything.

* * *

47

By the end of the morning's qualifying session, Marie felt even more rattled by Lawrie Samson. Time and again she had watched helplessly as the purple streak of his car flashed past her. He seemed to have no regard for the racing line. And she could only assume that he felt so confident in his car's performance that he could afford to circumnavigate the other vehicles.

Consequently, by the end of the session she found herself lying provisionally in second place on the starting grid, with Lawrie Samson in pole position. Which meant a lot of work for her during the afternoon just to hold on to her position, let alone improve on it.

As she pulled into the pits after her final lap – one which she would have been very pleased with under normal circumstances – she could not help noticing that Carla and the rest of the crew looked less than elated.

'I'm going to go and check that bastard out,' Marie said, stepping out of the car and pulling off her helmet angrily. She knew she didn't have to explain to whom she was referring.

'What good do you suppose that is going to do?' Carla responded as she climbed into the driver's seat, intending to back the car into the garage. 'You can't stop him competing.'

Marie pursed her lips as she ran her fingers through her hair. 'Well, we'll see about that,' she said defiantly. 'I intend to have a word with Ray Rumbold as well.' An ex-Pirelli Porsche Production Championship winner several times over, Ray was the chairman of the committee which governed the Xtreme Oil Championship.

'You're wasting your time and you know it,' Carla pointed out with a sigh, 'but far be it from me to try to stop you.'

Even as she spoke, Carla knew she was wasting her breath. Winning meant everything to Marie and her dearest friend had the determined glint in her eye that she recognised of old. It came as no surprise when Marie fixed her with a narrow-eyed stare.

'I'm glad you're not going to try and talk me out of it,

because you wouldn't be able to,' Marie said with conviction. And, with that, she turned on her heel and marched off down the pit lane in the direction of Lawrie Samson's garage.

The first thing Marie noticed when she reached the Samson garage was a team of half a dozen mechanics. Immaculately clad in purple and white overalls, they swarmed over the car. At the back of the garage, leaning nonchalantly against the wall, was a tall man. He was still dressed in racing overalls and wearing a matching purple and white helmet with the visor raised. He was talking to two young women.

Both were long haired – one fair, one brunette – and both were clad in pale mauve jeans worn with white short-sleeved blouses that clung to their enviably slim figures like a second skin. Their expressions were equally animated and even from a distance, Marie could see how they appeared to hang on Lawrie Samson's every word.

'Egotistical so-and-so,' Marie muttered to herself as she walked boldly into the garage.

'Excuse me. Mr Samson?' Marie called out, deftly sidestepping the mechanic who tried to block her path.

She watched as the racing driver slowly turned his head and felt her breath catch in her throat as he fixed her with a direct, grey-eyed gaze.

'Yes,' he said in a deep, penetrating voice, 'do I know you?' His fair eyebrows beetled slightly as he asked the question.

Marie shook her head, wondering why she was trembling all of a sudden. It must be rage, she told herself, while all the time recognising the all-too-familiar, helpless sensation of pure desire.

'No, I – er, well, that is, you should do,' she stammered. Trying hard to regain some vestige of self-control, she held out her hand as she walked right up to him. 'I'm Amber Barclay.'

Lawrie Samson appeared to hesitate for a moment, as though the name did not register with him. Then he, too, held out his hand and took Marie's in a firm grip.

'I do apologise, Miss Barclay,' he said, 'I should have recognised the woman currently leading the points championship.'

Marie seethed inside. It was impossible to ignore the inference behind his use of the word 'currently' and his arrogance. Despite her annoyance, as he dropped her hand, she felt curiously bereft of his touch.

'So,' Lawrie Samson said, leaning back to rest his shoulders against the wall and crossing his arms in front of him, 'what can I do for you?'

Marie found she was still gazing mutely at him and he at her. The two young women by his side were also staring at her, she realised, but more with amusement than anything else. All at once, she felt a fresh surge of annoyance. Was everyone involved in this team as bloody arrogant as Lawrie Samson himself?

'I'd like to talk to you – in private,' she stressed, glancing pointedly at the two women who were still smirking at her. Although she was determined to say her piece, she had difficulty getting the words out and cursed herself inwardly for it. For goodness sake, he was only a man when all said and done! 'I said, I'd like – ' she started to repeat, when he gave no indication that he intended to answer her.

He put up a hand. 'I heard what you said, Miss Barclay. There's no need to raise your voice.'

Marie was livid. 'I didn't raise my voice. I – '

'You're doing it again,' he said in a patient tone, as though he were talking to a child. Stepping forward, he took her by the elbow. 'Perhaps you would like to come into my trailer. Once you've calmed down we can – '

'I am calm, thank you,' Marie responded through gritted teeth. She tried to shake his hand off but found he had a surprisingly firm grip on her. 'Oh, come on then, if we must,' she added in a resigned tone. 'I haven't got all day.'

Lawrie had to fight back the urge to laugh as he gazed down into the angry face of the young woman. She obviously took racing very seriously, he thought, leading her to the door of his motor home, though perhaps that was no bad thing. Too many of the racing drivers he had come across during the past couple of years competing in classic and sports car events had irritated him with their casual attitude to racing and to life itself. It seemed all they wanted to do was play at motor sport, enjoying the glamour and the prestige, with hardly a thought for their own safety, or that of anyone else.

Some of them, he had discovered, were perfectly prepared to go out on track after a night spent drinking gallons of scotch or champagne. Somehow, they managed to get past the rigorous checks carried out by the race scrutineers. Although, he admitted to himself, the scrutineers were more interested in the condition of the cars than the drivers, who were clever enough to cover up their bingeing and lack of sleep.

'Come in and sit down,' he invited his guest, ushering her through the door and waving his hand toward a large square seating area at the far end of the motor home. 'If you think we've got something to discuss, which personally I do not, then I suppose we'd better get it over and done with.'

Chapter Four

The interior of the motor home was huge. Almost as big as her flat and far better equipped, Marie reflected as she sat down in a grey velour-covered armchair. While Lawrie Samson busied himself in the kitchen area, filling a Phillip Stark chrome kettle and spooning instant coffee into a couple of purple mugs, she contemplated her surroundings.

The decor was predominantly white and grey, with splashes of purple here and there. The large seating area at the far end of the motor home was surrounded on three sides by huge picture windows, obscured by slatted blinds. The seating area was furnished with free-standing furniture, rather than fitted: three squashy two-seater sofas, a low grey granite table and the armchair she was seated in now.

Divided from the seating area by open shelving, the white and grey kitchen was equipped not only with a cooker and dishwasher but a washing machine cum tumble dryer as well. Towards the rear of the motorhome were three doors which Marie assumed led to the bathroom and two bedrooms.

Looking around covetously, Marie's eyes took in every detail. Lucky bastard, there's real money involved here, she thought. Immediately, she felt annoyed and irritated by the surge of resentment her thoughts invoked. It wasn't normally like her to feel envious of others and as Lawrie Samson walked towards her, she glanced up guiltily.

He held two steaming mugs and his eyes were soft with a natural friendliness that made her feel even worse. She wanted him to carry on being nasty and arrogant. She wanted a good reason to hate him and so knock herself out to beat him on the track.

He paused to put the mugs down on the low grey granite table in front of her, before sitting opposite her on one of the sofas. When he had made himself comfortable he dragged off his racing helmet.

Through this simple action Marie felt such a rush of desire it was as though her whole being had been vaporised: every bone, every muscle, every antagonistic thought.

The finely sculpted face that emerged was the most beautiful she had ever seen. And as he pulled the helmet away completely and shook his head, she couldn't help letting her astonishment show. A beautiful combination of ash blond with streaks of copper and gold, his hair was a good two inches longer than her shoulder length 'Amber' wig.

'You're impressed, aren't you?' he commented, without a hint of modesty.

All Marie could do was nod dumbly. My God, she thought, trying hard to come back down to earth, he is the most perfect, desirable specimen of manhood I have ever seen; shame he's such an arrogant, self-opinionated so-and-so.

'I forgot to ask you if you take sugar,' he said, interrupting her judgment of him.

'I – oh, no. No, thank you,' she replied, still feeling distracted by his demi-god appearance and the way he scrutinised her so intently.

She realised abruptly she was gawking at him and hastily picked up her coffee and sipped it, scalding her mouth in the process. She grimaced and put the mug back down on the table.

'Too strong?' he enquired, a hint of amusement dancing in his dove grey eyes.

'No, too hot.'

'That's because I've only just made it.'

Marie opened her mouth to utter a suitably scornful retort, then shut it again, feeling foolish for almost rising to his bait. Damn the man, she thought as she watched him recline easily on the sofa, he was so cool she could get frostbite just by being near him. Either that or turn into a fireball of lust.

Splaying his arms across the back of the sofa, he regarded her steadily. He appeared to be biding his time, as though he was waiting for her to say or do something that would put her at a disadvantage. His appraisal certainly made her feel uncomfortable, which was not a state of affairs Marie was accustomed to.

'What did you want to see me about?' he asked finally.

For a moment Marie couldn't decide how to reply. All she could concentrate on was the movement of his wide sensual lips as he spoke, the continuing twinkle in his eyes and the undeniable chemistry between them. Unlike the slowly growing warmth she had experienced with other men, this was a fervent, sparking desire which gave her an intense, edge-of-the-seat feeling she couldn't ignore. Her only hope at that moment was that it wasn't wishful thinking on her part which made her certain he felt the same way.

Yet how could they possibly progress on a personal level? she asked herself in the next moment. He was a serious competitor, for goodness' sake; the enemy. With a sinking feeling, she wished her body could behave as sensibly as her mind. Reaching forward she picked up her coffee mug again and held it between her hands, as though she could draw strength from its comforting warmth.

'I want to know if you consider yourself a serious

contender for the Championship,' she asked, thinking she sounded far bolder than she felt.

There was a pause while he recrossed his legs. Then he said, 'Of course I am a serious contender. I never do anything without good reason.'

Marie felt tempted to tell him how pompous he sounded but instead she said challengingly, 'You know you're pushing your luck if you think you can win.'

His raised eyebrows accompanied an amused twist to his lips. 'Is that so?'

'Yes,' Marie persisted, 'there is no way you can hope to make up the points. We're halfway through the season already.'

He shrugged. 'So, what are you worried about?'

'I'm not worried.'

'Aren't you?' he said. He raised a quizzical eyebrow. 'Why did you want to see me? What was so important that we had to talk in private? Why can't you just be honest – with both of us?'

Yes, why? Marie asked herself, angry now that she had let the man get to her in the first place. If only she didn't feel so damned harassed all the time. If only Greg hadn't left her all those debts. If only she didn't feel as though she wanted to do Lawrie Samson some serious damage and yet ravish him all at the same time.

'I'm sorry, I'm obviously wasting your time and mine,' Marie said firmly as she put down her coffee cup and started to get up. 'There are things that – well – that you don't know about. None of your business really. I shouldn't have bothered you.'

'You haven't,' he replied. 'It's been a pleasure meeting the famous Amber Barclay.'

Marie glanced quickly at him to see if he was mocking her but saw straight away that he wasn't. Although he was smiling at her, his full lips were curved in a genuinely friendly, relaxed way that touched his eyes. With a jolt, she noticed how soft and appealing his gaze now looked. Despite herself, she felt herself melting.

'Do you have to rush off? he murmured beguilingly. 'I was about to offer you a sandwich.'

Marie felt torn by indecision. On the one hand she would like nothing better than to spend some time with him, especially on a more friendly basis. On the other –

Her indecision was suddenly interrupted by the arrival of the two young women who had been talking to Lawrie Samson in his garage. Having slammed the door shut behind them they stood in the kitchen area, each with their arms folded and one foot tapping impatiently.

'Lawrie, come on, we're waiting for you to take us to lunch,' the blonde-haired one said with a lilac-lipped pout.

'Pretty please, Lawriekins,' the brunette added in a little girl voice.

Her tight trousers gave her a mincing gait as she walked over to him. Lowering herself gingerly on to the arm of the sofa beside him, she brushed a possessive, talon-nailed hand over his blond head. Look at me, her expression seemed to say as she gazed steadily at Marie while twirling a strand of Lawrie's hair around her finger, I'm allowed to touch him and you're not. She smirked as Lawrie gave a resigned shrug and put his arm around her slender waist.

'OK, girlies,' he said, switching to a pronounced Scots accent which surprised Marie until she remembered that Lawrie was a Hibernian name, let's see what culinary delights the Dutch can come up with.' He turned to Marie who stood rooted to the spot. 'Will ye no come with us, hen? I mean – ' he reverted to his normal, accentless accent ' – would you care to join us?'

The two young women giggled for his benefit but looked daggers at Marie.

Marie felt tempted to accept his invitation just to spite them. And she was also enticed by the prospect of spending a little more time with Lawrie. But her pride got the better of her and she shook her head.

'Sorry,' she said, knowing she looked anything but,

'I've already made other arrangements. I'm sure you understand.' She wanted to elaborate, to pretend that she was lunching with a large, potential sponsor, but to her surprise found that she couldn't lie to him.

And somehow, she realised, as she wandered disconsolately through the pits a few minutes later, she didn't think Lawrie Samson would have believed her for one minute if she had.

'How did it go then?' Carla asked the moment Marie walked into their garage.

Marie shrugged. 'OK, I suppose.' Pausing to pick up a spanner and turn it thoughtfully around in her hands, she added, 'He is one hell of an arrogant so-and-so.'

'Well, I could have told you that and saved you half an hour,' Carla responded drily. Taking the spanner away from Marie she replaced it carefully in a large, red metal tool box. 'Now, if you could just give me five minutes to have a wash we can wander over to the restaurant for lunch.'

The licensed restaurant at Zandvoort, which is restricted to the élite who either have track or press passes, has a huge open-air terrace which directly overlooks the track.

As this particular qualifying session was open to the public, the organisers at the race track had arranged for various displays to entertain the spectators during the two-hour lunch break.

Having found an empty table on the far side of the terrace, Marie sat down and rested one elbow on the low wall beside her. Turning her head, she gazed down at the scene below. On the track, members of a motorcycle stunt team were going through their routine. Marie had seen it all before and was bored after only a few seconds. She looked away and glanced around the terrace instead. Everyone there seemed to be in high spirits, laughing and joking and generally making merry. And the balmy air was alive to the sounds of cutlery clattering upon china and the crystalline chink of glasses touching.

For once Marie wished she, too, could enjoy a glass of wine with her lunch. Or better still, she mused as she turned her attention to the uninspiring glass of iced orange juice in front of her, a whole bottle. Thanks to her encounter with Lawrie Samson she felt unusually ill at ease. It was as though her life were a house of cards and he had deliberately come along and blown gently at it. Not hard enough to cause complete destruction but with sufficient force to make her future seem that fraction more unstable.

She looked up as Carla returned from the ladies' lavatory.

'Food not arrived yet, then?' her friend observed as she sat down opposite Marie.

'No, I was just wondering if we should – ' Marie's words were interrupted by the arrival of a plump, ruddy cheeked waitress, who put two plates of honey glazed ham and french fries down in front of herself and Carla.

'So sorry to be keeping you waiting,' the waitress said, her chestnut curls bouncing as she bobbed her head apologetically. 'Can I be getting you another drink?'

Amber nodded and, draining the last drop of her orange, handed her glass to the waitress.

'Make it a double,' she said drily. Then she turned to Carla, who was spooning a dollop of mayonnaise on to the chips heaped up on her plate. She frowned. 'Carla, how could you? You've got no style.'

Used to Marie's mood swings, her friend gave a careless shrug. 'They all eat fries with mayonnaise here, haven't you tried it yet?' She paused as Marie shook her head. 'Well, don't knock it until you have,' she said.

Tentatively, Marie dipped the end of one of her french fries into Carla's mayonnaise. She bit it and crunched thoughtfully.

'OK, you win,' she conceded, her thoughtful expression broadening into a smile as she dunked another chip. 'You're right, they're delicious like this.'

Marie had just picked up her knife and fork when she noticed Lawrie Samson arrive and take a table at the far end of the terrace. The two girls were still with him, she noticed, feeling unaccountably irritated, and they were laughing their heads off at something he was saying.

When he caught Marie staring at him over Carla's shoulder, Lawrie stopped talking abruptly and simply stared back.

Marie felt her heart begin to pound behind her ribs. Everything and everyone else around her seemed to recede into insignificance. It was as though the rest of the world had been sucked in by a giant Hoover, leaving a vacuum which only contained herself and the golden god.

Having changed from her racing overalls into white shorts and a cropped T-shirt, Marie suddenly felt utterly naked under the intensity of his gaze. All at once she became aware of her breasts, particularly the size and shape of them. They felt heavy, warm and desirous. She could feel her nipples hardening, chafing against the thin cotton that covered them yet concealed virtually nothing. She knew the outline of her breasts was clearly visible through the T-shirt, as were the dark circles of her areolae.

Feeling self-conscious all of a sudden she deliberately crossed her arms in front of her, trying to shield her breasts from Lawrie's uncompromising gaze. But when she glanced down, she realised that all she had succeeded in doing was to create a noticeable cleavage for herself.

Across the table from her she saw Carla's mouth moving, making an indistinct noise that sounded as though it was coming from under water. Marie shook her head, forcing her own numbed lips into a shaky smile. Can't she see I've been hypnotised? she wondered. Surely I'm not still coming across to her as the 'normal' me?

Uncrossing her arms, Marie grabbed her glass of orange juice instead. She downed it in one go, gulping hastily. As a half-melted ice cube slithered down her throat she began to choke.

Even though he was seated at the opposite end of the terrace, Lawrie was on his feet in an instant. Dashing to Marie's side, he thumped her hard on the back. The ice cube shot out of her mouth and landed on the table-cloth, where it started to melt.

Marie felt mortified as she watched the transparent sliver of ice transform into a slowly expanding wet patch.

'I'm sorry,' she gasped, waving one hand frantically and clutching at her throat with the other, 'I'll be OK now.' She sniffed and picked up a napkin to dab at her watering eyes.

'Are you sure you're all right?' Carla leaned across the table. Her face wore a concerned expression.

Lawrie squatted down beside her, a broad hand patting her bare thigh in a comforting gesture.

'Here, drink this,' he said a moment later. He poured a little mineral water into an empty glass and handed it to her.

His hand, Marie noticed, as she sipped obediently, immediately went back to patting her thigh. Though this time the patting was more like stroking. Stroking and kneading, she realised blissfully. She continued to sip, pretending not to notice what he was doing so that he wouldn't stop. After a minute or so she reluctantly put down the glass and turned her head to smile properly at him.

'Thank you,' she said softly. 'I feel much better now.'

Their eyes met, their locked gaze falling to his hand, which now rested immobile on the bare brown skin of her thigh. His skin tone was golden, whereas hers was more olive where she had caught the sun, she noticed, feeling a distinct tightening in her stomach.

While her pulse raced and sensuality soared inside her, she scrutinised his broad hand with its long, tapering fingers. The clean pink and white nails had perfectly shaped half-moons. There were a few freckles on the back of his hand, and he wore a complicated looking Tag Heuer watch around his wrist. Her glance travelled up his arm which was golden brown and covered with a light, almost invisible down of pale hairs.

'Amber, for goodness' sake, our lunch is getting cold.'

Carla's voice interrupted Marie's reverie and she snapped unwillingly to attention.

'Yes, must go,' Lawrie murmured in her ear. His breath tickled her eardrum seductively, inciting an answering tingle of desire between her tightly compressed thighs.

All at once she felt like spreading her legs apart, then taking his hand and placing it on her hot, damp sex. She wore no knickers under her shorts and the fabric clung to the outline of her vulva. Wriggling slightly, she allowed the seam of her shorts to tantalise her throbbing clitoris.

Paralysed by the shame of her overwhelming desire, she felt the removal of Lawrie's hand as keenly as if he had ripped her skin away with it. Her bare thigh felt more naked and exposed than ever now he no longer touched it. Feeling envious, she watched him rub his palms along his own thighs. Then he straightened his legs slowly and stood up.

'Thank you again,' she murmured, glancing up at him.

She noticed he seemed to tower above her. His face was indistinct, his divine features blurred by the sharpness of the sun which created a nimbus of light around his blond head.

His voice floated down to her, deep and without inflection. 'Don't mention it. I'll see you later on track, no doubt.'

She found herself nodding dumbly as he loped away, back to his own table where the blonde and the brunette greeted him like a conquering hero. Oh well, Marie thought, turning her attention back to her lunch, her intimate connection with Lawrie had been nice while it lasted. Five more minutes in such close promimity with him and she might well have orgasmed.

Coming back down to earth, Marie realised that Carla was speaking to her.

'Sorry,' she said apologetically, 'I didn't catch that.'

'It was nothing much,' Carla said. 'I only asked who that gorgeous hunk of a guy was who had his hands all over you just now.'

'Guy?' Marie stared stupidly at her friend. 'Oh, him,' she said, trying to sound cool when she felt anything but. 'That was none other than the infamous Lawrie Samson.'

Six hours later, with qualifying over for the day and the starting positions unchanged as far as she and Lawrie were concerned, Marie stood under the pulsating spray of her hotel shower. While she showered she carried on an argument with Carla who was in their shared bedroom getting dressed.

'I don't really feel like going to a bloody party, Carla,' she called out. 'I'm shattered. I just want to go to bed.'

Carla appeared in the open doorway, blasting at her hair with the dryer. 'You've got to,' she insisted. 'Rooney is a nice guy. He'll think it really strange if we don't turn up.'

Stepping out of the shower, Marie paused to wrap a small towel around herself. Tipping her head forward she began to rub vigorously at her short, dark hair.

'Oh, all right then, if we must,' she mumbled, her head still hanging upside down, 'but I'm not staying long. I've got a race to compete in tomorrow, remember?'

'Yeah, so?' Carla said, clicking off the hairdryer and turning back to the bedroom. 'You and fifteen or twenty others who'll be there. Stop acting like you're Queen of the May.'

Flinging her head back, Marie laughed aloud. Whatever happened, she could always rely on Carla to bring her back down to earth.

Twenty minutes later, the two young women were dressed, made up and ready for the call from reception to tell them that their taxi had arrived. With her freshly washed hair tucked back under her 'Amber' wig, Marie was wearing a pair of straight turquoise hipster trousers in satinised cotton and a matching jacket which she wore fastened by a single button over a silver uplift bra. Carla was similarly attired but in lime green, with an orange satin bustier under her jacket. On their feet they each wore a pair of white strappy sandals with high, straight heels.

Now she was ready to go Marie found herself looking forward to the coming evening. Even though she'd only be able to stay for a few hours it would be worth it, because Swedish driver Rooney Svenson threw the wildest parties and in some of the craziest locations she had ever come across. The address printed on the invitation meant absolutely nothing to her but, Rooney had insisted, if she just handed it to the taxi driver he would know where to go.

The phone rang and Carla jumped up to answer it.

'OK,' she said to Marie, picking up a boxy white patent handbag and the swipe card for their room, 'we're on, let's go.'

During the taxi ride, Marie had to concentrate on becoming Amber again. She realised she was beginning to tire of the deception. For one thing the wig made her head itch, and if she got into any intimate situations while she was wearing it, she always worried that it would come off during the height of passion. Her multiple lives were becoming so confusing that Marie felt certain she would be caught out, or even give herself away one day soon. Provided she could just hang on until the end of the season she would be fine, she reminded herself. It was only another eight weeks until the final race and if she won the Championship –

She stopped herself suddenly, mid-thought. What was she thinking of – *if* she won the Championship? Until now it had only ever been a question of *when* she won it. With a sinking feeling, she realised that, somehow, Lawrie Samson had really managed to get to her.

'Are you thinking about that guy again?' Carla asked incisively.

Marie glanced round. 'What guy?'

'Oh, come off it,' Carla said, 'you've been behaving like a bitch on heat since lunchtime.'

Marie frowned at Carla's burst of laughter. 'That's not very nice – or true,' she said. 'I haven't given him a second thought.'

Liar, her reflection in the window accused her, as she gazed out of the taxi at the bright streets of the seaside town, which reminded her of Margate. She had hardly stopped thinking about Lawrie; imagining the two of them together. Ever since he had touched her at lunchtime she had been unable to stop fantasising about how his hand would feel if it touched other parts of her body. Or what his body looked like under the seven layers of his fireproof overalls. How did he behave away from his car, his motor home, his crew and his groupies? Was he just a normal man under all those protective layers, or was he still a demi-god?

'Are you all right, Marie? You're looking a bit flushed,' Carla said as the taxi drew to a halt outside a red brick windmill. Red bulbs flashed on the sails of the windmill in a curious parody of the Moulin Rouge.

'It's Amber,' Marie hissed back, feeling embarrassed, 'and yes, I'm all right. For God's sake, Carla, just stop fussing and give me a break!'

She felt instantly guilty for speaking to Carla that way and wasn't surprised when her friend climbed from the taxi and went straight up to the open door of the windmill without waiting for her. Loud music and party noises issued through the doorway and bright lights flashed through the tiny windows dotted about the tall structure, punctuating the darkening sky like strobes.

A good-looking man, with short fair hair, about five foot ten and broad shouldered, was waiting to greet people as they arrived. Marie stepped through the doorway and was immediately pulled into a quasi-passionate embrace by him.

'Rooney, you idiot,' she said, laughing as she twisted her head away from him.

'Kiss me, Amber, or I swear I'll kill myself,' Rooney declared. 'No, on second thoughts, I'll kill him instead, he is far better looking than me.' Rooney's green eyes alighted on a tall, lanky young man who had just entered.

The party-goer looked so startled by the Swedish driver's pronouncement that Marie laughed again and cupped Rooney's broad face in her hands.

'OK, I give in,' she said in a jokey manner. She pressed her lips hard against his.

To her surprise she felt herself melting against him as his mouth opened under hers for a proper kiss. For some time she had been harbouring certain fantasies about the Swede, which she had never had the opportunity to pursue before. Now, however, the situation seemed perfect. He was there. She was there. And, thanks to her frustrating encounter with Lawrie Samson, she was feeling as aroused as hell.

'Dance with me,' Rooney murmured, pressing his erection against her stomach as he walked her backwards into the circular main room where the party was taking place.

With a lascivious twinkle in her eye Marie continued to walk backwards, drawing him with her to the centre of the room where an open-tread staircase led up to a round hole in the wooden ceiling.

'Forget the dancing,' she said, her eyes following the length of the staircase. 'Take me up to the stars instead.'

The floorboards of the tiny platform at the top of the windmill were hard, splintered and covered in dust, though Rooney didn't seem to mind and nor did Marie. Rolling around naked, they finally broke apart to lie back, panting. With their hands cupping the backs of their heads, they stared up at the diamond-studded canopy of black velvet that was the sky.

'You're beautiful,' Rooney said after a moment or two. He cast an appreciative glance at Marie, his gaze travelling from her face to her breasts. With a devilish wink he added, 'Both of you.'

Marie laughed. Rooney had let it be known right at the start, as he unfastened the single button on her jacket to reveal the silver bra, that he was a breast man. Just in case she had been left in any doubt, the way he had groaned and buried his face in her uplifted cleavage had convinced her.

Now Marie glanced down to his cock where it curved ever so slightly on its nest of brassy-hued curls as it began to soften. Reaching down she pulled off the used condom carefully, disposing of it neatly in a tissue.

'You're ever so big,' she offered flatteringly.

She noticed he opened his mouth as if to protest and then seemed to decide against it. Instead he rolled on to his side and stroked a hand over her torso. Instantly, she felt her nipples harden and goosepimples spring up on her skin.

Where they lay could almost be considered alfresco, she thought, delighting in the caress of the warm evening air on her naked flesh. All that surrounded them was a wall which was a combination of bare red brick and square glass-less windows. Through the open squares she could see the starlit sky and hear the sounds of the surrounding countryside: the hoot of owls, the faint mooing of the black and white Freesian cows for which the region was renowned, the chirruping of grasshoppers and the bubbling sound of fish coming up to the surface of a nearby canal to feed. It was a far cry from the gaudy, tawdry atmosphere of night-time Amsterdam, which was only a couple of hours' drive away and which had been the alternative on offer to her that evening.

All at once she found herself wondering if Lawrie Samson had elected to visit what was, to her, one of Europe's sleaziest and, for that reason, most exciting of capital cities.

Perhaps, right now, she mused, determined to torture herself, he was seated at a table in some glitzy hostess bar, eyeing the jiggling breasts of the waitresses. Or maybe he and his two bimbo girlfriends were wandering through the red light district, gawping at the hookers who sat advertising their wares in the front windows of the houses that lined the streets.

No, she chided herself, Lawrie Samson was not the sort of man to gawp. He was far too sensual for that. She groaned aloud with desire at the mere thought of him.

'I am learning you are a greedy young woman,' Rooney said, mistaking the reason for her groan. Smiling with satisfaction, he cupped her left breast and squeezed it gently.

Marie arched her back, thrusting her breast further into his hand. Let him think what he liked, she decided; where was the point in correcting him? As long as they both got plenty of pleasure out of the experience, who was it going to hurt?

Pressing her shoulders and the soles of her feet into the hard wooden floor, she raised her hips and stroked a hand suggestively between her parted thighs. Her vulva felt warm and moist, her vagina aching to be filled once again. She felt her stomach tighten as Rooney's hand followed hers, his broad fingers stroking the length of her slit. Filled with renewed excitement she moved her hand away and lowered her bottom to the dusty floor-boards. Then she wriggled suggestively as Rooney's fingers spread her outer labia wide, his thumb circling the swollen bud of her clitoris.

Reaching down, she grasped his cock, her fingers stroking his shaft. She slid her fingers up and down it until she felt his cock begin to harden again. Rooney wasn't a young man by racing standards, perhaps 35, or even older, but time had been good to him. His body was trim and firm, without a hint of flabbiness. Golden curls covered his chest and a slightly darker line of hair arrowed down from his navel to disappear into his thick bush of pubic hair.

Although he was certainly good-looking, it was his personality which mainly attracted her. He was always full of fun and optimism, with a sheer exuberance for life and an irrepressible mischief that often ended up catching other racers unawares. It wasn't unknown for a driver's overalls to disappear overnight, only to be discovered flapping away at the top of a flagpole. Or for one of the track marshals to find himself as the butt of a joke which Rooney had devised.

Marie thanked her lucky stars that he raced more for the fun of competing than with a determination to win, otherwise she might have felt slightly guilty about beating him hands down every single time.

Rooney's movement beside her made her open her eyes. She had been so busy concentrating on the delightful sensation of her fingers wrapped around his hard, throbbing cock and the slowly growing warmth in her pelvis that she had blocked out everything else.

Below her she could feel the vibration of the music's heavy beat and could hear a symphony of animated party noises. It excited her to think that anyone could climb up to the platform and catch her and Rooney *in flagrante*. There was no way she could hide her nakedness if someone should appear. Her clothes were in a pile with Rooney's near the top of the staircase, too far out of reach for her to be able to grab them in an emergency.

'You know why I pick the number of my car, don't you, Amber?' Rooney was saying as he moved to his hands and knees.

She shook her head. 'No – I – ' Feeling a trifle ashamed, she realised she couldn't remember his racing number.

He turned around and swung one leg over her shoulders, positioning himself so that his cock brushed her lips enticingly. Parting her legs wider by applying a slight pressure to her inner thighs, he glanced over his shoulder at her.

'Three guesses,' he said, flashing her a wicked grin before lowering his head.

Marie groaned with pleasure as she felt his mouth encompass her vulva and the tip of his tongue circle her vagina before plunging into its musky depths. Whimpering, she caught his cock between her hands and guided the swollen glans between her lips. Of course, she realised as she began to suck him skilfully, how could she have forgotten so easily? Rooney's racing number had always been 69.

Chapter Five

The following morning at Zandvoort the sun came out and, along with it, all the beautiful people. As the stands were packed with spectators and the pits swarming with life, the noise around the track was almost deafening. With only half an hour to go before the start of the race, all the teams were assiduously warming up their engines, while the mechanics and drivers shouted last minute instructions to each other over the din.

For once Marie was a bag of nerves and it was no help to her whatsoever to know the reason for her anxiety. Lawrie Samson, she sighed to herself as she slid out of the driver's seat of her car and stretched, had become a major problem. Not only was he a threat to her championship hopes but he seemed ubiquitous. Everywhere she looked she caught sight of someone, or something, in his racing colours.

Like her own, his car was out of the garage being attended to. And his crew and band of hangers-on seemed to have tripled. Wherever Marie happened to glance she caught a flash of purple and white. Or perhaps that was simply her frazzled mind playing tricks on her, she decided, as she wandered into her garage to finish her fifth cup of coffee of the morning.

As she stood at the back of the garage, pulling on her racing gloves and adjusting the chin strap on her helmet, she felt a keen presence beside her. Without glancing up she knew it was Lawrie. Come to gloat, no doubt, she mused, feeling her stomach lurch. Unable to avoid him any longer, she deliberately composed her expression into one of pleasant surprise before turning around.

'I just came to wish you luck,' he said, totally disarming her before she had a chance to speak.

She felt herself start to tremble and had to grip on to the edge of the workbench to stop herself from keeling over with desire. No matter how badly she wanted to hate him, she found he had the opposite effect on her.

'Thank you,' she said eventually, her voice hardly more than a whisper, 'that's very sporting.'

He threw back his head and laughed, his blond hair rippling over his shoulders like a lion's mane.

'That's me,' he said, smiling broadly. 'Sportsman of the year. But seriously,' he added, his lips losing some of their curve while his eyes darkened slightly, 'I don't want you to imagine there's any unnecessary competitiveness on my part. Of course, I want to win but I wouldn't like you to think that it's the be-all and end-all for me.' He paused and narrowed his eyes. 'Somehow, I get the impression that success in this Championship means a whole lot more to you than it does to me.'

Wondering how he could have judged her so accurately when they had hardly exchanged more than a few words, Marie tried to shrug.

'I have my reasons for wanting to win, as I'm sure everyone else does,' she said, scuffing the toe of her racing boot on the concrete flooring. She couldn't bear to look at him properly. His eyes were doing strange things to her and if ever she needed every ounce of her normal self-possession it was now. 'Still,' she went on, forcing herself to glance up and smile brightly, 'it was nice of you to come over here and wish me luck. The same to you.'

She held out her hand to him shakily and felt her

breath catch as he took it between both his hands and simply held it for a long, heart-stopping moment. Beneath the layers of her fireproof kit she could feel the unmistakable warmth his touch created, causing small rivulets of perspiration to trickle down her shoulder blades and between her breasts. She felt feverish and almost had to drag her hand away from his to stop herself from saying, or doing, something stupid.

'Well, I'll see you out on the starting grid then, Amber,' he murmured, chucking her under the chin. 'So long.'

With a dry mouth, Marie watched him walk away. His loping stride and the confident way he held his broad shoulders and golden head made her long to run after him and fling her arms around him. More than anything she yearned to press herself against his lean, hard body and feel her naked skin touching his. Feeling dizzy with wanting, she leant against the wall for support.

After a moment or two, when he had disappeared from view, she felt sufficiently recovered to pour some mineral water into a plastic cup and gulp it down. Then she jammed her helmet on her head and fastened it with trembling fingers. It was time to forget all about Lawrie Samson and simply go out there and win.

Marie liked the Zandvoort track. Shaped like a reversed 'Q', it had just a few chicanes right at the start of the circuit. The longest straight was the one which ran from the final *Bos Uit* chicane, past the pits and into the first chicane after the grid, the *Tarzanbocht*. It was along this straight she hoped to lose the opposition by getting up to speeds of at least 140 mph. If there was one thing for which she was renowned, it was for having a heavy accelerator foot.

Strapped into the driving seat, while the tannoy blared a brass band's rendition of the Dutch national anthem, she tried not to glance sideways at Lawrie's car. Taking second place on the grid was bad enough but the thought of actually seeing him, of all people, sitting there in pole position would be more than she could bear.

Instead she concentrated on the lights above the grid. Like traffic lights, the sequence would tell her when to get ready and when to go. A few minutes later, the loudspeakers crackled and a disembodied voice announced that the race was about to start. Watching the red light come on, she thrust the gearstick into first. The split second the light changed to green she slammed her right foot down on the accelerator.

Changing quickly up and down the gears as she negotiated the tight series of chicanes at the start of the circuit, she felt the usual rush of adrenalin that obliterated every thought from her mind other than what she should be doing and when.

Lawrie had got off to a good start but she quickly caught up with him at the *Rob Slotemaker Bocht*. As the leader, he was happily following the racing line and Marie felt herself grit her teeth as she tried to get past him by cutting inside his car around the little 'S' bend of the *Marlborobocht*. She felt her car juddering as the nearside wheels rode the kerb. Damn, she wouldn't make it! She dropped back behind him again and stuck close to his bumper, making the most of his slipstream as they went over the *Tunnel Loost* and into *Panorama-bocht*. Again she tried to get around him on the chicane but was forced to concede defeat or go off the track.

For the next half dozen laps, nothing changed between her car and Lawrie's, though quite a few other drivers altered position, or went spinning off the track. At one point Marie almost lost her concentration as Darren Standish's car clipped her rear wing before going into a three-quarters spin and ending up on the grass beside the track. Knowing how much Darren had wanted to win at Zandvoort, above all other races, Marie felt a pang of compassion for him before quickly reverting to her single-minded intention to get past Lawrie at all costs.

Finally on lap eight she got her chance. Just as their

cars slid side by side around *Bos Uit* – so close they could have been Siamese twins – she dropped straight from fifth to third, then up to fourth and fifth again, making the gear changes in such rapid succession and accelerating so hard at the same time that she shot past him in full view of everyone in the pits.

From then on, she refused to give him an inch. Deftly avoiding his many attempts to overtake her again, she kept him behind her until the final lap. With a silent cheer of victory and a broad grin, which stayed hidden behind her helmet, she sailed over the grid. The welcome sight of the chequered flag was more thrilling to her on this occasion than it had ever been. After a lap of honour she coasted smoothly and triumphantly into the pit lane, coming to a halt beside a jubilant Carla and the rest of the crew.

As she stepped from the car, her crew and members of the press surrounded her and it was a full fifteen minutes before she was able to break away long enough to glance around. Now that she had succeeded in beating Lawrie, she wanted to see if he was watching her at all.

She had just about given up trying to spot him in the crowd when a firm hand on her shoulder startled her.

'Congratulations,' his familiar voice said in her ear, 'you won that race fair and square.'

'I know,' she responded automatically, intending to sound jaunty.

She turned, her face beaming. Just for the briefest of moments she felt tempted to kiss him, such was her elation at winning and her delight at having him so close to her again. Close enough to touch and to fill her nostrils with the delicious scent that was uniquely his. Her face fell when she noticed that he wasn't returning her smile. If anything his expression was one of contempt.

'I'll tell you what *I* know, Amber,' he said, the words dropping from his lips like acid, 'it wouldn't hurt you to learn a bit of humility. Yes, you drove a good race, there's no doubt about that. Your driving skills are

74

obviously first class but one day your sheer, bloody-minded arrogance is going to be your downfall.'

Marie felt her mouth opening and closing like a fish. Me? arrogant? she wanted to respond. Oh, no, mister, that's your speciality. But his hard-eyed look and the harshness of his words rendered her speechless.

'Amber, Amber. Come on, we need a piccy!' someone shouted out, interrupting her confused thoughts.

Swiftly bringing herself back to the reality of the moment, Marie glared at Lawrie before trying to push past him.

'Excuse me,' she muttered, 'much as I'm enjoying our little *tête à tête*, I can't stand here chatting all day.'

He stepped back and flung his arms wide, dramatically allowing her plenty of space.

'Away you go then, your highness,' he said, his Scots accent returning with a vengeance, she noticed, although she felt too upset to think anything of it at the time. 'Far be it for me hold you up when the good gentlemen of the press await you.' His eyes glittered for a moment. Then he let his arms drop and he shook his head, his expression clearly one of disappointment. 'Go on, go,' he continued gruffly. 'I don't know why I wasted my time talking to you in the first place. You're not a woman, you're a machine, like your car here.'

He raised a fist and for one terrible moment Marie wondered whether he intended to punch her car – or her. Instead he smacked it into the palm of his other hand before turning on his heel and striding away angrily.

With a crowd of journalists and photographers surging around her again, Marie didn't have the time to feel anything about his outburst. It was only later, when she managed to escape to the relative sanctuary of the team van, that she allowed herself to sit and contemplate Lawrie's dreadful opinion of her – and why it mattered so much.

* * *

For once she declined to stay at the track to watch the afternoon's racing – a round of the German Touring Car Championship. Instead, she slunk back to the hotel, feeling so low that she couldn't summon enthusiasm for anything. Not even the lap of victory she had taken – standing up in the back of an American pick-up truck decked with flowers and laurel wreaths – nor taking first place on the podium and spraying her crew with the customary bottle of champagne had managed to lift her spirits.

Eventually she fell into a fitful doze, during which she enjoyed a passion-filled dream about herself and Lawrie, only to wake up later and realise that that was all it had been – a dream.

'What on earth is the matter with you?' Carla asked as she let herself into the room a little while later. 'You look like your dog died.'

'I haven't got a dog,' Marie mumbled into her pillow.

'I know that, you idiot. I – oh, for goodness sake, what is it?' Carla sat down heavily on the bed next to Marie and touched her shoulder sympathetically.

'Nothing,' Marie insisted, sitting up and pushing her hair away from her face. 'I'm just tired, I suppose.'

Carla snorted with disbelief. 'Tired – you? Don't give me that. Normally when you've just won a race you're like a cat with two tails.'

'I said I was tired.' Marie tried to glare at her friend but failed dismally. Her lower lip trembled and she felt the unaccustomed sting of tears.

'It's that Samson guy, isn't it?' Carla said gently, after a moment.

Marie shrugged. 'A bit – sort of.'

'A lot,' Carla said firmly. Reaching down she picked up an unopened bottle of Dom Perignon which she had put down by her feet. 'Prezzie,' she announced, handing it to Marie, who studied it blankly for a moment.

'Who from?' she asked.

'A magazine editor, no less,' Carla said. Standing up,

she walked into the bathroom and helped herself to a couple of tumblers before sitting back down on the bed again. 'Are you going to just look at that, or drink it?'

Smiling despite her black mood, Marie held the cork and twisted the bottle until the two parted company with a loud pop. Pouring some of the effervescent liquid into the glasses, she put the bottle on the floor again.

'So,' Marie said after she had taken a couple of sips, 'what magazine was this?'

Carla tossed her head airily. 'I can't remember what the editor said it was called. Only that it's some kind of Dutch soft porn mag, but for women rather than men. She's invited us to a party tonight, with you as the guest of honour.'

Marie laughed thinly and drained her glass, refilling it immediately. With a sorrowful glance at her friend, she said, 'I'm not in the mood.'

Carla frowned. 'Well, be in the mood,' she retorted firmly, 'because they want to talk to you about sponsorship.'

'Sponsorship?'

'Yeah.' Carla snorted into her champagne, making Marie wrinkle her nose with disgust; her friend always had trouble holding even the tiniest amount of alcohol. 'They think you'd make a good sales tool – emancipated lady racer and all that.'

'Well, well, well. Tell me more,' Marie murmured as she reclined against the headboard of the bed. She felt more than a slight stirring of interest. Suddenly, Lawrie Samson and his stupid remarks didn't seem all that important any more.

'It seems they want to do a photo spread of you with the car,' Carla explained, 'with all these half-naked guys draped all over it.'

'Interesting variation on an old theme,' Marie cut in.

'Exactly.' Carla waved her glass in the air, spilling some champagne on the bed in the process.

'Hey, watch it. I've got to sleep in this tonight,' Marie protested.

She grinned as Carla winked at her. 'Not if you play your cards right. By the sound of this bash we're going to, you'll be lucky if you get any sleep at all before the sun comes up.'

'Sounds like my kind of party,' Marie agreed, getting up and making for the bathroom.

Carla grinned after her and lay down in the space her friend had vacated. She stared bleary-eyed at the ceiling, wondering why it was going round and round.

'I thought you'd say that,' she called out.

Although it was surrounded by acres of flat farmland, there was no mistaking the huge Dutch barn where the party was being held. Barely a kilometre from the track, the front entrance was marked by two flagpoles, ten metres high, from which a couple of chequered flags fluttered in the warm evening breeze.

As they drew close to the building Amber noticed that a huge yellow banner was strung across its whitewashed façade. In bold scarlet lettering the banner proclaimed the word VERVAL!

'That's the name of the magazine,' Carla said quickly, before Marie had a chance to say anything. 'I remember it now.'

'It's a bit of an odd name,' Marie declared as she climbed from the taxi.

Carla punched her lightly on the arm. 'Of course it seems odd. It's in Dutch, you idiot!'

Just as Marie swung round to offer Carla a suitable retort, she was stopped in her tracks by the appearance of a tall, cropped-haired brunette. The woman, who looked to be somewhere in her late thirties, was dressed in a green catsuit, the narrow legs tucked into matching knee-high boots. In the centre of a long, angular face the tip of her straight nose sported a pair of schoolmarmish spectacles. She was so thin and so green she reminded Marie instantly of a praying mantis. With difficulty, Marie forced herself not to laugh aloud at her own thoughts.

'Hi, there, I'm Bette Bezuidenhout,' the woman said in heavily accented English, 'but everyone calls me BB. I'm the editor of *Verval* and hostess of this party, for my sins.' She giggled like a naughty schoolgirl.

Strange though BB was to look at, Marie found that she warmed to the woman straight away.

'What does *Verval* mean?' she asked as they climbed the steps to the front door of the farmhouse.

'In English?'

Marie nodded.

BB smiled. 'In English it means – uh – '

'Decadence,' a newcomer supplied for her.

Marie glanced up, liking what she saw instantly. The interloper was male, slightly taller than herself, dark haired, swarthy and very, very good-looking.

'Decadence, eh?' Marie murmured, treating the man to her best come-hither smile. 'You must have been the inspiration.'

To her delight he laughed hugely, throwing his head back, his shoulders shaking. When his laughter faded to a chuckle, he straightened up and held her gaze in the olive grip of his own.

'My, my, BB,' he said, his accent indeterminable, 'you have found yourself a woman who flirts even more outrageously than me.'

Marie smiled as BB pretended to look disbelieving. 'That is impossible, Laurent, you are the master *libertijn*.'

This time, Marie had no need of a translation. Deciding that she liked Laurent a great deal, she agreed to go with him to the bar, leaving Carla to fend for herself. Although, Marie noticed, as she eyed the crowd of young men already gathered around her friend, Carla was hardly being left in the lurch.

While tequila slammers kept on coming with brain-numbing regularity, BB explained that the publisher of her magazine was so impressed by Marie's performance that season she was regarded as the ideal woman to represent it.

'You are perfect, Amber,' she said expansively, 'sophisticated, dedicated, emancipated – '

'Inebriated,' Laurent cut in, noticing the way Marie's eyes were beginning to glaze over. 'Excuse us, BB, but I'm going to take this young woman away from you for a while. I think she needs very badly to dance with me.'

'I do?' Marie gazed at him, feeling a powerful surge of desire that almost rocked her on her Russell & Bromley black satin slingbacks. It was true, she conceded, she did need to dance with him. Or at the very least feel his arms around her, his body pressed hard against her own.

As she walked hand in hand with him to the dance floor, she couldn't help noticing the appreciative glances other men gave her. It wasn't surprising, she thought immodestly, she did look good in the outfit she had chosen to wear. It was one of her old favourites, a plain black silk dress with a strapless, boned bodice and straight, wraparound skirt. Best of all, the creases fell out almost from the moment she unpacked it, making it her preferred standby party dress whenever she travelled anywhere. Underneath it, all she wore was a tiny black silk G-string and hold-up stockings.

Tonight, she decided, as she floated into the welcoming circle of Laurent's arms, she felt like a femme fatale. At long last she was high on success. Her win and the ten thousand pounds sponsorship deal BB had offered her – which she had accepted immediately, before the other woman changed her mind – combined to make her feel on top of the world.

'You smell divine,' Laurent said as he nuzzled the side of her neck. His lips pressed against her skin, warm and wet and inviting.

Marie shivered with arousal. Allowing her hands to glide over his back and shoulders, she felt the hard muscle beneath his black dress suit. All the male guests were similarly attired, she noticed, glancing around as she and Laurent danced, but none looked as good to her at that moment. She felt her stomach lurch into a double somersault as his lips continued to lay a trail of kisses down the length of her throat and along her collar bone. He nipped her bare shoulder, one hand squeezing her buttocks when she gave a slight yelp.

'You like a little pain?' he said darkly.

She shook her head and smiled provocatively at him. 'Not usually but I'm open to suggestions.'

His eyes widened and he said, 'Ah!' as though her simple statement had told him everything he needed to know about her.

Marie felt her insides liquefy, the juices trickling from her body, soaking the scanty crotch of her G-string. Her body felt hot, her mouth dry. Tonight, she realised, with a certainty that set her senses aflame, was going to be more fun than she could have hoped.

At the front of the darkened room, the sudden brilliance of a series of spotlights coming on served to highlight the smoke-filled atmosphere as well as cast a silver trail across the stage and down the catwalk.

'Are we going to watch a fashion show?' Marie whispered to Laurent as they took the couple of seats reserved for them to the right of the catwalk.

'Hardly.' Laurent laughed throatily as he glanced across Marie to BB.

The other woman smiled knowingly at him. 'Don't let him tease you, Amber,' she warned with a hint of amusement in her tone. 'He knows what is about to happen. After all, he helped me to organise it.'

'Well,' Marie said, glancing from one to the other, 'aren't either of you two going to elaborate?'

'No,' Laurent replied, patting her knee and letting his hand stay there. 'You'll just have to wait and see.'

Marie shrugged, pretending she couldn't care less. Then she glanced up as loud music started to blare from a couple of huge amplifiers set up at the corners of the stage. The music was raunchy, with a heavy, hypnotic beat that filled her with expectation. She was fully aware of Laurent's hand still resting on her knee and was hardly surprised when it started to slither higher up her stockinged leg. Shifting slightly in her seat, she allowed her thighs to part a little. Immediately, Laurent's hand slid over the bare portion of her thigh above her stocking top, his fingers describing tiny circles in the little dip where her inner thigh met her groin.

She let out the breath she was not aware she was holding in a quiet hiss. With the music playing so loudly she was certain no one could have heard it. Yet when she happened to glance sideways at Laurent she caught his wolfish smile. His eyes were dark; the dilated pupils almost obscuring the olive irises. She wondered if her eyes similarly conveyed the extent of her own arousal. All her emotions were held in check, bubbling just below the surface of her outwardly calm exterior.

He knows how I'm feeling, she thought, sensing the animal interest he conveyed silently to her. Their contact was primaeval. Lust for the sake of lust. Nothing and no one existed outside their state of wanting; each waiting for the right moment, when the full extent of their mutual passion could finally be unleashed. She felt overwhelmed by it. As though she were drowning in inevitability. Their bodies were mere shells; fragile containers for the desire that burned inside.

Forcing herself to concentrate on something else, something outside herself, Marie gazed across the polished wood catwalk and noticed that Carla sat almost opposite her. They shared a conspiratorial grin. Carla looked happy, Marie thought to herself. She couldn't help noticing the two young men seated either side of her friend, or the way their shoulders pressed meaningfully against hers. Both were just Carla's type. Very young, barely in their twenties, with floppy, unstructured hairstyles that probably cost a fortune to create. They looked as though they spent their whole lives working out at the gym, watching MTV or bungee jumping.

'Attention, Amber,' Laurent said in her ear, 'the first part of this evening's entertainment is about to begin.'

Flashing him a brief smile she turned her attention to

the stage where a procession of young men – clothed in dress suits like all the others at the party – appeared, dancing, from the wings. They gyrated along the cat-walk, moving in choreographed sequence.

Her face raised to the dancers, Marie couldn't help giving a gasp of surprise as, one by one, the young men started to discard their clothing. Never missing a beat they ripped away bow ties, jackets, shirts and trousers to reveal outstandingly muscular torsos. She was aware that Laurent was watching her but couldn't tear her eyes away from the spectacle. As the men turned she noticed that they wore thong-backed briefs. With the eye of a conoisseur she eyed their buttocks – firm, smooth and rounded – as they continued to bump and grind.

'Oh, my God!' Marie exclaimed in a shocked whisper as the skimpy garments were whipped away. The dancers displayed such an astonishing array of semi-erect penises that she almost covered her face in embarrassment.

'Don't tell me you're shocked,' Laurent said beside her. 'You're loving every minute of it. You can't fool me, I can feel how wet you are.'

Her cheeks burning with shame, Marie tried to ignore him. But it was impossible to deny the fingers slipping skilfully under the thin gusset of her G-string and stroking her blossoming sex.

'As smooth as a baby's bottom,' Laurent continued mercilessly. 'How charming.'

To Marie's humiliation she noticed that one of the dancers was watching her, or rather Laurent's hand as it massaged the moist, swollen flesh between her thighs.

Tossing his head, so that his silky chestnut hair swung over his shoulder, the young man dropped to his knees in front of her. Immediately, he parted his thighs and started to churn his hips, lewdly offering her an unob-structed view of his stiffening cock and swinging balls. Grasping his cock with both hands he began to mastur-bate, then slowed his movements and offered his cock to Marie.

Unsure what he wanted her to do, Marie shook her head slowly.

'Go on,' Laurent encouraged, removing his hand from between her legs, 'I think he wants you to finish him off.'

'I can't,' Marie whispered, appalled. 'Not in public.'

She glanced around as BB tapped her on the arm. 'This is not public, *lieveling*,' BB prompted her. 'This is a private party. Go for it. Enjoy. That is what they're here for.' She nodded meaningfully at the stage full of young men before adding, 'That is what we are all here for.'

Feeling her heart pound, Marie rose unsteadily to her feet. Standing up, she found the dancer's cock was level with her face. Taking a deep breath, she reached out and grasped it. A cheer rose from the audience.

'Go, Amber go!' she heard some of them shout out.

She glanced around, noticing the blatant looks of encouragement on everyone's face, including those of BB and Laurent. Finally, she looked up at the dancer.

His eyes were glazed with an expression she recognised instantly as lust. Her hand tightened around his thick shaft, delighting to the sensation of the hard muscle throbbing away beneath her fingers. Right, she thought, if they all want a show, they'll get one. Leaning forward, she glanced up at the dancer once more and licked her lips deliberately. Then, forming a perfect 'O' with her lips, she went in for the kill.

Chapter Six

The dense, musky aura of sex, combined with raunchy music and the heat of many bodies, launched Marie on a hitherto uncharted voyage of erotic discovery. She thought she had already seen and done most things but the party at the barn was far and away the most exciting event she had participated in so far.

Heedless of the audience around her, she concentrated solely on the delicious length of the dancer's proud member as it reared up in front of her from between broad, muscular thighs. Relaxing her throat, she slid her lips all the way down his shaft to encompass every last millimetre of him. Then, gazing intently at the flat, golden-toned stomach in front of her eyes, which was covered with a thin sheen of perspiration, she concentrated all her efforts on reducing the rest of him to a helpless wreck; one who writhed and groaned and who clutched fervently at her hair in desperation.

She gripped the base of his shaft with one hand and stroked his thigh with the other. She felt supremely powerful as her fingertips traced the tautness of his muscles, delighting in the way they quivered unmistakably, proving how desperately he was trying to hold himself back. As she allowed her hand to travel up over his flat belly and down and around the base of his cock to cup his hard balls, she could sense the virility surging inside him. The taste of him and the musky scent touching her nostrils provoked an intoxicating sensation of animal lust that drove her to double her efforts.

Determined to make him cede to her, she drew him deep into her mouth, sucking and licking, until, at the very last moment, she felt his throbbing cock swell to bursting point. Pulling her head away just in time, she gripped his shaft and watched with undisguised triumph as his semen jetted up and arced over the chest of one of the other dancers in a milky-white cascade. Satisfied with the result but even more desperate to assuage her own desire, she climbed up on to the catwalk, pulled off her g-string and straddled him in full view of everyone.

As if she had given a cue for inhibitions to be unleashed, several women in the audience followed suit, while the eager hands of others reached up to the stage to fondle the nearest piece of naked masculine flesh. As willing victims to the liberated passions of the assembled *cliterati*, the vigorous dancers gave in to the women's desires with rampant enthusiasm.

Marie was pleased to note that despite the violence of his orgasm her chosen hunk of beefcake was still rock hard. And she was wet, she realised, caught up in the thread of lascivious intent. So very delectably wet.

Grasping the dancer's thick rod she guided it inside her, her vagina almost sighing with relief as she did so. She gripped his cock tightly with her internal muscles as she ground herself on top of his hard body, aware of but indifferent to the fact that she was merely using him for her own gratification. Totally abandoned now in a desert of sexual longing, she thirsted only for fulfilment.

Cursing the restriction of her clothing, she only wavered for a moment before hitching her skirt up around her waist. Fingers working feverishly, she tucked it under the hem of her bodice, freeing her lower body. To her relief, the dancer's hands were on her in an instant, his broad fingers spreading her swollen labia wide apart and rubbing her throbbing clitoris.

She moaned aloud as she felt a second pair of hands slide around her, pulling down the front of her bodice and exposing her aching breasts. Even in the heady moment of near-ecstasy it was easy for her to recognise the owner of the hands as Laurent. She smelled his unique scent: tangy aftershave mingled with hair gel and the enticing musk that symbolised his arousal. His mouth was upon her bare shoulder, his hair tickling her skin, his fingers playing with her swollen nipples as he cupped her breasts.

'Sexy woman,' he breathed in her ear. 'You come with him then I take you and give you more pleasure.'

With his words tantalising her and reverberating erotically throughout her body Marie felt like crying out, 'Oh, yes, please!' As it was she heard herself groaning, craving satisfaction. Her whole body was sizzling with desire. With her pelvis rocking and churning on the hard body beneath her, she arched her back, thrusting out her breasts which were were full and heavy, burning with lust.

She felt greedy, hungry for Laurent's mouth on her aching nipples. Reaching up as she arched her back further, she pulled his head down to her breasts. She let out a long moan as he squashed them together and began to lathe them simultaneously with his tongue.

All at once she felt her sex spasming, forcing ripples of hot passion to spread outwards from its core. Her clitoris throbbed mercilessly. The hard bud was so swollen and exposed by the dancer's fingers which kept her labia spread wide apart that she felt a burning wave of shame at the blatant proof of her arousal. She was aware that people were watching her, looking at her breasts and between her legs, at the hugely swollen berries that were her nipples and clitoris. Humiliating though it was, it only added to the thrill.

Desire rampaged through her, trampling every last inhibition she might have held. And a moment later she came, viciously, overwhelmingly, with an almighty groan of triumph that seemed to shake the very rafters of the old barn. With every tendon in her thighs quivering she slowed her movements to a gradual halt and climbed off the dancer, spent for the moment but elated.

'Come,' Laurent said a minute or so later, dragging her limp body from the stage.

'I thought I just did,' she joked weakly.

She gazed at him, wondering why, despite the monumental orgasm she had just enjoyed, she felt once again as though her erotic touchpaper had only just been lit. Turning in his arms as her feet touched solid ground, she churned her half-clothed body against his and pressed her lips to his surprised mouth. Her tongue darted avidly here and there in that wet, unexplored cavern. It captured his tongue and caressed his gums and the sensitive flesh behind his lips.

They continued to kiss for a long time, then Laurent took her by the hand. Pausing only to tug down her skirt and right her bodice, he led her away from the party-goers, through a large kitchen and up a narrow wooden staircase.

'The old hayloft,' he explained to Marie as they reached the top of the staircase.

'But no hay,' she observed.

For a moment, Marie stood gazing around the small room with its slatted wood walls, varnished floorboards and low, sloping ceiling. All at once she smiled, her eyes twinkling mischievously.

'Thank goodness there just happens to be a bed in here instead,' she added.

The bed to which she referred looked surprisingly comfortable for such a spartan room. A four-poster, it matched the rest of its surroundings in that it was crafted from solid wood. From it hung floral cotton drapes, and the thick mattress and linen sheets were covered by a white crocheted throw. The fine, lacy confection looked to Marie as though it had been worked by hand.

'I think I'm a bit tipsy,' she declared, throwing herself

face down on to the bed and glancing coquettishly at Laurent over her bare shoulder.

He raised a black caterpillar eyebrow. 'Tipsy?'

His apparent confusion made her laugh. 'Yes, you know? A bit drunk.' For a moment she looked sober as she sighed, then she chuckled again and wriggled her bottom cheekily. 'Too many tequilas and not enough slamming,' she added, noticing how his gaze seemed to darken as she said it.

'Speaking of slamming,' he said as he sauntered over to the bed to sit beside her, 'I was very impressed by your performance with that dancer.'

Marie had the grace to blush. She shivered as his fingertips walked a lazy trail across the back of her shoulder blades. 'I don't usually behave so badly,' she admitted.

'That is too bad,' he said. 'I was beginning to think you were my kind of woman.'

Turning over, she lay on her side, her head supported by her hand. 'What kind is that, then?'

'Wild, sexy, fantastic-looking, totally outrageous.'

'Oh, I don't know,' Marie said, her cheeks dimpling. 'I think I fit the bill on most of those counts regardless.'

'I think you do too,' Laurent replied with a wicked smile that made her burn inside, 'but just to make absolutely certain – '

Marie gasped as he suddenly grabbed her and pulled her against him. Falling back on to the bed he pulled her down with him until they lay, noses, lips and hips touching. Laurent reached behind her back as they kissed, and pulled down her zipper, easing the fabric of her dress apart with his hands to stroke her back.

'Mmm,' she sighed delightedly, 'you make me feel wonderful.'

'You are wonderful,' he said immediately. 'Wonderful and very fuckable.'

Even though she felt her stomach clench with longing, she managed a light laugh. 'Your English is very good,' she said, 'and I think you're very fuckable, too.' With a soft sight, she began to unfasten each of the tiny pearl buttons down the front of his shirt, pausing to kiss each patch of flesh as she exposed it.

As she reached for the buttons on the waistband of his trousers, he stopped her with a gentle hand.

'Let me make love to you,' he said softly, 'I don't want to rush this. I would prefer to savour every moment.'

'OK,' Marie conceded with a gentle smile, deciding that it might be quite nice to let her partner take the lead for once.

Laurent, she thought as he finished undressing her and then slowly undressed himself, was an exceptional man. Great-looking. Superbly built in a slim, finely boned way. Not to mention kind, warm and thoughtful. Quite unlike that supercilious bastard Lawrie!

The unprovoked and rather hostile recollection of her new track rival shocked her. It wasn't like her to let a man – any man – get to her to the extent Lawrie had. The only other male she had vile thoughts about was Greg and, thankfully, he was long gone.

'You've disappeared somewhere; come back,' she heard Laurent say.

Marie shook her head vigorously in an effort to dismiss the image of Lawrie smiling at her over a cup of coffee, then almost hitting her after she had won the race and effectively snubbed his generous congratulation. An image of him filled her mind: his face; the delicious colour and texture of his hair; his lean, well toned body and the way he carried himself – so confident, so relaxed. She imagined him liking her instead of despising her. What would it be like to be on the receiving end of his warm smile, she wondered, and to feel those eyes upon her again, but filled with lust instead of loathing?

What a bloody ridiculous notion, she told herself forcefully, trying hard to concentrate on Laurent's words, which seemed to be coming from a long way off. There was no way on the face of this earth that she and that snake, Samson, were going to be anything more than bitter rivals.

'I said, would you rather not go through with this?'

'What?' Coming out of her reverie, Marie glanced up at Laurent in surprise.

Pausing only to sit down on the edge of the bed first, Laurent reached out to her and stroked a delicate hand across her bare stomach.

'I don't know what I've said or done,' he murmured, 'but you don't seem to be enjoying yourself any more. You were frowning just then when you should have been smiling, or better still looking dazed with lust.'

'Oh, God, Laurent, I'm sorry,' Marie cried, struggling to sit up. 'My mind does that to me sometimes. It goes off on a tangent before I can stop it. Really,' she urged, 'don't stop. I don't want to stop. I want you. Honestly. Feel.' Taking his hand she thrust it between her thighs, pressing his fingertips into the moist entrance to her vagina.

He looked more or less convinced, she noticed with relief. She did like Laurent. She did want to carry on and make love with him. Most of all, she wanted someone and something to take her mind off Lawrie Samson.

'OK, you've persuaded me,' Laurent said with an engaging smile, that made Marie relax instantly. 'But promise me one thing?'

She fluttered her eyelashes dramatically as she gazed at him, a smile playing about her lips. 'What's that?' she asked.

'Promise me you won't think any more,' he said, 'or if you must, try thinking about this – ' Suddenly, he wrenched her thighs apart and dived between them, his skilful lips and tongue immediately rekindling the smouldering embers of her desire.

Marie's climax was slow to peak yet devastating in its intensity. She cried out as sharp darts of pleasure pierced her. Gripping Laurent's head hard between her thighs, she churned her pelvis and urged her swollen clitoris against his mouth. She kept on rubbing until she had extracted every last ounce of enjoyment. Eventually, as the gratifying waves began to recede at last, she watched through heavy-lidded eyes as Laurent raised his head and gazed at her.

His expression was one of satisfaction mingled with desire. His eyes were heavily laden with lust, his mouth and chin glistening with her juices.

Putting her arms out to him, she pulled him close, kissing him and relishing the taste of herself upon his lips. As they continued to kiss, she revelled in the sensation of his hands as they travelled over her torso and caressed every portion of her glowing flesh. Sighing with pleasure, Marie reached down between their bodies to grasp the hardness that she could feel pressing into her belly. His cock was quite thin, she noticed, graceful like the rest of him, with a slight kink.

Relinquishing his lips, she pushed him gently so that he rolled on to his back. Then she slithered down the bed to take him in her mouth. His taste was a delight to her, tangy and salty, and she loved the sensation of his hardness between her fingers and her lips. For long moments she teased and played with him, sliding her wet lips up and down his shaft, wrapping her tongue around him, licking and dabbing at his glans with the flat of her tongue and then the tip.

She felt him stiffening further, her senses picking up the restlessness in him. His hands clutched at her hair, his back arching as he tried to force more of himself into her mouth. But Marie was in control and let him know it. Through the tightening of her grip around the base of his shaft and the way she changed the pace of her oral caresses at just the right moments, she governed his pleasure.

'Oh, no,' she said, grinning wickedly at him as she raised her head, 'you're not coming, not yet.'

She couldn't help noticing Laurent's expression looked almost pained as he stared back at her and that sent a jolt of intense excitement through her. Aside from driving powerful cars, causing men pain – pleasurable pain – was the one thing she was particularly good at, and enjoyed to the hilt.

Ignoring his erection, which nudged her insistently as she changed position, she worked her way up and down his body, licking and nipping at his satin smooth skin. Every so often he grasped at her shoulders, or clutched at her hair, begging her to stop, to let him fuck her. But her intense, determined expression denied him the opportunity far better than words ever could.

Eventually, as she glanced up at the window and noticed that the sky had lightened to a pale grey, streaked with shades of red, she granted him his desire. Sliding up his body, she rolled on to her side, pulling him with her so that they lay face to face. Then she hooked her leg over his hip, felt for the yearning hardness of his penis and guided it into her hungry body.

He filled her well, she noticed with a surge of pleasure, and all at once she decided to abandon herself to him, to let him orchestrate the final opus of their night together. They moved together as one, tantalising and gratifying each other until their skin became soaked in perspiration and they were left gasping for breath. Totally spent, they surrendered to the fallibility of their own bodies and collapsed against the lacy coverlet, arms and legs sprawled carelessly, chests heaving.

As the gathering warmth of the new day stole over her, Marie felt drowsiness tugging at her eyelids. Moments later her body sank into blissful repose.

Humdrum was one of Marie's least favourite words but it seemed to sum up the rest of her week. By the time she returned home from Zandvoort, the elation she had felt at winning that particular round of the Championship had already diminished to virtually nothing. Appointments for her freelance computer sales had ground to a halt, and although she anticipated a phone call from Chantal, nothing came, which only served to add to her boredom. She felt restless, yet had nothing and no one to divert her; nothing to get out of bed for.

On Friday morning Carla popped her head round Marie's bedroom door with the bright-eyed announcement that she was off to work. Her friend seemed disgustingly cheerful, Marie thought, as she felt herself sliding further under the duvet. She wriggled uncomfortably under Carla's uncompromising gaze.

Carla continued to stare accusingly at her. 'Aren't you planning to get up at all today?' she said in a world-weary voice. 'All this lying around in bed isn't going to do you any good, you know.'

'Shut up,' Marie said crossly, 'you sound just like my mother.'

She watched, feeling guilty as Carla narrowed her eyes. 'Just snap out of this, Marie. I don't know what's the matter with you lately but whatever it is, get it sorted out and move on.'

Raising a feeble arm from under the warmth of the duvet, Marie saluted her friend. 'I promise I will,' she said, 'just as soon as I've had a bit more sleep.'

She winced inwardly as Carla made a sound of disgust and slammed the door behind her. Then she tucked her arm back under the duvet, pulled the thick quilt up to her chin and closed her eyes. Immediately, her mind became filled with the unwelcome image of Lawrie Samson.

Oh, no, not you again, she thought in despair. These days it seemed that, unless she deliberately concentrated on something else, that infuriating man intruded on her thoughts. Not that it was always an unpleasant intrusion. Sometimes, while she was asleep, she dreamed that he was actually nice; that he was capable of smiling and joking and saying things that flattered rather than accused. But more often than not, she recalled him as he really was: bombastic, arrogant, sarcastic and without a decent bone in his body.

Just as she started to drift off to sleep again, she was roused by the insistent chirruping of her mobile phone. Reaching out a lazy hand, she picked it up from the bedside table.

'Yes, can I help you?' she said as she shuffled into a sitting position.

Although still sleepy, she soon became alert as she recognised the efficient tones of Melanie Dwyer, one of the telesales personnel at SmartTech Computers.

'Hi, Marie. I've got an appointment for you this morning if you can make it.'

Half of Marie thought: oh, no, I can't be bothered, I'll have to shower and get dressed, while the other half was thinking: great, I could do with the money.

'Of course,' she said into the receiver. 'When and where?'

Reaching out to the bedside table again, this time for a notepad and pen, Marie jotted down the details Melanie gave her. The appointment was for eleven-thirty, which gave her plenty of time to get up and moving.

As she stood in the shower she found herself thinking about the name of the company, Larchlap Landscaping, and wondered why it sounded familiar to her. Perhaps it was something to do with a member of Chantal's group, The Inner Sanctum. Or maybe she had simply seen an advertisement for them.

Well, she decided, shrugging her still damp body into her usual smart black dress and red jacket, whoever they are, they're going to order a SmartTech computer system even if I have to offer them my body as part of the package. Smiling at the thought, she picked up her portfolio of sales literature, slung her bag over her shoulder and headed out of the door.

The Victorian house standing in its own, beautifully tended grounds was far removed from the smart office block Marie had been expecting. Though there was no mistaking that she had come to the right place. As the minicab she had hailed at the station swung into the driveway that led up to the house, she couldn't help noticing the words LARCHLAP and LANDSCAPING worked in wrought iron in the centre of each huge black iron gate.

There was an entry-phone system on the wall by the

glossy, Lincoln green front door. As she pressed the button to announce her arrival, she felt a familiar stomach-clenching anticipation. Being a sales person was similar to being an actress, she always thought. Making her first entrance into the client's office and going through the ritual of hand-shaking and pleasant introductions was akin to making her debut on stage.

As a buzzer sounded to admit her entry and she pushed open the door, she imagined herself speaking as the Prince in Henry IV: 'Before God I am exceeding weary.' And weary she certainly felt as she climbed the long staircase directly in front of her, as the disembodied voice on the entry phone had instructed.

She felt tired of trying against all the odds to pay off her debts and make ends meet. For the umpteenth time in the past six months she found herself longing to be just like any other single young woman – working nine to five and using her spare time to have fun. How wonderful it would be to have no other worries and no constant battle to fight. Simply being able to live carelessly until either Lady Luck or Mr Right stepped into her path and led her in another direction would be like a holiday.

The fact that she had been offered a sponsorship deal by *Verval* magazine was some consolation, she supposed. At least the money would cover her running expenses for the remainder of the season. Though the deal didn't come *that* cheaply. In return, the magazine wanted her cooperation with regard to publicity shots.

A full colour photospread, to be taken after the Hockenheim meeting the following weekend, was the least that was expected and agreed upon. And it went without saying that the onus would be on her to produce consistently high placings during the rest of the season. Sponsors weren't interested in losers, only winners. But then, Marie reminded herself as she paused for breath before turning right at the top of the staircase, she had absolutely no intention of losing the Championship. Not at any cost.

The corridor she was in was narrow, well lit by natural light and very long. She trudged wearily along the strip of thick floral carpeting that ran the length of it. The cream-painted wall to her left was punctuated by tall sash windows which overlooked a couple of acres of beautifully tended, striped lawns. In the centre of the lawns a lake, edged by weeping willows, sparkled invitingly under the hot sun. More than anything at that moment, Marie longed to run back downstairs and out into the grounds. There she would kick off her shoes, pull off her tights, which were sticking uncomfortably to her, and plunge her feet into the refreshing water. The summer was growing hotter day by day. And with no prospect of a proper holiday, the idea of immersing herself in the lake seemed almost too inviting to resist. But resist she must.

'Penny for them.'

Marie whirled around, embarrassed that she had been caught daydreaming when she was supposed to be on the ball. As she did so, her eyes widened and she felt every last ounce of breath leave her body simultaneously. Lawrie Samson – what on earth . . . ?

Marie struggled not to voice her disbelief. Of all the rotten luck, she thought, to bump into the man she least wanted to see ever again. And at a time when she needed all her wits about her. Her heart was thumping wildly and she felt her portfolio slipping from the palm of her hand, which had suddenly become damp.

'You!' she declared, for want of something better to say.

He raised an amused eyebrow. 'Do we know each other, Miss – er – Miss Gifford?'

Of course, Marie realised suddenly, to all intents and purposes she was a complete stranger as far as he was concerned. Amber was the woman he knew and despised, not her real self, not Marie. The relief she felt was as keen as her determination that he should never discover her secret. She clung on to her portfolio and the realisation that she could – would have to – play this scene out to the best of her ability.

'I'm sorry,' she said with a forced smile. 'I was miles away just then, please forgive me.'

'Of course.' He smiled back at her far more naturally while extending a hand. 'My name's Lawrie Samson, by the way. Perhaps we should go into my office.'

He glanced over his shoulder at the open door behind him and grinned to himself as Marie offered him her own trembling hand. Looking back at her, he realised there was no mistaking the small, heart-shaped face, or the huge azure blue eyes that dominated it. The only real difference was her hair. Now that would take a bit of getting used to.

Taking her hand and holding it just for a moment longer than necessary, he debated whether to come clean straight away and let her know that he realised she and Amber Barclay were one and the same. It was either that or simply play along with her deception. Whatever he decided to do, he'd better do it fast or the moment would be lost.

It was unusual for him to be torn by indecision. He had never met a schizophrenic before and couldn't help wondering how far she would take things. Or if she even realised that she had a dual personality. Perhaps she was genuinely insane, in which case he didn't want to risk upsetting her. If that was the case she could be capable of anything and therefore it would be safer, he decided in that instant, to let her take the initiative for the time being.

With her mind whirling at pretty much the same rate as Lawrie's, Marie followed her 'client' into his large, high ceilinged office. She glanced around, noticing the décor's tendency towards the colour green. Everything was a different shade of green. The sage walls were lighter than the bottle green stained floorboards, which were strewn with abstract patterned rugs. The curtains and pelmets framing the wide, high windows behind his mahogany desk were finely striped in mint and pistachio. Even the deeply buttoned leather chairs either side of his desk were bottle green in colour.

'You're obviously a very green person,' she said with a hesitant smile.

She realised her observation was probably the most inane thing she could have come out with and blushed again. Still, she reasoned, it was better than acting as though she had been struck dumb. She had to keep reminding herself that he had never met her before. Amber was someone else. Marie was the computer salesperson and it was Marie with whom he was dealing now.

Accepting his offer to sit in one of the visitors' chairs in front of his desk, she crossed her legs demurely. The realisation that Amber might well have done a Sharon Stone *Basic Instinct* impersonation at that point almost made her laugh aloud. But Marie was not like Amber at all. For one thing, she was much more refined – possibly even repressed. Never in her wildest dreams could Marie imagine herself indulging in the sorts of things either Amber or Portia got up to.

My God, she thought, shaking her head to rid herself of her conflicting observations, this whole double-life business is getting out of hand. Now I can't even work out which is the real me any more.

She glanced up as she realised Lawrie was speaking to her. 'I'm sorry,' she said, 'I didn't catch that.'

'I asked if you would like tea or coffee,' he offered, amusement tugging at the corners of his mouth, 'or you could always have a soft drink if you prefer. It is a very hot day, after all.'

'No, thank you, tea will be fine,' Marie muttered. To calm herself down she began to fiddle with her portfolio. Unzipping it, she took out a sheaf of promotional litera-ture and spread it out on the desk. 'Did you have a particular type of computer system in mind?' she asked, glancing up at him.

He shook his head. 'Not really,' he replied. 'Computers are a closed book to me. All I need for my own personal use is something that is idiot-proof and reliable. You can speak to my secretary afterwards to define what sort of system is needed for the rest of the staff.'

Feeling more secure now that she had the upper hand, Marie smiled easily at him.

'Then you might feel most comfortable with a networked ST2125 system for the company, linked to an ST2000 for you,' she said as she passed him an information sheet. 'It comes complete with a word processing package, spreadsheets and a databasing facility. Although it's a very basic model, you can still connect it up to a CD-ROM and modem. You shouldn't underestimate the usefulness of e-mail in this day and age and the – '

Lawrie Samson put up a hand to silence her mid flow. 'Stop,' he said, looking bemused. 'Now, rewind please. I can't take it all in. I told you I'm not computer literate and you're baffling me with just the sort of technical double speak that gives a creative man like me nightmares.'

Feeling suitably chastened, Marie opened her mouth to offer an apology but was interrupted by the arrival of a comfortable-looking middle-aged woman who bore a tray of tea and biscuits.

'Thanks, Mrs Mac,' Lawrie said to the woman. 'You can put the tray down on my desk. I'll be mother.'

With a tightening in her stomach which Marie recognised as envy, she noticed the way his eyes took on a certain warmth as he smiled at the older woman. Not recognising her as Amber – the enemy – he had almost smiled at her that way a couple of times, she recalled. All at once she became aware that she was considering him as simply a man and not a loathsome beast.

Get a grip, Marie, she warned herself. There are plenty of men out there in the big wide world, don't even think about getting involved with this one. Do yourself a favour and leave Lawrie Samson well alone.

Chapter Seven

*T*he trouble was, Marie acknowledged as she accepted a cup of tea and a chocolate digestive biscuit from Lawrie, her body seemed to be ignoring her well-intentioned mind completely. Concentrating on nibbling her biscuit, she tried to disregard the growing wetness between her thighs and the way her nipples chafed at the black lacy bra she wore underneath her dress.

Beneath the red jacket she felt unbearably hot. Her armpits were damp, despite a good spray of antiperspirant, and as for her dress – she paused in her thoughts to glance down. Yes, just as she feared, it was badly creased. Blow this weather! All she wanted, right at that moment, was to strip all her clothes off and stand in front of a large electric fan, or under a cool shower. Ah, what bliss that would be.

All at once her daydream began to involve the presence of another, unseen, person. All she had was the sensation and image of arms circling her waist then entwining her naked body. Sun-browned, slightly muscular masculine arms, with just the vaguest covering of golden down.

Oh, bloody hell! She cast a surreptitious glance across the desk to where Lawrie Samson sat, sipping his tea and studying one of the leaflets she had pushed across the polished wood to him. The arms in her fantasy belonged to him, of all people. The taut nipples brushing her shoulders were his. The erect penis nudging between her buttocks was a part of him she had yet to see. Suddenly, she felt a tremor of lust so powerful she wondered if Lawrie could see her trembling in her seat.

If he had, the object of her inopportune desire gave no indication that he had noticed anything untoward. Just as she gave him another surreptitious glance, Lawrie stood up.

Without saying a word he walked over to stand in front of the window. Resting the tight, nicely round bottom that Marie had only just begun to appreciate upon the sill, he crossed his long legs casually at the ankles and gazed over his shoulder out of the window.

As Marie found herself scrutinising him, she saw him illuminated by the midday sun. Dressed in simple but well cut cream trousers and a pale lavender polo shirt, he looked almost ethereal. His tall, lean body appeared blurred at the edges, his fair head surrounded by a nimbus of light.

The glare of the sun forced her to squint slightly as she concentrated on him, wondering what was going on in his head to cause his faraway expression. Obviously he was even more baffled by the complexities of computers than she had realised.

'Are you all right? Shall I draw the curtains?' Lawrie asked, his deep voice shattering the heavy silence as he turned to look at her.

Marie noticed his faraway expression had disappeared now. Hardly able to think straight any more herself, she nodded and said, 'Yes, please. If you don't mind. My goodness, that's sun's a bit strong, isn't it? I don't remember it ever getting quite so hot in this country before. I – '

If she was embarrassed to find herself babbling she was even more embarrassed when she found she couldn't stop. Instead of talking about the weather any longer, she forced herself to revert to the subject she

103

knew like the back of her hand: computers. As Lawrie Samson turned and carefully drew the curtains across the window behind his desk, Marie found herself describing in minute detail the many functions he could expect from a ST2000.

'Enough,' he commanded gently as he sat back down in his high backed leather chair. 'I can't take it all in.' He paused to glance over his shoulder at the shielded window and then back at her. 'Is that better?'

'Yes, I – oh, goodness, it's much darker in here now, isn't it?' she twittered, annoyed with herself for her lack of composure.

Glancing around she noticed that while she had been jabbering on about computers, like an excitable but well informed chimpanzee, he had drawn the curtains at all three windows in his office. The diffused light coming through the fine drapes shadowed the room in a very intimate way and was barely enough for her to read the wording on the literature she had brought.

'Should I just leave these for you to look through at your leisure?' she asked as she put down the sales sheets again and picked up her untouched cup of tea.

'I think that might be a wise idea,' he said with a yawn. His hand flew to cover his mouth. 'Oh, God, sorry about that. I had a bit of a late night last night.' He arched his neck and flexed his shoulders, as if to demonstrate to her that his body felt stiff as well as tired.

Without thinking, Marie stood up and walked around to the back of his chair. 'Allow me,' she said, sounding more authoritative than she had so far that morning, 'I'm quite good at massage.'

Resisting the urge to quip, 'I'll bet,' Lawrie simply nodded. By silent assent he allowed her to get to work on his knotted muscles. And work them she did. God, her fingers felt good, he thought blissfully; so deft and yet so strong. It had been ages since he'd had a massage as expert as this. Almost against his will, he found himself relaxing under her practised touch, to the point of dozing off.

He was finding it difficult to control himself. All his concerns about her being schizophrenic had evaporated almost instantly, to be replaced by a growing awareness of her as Marie. Whereas Amber was beautiful but aggravating, he decided, Marie was beautiful inside and out. Assertive rather than aggressive, she delighted him by the way she conveyed her knowledge about computers simply and without a hint of Amber's arrogance. He admired her professionalism as much as he admired her figure in the simple dress and jacket she was wearing.

He thought she must be feeling hot and, at one point, had almost suggested she take her jacket off. But then he knew he wouldn't be able to disguise his interest in her as a woman any longer. Walking over to the window had been the only way he could stop himself saying something too personal. He had noticed a certain look in her eyes: dark and enigmatic, yet also lustful. No doubt she had been thinking about her boyfriend. Lucky guy, whoever he was.

And now Marie had her hands on him, the warmth and pressure of her fingers driving the tension from his shoulder muscles but creating a familiar tension somewhere else in his body. He hoped to God she wouldn't notice what was happening to him. With any luck it was too dark for her to see properly. Just to make certain he clasped his hands loosely in his lap, hoping they shielded his growing tumescence.

As Marie stood massaging the nape of Lawrie's neck and shoulders over the top of his shirt, her fingertips easing the hard muscle beneath the thin textured cotton, she found herself wondering what the hell had got into her. Her behaviour was far too intimate for a client/salesperson relationship and yet, at the same time, it felt entirely natural.

The only thing that had prompted her was her own

instinct, she realised. And now she was there, with Lawrie Samson at the mercy of her fingertips, all her negative thoughts about him seemed to have flown out of the curtained window behind her. So far that morning all he had been was pleasant and ordinary. An ordinary guy, in an ordinary situation, with an ordinary woman. Not two people pitted against each other as adversaries, in a setting where adrenalin ran high and tempers flared.

What a shame we couldn't have met like this in the first place, she found herself thinking. Things might have been so different.

When Lawrie's chin sagged to his chest and he began to snore softly, Marie stopped massaging him and simply returned to her seat. There she sat and contemplated him as he dozed. Time seemed suspended in that shadowy room, where the only movement was the rhythmic rise and fall of Lawrie's chest and the slight billowing of the curtains whenever a breeze caught them. Presently, she shrugged off her jacket and hung it over the back of her chair. Making herself more comfortable she gazed at the beauty of Lawrie's slumbering face and wove a scenario in her mind that took both of them away from the airless office and down to the edge of the lake.

They walked barefoot and hand in hand, their fingers entwining while their toes splayed out on the springy grass. The scent of fresh flowers was intoxicating, the humidity enervating. By the edge of the lake they sat down. Marie felt the short blades of grass tickling the backs of her knees and sighed with pleasure as she reclined and turned her face up to the sun.

'You look beautiful, Marie,' Lawrie murmured in her fantasy. His hair flopped over his brow as he leaned over her and began to follow the contours of her face with the feathery end of a long blade of couch grass. 'I don't know how I've managed to keep my hands off you so far.'

Stretching luxuriously, Marie's eyes twinkled as she

gazed up at him. 'Nor do I. You've wanted me ever since I walked into your office, I could tell.'

'You're right, of course. How could I not want you?'

Marie felt her breath catch as she heard the lustful timbre of his voice and saw the way his dove grey eyes darkened to slate. His expression was one of gentle lasciviousness. A promise of seduction, of sensuality and all things deliciously erotic.

Somehow, in her fantasy, their clothes simply melted away. There was no fumbling, no, 'That's OK, I'll do it,' or, 'Here let me help,' as fingers reached for zippers and belt buckles. Everything happened as if in dream and indeed, that was precisely what it was. As in all the best fantasies, the grass below their naked bodies was as soft as a blanket, the earth beneath as giving as a down-filled mattress as they lay down together.

Lawrie's caresses were gentle yet inflaming, his hands light as they skimmed her torso and stroked her sun warmed breasts. Marie felt her nipples spring to attention, the raspberry buds ripening as his slender fingertips toyed with them.

'Suck them,' she urged while cupping her breasts and offering them to him, 'please.'

As he bent his head and took one nipple between his soft lips, Marie felt the tight coil of desire in her belly slowly unravel. She felt the wetness between her legs, trickling out of her hot, honeyed vagina to dampen the grass beneath her. She imagined the emerald blades of grass glistening under the strong sunlight where her dew coated them. The gentle, lapping sounds of the water in the lake played a harmonious rhythm to the lapping of Lawrie's tongue which lathed and dabbed at her nipples, exciting them still further.

A light breeze wafting in from the lake snaked around her pouting vagina, drying the wetness there. It tickled the sensitive membranes of her most intimate flesh, making her groan with arousal. Bending her legs at the knees, she let her thighs fall wantonly apart. There was no one there but Lawrie and herself to view her blatant nakedness. And only Lawrie would be able to see the way the moist petals of her sex unfolded, her clitoris swelling, yearning for his touch.

'So wet,' he murmured in her ear as he slid a hand over her pink, hairless mound and between her legs. 'Rude little thing, Marie. Naughty girl . . .'

Back in the reality of Lawrie's office, Marie shivered involuntarily, wondering where that thought had come from. It wasn't like her to be submissive or shamed by her body's responses. Yet, she reasoned, her mind still encapsulated by the fantasy, it wasn't like her to enjoy sex as Marie. Usually she was Portia the dominant, or Amber the assertive, or any of a dozen or so others created at random from her vast collection of wigs and characteristics.

Marie – as Marie – hardly ever indulged in sex. Certainly not since Greg had managed to destroy Marie as a woman. Thank goodness the 'others' were there to save her. Heedless of the restrictions of real life, her invented characters rushed in where earth-bound entities like Marie had long since feared to tread.

So was this how Marie saw fit to cope with her sublimated desires – by pretending sex was all very naughty and beyond her control? She shifted uncomfortably on the leather chair, abandoning the lakeside scenario to ask herself a few more searching questions. In the unlikely event that Lawrie should ask to see her away from the business environment, could she cope with that as Marie? Was Marie ever going to enjoy a normal sex life again, whatever that might be? Or would one of her other personalities intrude, or even take over?

Glancing up, she noticed Lawrie was stirring in his sleep. He looked beautiful in repose, she decided, watching the way his full lips curved slightly in an enigmatic half-smile. She couldn't help noticing the feathery shadows his long, pale lashes cast upon his high cheekbones. And his hair looked so soft she longed to reach across the desk and touch it. Similarly, her fingers itched to raise his shirt and explore the satin soft skin she was certain lay beneath. Her greatest longing was to trace the bumps and ridges of his musculature and slide her hand down over his belly and below the waistband of his trousers.

She noticed, though she had to crane her neck slightly to see, that the bulge in the front of his trousers was intriguingly large. She knew that didn't necessarily mean anything; expertise was far more important than size. But put the two together and the results were mind-blowing!

Without realising it, Marie's face was still wearing a broad smile when Lawrie suddenly awoke with a start.

Looking startled, he glanced around.

'My God, I didn't fall asleep, did I?' he asked, his eyes pleading with her to deny what he knew to be true. When she nodded – her lips and eyes still smiling – his cheeks flushed slightly. 'I don't know what to say,' he continued. 'I am sorry. It's not that you were boring or anything. I spent hours working on a problem with my car last night and – '

'It's OK,' Marie interrupted him gently, 'my massages usually have that effect on people. Don't worry about it.' She deliberately tried not to think about his car problems. That was something for Amber to gloat over, not her.

He glanced at his watch as he straightened up. 'Look at the time. I've kept you far too long already and I still want you to have a word with my secretary.'

Marie shrugged. 'I'm in no hurry,' she said. 'Friday is usually a quiet day for me workwise. I haven't got any other appointments.'

'In that case,' he suggested, 'shall I take you along to Sheree's office? Then when you've finished discussing computers with her I'd like to take you somewhere for a late lunch. I think it's the least I could do under the circumstances.'

Glancing surreptitiously at her own watch, Marie noticed it was almost three o'clock. Her stomach growled, telling her in no uncertain terms that she should accept his invitation.

As she nodded, her face broke into a smile. 'OK, thanks,' she agreed happily. 'I'd like that.'

Bracing his hands on the arms of his chair, he pushed himself to his feet. 'Great,' he said as he led her to the door, 'just tell Sheree to buzz me when you're finished.'

To Marie's surprise almost two hours flew past as she explained the different types of computer systems to Lawrie's secretary and the way they could be linked together to service the whole firm. The company, she discovered, was much larger than she first realised. And Sheree turned out to be quite a computer buff. She asked a lot of searching, intelligent questions which, fortunately, Marie had no difficulty in answering. When the final package had been decided upon, Sheree buzzed Lawrie on her intercom.

'He'll be along in about five minutes,' she said to Marie.

'In that case,' Marie replied, zipping up her portfolio, 'would you mind telling me where I'll find the loo? I think I need to freshen up a bit.'

'No problem.' Sheree took her out into the corridor and pointed. 'Down there, third door on the left,' she said.

When Marie returned to Sheree's office Lawrie was waiting for her. He was holding a smart, crocodile skin briefcase – which Marie hoped was fake – and a cream jacket to match his trousers was slung carelessly over his shoulders.

'Shall we make it the pub instead?' he suggested to Marie. 'I know a nice one at Hampton Court. It's right on the river.'

Marie noticed how Sheree flashed Lawrie a look of surprise but said nothing. Though she began to juggle the sheaf of papers in her hands with more vigour than Marie thought was absolutely necessary.

'Sounds lovely,' Marie replied, ignoring Sheree's

response to Lawrie's suggestion. 'I just fancy a nice cold lager.'

Because she had arrived by taxi, Marie readily accepted Lawrie's offer of a lift. He also drove a Porsche on the road, she noticed a moment later as they strolled across the small gravelled area to the side of the house that served as a car park. Brand new, the red paintwork of the convertible gleamed in the sunlight, the glare almost blinding in its intensity.

'Nice,' she murmured, running her hand appreciatively over the curvaceous bodylines of the Porsche 911 Sportster. 'My dream car.'

'Is it?' Lawrie gave her a quirky grin and Marie had to remind herself who she was and that she didn't own a car at all, let alone a Porsche.

Forcing herself to smile nonchalantly back at him, she said, 'One day perhaps. If I sell enough computers.'

As he opened the passenger door for her, she slid into the seat. Her bare legs stuck to the hot leather, making her wince. She had decided to dispense with her tights while she was in the loo but now she wished she hadn't.

'Sorry, I should have parked in the shade,' Lawrie said as he climbed into the driver's seat.

He glanced sideways at Marie, his gaze straying to her bare, tanned legs.

'I was too hot in tights,' Marie explained, in answer to the question he had only asked with his eyes.

'Quite right. I feel sorry for you women having to wear such dreadful things,' Lawrie murmured. Putting the car into gear, he suddenly floored the accelerator and the car shot out of the car park and down the driveway, the spinning rear wheels throwing up a hail of gravel. He shrugged and flashed her a disarming smile as he slowed down a little. 'I can't help doing things like that,' he explained. 'I suppose it's the kid in me. I have to show off, even if it's only to myself most of the time.'

Marie grinned back at him. She decided she liked this version of Lawrie a whole lot more than the one she had met at the race track. Today he seemed very human, with a vulnerability that she found engaging and also undeniably attractive. For a moment she wished the broad, tanned hand that hovered over the gearstick would slide up her leg instead. Although her body had calmed down considerably since the onset of her fantasy earlier that afternoon, the desire she felt had by no means abated. It was simply simmering, waiting for the right word or the right touch to send the heat inside her back up to boiling point again.

Though it was a hot day, with the top down on the car there was enough of a breeze to ruffle Marie's dark hair. Presently they left the countryside behind them, heading in the direction of Hampton Court. Eventually, a glimpse of the winding grey-blue ribbon of the Thames told Marie they had almost reached their destination.

As a large, ivy-clad pub loomed on their right Lawrie slowed and pulled into the packed car park. Finding an available spot right in the far corner he parked and immediately rushed around to the passenger side of the car to open the door for Marie.

It was little gestures like that which Marie really appreciated about Lawrie. So far that day he had, in turns, been charming, thoughtful, respectful and incredibly likeable. Although she had been attracted to him from the start – more often than not despite her better judgement – she now realised that this version of him was irresistible. The question was whether she intended to try to resist him, or simply go with the flow?

They walked straight through the busy pub, decorated in traditional style with dark wood and horse brasses, to the bar, where Lawrie ordered two half pints of lager. Then they carried on through to the pub garden where they found a table right by the edge of the river. For a moment or two they sat in silence, contemplating a flock of ducks as they swam down river and sipping their ice cold drinks.

Marie was the first to break the silence. Putting her glass down on the wooden table, she reached out to

Lawrie, who sat beside her, and wiped her finger across his top lip, removing a layer of froth.

'I prefer you without the moustache,' she said, laughing.

She realised it was a very intimate gesture but there was something about the way Lawrie had elected to sit beside, rather than opposite her, and the way his body inclined slightly towards hers as they sat – as though attracted by a magnetic force – that invited such a display of intimacy.

She put her froth-coated fingertip in her mouth and sucked it. As she did so she raised her eyes and captured Lawrie's interested gaze. Time seemed suspended as she sat, finger in mouth, and simply stared at him. Communication between them was silent yet screamed of their desire for each other. She still felt the tingles in her fingertip from the jolt she had received when she touched him. Now those tingles and the sensuous expression in his eyes caused her stomach to lurch and her sex to moisten between her tightly clenched thighs.

Trying to assuage her arousal, she recrossed her legs and shifted uncomfortably on the hard wooden bench. Taking her finger out of her mouth, she picked up her glass and sipped her drink before returning her gaze to his face.

Lawrie felt compelled to say or do something to convey the desire he felt for the young woman seated next to him. He was certain she already knew, but not quite as confident that his interest in her would be reciprocated. He sensed, from the tautness of her body and the way she held her head stiffly erect, that she was trying to contain something within herself.

Was it lust or loathing? he asked himself. Obviously, she knew who he was and remembered the conflict they had experienced the previous weekend at Zandvoort. To her he was a rival. To him she was simply a young woman who sold computers. Having realised all that, he

113

was almost convinced that the flicker in her eyes was one of erotic intent.

Because he was driving, Lawrie switched to drinking mineral water after their first drink but Marie was happy to move on to tall glasses of gin and tonic packed with ice. She felt supremely relaxed after her third drink and had no hesitation in voicing her feelings to Lawrie.

'I can't believe how good I feel,' she said as she stretched her arms and then her legs, which she crossed at the ankles. 'It's been one hell of a stressful week.'

'Lots of work?' Lawrie enquired, glancing at her over the rim of his glass.

Marie shook her head. 'No, quite the opposite, unfortunately. But I find boredom far more stressful than activity.'

'Well, if it's any consolation, you can expect an order from my company,' he said as he put down his glass and leant forward. Resting his elbows on his knees and clasping his hands loosely, he glanced sideways at her. 'I am very impressed – by the computer equipment as well as your professionalism.'

Marie felt herself blushing. 'Thank you,' she murmured, embarrassed as always when she received a compliment. She felt the keenness of his gaze as he turned in his seat to face her.

'Credit where credit's due,' he said. He glanced at her almost empty glass. 'Want another?'

'No.' She shook her head and regretted it instantly. Her head was swimming, she realised, and then it occurred to her that she hadn't eaten at all that day. 'Sorry,' she said, placing a palm flat against her clenching stomach, 'what I meant was, I really shouldn't, not on an empty stomach.' The minute she said the words she realised that it might sound as though she was angling for an invitation to dinner. She blushed again, even harder. 'That wasn't a hint or anything,' she added hastily.

He smiled kindly at her and, to her surprise, placed

114

his hand over the one that still covered her stomach. 'I'm sure it wasn't,' he said softly, 'and you've just made me realise that I haven't eaten anything since breakfast, either.' He laughed, still keeping his hand pressed to hers. 'This computer business can certainly take up a lot of time, can't it?'

Reeling from the imaginary sensation of his hand burning through hers and searing a hole in the flesh beneath, Marie nodded wordlessly.

'Then I propose we go inside and eat,' he said, taking her hand and hauling her to her feet. 'Either that or we can go on somewhere else.'

'Oh, no,' Marie mumbled as she started to shake her head again, 'I couldn't. I've taken up far too much of your time already.'

From his lofty height Lawrie smiled down at her while gripping her hand even tighter.

'I insist,' he said firmly. 'It's as much for my own benefit as it is for yours. If you don't agree to eat with me now, I'll only end up going home and making do with beans on toast.'

Marie pursed her lips disbelievingly. She couldn't picture Lawrie Samson as a beans on toast man. She imagined he was the sort of person to have a motherly cook-cum-housekeeper; a bit of a Mrs Mac. Feeling daring, she voiced her thoughts, to which Lawrie laughed out loud.

'Oh, my God, you do have a warped image of me, don't you?' he said, wiping the tears from his eyes with the back of his hand. He paused to push open the door to the pub and ushered her inside. 'Come on. Let's get a table, then you can tell me all the other preconceived notions you have about me.'

What can I tell you? Marie wondered, as she pretended not to stare at him across the small wooden table they had been shown to. Should I reveal my real thoughts? That I think you are the most sensual, desirable, enigmatic man I have ever set eyes on. That I can't stop imagining you naked. That I keep picturing us both locked together in an erotic embrace, our bodies pouring with sweat as we strive for mutual pleasure. That I think you would probably prove to be the best lover I, or any of my alter egos, have ever had . . .

She paused in her deliberation, unable to carry on without fainting from sheer desire. The longing to touch him was overwhelming. His hand, laid flat on the table top, was almost too temptingly close to resist. She wanted to rest her hand on top of his. Entwine their fingers. Raise his hand to her lips, her breast. Slide it into the hot wetness between her legs. Oh, God, Lawrie, she breathed silently, I want you to sweep everything off this narrow little table, throw me across it and fuck me senseless!

'Avocado salad, madam?'

Marie glanced up, startled, as the waitress to whom she and Lawrie had given their order hovered at her side. She nodded dumbly, watching as the plate was set down in front of her. Although she was aware of the weight of the silver knife and fork as she picked them up, she hardly tasted the food as she cut it, put it in her mouth and chewed mechanically.

Everything in her, every fibre of her being, screamed out her desire for him now. Wanting him was no longer a passing fancy; the need to have him was far more than simply a fleeting thing which could be suppressed, ignored. Sod convention. Sod client relations. Sod everything. All she wanted now was to hear him say he wanted her in return. Then her answer would be an unequivocal yes.

Lawrie glanced up at her. His eyes scanned her face as though he could read her thoughts. 'Are you enjoying your meal?' he asked her, in a voice thick with emotion and longing.

She nodded and forced a smile. 'Yes, it's – er – lovely. – I – '

With a single look that turned her insides to jelly he interrupted her.

'Hell, Marie, I don't know how to say this nicely, or

discreetly, so I'll just come out with it.' He almost faltered at her questioning look, her eyes wide, reflecting a combination of surprise, alarm and something else – something he couldn't quite fathom but hoped he understood. 'I want you, Marie,' he said gruffly. 'I don't want to waste a minute longer in here, eating, making small talk and pretending nothing's happening between us. I have to have you – as soon as possible. I only hope you feel the same way.'

Chapter Eight

The evening air was still warm, the soft lapping of the river and the sounds of traffic going past on the road the only noises to be heard in the otherwise packed car park. Outside the pub, Marie and Lawrie walked quickly, almost stumbling in their haste to get to the car.

'Where can we go?' Marie asked. 'My flatmate will probably be home which will make things a bit awkward.'

'My place,' Lawrie replied, 'but it seems too far away right at this moment. I don't think I can wait.'

His impatience overwhelmed Marie, who gazed longingly at him and muttered breathlessly, 'Nor me,' as he pulled her into his arms and crushed his lips against hers.

Their hands roamed each other's body feverishly. Both could feel the heat of the other's desire and the pounding of hearts behind ribs. Breaking away, Lawrie glanced around then grabbed her hand.

'Come on,' he said gruffly, 'in the car. No one will see us.'

'Oh, God!' Marie half giggled, half gasped with desire. Somehow the thought of being fucked in his Porsche seemed risky and yet incredibly apt. The one thing that linked them, apart from their urgent need for each other, was a love of the sleek, powerful cars.

Lawrie flung open the passenger door and squatted down to reach under the passenger seat. Releasing the lever and pushing at the same time, he moved the seat as far back as it would go.

'It's going to be a tight squeeze,' he said, glancing lasciviously at her as he straightened up.

Marie felt her insides melt. Reaching under her skirt, she pulled her black lacy knickers down swiftly and stepped out of them before tossing them on the driver's seat. Then she slipped into the passenger seat, hitching her dress up as she did so. She waited as Lawrie hesitated for a moment, simply looking down at her. She flamed, feeling his eyes skimming her bare thighs to alight upon the compressed pouch of her sex, which peeped enticingly from under the black fringe of her hem.

'Christ, what have you done to yourself?' Lawrie exclaimed. 'A hairless pussy; whatever next?'

Marie felt like giggling again. For the first time in a long time she felt nervous about displaying herself to a man.

'Don't you like it?' she asked hesitantly.

She drew in her breath sharply as he dropped to his haunches and reached out a hand. His palm stroked the tops of her thighs. His fingertips brushed the smoothness of her labia which swelled at the intimacy of his caress. When he glanced at her face, she noticed, with a sharp clenching of her stomach, that his eyes were brimming over with desire.

'I love it,' he said huskily. 'God, Marie, you're fabulous, every inch.'

Marie sucked in her breath again as his hands spread her thighs apart, as far as the dimensions of the car would allow. Then his fingers were stroking her sex again, easing her labia apart and peeling back fold upon pink, wrinkled fold of flesh until her clitoris was revealed to his lustful gaze. Alive with erotic yearning, it swelled and pulsed mercilessly.

Lawrie knelt on the tarmac, not caring that his cream

trousers would get filthy. The ground couldn't be dirtier than his mind right at that moment, he was sure, as he bent his head forward and inhaled Marie's delicious scent. The musky dew that glistened around her pouting vagina beguiled him, encouraging him to taste the sweetness of her honeyed flesh.

'Ah!' Marie threw her head back and clutched at his hair as she felt his tongue slide around her moist opening and delve inside like a hot spear. His fingers were still holding her labia wide apart, one thumb now stroking the swollen bud of her clitoris. 'Oh, God, I can't – ' she moaned as the first hot waves of orgasm crashed in on her. There was no way she could hold back. Gratification was instantaneous and mind blowing. She could feel the juices flowing from her as her sex throbbed under Lawrie's exploring tongue.

Still holding the puffy folds of Marie's labia wide apart, the pad of his thumb pressed hard against her pulsing clitoris, Lawrie climbed awkwardly into the car. He knelt in the footwell between her widespread legs. Sliding his hands around her hips, he slipped them under her buttocks, gripping the taut mounds of flesh and pulling her to the edge of the seat. Raising her legs, he urged her to bend them at the knees and hold them wide apart while he unfastened his trousers and pulled down the zip. He slid his trousers and jockey shorts down to mid thigh, watching Marie's lustful expression as his rigid cock sprang free.

Marie gazed at him, her eyelids heavy with erotic desire as she admired the dimensions of his erection. She licked her lips while silently bemoaning the fact that they had no time to linger. Otherwise she would have liked to take that stiff shaft in her hand and feel its proud hardness. She yearned to taste him; to lap up the little drop of fluid that oozed from the slit at the tip of his plum-like glans.

Holding her legs apart, wantonly displaying herself to him, she had no option but to content herself with admiring him visually. Her time would come, she promised herself, later, when they could be alone somewhere more comfortable. Then she would give herself free rein to explore his body properly. Right now, her powerful orgasm reduced to a dull throbbing, she yearned to take him inside her.

'Fill me, fuck me,' she gasped, pulling her thighs back further towards her chest, thus making him a blatant offering of her wide open sex.

Her ears vibrated with erotic delight to the sound of Lawrie's groan of desire as he lunged forward, grasped her hips and plunged himself deep inside her up to the hilt. Soon her whole body was sizzling, her brain numbed by the mindless desire that gripped her. He filled her magnificently, exceeding her expectations; once again driving her instantly to the point of orgasm.

She felt herself convulse, her vagina spasming madly as she writhed and bucked against him. The way his fingers gripped her buttocks drove her wild with lust, as did the sensation of his groin rubbing her labia mercilessly. Her clitoris felt as though it was being stimulated almost unbearably as he thrust into her with fast, measured strokes, the action tugging at her sensitive folds.

She knew her juices were flowing copiously, snaking down the sensitive, stretched skin of her perineum and trickling between her buttocks. From somewhere in the distance she could hear voices and footsteps. Other people were in the car park, she realised, the knowledge filling her with a burst of urgent excitement. She and Lawrie could be discovered at any moment. With a final surge of molten desire she came again, grinding herself against him until the waves of her orgasm started to ebb.

A moment later Lawrie withdrew from her, his cock still hard and glistening with their combined juices. She could see her creamy nectar clinging to the golden curls of his pubic hair and sighed gloriously as she lowered her trembling legs.

'I didn't feel you come,' she murmured, pouting a little with disappointment.

Lawrie smiled at her. 'I'm not surprised,' he said. 'You got a bit carried away.'

Despite her lack of shyness with him now, she still blushed. And, when Lawrie reached out a hand and stroked her cheek gently, she felt suffused by passion for him all over again. She nuzzled his hand, smiling softly up at him.

'That was amazing,' she said.

Taking his hand away so that he could pull up his trousers and fasten them again, Lawrie said, 'It was more than amazing. I hope that was just the start of things to come.'

They both chuckled softly at his unintentional pun. Then Lawrie climbed from the car and walked around it to slide into the driver's seat beside her. Picking up her discarded knickers, he handed them to her.

'Better put these on again for now,' he said, still smiling, 'otherwise you'll ruin the upholstery. Only joking,' he added quickly when he noticed a flicker of alarm cross Marie's face. 'I don't know if it's been scientifically proven, or anything, but I should think it's good for the leather. Probably makes it more supple if you rub it in.'

'Shall I try?' Marie responded cheekily.

She rubbed her fingertip upon the soft leather between her open thighs. Then she put her knickers on, though she didn't bother to pull her dress down again. It would be exciting to tantalise Lawrie with the sight of her slender thighs while he drove, she thought, not caring that any truck driver they might happen to pass on the road would also have a good view.

The idea of other men ogling her body gave her a vicarious thrill. She and Lawrie hadn't been caught *in flagrante* in the car park but if they had, Marie was certain she would have derived a perverse enjoyment from that as well. Perhaps there was more of the real her in her characters than she realised. Perhaps Marie, Portia and Amber were one and the same, after all.

She was surprised to find them driving back down

familiar roads and when they arrived at the gateway to the house where Lawrie's offices were located, she gave him a sideways glance.

'I live here as well,' he said, answering her unspoken question. 'I had the stable and garage block converted to residential quarters.' Turning into the driveway, he drove down to the house and continued around the side. Finally, he parked at the rear of the house and once again sprinted around to the passenger side to open the door for Marie.

'I could get used to all this chivalry,' she joked as she climbed out.

Her legs had stopped trembling but the rest of her body was unchanged in that it still yearned for more of him. She noticed his expression was enigmatic as he glanced at her while he locked the door.

'Take my arm,' he said. 'This gravel is bound to cause you a few problems with those shoes.'

They looked down at Marie's feet simultaneously. She was wearing a pair of ordinary black leather court shoes but the heels were narrow and quite high. Marie took his proffered arm happily and they walked down the path, which was edged by perfect lawns, to a long, two-storey building. Pausing at a stable-type door located centrally at the front of the building, Lawrie took a bunch of keys from his pocket and inserted a long silver key in the lock. As the door swung inwards he urged Marie inside.

By this time, the light was beginning to fade a little. They entered a large galleried room; Lawrie walked around switching on table lamps and pulling down blinds. At once, the vast open-plan area was flooded with a soft, hazy glow that made it seem cosier and more intimate. He indicated that Marie should sit down on one of four long sofas covered in mint-coloured cambric. The sofas formed a square island in the middle of the huge, polished wood floor.

As she sat and waited for him to return with a promised bottle of wine, Marie surveyed her surroundings properly. The first thing she realised was that her flat would probably fit into the living space several times over. And that was just the ground floor, she mused, glancing up to the galleried landing that ran all around the perimeter of the high-ceilinged building. The walls were all roughly plastered and painted a stark white, their bareness relieved by tasteful displays of abstract art. The paintings surprised Marie, who had suspected that Lawrie's domain would be devoted to cars, particularly Porsches. As it was, there was no indication that the man who occupied this wonderful abode was even remotely interested in motorsport.

No doubt racing is just a game to him, Marie found herself thinking ruefully; like all rich little boys he just wants to amuse himself with something before moving on. The thought angered her a little. Porsche racing meant so much to her and could cost her everything she held dear. Reclining back against the thickly padded cushion of the sofa, she sighed. Life just wasn't fair sometimes.

'Hey, you look very pensive all of a sudden. What's up?'

Lawrie surprised Marie by entering the room from the opposite end to where he'd left it. He took a few long strides, and sat down on the sofa beside her, placing a bottle of champagne and a couple of glasses on the low table in front of them as he did so.

She shook her head quickly. 'Oh, nothing, not really.' It didn't take too much effort to give him a bright, reassuring smile and she patted his hand while glancing at the bottle on the table. 'Champagne?' she remarked as she raised her eyebrows in surprise. 'What are we celebrating?'

Reaching forward, Lawrie smiled back. 'That's easy,' he said, handing her a glass and uncorking the champagne. 'I thought you'd realise. I want to toast you, or rather us – our future.'

Marie sighed with pleasure as she watched the effervescent liquid foam in her glass as he poured. Us, he'd said, and the future. Did that mean he seriously thought they had a future, or was he just getting carried away by the moment?

'I suspect,' she said, pausing to sip her wine, 'that you're really an old romantic at heart.' She held her breath, wondering if her comment was a bit too personal. It was a relief when he chuckled.

He held his hands up, palms facing her. 'It's a fair cop,' he said, 'and there was I, trying to convince the world that I'm just a lascivious rake, not to mention playboy and motorsport superstar.'

She laughed at the image. Then she remembered how he had appeared to her the moment she had first set eyes on him: handsome, successful; rich; with a beautiful, leggy girl hanging off each arm and on every word that dropped from his sensuous lips.

'Perhaps you are a bit of everything,' she murmured, her eyes smiling at him over the rim of her glass. She felt her breath catch as Lawrie's gaze darkened with erotic promise and he took her glass away from her, placing it next to his on the table.

'Let's see, shall we?' he said softly. Wrapping one arm around her shoulders, he pulled her tightly against him.

Time seemed suspended in that hushed, softly lit room as Marie and Lawrie kissed. This time their kiss was less urgent and more exploratory. As their tongues thrust and parried, she slid her hands up under his shirt, feeling for the first time the smooth hardness of his body, making the delicious contact of skin upon skin.

She felt him reaching behind her and pulling down the zip at the back of her dress. Wriggling slightly, although not releasing his mouth for more than a fleeting moment, she helped him to remove the dress. Then she pressed herself to him again, pushing his shirt up to his armpits and feeling their bare stomachs brush against each other.

The sensation was electric. An erotic charge went through her, touching every nerve-ending and causing a rivulet of moisture to run from her tingling vagina. She could feel her clitoris swelling, rubbing against her lacy knickers as it forced its way between her blossoming labia.

Holding her away from him a little, Lawrie ran an appreciative eye over Marie's scantily-clad body. He stroked a hand across the lightly tanned mounds of her breasts where they swelled above the black lacy cups of her bra. He heard her breathe in sharply and noticed the automatic parting of her thighs as he caressed her. It was difficult for him to hold his desire in check, but now they had finally reached the moment when they could be alone and were able to indulge themselves completely, he wanted to savour it.

'Christ, Marie, you're so beautiful,' he murmured huskily.

The way her cheeks flushed and her eyes sparkled entranced him. It was a pleasure to compliment her and to witness her reactions. Almost as much of a pleasure as touching her exquisite body, he thought.

Sliding his hand over the satin smooth skin of her torso he stroked the swell of her breasts again, then slipped his fingertips under the black lace to touch her bare skin. As his fingers brushed the wrinkled bud of her nipple he felt it harden. He caught the nipple and for a few pleasurable moments he toyed with it. Tugging at the hard nub, he rolled it gently between his fingertips, delighting in her body's response to his caresses.

Marie moaned softly, arching her back, thrusting her breasts towards him. The way he was taking things so slowly was exquisite torment. Her whole body yearned for him. Swelling. Pulsing. Tingling. Moistening. Take me! she wanted to cry out, like an old fashioned heroine. Take me, do what you want with me. Strangely, she now felt hesitant about caressing him in return. It was as though he had taken command of her body. Without speaking he had willed her to remain submissive to him, to let him dictate the pace.

For once, Marie felt happy to cede to a man. It was a relief not to feel as though she had to give in equal measure to what she received. His whispered comments thrilled her, made her feel beautiful, adored. She held her breath as she watched Lawrie reach out to pick up a crystal glass of champagne. Through heavy-lidded eyes she watched it tip. The clear, fizzing liquid trickled on to her bare stomach. As it touched her feverish skin the chilled liquid seemed to sizzle.

Then Lawrie's mouth was upon her yearning flesh, lapping up the champagne where it ran in tiny rivulets. A small amount pooled in her navel and a moment later Lawrie's tongue was there, swirling around and around the tiny indentation, his soft hair brushing her skin at the same time. Soon Marie was gasping urgently with arousal.

'Oh, please,' she breathed, 'I want you. I want you to – ' She broke off, clutching urgently at his hair, sliding her hands under the collar of his shirt to knead his muscular shoulders.

'Patience, sweetheart,' Lawrie said, chuckling softly, 'we've got all night. And all tomorrow if you want it.'

Oh, God yes, Marie thought, half out of her mind with wanting.

'I ought to call my flatmate,' she muttered, suddenly remembering Carla. 'We usually let each other know if we're not going to come home.'

Pressing her back against the soft cushions, Lawrie smiled down at her. 'Later,' he said, 'I promise. But not yet, don't let's spoil the moment.'

No sooner were the words out of his mouth and Marie felt the tension flow out of her body again than there was a knock at the door.

'Damn it,' Lawrie muttered crossly, getting up. He glanced back down at Marie, his chest constricting as he saw her sprawled there in her black underwear, legs wantonly splayed apart. 'Stay there,' he ordered. 'Stay just like that. I won't be a moment.'

Feeling happy and relaxed, Marie closed her eyes and

listened to Lawrie's footsteps as he crossed the timber-floored room. She heard the door opening and then muffled voices, some male, others female.

A moment later she realised the voices had become progressively louder and there was the sound of more heavy footsteps. These were interspersed with the distinctive click of high heels on the wood flooring.

Tipping her head back Marie surveyed the scene upside down. The blonde and brunette at the far end of the room she recognised as Lawrie's pit groupies from Zandvoort, but the two fair-haired men she didn't recognise at all. Glancing around wildly for her dress, she noticed it was on one of the other sofas – too far away for her to be able to grab without being seen by Lawrie's visitors. Snuggling back down on the sofa, she prayed they wouldn't come any further into the room and see her lying there, half undressed.

'Well, well, darling,' she heard one of the women say, in a clipped tone that sounded falsely bright to Marie's ears, 'what have we here – Or should I say, who?'

Marie cringed as she felt unseen eyes upon her. She didn't dare look up. To do so would acknowledge the unwelcome existence of the other woman and also put herself at a disadvantage.

Lawrie muttered something that Marie didn't quite catch but it seemed his visitors were undaunted.

'Come on, Lawrie,' one of the men said. 'We've come over here to party. The car's all fixed. We've been working our whatsits off all day, surely we deserve a bit of fun now.'

'Not now, Blair. I'm busy.' Lawrie's voice was stern but it seemed that his tone cut no ice with the unwelcome guest.

Unwillingly, Marie turned her head and saw that the small group were now standing barely three feet away. Both men were craning their necks to get a good look at her and one of the women, the blonde one, was reaching down and tugging off one of a pair of grey ankle boots.

Her pink jacket was already discarded and hanging on the back of a chair.

'We won't disturb you, sweetikins,' the woman said as she straightened up and unzipped the pair of grey leather trousers she was wearing. 'We just want to soak in your jacuzzi.'

There followed a long sigh from Lawrie. 'Oh, all right,' he said, 'just keep your fun and games confined to one room, OK? Don't come back in here to bother us.'

Both women laughed at this and the blonde said, 'Oh, I'm sure we'll *come* plenty of times, won't we, boys?' She reached up and stroked a slender, pink-taloned fingertip from the base of Lawrie's throat to mid thorax. 'Why don't you change your mind and join us, darling? I'm sure your little friend won't mind. There's plenty to go round. Blair and Peter are big boys, they can handle an extra woman.'

The two men – both bronzed gods like Lawrie, though slightly younger with shorter, darker blond hair – nodded eagerly, and Marie felt herself cringing again. She hoped Lawrie wouldn't agree.

'No thanks, Fiona,' Lawrie replied, to Marie's relief, 'Marie and I are quite happy as we are. Or at least we were, until you four turned up.'

At that point the brunette, who had in the meantime stripped down to a blue silk teddy that barely contained her voluptuous body, pouted at Lawrie. 'For goodness' sake, darling,' she said, 'you're so tetchy this evening. Where is your sense of adventure? It's not like you to turn down an orgy.' Throwing back her head, so that her long, dark hair cascaded down her spine, she gave a tinkly laugh.

Marie grimaced inwardly. She was certain that the young woman's laugh was as false as her large, thrusting breasts appeared to be. You're such a bitch, Marie, she reprimanded herself silently, I thought only Amber made unfounded suppositions like that. And it struck her again that perhaps there was more of Amber and Portia in her than she had previously realised.

Contemplating the situation for a moment, she reached an instant decision. Rising as gracefully as possible from the sofa she sauntered with deliberate nonchalance over to Lawrie. As soon as she reached his side she slid a possessive arm around his waist and smiled up at him.

'I think if your friends want us to join their party, we shouldn't disappoint them,' she said, enjoying the amazed stares of everyone else in the room, including Lawrie himself.

'I don't know – ' Lawrie started to say, gazing down at her with a mixture of disbelief and desire.

Marie's suggestion had not only surprised him, but also excited him like crazy. The idea of watching her with Fiona and Dorinda was extremely alluring. Although he wasn't too sure about allowing Blair and Peter to get their hands on her. Still, he supposed all was fair in sex and jacuzzis.

Taking Marie to one side, he whispered, 'Are you sure about this, sweetheart? I can get rid of them. Or we can lock ourselves away in my bedroom if you prefer.'

Marie shivered at the thought of being locked in Lawrie's bedroom with him. It certainly was tempting. But there was no way she would allow herself to be demoralised in any way by a couple of man-eaters like Fiona and Dorinda. She chuckled inwardly; they were a pretentious couple of names for a pretentious couple of young women, she decided. If necessary, she would have to allow her Portia character to take over a little and put everyone apart from Lawrie properly in their place.

It surprised her to realised that she could never consider dominating Lawrie. More like the other way around. Being submissive was not an option she had given any serious thought to before but Lawrie had a way of making her feel excited by the idea.

Just as Lawrie bent his head to kiss her, they were interrupted by Fiona. 'Lawrie, darling, do stop canoodling in the corner and come and join us. The water will be getting cold.'

'Silly bitch,' Lawrie murmured out of the corner of his mouth.

Marie giggled and muttered, 'My sentiments exactly.' Then, in a louder voice, she said, 'Yes, come on, darling, mustn't keep your little friends waiting, must we?'

Stressing the words *darling* and then *little*, she cast an imperious eye over the two women and then the men. She was pleased to note they all looked suitably taken aback. My goodness, she thought, with a grin, now Portia is really starting to take over.

Chapter Nine

Soft music and natural warmth filled Lawrie's huge, stark white bathroom. As Marie entered, her bare feet leaving impressions in the thick white carpeting, the first thing she noticed was the room's centerpiece – a round jacuzzi edged with white marble. A shudder of apprehension passed through her as she stood gazing down into the foaming water. This will take the six of us quite comfortably, she thought, wishing she hadn't been quite so bold.

She felt a little nervous now it had come to the crunch, and cursed her impetuous nature. She would much rather have had Lawrie to herself that evening. Marie raised her head, her sweeping glance taking in the rest of the room. Though there was very little else in the windowless room apart from the usual bathroom fittings, which lined the far wall, and a few thick slabs of marble which bore clusters of fat, creamy candles, it still felt luxurious. The only furniture was a white, towelling-covered divan upon which Blair and Peter were already lounging casually, their hard, naked bodies glowing in the flickering candlelight.

Marie managed to catch Lawrie's eye as he lit the last group of candles from a long taper. Raising the taper to his lips he blew softly. His eyes questioned her, asking her if she was OK. And in reply she nodded, adding a tremulous smile for good measure.

The spell between them was broken when Fiona and Dorinda walked into the room. By this time both women were naked and they glanced contemptuously at Marie who was still wearing her black underwear.

They reminded her, Marie decided, as she reached behind her to unclasp her bra, of the Siamese cats in Disney's *Lady and the Tramp*. The very idea made her face crease into a smile. Thank goodness that even in the face of adversity, she could always see the funny side.

All thoughts flew out of her head as Lawrie walked over to stand behind her. Sighing with desire, she allowed him to move her hands out of the way and unfasten her bra for her.

'Here, allow me,' he murmured in her ear.

His warm breath was seductive, making Marie shiver with pleasure. She trembled at the sensuousness of his caress as he slid each strap slowly down her shoulders, then slid his hands around her to cup her breasts. His fingertips toyed lightly with her hardening nipples and she groaned deeply.

'Beautiful,' he murmured. 'So, so delicious.'

Feeling a telltale wetness seep out of her, Marie shrugged off her bra and turned in his arms, crushing her yearning breasts against his naked torso. For a moment they abandoned themselves to a deep, sensuous kiss that left them panting with arousal.

They were interrupted by a tut-tutting from Fiona. 'Come on, you two,' she said briskly, adding, with a swift turn of her head, 'and you boys over there. Dorinda and I haven't got all night.'

Marie chuckled quietly as Lawrie muttered, 'Thank Christ for that.' Then she stepped back from him so that she could pull down her lacy knickers.

Her ears couldn't fail to pick up the combined sharp intake of breath as the others set eyes on her shaven mound for the first time. Feeling pleased with the sensation she had just caused, Marie executed an impudent twirl. With her arms held out wide to the side of her body, she showed herself off to her audience.

'Will I do?' she asked of no one in particular.

'You'll do for me, baby,' Blair enthused.

Jumping to his feet, he bounded across the room like an eager puppy. He tried to grab at Marie but Lawrie blocked him.

'Down boy,' Fiona said tersely from the doorway. 'Let's get into the water first.'

Climbing into the warm, swirling waters of the jacuzzi, Marie settled back in idle luxury to watch Fiona and Dorinda cross the room. Both women were tall and well proportioned, though Fiona was far slimmer than her friend. Her figure was very slight and quite angular, with a tiny waist, flat, barely existent buttocks and small pointed breasts.

Dorinda, on the other hand, was far more sinuous. Her breasts which, by now Marie was totally convinced owed more to plastic surgery than Mother Nature, were large and gravity defying. They were tipped by big, juicy nipples that were almost the same diameter as her areolae. Her narrow waist flared out to generously curved hips and her bottom was high and nicely rounded above slightly heavy thighs.

Marie was aware that her gaze followed Dorinda as she climbed into the jacuzzi and sat opposite her, with Blair and Peter settling themselves either side. Unlike Fiona, who she found rather too brittle for her liking, Marie was rather attracted to the brunette. Dorinda had hardly spoken and had an air of quiet submissiveness about her that excited Marie's dominant inclinations. All at once she imagined herself chastising the young woman, bending her over her knee and smacking those deliciously plump buttocks until they glowed bright red.

'Are you OK, sweetheart?' Lawrie asked Marie as he sat down beside her.

'Fine,' she murmured, flushing slightly at her lascivious thoughts and feeling glad that he couldn't read her

134

mind. She swirled her hands idly in the water for a moment before dipping one hand deeper and seeking out the semi hardness of Lawrie's cock. 'And what I'm feeling makes *me* feel even better now,' she added, grinning pertly up at him.

Straight away, she felt his cock stiffen in her hand and she began to caress it rhythmically, sighing with pleasure as one of Lawrie's hands slipped between her thighs and began to return the compliment.

Fiona was the last to climb into the jacuzzi. She was obviously intent on making a grand entrance, Marie thought wickedly. And she watched in amusement as the blonde woman minced across the tiled floor, making a great fuss about dipping her toes in the water before finally sliding gracefully into the space between Blair and Lawrie.

A moment later Marie felt Fiona's fingers brush her own as the other woman sought out Lawrie's cock. Marie held on to his stiff shaft possessively. She resisted the urge to glare at Fiona, who quickly snatched her hand away when she realised Marie had already beaten her to the prize she sought.

Obviously undaunted, Fiona pulled Lawrie's head down to hers, devouring his mouth in a long, passionate kiss.

Marie was gratified that Lawrie continued to stroke her throbbing sex as he kissed Fiona. She could feel her clitoris burgeoning under his skilful caresses and spread her legs wider apart to make things easier still for him. Stretching out one leg, she pointed her toes and insinuated them between Dorinda's thighs. Straight away her toes encountered the soft springiness of the other woman's lush pubic hair. Wriggling her toes, she worked them between Dorinda's swollen labia to tease and tantalise her hard little clitoris.

Gazing straight into Dorinda's face, Marie felt a warm surge of arousal as she caught the other girl's blissful expression. Working her toes down the sensuous flesh of the brunette's slit, she pressed her big toe into her slippery vagina, using it like a tiny cock.

Dorinda gave a long moan. Peter was cupping one weighty breast and Blair the other. Simultaneously, the two men bent their heads and sucked her nipples into their mouths. Throwing her head back, Dorinda closed her eyes and Marie watched with pleasure as the other woman gave herself up to the beauty of the multiple caresses she was receiving.

Releasing Lawrie's mouth at long last, Fiona glanced up, looking firstly at Dorinda and then at Marie. Marie followed the woman's keen-eyed gaze as she looked down into the water where her own slender leg could clearly be seen stretching out towards Dorinda. What about me? Fiona's expression seemed to say.

Immediately, Blair noticed Fiona's downcast expression and turned his attention to her instead. Reaching around her, he pulled the other woman on to his lap and a moment later Marie noticed how her eyes widened and then fluttered closed.

Having watched Fiona bounce rhythmically up and down for a few moments, Marie turned to Lawrie, removing her foot from between Dorinda's thighs at the same time. She smiled knowingly and slid herself on to Lawrie's lap so that she was facing him. Reaching for his stiff cock again, she guided it into her aching vagina and began to grind her pelvis against his.

'I didn't expect our evening to turn out like this,' Lawrie murmured in her ear as his hands slid up her torso to her breasts and massaged them gently.

'Nor did I,' Marie said honestly. She gazed properly at his face, feeling the pull of his soft grey eyes. Like the downy feathers of a duckling, they were warm and inviting. She felt herself sink into them as his cock drove deeper and deeper inside her. 'You don't mind, do you?' she asked.

He shook his head. 'Mind? No, I don't mind but I couldn't help wondering if you were disappointed.'

'Do I feel disappointed?' she countered gently, clenching her internal muscles so that they gripped his cock even harder.

His immediate laughter finished on a groan of arousal. 'No,' he said, 'you certainly don't.'

Releasing her breasts, he slid his hands around her wet, slippery body to clasp her buttocks. He eased them apart and his finger sought her tight little nether hole.

'Ah!' Marie let her head drop back as she let out a long moan of desire. She could feel her swollen clitoris rubbing against the wiry bush of his pubic hair and the membranes surrounding her anus were so sensitive she felt supremely stimulated.

A moment later she felt more hands sliding up her back and across her shoulders. They slipped around her and covered her breasts, the fingers plucking and tugging at her distended nipples. Catching a whiff of perfume and the sensation of long, wet hair tickling her shoulder, Marie turned her head slightly. She knew who she expected to see and felt a rush of exhilaration as she found herself gazing into a pair of soft hazel eyes.

'You're a naughty girl, Dorinda,' Marie said in a low but stern voice, 'and in a moment I'm going to punish you for this.' Hearing Dorinda's answering whimper and feeling the way the young woman's fingers started to work even more feverishly on her nipples, Marie felt swamped by arousal. She had known it all along. Dorinda *was* submissive and that was going to make the evening a lot more fun. 'Pinch my nipples,' Marie urged her. 'That's it; go on, pinch them hard – harder.'

As Dorinda's fingertips clamped her nipples like two tiny vices, Marie let out an agonised groan. The pain was exquisite. Sharp. Bittersweet. She could feel the warmth in her body expanding, the heat from her nipples travelling down to her sex where the wonderful sensations in her stimulated clitoris, anus and vagina all culminated in one huge, delicious climax.

She ground herself down harder on Lawrie's cock, her breath shortening as she felt him swell inside her and then explode. At the last moment she covered his open mouth with hers, tasting his gasps of pleasure, breathing them in.

As the violence of their orgasms began to abate, Marie slowed down to a gentle rocking motion, delighting in the blissful expression on Lawrie's face. Dorinda's grip on her nipples slackened and after a moment Marie was able to turn her head and order Dorinda out of the jacuzzi.

'Sit on the side,' she said sternly, 'legs spread.'

Ignoring the amazed expressions on the faces of the others, Marie slipped gently off Lawrie, dropped a light kiss on his shoulder and murmured, 'That was wonderful,' in his ear, before standing up fully and turning around.

The warm water reached the tops of her thighs as she stood up and watched Dorinda climb awkwardly from the jacuzzi. It was obvious to Marie that the young woman was beside herself with excitement. Her movements were clumsy, her hands and knees slipping on the marble tiling around the edge of the bath in her haste to do Marie's bidding. Marie allowed a slight smile to touch her lips as she saw Dorinda's bottom wobble slightly as she moved. It was so round, so plump and glistening, with droplets of water clinging to the rosy flesh, that Marie felt her palms tingle with anticipation.

'On second thoughts, stay just like that,' she ordered the young woman, as she crouched on her hands and knees on the side of the jacuzzi, making ready to stand. 'Thrust that bottom in the air. That's right. Now arch your back more. Lovely, darling, just right.'

As Marie spoke she waded the few steps that took her to the side of the bath and stroked her hand assessingly over Dorinda's buttocks. Her fingers slid crudely into the exposed cleft between them. Stroking the small, puckered hole that nestled between them, she pressed her fingertip experimentally against it, enjoying the way the taut muscles around the opening yielded to the pressure.

She heard a collective gasp as her finger slid inside

Dorinda's anus and didn't have to look around to know that the eyes of Lawrie and his friends were riveted to her actions. Dorinda also gave a tiny gasp that changed to a whimper as Marie twisted her finger deeper inside the tight channel. After a moment she withdrew her finger slowly and dabbled her hand in the water to cleanse it before stroking the inviting pouch of Dorinda's sex.

Her dark bush was thick and glossy but there was no mistaking the visual signs of her arousal. Her thickened sex lips were parted to reveal the juicy folds of her inner flesh and her vagina pouted openly. The flesh was red and glistening with the copious juices that flowed from it.

Unconsciously, Marie licked her lips at the sight of such succulent abundance. Everything about Dorinda was sensuous and voluptuous, from the lush curve of her hips to her pendulous breasts, the tips of which brushed the cold marble.

'You're a naughty, greedy girl, aren't you, Dorinda?' Marie said in a low voice. Her fingers skimmed the slick entrance to the young woman's vagina, eliciting another whimper. 'I'm going to punish you for your bad behaviour. Don't you know that everyone is looking at you? Everyone can see how aroused your naughty body is. They're all looking at you, Dorinda, my love.' She paused to spread the young woman's vaginal lips wider apart. 'They can see everything,' she continued mercilessly. 'All your rude little places.' Dorinda gave an anguished groan but Marie carried on. 'Should I let one of the others touch you, Dorinda? You're so wet and open. Should I order Blair to come over here and finger you? Or maybe I should allow Peter to play with your swollen little clitoris – would you like that?'

'Ah! Oh, no – yes – please – ' Dorinda was barely coherent as she shook her bowed head from side to side.

Reaching forward, Marie lifted the curtain of hair away from one side of the brunette's face and noticed, with satisfaction, that the cheek she revealed was glowing bright red with shame.

'Maybe I'll finger-fuck you,' Marie said in a stage whisper, leaning over the edge of the bath until her mouth was level with the young woman's shoulder. 'No,' she amended, moving back again, 'on second thoughts, I think I should punish you instead. Don't you agree, my darling? Don't you think you deserve to be punished for such lewd behaviour?'

Her lips curved with satisfaction as Dorinda nodded wordlessly. Standing up straight, Marie slid her hand up from the young woman's sex to stroke her bottom again. At the same time she gazed at Lawrie and the others. Each remained completely silent, their faces rapt with attention, as though transfixed by the scene being played out right in front of their very eyes.

Inside, Marie glowed. There was nothing she enjoyed better than an audience. Or at least, she reminded herself wryly, there was nothing Portia enjoyed more. It was difficult for her to tell now where one character ended and the others began.

She stroked Dorinda's plump, quivering buttocks for a moment longer. Then she raised her hand and brought it down hard to deliver a sharp smack which she knew would sting like crazy on the damp flesh.

Dorinda gasped but didn't protest as Marie repeated her action again and again until both buttocks were glowing. Presently, the young woman's gasps turned to whimpers and then groans of arousal. Glancing down, Marie could see how swollen her sex had become. The puffy lips seemed to open out like a huge bloom, the nectar trickling from her gaping vagina in a steady flow.

Her clitoris was long and extremely swollen. Like a tiny cock, it seemed to cry out for attention and, ultimately, relief. Taking pity on the poor girl, Marie stroked the hard bud. Expertly, she slid its little cowl of flesh back and forth over the sensitive tip until Dorinda reached a shuddering, tumultuous climax, her cries of pleasure reverberating around the stark white walls.

Feeling satisfied with her efforts, Marie watched as Dorinda's arms and legs trembled for a moment before the young woman collapsed face down on the cool marble. Her bottom was still red and glowing, Marie's hand prints clearly visible, and her swollen sex was awash with her own juices.

'I think what she needs now is a good fucking,' Marie stated as she glanced at the three men. 'Any volunteers?'

She noticed Lawrie and Fiona still appeared stunned but Peter was marginally quicker than Blair about leaping into action. Crossing the jacuzzi in a couple of strides, his stiff cock rearing proudly from its nest of sandy-coloured hair, he stood behind Dorinda, spread her quivering thighs insolently apart and entered her without preamble.

A bolt of pure desire shot through Marie as she watched the spectacle. Savage and undeniably carnal, Peter's actions and Dorinda's responses to them were almost bestial in their simplicity. Turning to Lawrie, she gazed at him, her eyes heavy-lidded with lust.

'Take me,' she said, almost in a whisper. 'Take me again now before I erupt.'

This time Lawrie swept her up in his arms, carried her out of the bath and over to the divan, where he laid her down gently. Covering her with his lean, hard body, he caressed her for a moment before sliding effortlessly into her soaking wet vagina.

Her body grasped at him eagerly and she wound her arms and legs around him, latching on to him like a limpet. Abandoning herself totally to her body's needs, she grunted and groaned as she thrust her pelvis up against him urgently. Just for a moment she glanced sideways and noticed that Fiona and Blair were thrashing about in the jacuzzi, while Peter was still driving into Dorinda's squirming body with long, measured strokes.

It wasn't the first time, by a long shot, that she had indulged in such orgiastic revelry, yet she couldn't remember ever having felt so totally and utterly abandoned. Whenever Marie was to look back on that night, she recalled it as though it were one long, erotic dream. One in which, although the action and the players kept changing, the libidinous pleasure always managed to reach the same dizzying heights.

Now, almost a week later, Marie couldn't be sure if it was the noise or the strong sunlight that woke her. Since she and her crew had reached the other side of the Channel they had been driving for over eight hours, with only short breaks for calls of nature. For the past four hours she had been sleeping solidly and was thankful that – for once – she and her team mates were able to enjoy luxury on a grand scale.

Thanks to the sponsorship money she had received from *Verval*, the team had been able to afford to lash out on the hire of a motor home for this extended trip. With the last three race meetings – one in Germany and two in Italy – all so close together in terms of time and location, it had made sense not to bother returning to England in between races. Only Frank and his brother would be flying back and forth because they had a business to run.

For Marie and Carla the coming three weeks in mainland Europe would be like a holiday, especially as they didn't have to do any of the driving. Sitting up on the long sofa that spanned the back of the motorhome and doubled as a single bed, Marie glanced out of the window. On a trailer behind them was her beloved car, its fabulous new blue and black livery covered by a plain black weatherproof cover.

Marie felt a strong surge of pride and exhilaration as they entered the Hockenheim track, drove down the pit lane and pulled to a halt at the back of their assigned garage. Though the actual race meeting wasn't until the following day, the famous German track was seemingly packed to the gills with spectators.

If there was one thing Marie had learned during her brief career as a racing driver, it was that on the whole the German people loved motorsport with a passion and were ardent supporters of their own countrymen.

It was then she felt a flicker of doubt. Kurt Jurgens was one of the German contingents and a formidable opponent. Although he hadn't competed in all the race meetings in the Championship and therefore didn't have a hope of winning overall, he could easily scupper her chances of taking first place at this meeting.

Then there was Lawrie to contend with, she remembered with an equal mixture of lust and apprehension. Between Lawrie and Kurt she could easily find herself relegated to third place. And that wouldn't do her overall prospects for winning the Championship any good at all.

She had worked out that she could only afford to come as low as third place once during the remainder of the Championship. She was still leading on points at the moment but one of the Spanish drivers, Guillermo Castillos, was only two points behind her. An American driver, Tony Bertorelli, was her next serious competitor, with a deficit of only four points. Then came Darren Standish, an Italian and a Swede. They were followed closely by Lawrie – who had already distinguished himself despite his late entry into the Championship – and Kurt, both lying at equal sixth place. Although they were all behind her at the moment, in terms of points there really wasn't all that much in it.

The pits were buzzing with people and, despite her apprehension, Marie had to force herself to banish all negative thoughts from her head. It wouldn't do to dwell on possible misfortune. Positive creative visualisation was what was called for, she told herself firmly. Particularly as she now had to concentrate her efforts on transforming herself into Amber Barclay again.

Drawing the curtains around the rear of the motorhome to shield her from prying eyes, she quickly pulled on her wig. Then she stripped off her clothes, heedless of the presence of the crew – who had seen her quick change act so many times it had ceased to be of any interest to them – and pulled on a short navy skirt, which she teamed with a white cropped top. She wore no bra under the clinging top and was aware how clearly the outline of her nipples could be seen through the thin cotton, and how brown her bare midriff seemed in contrast.

Next she turned her attention to her make-up, only slightly darkening her bleached eyebrows with a feathering of red-brown pencil and coating her lashes with a single coat of brown mascara. Around her eyes she smudged a small amount of taupe eyeliner pencil. Then she finished off her 'barely there' look by slicking a browny-pink lipgloss over her lips.

'All done?' Carla asked as she sat down next to Marie.

Closing her compact and zipping up her make-up bag, Marie nodded.

'All hail the return of Amber,' she said in an ironic tone, a smile curving her shiny lips. That same smile faltered a little as she gripped Carla's hand which rested on the seat between them. 'I hate to admit it but I'm nervous, Carla. The competition seems so fierce all of a sudden, I don't know if I can cut it.'

Carla raised her eyebrows and stared at Marie as if she'd gone mad.

'Don't talk rubbish, girl. What is all this?' she said firmly. 'You're as good a driver as you ever were and the car's in tip top condition. Plus this is one of your favourite tracks. How could you fail to feel confident?'

'That's easy, ' Marie replied, shrugging. 'I can sum it up in two names: Guillermo Castillos and Lawrie Samson.'

'Oh, them.' Carla was quick to dismiss her fears. 'They're only men. You're you, remember.'

Marie's first impulse was to agree laughingly. Then she suddenly became serious again.

'To tell you the truth, Carla,' she admitted, 'just lately I've been beginning to wonder who I really am.'

Carla looked confused. And rightly so, Marie realised.

'What do you mean?' she asked.

'I mean,' Marie said, 'that my characters don't seem like separate people to me any more. That night at Lawrie's house – '

'Oh, for goodness' sake, stop harping on about that night,' Carla interrupted forcefully. 'All you've done is go over it a million times. You've analysed it to death, love. But at the end of the day all it was was an experience like any other. Fun, yes. Pleasurable, yes. But you've had loads of those sort of experiences. What's so different about this one?'

Marie fell silent. She knew what the difference was but didn't like to admit it, least of all to Carla who, she knew, would only sigh and tell her she was being a bloody idiot. Instead of saying, 'Lawrie Samson, that's the difference,' she simply shrugged again and forced a smile.

'I know,' Marie said at last with a sigh. 'I am being a bloody idiot about all this. You don't have to say it. It was fun while it lasted but that's as far as it goes, right?'

She looked to Carla for confirmation of something she didn't actually believe. Although she was loath to admit it, the fact that Lawrie had made no attempt to see her since that night, or even call her, hurt like hell. It was just typical male philosophy, she had tried telling herself on more than one occasion. All I was to Lawrie was an easy lay. Now he's moved on and so should I.

The trouble was, she mused as she slipped her feet into a pair of low-heeled tan leather sandals, it wasn't going to be easy trying to forget about Lawrie, particularly as she was going to be spending the next few weekends in competition with him. And to make matters worse she couldn't even speak to him on a personal level. As far as he was concerned, Marie and Amber were two entirely different women.

After breakfast in the pit area café Marie decided to leave the team to unload the car and give it the once-over while she did her usual track walkabout. Pausing only to wave at some of the teams as she passed by their garages, she wandered up the pit lane and out on to the track itself.

At the moment it was totally deserted. Practise and qualifying wouldn't take place until the afternoon. As it was only just past eight, she had plenty of time to familiarise herself again with the track layout and its varying curves and changes in camber.

The Hockenheim circuit is almost an oval, with several gentle chicanes, one killer chicane in the form of a tight 'S' and an extremely long straight which makes it a fast track.

As it was another blisteringly hot day, without a cloud in sight, Marie expected to get a lot of traction, which meant that the heat would make her tyres sticky and therefore grip the track surface nicely. Her worst night-mare was racing in wet conditions, when the track became as slippery as sheet ice, causing no end of hazards.

By the time she had walked the entire circuit – a distance of four and a quarter miles – and returned to the pits, Lawrie's team had arrived. Once again his mechanics in their purple and white overalls seemed to be everywhere, and a huge crowd had gathered around his car. Lawrie himself was nowhere to be seen and Marie took a perverse delight in wandering over to his garage and studiously pretending not to be looking for him.

Just as she was about to give up and go back to her own car, she saw him. In truth, she couldn't fail to miss him. Not his long, loping stride, nor his white blond head towering over everyone else in the pits. Further-more, the two young women walking either side of him, their arms wrapped around his waist, were unmistak-ably Fiona and Dorinda.

Although she had promised herself that she would remain aloof, Marie felt her heart miss a beat. Then it seemed to stop altogether as Lawrie looked directly at her. A flicker of something passed across his face and, just for a fleeting moment she felt a surge of elation, thinking that he had recognised her, despite her disguise. But to her disappointment he looked away and, a moment later, began talking earnestly with a TV journalist who was accompanied by a cameraman and sound man.

She stood watching the exchange for a moment, noticing Lawrie nod his agreement to something. Then she remembered that she had agreed to accept every available opportunity to get TV coverage for herself and *her* car.

Publicity on the largest scale possible was part of her agreement with *Verval*. And they had managed to talk her into spending the following Monday at a local studio, where they wanted to do a photographic shoot for the magazine. Anxious to get the sponsorship deal at any cost, Marie had blithely agreed to everything they suggested.

Now she regretted her impulsiveness. She was always worried that someone would recognise her, that one of her creditors would see through her disguise and insist on repossessing her precious car. All she could hope for was to hold the vultures at bay until she had won the Championship. Then all her troubles would be over and she could drop her charade for once and for all.

Chapter Ten

Marie was halfway round the tight triple chicane, just entering *Sachs Kurve*, when disaster struck. The previous day's practise and qualifying had gone extremely well, putting her in pole position, with Guillermo Castillos in second and Lawrie in third. Time and again during the race Guillermo had tried to get past her, nudging at her bumper around *Bremskurve 1* and *Bremskurve 2* and then almost forcing her into the gravel at *Ostkurve*.

He was doing it again now and the only way she could hold him off was by riding the kerb, thereby forcing her car to slew across in front of him. Slamming her foot down on the accelerator, she pulled out a quick lead of about two car lengths and smiled to herself as she imagined the Spanish driver mentally shaking a fist at her.

Through her headset Marie heard Carla's voice congratulating her. Smiling faintly, she switched all her concentration to the next chicane, which she was dreading. No sooner was she into the first bend, *Agip Kurve*, than Guillermo was close behind her, putting the pressure on again. Managing to hold him off, Marie deliberately veered from the racing line in order to confuse him.

And confuse him she had, she realised as she glanced

in her wing mirror. She had hardly felt the clip on her back wing from the front of Guillermo's car but couldn't fail to notice him scream past her, closely followed by Lawrie, Darren and one of the Swedes, as she spun wildly off the track. She clenched her teeth as she felt her car sliding across the edge of the gravel and on to the grass before coming to a standstill at right angles to the track.

'Of all the slimy, cheating little ..!' Marie muttered angrily to herself. Ignoring Carla's instructions through her earpiece to calm down and take things easy, and cursing under her breath, she slammed her foot down hard on the accelerator. Instead of driving smoothly off the grass and on to the track, the Porsche reacted by doing a complete one hundred and eighty degree turn, throwing up a cloud of smoke and grass. With her heart thumping, Marie managed to wrestle with the car to get it back on track. She ended up just behind one of the Italian drivers, yelling, 'Out of my way, you dickhead!' as she accelerated up close behind him.

The Italian's car – a white and orange 928 – was like a red flag to a bull as far as Marie was concerned. To say the sight of it irritated her would be an understatement. Try as she might she couldn't get past him and finally, when the chequered flag came down, it was Lawrie who did the lap of honour. Guillermo came a close second, leaving Marie embarrassingly in sixth place.

'Where is that cheating Spanish bastard?' Amber fumed to Carla and the rest of the crew as she leapt from her car the moment she pulled into the pits. 'Let me at him.' Furiously, she began dragging off her helmet and racing gloves. 'Did you see what he did? I mean – can you believe it?' She gesticulated wildly as she spoke and flung her helmet and gloves inside the car.

'You would have done the same given half a chance,' Frank said, so evenly he made Marie want to scream. 'Let's face it, he's a good driver, one of the best.'

'He's a shit! And a grade A – ' Marie was almost

beside herself with indignation but Carla interrupted her.

'Come and have a drink, love,' she said, putting a consoling arm around her friend's shoulders.

'I don't want a fucking drink, I want to go and rip that bastard's balls off and make him eat them.' Marie shrugged off Carla's arm, then felt herself sag. As quickly as it had erupted, her anger dissolved. 'Bugger it,' she said, kicking the garage wall and pretending it was Guillermo's shin. 'I deserved to win that race.'

Wandering disconsolately into the garage, she sat down on top of a large red metal tool box and unzipped her racing overalls. Shrugging them down to her waist, she pulled off her fireproof vest and sat there, the top half of her body clad only in a pale blue silky bra edged in ecru lace. A moment later she heard footsteps but she felt too downcast to bother looking up.

'Very fetching,' a voice said beside her. 'I wish I was coming in here to congratulate you on an excellent win. The race should have been yours.'

For a moment Marie felt stunned. Then the familiarity of the voice broke through her confused thoughts. Turning her head, she glanced up, her eyes widening with pleasure as she saw Lawrie looming over her. Shielded from the bright sunlight, the interior of the garage was heavily shadowed and she could barely make out his features. However, there was no mistaking his voice, or the endless legs and long lean torso clad in purple and white racing overalls.

'I suppose you've come in here to gloat,' she said dully, returning her gaze to the concrete floor.

'Not at all,' Lawrie replied, moving to squat down in front of her. 'I told you, I thought the race was in the bag. But let's face it, that Castillos character only did what any of us would have done under the circumstances.'

'He's a shit,' Marie said, repeating her earlier phrase but this time without the venom.

Lawrie's face broke into a broad smile. 'Yes, he is,' he said, nodding his agreement, 'but it's only a race.'

Only a race! Marie stared at him in disbelief. She felt like screaming, or laughing hysterically, or crying, or all three. *Only a race.*

'It means a lot to me,' she murmured dully. 'Sod it, it means everything.'

When she felt the consoling touch of Lawrie's hand on her bare shoulder she had to force herself not to turn her head and nuzzle it. More than anything she longed to pick up his hand and kiss its palm, then to place it against her breast.

'Well, I can't sit here all day feeling sorry for myself,' Marie declared a moment later, ignoring her erotic thoughts and rising stiffly from her makeshift seat.

Pausing to slip her arms back into the racing suit and zip it up she glanced down at Lawrie. More than anything she wanted to run her fingers through his soft blond hair, then pull him to his feet and hold him.

All at once her blank expression crumbled. 'I don't think I can bear the idea of seeing him climbing on to that rostrum and standing there in second place,' she admitted. 'And God knows what this is going to do to my Championship hopes.' Although she hardly realised it, a solitary tear slid slowly down her cheek.

'You can do it,' Lawrie murmured gently. Standing up, he reached out and caught the teardrop on the end of his finger. They both stared at the drop and watched it slowly dry out in the heat. 'You're a strong woman, Marie. You'll find it in you to win.' With that he turned on his heel and strode quickly out of the garage, as though he thought he had gone too far.

It was only after Lawrie had well and truly melted into the crowd in the pits that Marie realised what he had said. Bloody hell, she thought, gazing blankly out at the crowd in the pits, what a fool I've been to think I could keep my identity a secret from him!

* * *

Fear had replaced Marie's fury by the time she joined the others in front of the winner's podium. Somehow she forced herself to go through the rigmarole of being showered with champagne and smiling for the cameras.

'Amber, could you spare us five minutes for an interview?' an German-accented voice asked.

Glancing sideways, Marie noticed a stout man dressed in knee-length khaki shorts and a black T-shirt. He was holding a microphone and had a cameraman in tow. The initials displayed on the front of the large video camera told her that she was dealing with one of the major German news stations.

Ever the professional, Marie forced a sunny smile as she replied, 'Sure, no problem.' Glancing around the busy pits she added, 'Where do you want to do the interview – here?'

'No, next to your car,' the German said as he motioned to the cameraman to follow them.

By unspoken agreement they began nudging their way through the crowd and walking back towards her garage.

Fortunately, the car was still outside in the pits, its new paintwork gleaming in the sunlight. Only the small dent in the rear wing, which Guillermo Castillos had caused, marred its otherwise pristine appearance.

'We'll soon get the bodywork sorted,' Frank assured Marie as he walked around from the front of the car, cleaning his hands on a piece of white cloth.

'This is your crew chief?' the reporter asked.

Marie grinned wryly. 'No,' she said, '*that's* my crew chief.' She pointed to Carla, who was dragging a trolley jack from the garage.

Although her mechanic's overalls were dirty and her face was streaked with grease, there was still no mistaking Carla's femininity. Consequently, Marie enjoyed the reporter's double take.

Turning to the cameraman, he muttered something in German, then glanced back at Marie, his pudgy face beaming. Taking a handkerchief from the pocket of his shorts, he wiped it across his brow.

'The heat,' he explained needlessly. He tucked the handkerchief back into his pocket, and added, 'Do you think we could interview both of you?' He nodded in Carla's direction and Carla glanced up inquiringly.

'Want to be a TV star, Carla?' Marie called out to her.

Carla pulled a face, which Marie took to mean, 'What – with me looking like this?'

With a broad grin Marie nodded and beckoned her friend over.

Looking truculent, Carla thrust her hands in her pockets and trudged around the car to join Marie and the camera crew.

'This is good,' the cameraman, who was tall, with straggly light brown hair, observed as Carla and Marie posed side by side at the front of the car. 'Now, just move around a bit, you are both squinting.'

Marie and Carla dutifully shuffled around the car until the sun was no longer in their eyes. Then, leaning casually against the front wing, they composed their faces into serene smiles. The interview was short and predictable. Marie gave her viewpoint of the race and Carla backed her up with more technical details about the car's performance.

'And now,' the reporter said at last, 'just a couple more questions. Amber, how do you feel about Guillermo Castillos?'

Marie felt her hackles rise at the question and sucked in her breath until she felt the calming touch of Carla's fingers on hers. She breathed out slowly, allowing the words to form in her mind before giving her answer.

'Guillermo Castillos is an excellent driver,' she said, almost as if she were reciting a well rehearsed script. 'We were both in heavy competition from the start but he managed to get the edge on me at Sachs. You can't blame a driver from doing what he did. Any one of us would have done the same.'

153

She gave a faint smile as she heard Carla whisper, 'Well done.'

The reporter nodded, then added, 'Just one last thing, Amber. You have recently signed a sponsorship deal with *Verval*, is that correct?'

Feeling that she was back on safer ground, Marie's tentative smile broadened. 'Yes, that's right,' she said, 'as you can see for yourself.' Her casual wave indicated the Porsche in its new livery.

'So you don't think the magazine is an unusual sponsor to have?' the reporter asked.

'No, I – '

Marie felt her confidence falter as she shook her head. All at once her legs seemed to turn to water when she noticed the reporter's sly smile. She recognised that expression of old. He looked every inch as though he was about to go in for the kill.

'Then you have no problems posing for the magazine?' he continued, interrupting her. 'A nude photo-shoot is a very unusual thing for a racing driver, don't you think, particularly an Englishwoman?'

Feeling the colour drain from her face, Marie simply shook her head dumbly. What was all this about nude photo-shoots? she wondered. Quickly, she managed to compose herself.

'No, of course it's not a problem,' she responded, smiling defiantly into the camera. 'Why should it be?'

The reporter grinned and held out his hand to her. 'Thank you very much, Miss Barclay,' he said greasily. 'I think that is all we need.'

As soon as the two Germans had disappeared into the crowd – no doubt on the trail of a new victim, Marie thought grimly – she grabbed Carla's arm and dragged her friend into the garage where they could talk privately.

'What the hell was all that about?' she asked as soon as they were alone. 'Do you have any idea?'

Carla shook her head, looking genuinely confused. 'No, none at all,' she said. 'This nude thing is news to

154

me. When I took that call from BB she simply said she wanted a photospread of you, with the car in its new colours. She didn't mention anything about what you would be wearing. I suppose I just assumed it would be racing overalls as per usual.'

Marie gave a wry laugh. 'She probably didn't mention clothes because there aren't any involved.'

'I'm sorry, love, I should have asked,' Carla muttered, looking downcast.

Putting a reassuring hand on her friend's shoulder, Marie smiled.

'Don't be daft,' she reassured her gently, 'you're not my press secretary. I should have rung BB back and got all the details myself.'

Carla gave a sigh of relief. 'So, what are you going to do about it?' she asked.

Raising a querulous eyebrow, Marie stared hard at her. 'I thought you would know me well enough by now, Carla,' she said. 'I'm going to pose for them, of course. What else?'

After a moment's shocked silence the two women burst into laughter.

Typically, that night there was a party for the racers. This time it was organised by the Championship's sponsor and held at a bar-cum-restaurant unoriginally named Der Bier Keller. Marie had been in two minds about whether to go but, having had such an horrendous day one way and another, she thought she deserved the opportunity to let her hair down.

Plus, she mused, as she dressed herself carefully in a pair of cream silk trousers and matching jacket, Lawrie would be there. Against her better judgement, she had decided that she had to face up to him about his having seen through her disguise. There was no reason why he should deliberately blow her cover, she told herself, so why not simply brazen it out?

When Marie and her team first arrived at the party, Lawrie and his entourage were nowhere to be seen.

Guillermo Castillos was there though, Marie noticed grimly. And he was holding court over a bevy of beautiful women – all long-legged, with streaked hair and sleek bodies draped in the skimpiest of clothes.

'Look at him,' Marie murmured as an aside to Carla. 'Doesn't he just make you want to throw up?'

'Leave it, love,' Carla warned. 'If you make a scene, the only person who'll end up looking bad will be yourself.'

Marie clapped a hand to her breast, her wide-eyed expression saying, 'Who me?'

'I wouldn't dream of it,' she reassured her friend. 'I was just making an observation, that's all.'

Fortunately, at that moment Lawrie arrived and Marie was pleased to note that, for once, he didn't have Fiona and Dorinda in tow.

'Now there's the man I really need to speak to,' she said to Carla. She proceeded to tell her friend all about the conversation she and Lawrie had had earlier that afternoon.

'Just watch yourself with him as well,' Carla warned when Marie had finished. 'I know I sound like an old fusspot but you can't afford to be careless. Just a few more weeks and the Championship will be in the bag.'

'I hope you're right, Carla,' Marie muttered as they headed for the bar, 'otherwise I'm done for.'

The music was loud and the chatter even louder as everyone got up from the tables where a sumptuous dinner had been served by buxom fraüleins in traditional dress and butch Aryan men in lederhosen. Marie and Carla had enjoyed themselves immensely, drinking gallons of wine and sharing wicked comments about the tackiness of the place, which was obviously heavily targeted at the tourist market.

Leaving her friend in the eager clutches of a Swedish mechanic who had been trying to catch Carla's eye constantly during dinner, Marie wandered back into the bar area. She immediately spotted Lawrie sliding his gorgeous bottom on to the seat of a high bar stool. As she approached the bar she appraised him, as usual liking what she saw. On this occasion he was dressed in a loose sage green jacket over black trousers and a black shirt.

She felt her insides melt as he suddenly glanced up and trapped her instantly in his uncompromising gaze.

'Mind if I sit here?' she asked brightly as she pointed to the empty chair next to him.

His answering smile was slow and easy. 'Not at all,' he said. 'Feel free.'

Marie realised that whenever she was with Lawrie she did feel free. Or at least she felt a certain sense of freedom. Now, she couldn't help wondering if that would all change.

Without asking her what she wanted to drink, Lawrie ordered two scotch and sodas and a couple of glasses of kirsch schnapps.

'I know everyone else is drinking beer or Hock,' he said, 'but I prefer a glass of the real amber nectar. A taste of the old country.' He laughed softly and Marie couldn't help noticing that his Scots accent was again more pronounced than usual. He also stressed the word *amber*.

'You figured out who I am, then?' she said after she had knocked back her schnapps in a single gulp. The alcohol was so strong it made her eyes water.

Lawrie nodded. 'Yes, how could I not? I know you intimately, remember.' He broke off as Marie blushed. 'But there's no need to get agitated about it, I'm not going to give the game away to anyone,' he added swiftly. 'You obviously have your reasons for taking such drastic action.'

'Yes, I do. Very good ones,' Marie agreed mysteriously, not wishing to expand on her *modus operandi*. She reached out a tentative hand and placed it on top of his, which rested on the bar. 'I do want to thank you, though.'

He shrugged. 'No need. What you choose to do with your life is no concern of mine. I believe in give and take.' His mouth curved into a knowing smile which touched the corners of his eyes. 'And so do you, if I remember rightly.'

Blushing again, Marie cursed the way her own body betrayed her. If her flaming cheeks did not reveal how deeply he affected her, the senstion of her nipples hardening and thrusting against her silk jacket certainly did.

'I wasn't feeling myself that night,' she quipped lightly.

Lawrie's smiled changed as the gleam in his eyes turned to something far darker and more promising.

'Oh, I think I'd have to disagree with you there,' he murmured. 'I would say the person I enjoyed that night most definitely felt like the real you.'

Marie tried to fob off his salacious comment with a shake of her head but found herself quivering. Excitement overtook anxiety as his hand moved from the bar to her thigh. As he squeezed her leg gently, his fingers seemed to sear her flesh through the silk of her trouser leg.

'Let me take you away from all this,' he urged her. 'I want you.'

Unwilling to tear her eyes away from his, Marie nevertheless glanced around. Carla, Frank and the others were enjoying themselves, she realised straight away. They wouldn't miss her if she left with Lawrie.

Her voice was barely more than a hoarse gasp as she answered him. 'OK.'

Outside Der Bier Keller a black Ferrari was parked by the kerbside.

'Would you believe I couldn't hire a Porsche in Germany?' Lawrie said lightly, leading her over to the car.

'Oh, dear,' Marie responded drily, 'so you've had to make do with this old thing instead?'

He grinned at her as he opened the passenger door and waited for her to climb inside.

'Sarcastic bitch,' he murmured.

They hardly exchanged two words during the drive. As soon as he got in the car Lawrie slipped a CD into the player and, to a background of Mozart, Marie concentrated on staring out of the window at the dark shapes of the square houses and tall, thin trees that lined the roads.

His place turned out to be a fabulous house from the 1930s. All curves and glass, it was surrounded on three sides by tall fir trees.

'*Bauhaus*,' Lawrie said simply as he stopped the car in front of the stylish building. 'Isn't it fantastic?'

Marie nodded. 'It's fabulous and seems very appropriate for you.'

'How's that?'

'It reminds me of a Porsche somehow.'

With a conspiratorial smile, Lawrie said, 'I never thought of it that way, to be honest. But now you come to mention it – ' He broke off and gazed at her for a long, stomach-clenching moment. Then he broke the spell by changing the subject. 'Fancy a walk before we go inside?'

Although her heart was thumping, Marie forced herself to sound nonchalant as she replied, 'OK, I don't mind if I do.'

As she climbed awkwardly from the car Lawrie took her hand and she noticed how he looked down at her feet, which were clad in fairly low wedge-heels.

His glance shifted to her face and he smiled warmly at her. 'At least your shoes look a bit more comfortable this time,' he observed.

'They are,' Marie agreed. 'It must be fate.'

Her perky grin faded as she gazed at him. His hair seemed so pale it looked almost ghostly in the moonlight. Anticipation gripped her. She already knew Lawrie was a skilful lover and that knowledge heightened her desire for him. For someone who had always preferred the thrill of the chase, she was surprised to find herself looking forward to extending their liaison and taking their mutual desire to its limits.

Skirting the side of the house, they followed a path

that took them through a dense area of fir trees. Between the trees, bluebells and other wild flowers sprouted in thick clumps.

'I'll bet this place is lovely in the daytime,' she remarked, breaking the relaxed silence they shared.

Lawrie gave her hand an answering squeeze. 'It is,' he said, 'but I haven't seen much of it. I've been too busy at the track.'

'So why aren't you staying at the hotel with the others?' Marie couldn't help asking. She had noticed his crew members in the hotel foyer and restaurant the previous night.

'Because I like my privacy,' he said. 'Racing talk is OK but you can have too much of a good thing.'

Marie laughed softly. 'I know. Sometimes I wonder if the people I meet have a life outside the track.' She paused as she remembered something. 'Oh, yes,' she said, 'I meant to ask you. Where are Fiona and Dorinda tonight?'

'Returned to England,' Lawrie replied, sounding as though he couldn't care less. 'I'll be flying back on Tuesday.'

Unaccountably, Marie felt her spirits slump. For just one brief, mad moment she had hoped that he, too, would be spending the next three weeks in Europe.

'I'm staying over here,' she offered. 'It hardly seems worth going back when we're going to be in Italy for the next couple of weeks.' She glanced up at him. 'I take it you will be competing at Monza and San Marino?'

For once his nod came as a relief to her. 'Oh, yes. Wild horses wouldn't keep me away. Although,' he added with a wry frown, 'I don't know if I'm proving very competitive. Next year should be different.'

'I don't know what you're talking about,' Marie countered, 'thanks to that cock-up of Guillermo's and Tony's accident you've moved up into third place just behind me now, haven't you?'

For a moment they both recalled the collision between Tony Bertorelli and the Swedish driver. This had resulted in the Swede's car spinning wildly off the track, spewing a hail of debris from his car. It was doubtful whether, with so much damage to contend with, his car would actually be repaired in time for the next race meeting.

Tony's car hadn't fared much better. He had lost a rear wing and there was speculation that the chassis on his car was now bent. In addition, one of the leading Italian drivers had been forced to retire from the race due to steering problems. Only ten points separated Marie from Lawrie in the points Championship now.

'This is true,' Lawrie said, sounding very Scottish again.

Slowing his pace, he led Marie away from the path and over to a patch of soft, springy grass. There he stood, gripping her shoulders lightly and gazing down at her.

Maire felt her heart begin to beat wildly. It was a sultry night but that wasn't the reason why her trouser suit suddenly seemed to be sticking to her. She could feel the delicate silk sliding into the cleft between her buttocks and slinking into the slit that divided her labia. Earlier, when she had dressed, she hadn't bothered to put on any underwear, just the trousers and jacket.

Her breathing became shallower and shallower as Lawrie continued to gaze at her. Presently, he stroked a questing finger along her jawbone and down her throat. His hand slid under the neckline of her jacket, covering her naked breast.

Marie let out her breath slowly. She felt her nipple harden immediately and a rush of moisture soaked the crotch of her trousers. She felt weak. Weak with desire and the helplessness of that desire. It seemed to control her, to overtake every other thought and emotion.

'Please,' she whispered hoarsely.

Lawrie smiled a knowing smile and began to unbutton her jacket. Then he bared her breasts. With a soft groan of desire, he lowered his mouth to consume first one rosy nipple and then the other.

In the stillness of the moonlit night Marie heard herself

161

panting with arousal. The sounds of their breathing seemed to echo around the dark shapes of the trees which surrounded her and Lawrie like sentries. She felt hot. So hot.

She threw her head back and arched her spine, thrusting her breasts into Lawrie's face. She sighed as he nuzzled them and lathed them with his tongue. Every so often he flicked the pointed tip of his tongue over the straining buds of her nipples, sending frissons of desire coursing through her.

Straightening up a little, she reached for him, her hands tugging at the bottom of his shirt, freeing it from the waistband of his trousers. She breathed in sharply as she made contact with his bare skin. Sliding her palms up under his shirt she caressed his back, her nails scraping lightly against his silky skin. In her ear, she heard him groan softly. The air surrounding them was so warm it was like a caress and the combined scent of lush grass, pine needles and wild flowers was a heady medley, driving Marie's senses wild with desire.

Sliding her hands down his strong back and under his waistband, she stroked his buttocks, her palms covering them, her fingertips palpating the taut flesh.

Similarly, his hands slipped around her, under her jacket, stroking her sides, her back, her shoulders.

Marie could hear her breath coming in short gasps. She could feel the hardness of his cock nudging her stomach. They were taking things so slowly she could hardly bear the intensity of the suspense.

Slipping her hands out of his trousers, she fumbled for the drawstring that tied her own trousers loosely around her slender waist. As she tugged gently at the ends of the string she stepped back a little, wanting him to witness the moment when she revealed herself to him. Suddenly, the drawstring loosened. Slowly and tantalisingly her trousers slithered over her hips and down her thighs to form a silken pool around her feet. Shrugging off her jacket, she stood before him in that shadowy glade, naked as a nymph, the white, hairless mound of her sex a stark contrast to the rest of her deeply tanned body.

Transfixed, Lawrie gazed at Marie. Her nakedness was splendid: a living, breathing embodiment of womanly perfection. And that wonderful part of her at the apex of her thighs seemed to gleam in the moonlight, as though a spotlight touched that delectable portion of her body and illuminated it. He stared at her, his passion for her flaming as his eyes feasted on that small pouch of flesh with its intriguing slit and neat, fleshy lips. Like a vertical mouth it seemed to call to him to look, to touch, to explore. Press your lips against mine, it urged, taste my sweetness for yourself.

Exhaling slowly to release some of his pent up arousal, Lawrie dropped to his knees in front of her. Silently, he worshipped the naked goddess, longing to slake his thirst at the fountain of her femininity. He clasped her buttocks and pulled her hips to his face so that he could press his lips against those which tantalised him. Breathing in deeply, he inhaled her special, musky scent. Then he flicked out his tongue and allowed it to travel down that intriguing slit. He licked her slowly, the tip of his tongue delving deeper, separating the delicate folds until it encountered the tiny pearl of her clitoris. Rolling it around with his tongue he tantalised her, delighting in the way her clitoris swelled and grew harder.

Beneath his hands he felt her buttocks quiver. He could sense the erotic tension inside her; hear her soft moans and whimpers. Simply by using his face he nudged her thighs apart and immediately allowed his mouth to explore further. The moonlight enabled him to see the strands of her feminine juices streaking her inner thighs and glistening on the soft pink folds of her labia. Greedily, he lapped at her flesh, drinking in the honeyed sweetness of her. He nibbled lightly at her puffy outer lips then drove his tongue into the warm, wet channel of her vagina.

'Oh, God!' Marie moaned and clutched at his head. Her fingers raked through his hair as her mind whirled aimlessly in a vortex of eroticism.

She felt as though she were poised on the brink of ultimate pleasure, teetering, anticipating the moment when she would plunge into the dark pit of her own desire. Pleasure spiralled through her, creating its own warmth, making her body throb with unrestrained passion.

As gracefully as their urgency for each other would allow, they lowered themselves on to the lush, springy grass. Lawrie was inside her in a moment, his hard cock plunging deep, driving her mad with renewed desire. He knelt between her thighs and she raised her legs, wrapping them around his neck, pulling him even deeper inside her. Her fingers grasped wildly at his forearms, her short nails grazing his flesh as she urged her body against his.

Lawrie gazed into her eyes as she thrashed and writhed against him. Her vaginal muscles were gripping him so hard he could hardly contain himself and the sight of her. Oh, God, the sight of her; so abandoned, so unrestrained! It drove him quickly over the edge. His passion exploded, the heat of his lust all-consuming as he continued to thrust inside her.

However much he had of Marie it never seemed to be enough, he thought hazily. Slowly, he allowed his gaze to drift lower to feast on the perfect mounds of her heaving breasts and the rest of her small, taut body.

Without withdrawing from her he disengaged her legs from around his neck and turned her lower body sideways. Stroking her buttocks reverently, he started to move inside her again, delighting in the sight of his cock disappearing into the glistening tunnel of her vagina. The night was perfect, as pleasing and as sultry as the woman to whom he was making love. And her blissful gasps were music to his ears.

Chapter Eleven

*T*he night Marie spent with Lawrie, their bodies locked together in sex and in sleep, was the most blissful she had ever known. Bathed in moonlight in that tiny forest glade, they had eventually exhausted themselves. And after a brief period of recovery they had moved inside the house, where they started all over again on the huge round bed that dominated the master bedroom.

Marie awoke to find her body tangled in a smooth linen sheet. Sunlight streamed through the curved, uncurtained window, casting a shaft of brilliance across the bed. It took her a few moments to surface fully and to realise that Lawrie wasn't there. She stretched luxuriously, kicking off the sheet and spreading her arms and legs wide across the bed's generous diameter. The warmth of the sunlight bathed her naked body, which felt stiff and aching from so much sex. Between her thighs she felt a little sore. Allowing her fingers to investigate, she felt the sensitive flesh of her labia, which were still a little sticky from her own juices.

'Hey, what's this, starting again without me?' Lawrie joked from the open doorway.

Lazily, Marie raised her eyes to look at him. Gloriously naked, his body gleaming like burnished gold, he stood holding a tray.

'Just assessing the damage,' she murmured. 'What's all this?'

Lawrie carried the tray across the room and set it down in the middle of the bed.

'Budge over a bit,' he said. 'I thought you might fancy a bit of breakfast after all that energy you used up last night.'

'Mmm!' Marie murmured as she eyed the tray greedily.

There was fresh orange juice; bowls heaped with nutty muesli; plump strawberries mixed with sliced kiwi fruit, and a glass bowl of thick yoghurt. A generous swirl of honey glistened like melted gold in the middle of the yoghurt.

Her gaze then drifted to the place at the top of Lawrie's thighs where his cock slumbered on its blond, furry nest. 'German wurst, my favourite,' she said, licking her lips lasciviously.

'Coarse Highland sausage, if you don't mind,' Lawrie responded, laughing. 'And don't go getting any ideas about having that for breakfast, I think you've worn it out.'

Marie's mouth formed a moue, although her eyes twinkled mischievously at him. 'Guess I'll have to trade you in for a new model,' she threatened jokingly.

Lawrie pretended to glare at her as he said, 'You dare! I haven't finished with you yet, young lady, not by a long shot.' Selecting the largest strawberry, he dipped it in the yogurt and pressed it to her lips.

She opened her mouth obediently, uttering pleasurable sounds as she tasted the sweet, juicy fruit.

Their breakfast was decadent but short lived. Halfway through licking a dab of honeyed yoghurt off each of Lawrie's nipples Marie suddenly remembered the *Verval* photo-shoot.

'Bloody hell, what time is it?' she asked as she glanced around wildly, looking for a clock. The photo-shoot wasn't scheduled until two but she could tell from the position of the sun, high in the clear blue sky, that it must be quite late.

'Twelve-fifteen,' Lawrie said, consulting the watch he had left on the bedside table. 'What's the rush?'

Marie told him, leaving out nothing. To her amused irritation he simply laughed.

'So, you're going to be posing naked, are you?' he said. 'Can I come and watch?'

With a shrug Marie said, 'I don't see why not.' She glanced at him. 'Haven't you got something better to do?'

His raised eyebrows made her laugh again. 'Something better than seeing your naked body sprawled across the bonnet of your Porsche?' he said. 'What do you think I am – mad?'

She laughed harder, picking up a pillow and throwing it at him. 'Not mad,' she said, 'incorrigible.'

After a quick, mutually pleasurable shower and an even quicker telephone call by Marie to Carla at the hotel, they set off for the studio in the Ferrari.

BB was waiting just inside the studio to greet them. This time her tall, thin body was clad in a long black and white striped skirt, with a split at the front which allowed a glimpse of her bony knees. She had teamed this with a matching jacket.

Marie, dressed in the cream trouser suit she had worn the previous evening – which, thankfully, didn't look as though it had been carelessly flung off in the middle of a forest – and wearing her usual Amber disguise, recognised BB's suit as Armani.

'Nice to see you again, Amber,' BB said. She smiled her customary thin lipped smile as they shook hands. 'Ooh, and who's this? As if I didn't know.' Spidery eyelashes fluttered behind owlish spectacles as she glanced over Marie's shoulder at Lawrie.

'Lawrie Samson,' Lawrie said needlessly, offering BB his hand. 'I'm a friend of Amber's. I hope you don't mind me tagging along.'

'Mind?' BB looked as though she were about to burst into flames. The woman's veiny cheeks flushed a bright scarlet. 'No, joking you must be,' she said, before adding sheepishly, 'Please excuse my poor English.'

Marie noticed Lawrie gave BB his most devastating smile. 'You're excused,' he said. 'And anyway, your English is far better than my Dutch. I can't speak a word of it.'

'You are so kind,' BB responded, positively simpering.

Just then another familiar figure approached. This time it was Marie's turn to feel slightly uncomfortable as she took his proffered hand.

'Laurent,' she managed to gasp out, 'how nice to see you again.'

'And you, Amber,' he said, smiling lasciviously at her. 'I haven't forgotten.'

'Forgotten what?' Lawrie murmured in her ear as they followed Bette and Laurent through the studio and out the back where Marie was shown her dressing room.

'Oh, Laurent and I spent a rather memorable evening together at Zandvoort,' Marie said airily. Changing the subject swiftly, she added, 'I like the way they called this my dressing room. It should be undressing room.' She glanced around the small, pearl grey painted room which was bare apart from a wide shelf that ran the length of one wall – in the centre of which was hung a square mirror – and two uncomfortable looking chairs covered in grey tweed.

Lawrie sat down on one of the chairs. 'If you can manage a striptease in a forest – ' he began, reaching for her and starting to unfasten the buttons on her jacket.

Marie threw back her head and laughed. 'Yes. OK,' she said. 'I was just expecting a bit more of the star treatment, you know.'

'Uh-huh.' Lawrie nodded, his expression one of rapt concentration as he started on the drawstring that held up her trousers. 'You seem a little tense; perhaps I can help you to relax.'

Just as he began to lay a suggestive trail down her

torso with his tongue, they were interrupted by a knock at the door, followed by the sound of it opening.

As Marie whirled around, her loosened trousers fell straight to her ankles.

'*Mon dieu*, what a greeting, Amber.' It was Laurent, looking even more swarthy than before as he leant against the door jamb, his arms folded.

Marie felt a blush rise from the tips of her toes to the roots of her hair. Considering the colour of her wig, she didn't think the overall effect would be particularly devastating. Laurent's dark eyes flickered to her denuded mound and she blushed even deeper.

'Hello, old friend,' he murmured.

Behind her, Marie heard Lawrie's burst of low laughter. Oh, hell, she thought, I should have realised this was going to be difficult. Feeling as though she were a fly caught in a web between two spiders, she tried to free herself by assuming a haughty manner.

'If you don't mind, Laurent,' she said pointedly, 'I am here in a professional capacity.'

Appearing totally undeterred by her frostiness, Laurent merely continued to smile as he appraised her half naked body.

'So, am I, darling,' he said, straightening up. 'If you wouldn't mind slipping the rest of that off – ' he nodded at her unbuttoned jacket ' – they're just bringing the car into the studio now.'

'I'll be right with you,' Marie muttered. She waited until he had gone and closed the door behind him before turning to Lawrie. 'I feel a bit uncomfortable about all this – '

Lawrie interrupted her by placing a finger against her lips. 'Please don't feel embarrassed because of me, Marie,' he said gently. 'One of the things I find most attractive about you is that you're a free spirit.'

Relieved, she smiled back at him. 'That's the other thing that bothers me,' she said. 'Do you think you could remember to call me Amber when there are other people around?'

He grinned disarmingly. 'Sure, no problem.'

Reaching out, his hands spanned her waist, his fingers gripping her lightly as he pulled her towards him. For a moment he nuzzled her stomach, then he surprised her by releasing her torso and giving her bottom a playful smack.

'Go on, get on with you,' he said, his voice sounding oddly thick. 'Your public awaits.'

As Marie shrugged off her jacket and hung it on the back of the other chair with her carefully folded trousers, she wondered why she had found the smack Lawrie had given her so enjoyable. During her initiation at Chantal's house she hadn't particularly liked being chastised, not even lightly. But now, she reflected, still able to feel the slight sting of Lawrie's palm on her right buttock, she felt as though a whole new realm of pleasure had been opened up to her. The pleasure of submission.

Much as she wanted to, she didn't have time to dwell on the idea of being chastised properly by Lawrie. On the back of the dressing room door hung a pale blue silk robe and she slipped it on, tying the belt tightly around her slender waist.

'Come on then,' she said as she held her hand out to Lawrie, 'let's go and get this thing over and done with. Then we can have some proper fun.'

The promise of what was to come later clung to them as they wandered down the corridor in the direction of the studio. And, unbeknown to Marie, an idea had began to germinate in Lawrie's mind.

The first thing that struck Marie as she entered the studio was how magnificent her car looked under the studio lighting. Against a plain black backdrop, it appeared very moody and powerful. And knowing that she was the one in charge of all that power gave her a special thrill.

All at once, the possibility of winning the Championship seemed very real to her. Both she and her car had the capability of outplacing the rest of the competition, she realised now. Even competitors like Lawrie, Guillermo Castillos and Tony Bertorelli, who had brand new cars, still couldn't hold a candle to her driving skills. And it was those skills which counted for far more than simple mechanics.

'The car looks superb, doesn't it?' Lawrie murmured to her, echoing her own thoughts.

She turned her head and smiled at him. How could she have ever thought of him as arrogant? He was one of the most generous-spirited men she had ever met. Just as she opened her mouth to reply they were interrupted by an anxious-looking BB.

'Are you ready, Amber?' she asked, her eyes flicking momentarily over the blue dressing gown.

Marie forced herself to smile. 'Underneath this I am,' she said. Then she allowed her nerves to show a little by adding, 'How will you want me to pose exactly?'

BB's thin lips stretched wide over her teeth. 'Nothing too outrageous, my darling, I promise you. The boys will be the main focus when it comes to – ' She broke off as the studio suddenly filled with the sound of raucous laughter and deep, masculine chatter.

Following her glance, Marie saw that about half a dozen male models had just trooped into the studio. All pretty boys, they were dressed in pale blue mechanic's overalls which had been carefully streaked with grease. Half of them wore the overalls unzipped, while the other half had the tops pulled down and tied around their waists so that their well-oiled, muscular torsos were bared.

'Hmm,' Marie murmured appreciatively, 'nice.'

'Aren't they?' BB enthused, looking pink again. 'Oh my, I just love this job.'

Marie couldn't help noticing how much emphasis the older woman put on her words. But then, arranging good-looking young men to pose in various states of undress must be a dream job for a lot of women, she mused.

Just then Lawrie murmured in her ear, 'I think I'll go

and take that seat over there at the back.' He glanced over his shoulder and gave Marie a quick squeeze and a peck on the cheek before sauntering off.

'He is so gorgeous,' BB enthused, as soon as Lawrie was out of earshot. 'I wouldn't mind getting him as a *Verval* centre spread. Do you think he would, Amber?'

'I – er – I don't know, to be honest,' Marie replied, glancing at Lawrie as he sat down on one of a line of chairs at the back of studio, sprawling his long legs out in front of him. 'Probably. Why don't you ask him?'

'Ask who what?' It was Laurent, appearing out of nowhere as usual.

Briefly, BB explained and Marie was surprised to notice that Laurent looked inexplicably irritated by his colleague's suggestion.

'Too old,' he said uncharitably.

'Rubbish,' BB countered, 'he would be perfect. Not all our readers want to see models who are barely out of puberty.'

Marie sniggered at this remark and was about to agree with BB when Laurent launched into a tirade in Dutch, to which BB responded equally vociferously.

The moment was saved by the arrival of the photographer, a small, thin man with greying hair and a goatee beard. He was dressed all in black – a universal costume which Marie had learned to associate with photographers and film directors.

'We are ready to start,' the photographer said in a thick, indistinguishable accent, 'Miss, if you please, I would like you naked.'

Marie felt a slight leap of apprehension. It wasn't the first time someone had propositioned her so directly. But his order was delivered in such a deadpan way that she was reminded of her gynaecologist. She glanced around, half expecting to see a pair of stirrups and a tray of chrome implements somewhere to hand. Feeling like a medical specimen, to be appraised and visually dissected, she untied the belt around her waist and shrugged off the robe.

The photographer took a step back and rubbed his beard thoughtfully as he looked at her.

'Hmm,' he murmured, turning Marie's insides to water, 'splendid, absolutely splendid. Now, miss, hop up on to the bonnet of the car.' As Marie walked over to her car, he clapped his hands briskly. 'Come on, *lieblings*, around the car, please. You know what I want.'

Bent as the proverbial, Marie thought to herself as she hoisted herself on to the car, taking care not to damage the bodywork. As she sat drumming her heels casually on the wing she heaved a sigh of relief. Posing naked for a gay photographer did not seem nearly so bad. The male models draped themselves around her as she sat stiffly with an enigmatic smile on her face.

'Lean into them, darling,' the photographer called from behind his camera. 'That's it, all of you, get closer together.' He glanced up. 'Now, Perry, put some grease on your hands. *Ja.* OK. Now clasp her breasts. Leave some nice clear handprints.'

Marie gasped as two slippery hands enclosed her breasts. The grease was warm, igniting a spark of desire inside her instantly.

'More on her thighs,' the photographer called again. 'That's it, keep it artistic, *liebling*.'

The model who daubed Marie's naked body with grease was lean and blond, his hair a few shades darker than Lawrie's. He looked all of nineteen, she thought as she gazed at his profile. He was intent on parting her thighs a little so that he could get the hand prints just right.

Obediently, she spread her legs, once again breathing in sharply as she felt the model's greasy fingers come into contact with her skin. The bonnet of the car beneath her bottom was warm from where the engine had been run and now she felt as though she were melting. Her juices flowed from her as proof of her mounting desire. As the model glanced up at her face he gave her a triumphant smile.

Oh, God, Marie prayed silently, please let me be

professional about this. For a moment her imagination feasted on scenes of a wild orgy taking place on the bonnet of her car. Herself and six horny guys: what bliss! Perhaps Lawrie, Laurent and BB would join in, all of them stripping off their clothes and climbing on top of her. The Porsche's bodywork would never stand the strain. Carla and Frank would go spare.

'Smile now,' the photographer ordered, his voice breaking through Marie's wild reverie and bringing her back sharply to reality. 'Don't look at the camera. Look at *her*.'

All at once, Marie realised a dozen eyes were on her body – twenty if you counted those of the people behind the camera. She felt her desire climb higher and she flung back her head, revelling in the attention and thrusting her nakedness towards the unseeing lens of the camera. The audience no longer existed. In that brief instant she was alone in her private glory.

The moment didn't last long enough as far as Marie was concerned. The motordrive of the camera whirred and then the photographer was clapping his hands again and speaking to the models in a mixture of Dutch, German and French, as though he had tired of English already. Flashing a glance at Lawrie, Marie was relieved to get a warm smile and a thumbs up in return.

Laurent sauntered up to the car. 'Can you climb on to the roof, Amber?' he said.

Marie flashed a surprised glance at him. 'The roof?'

He nodded. 'Yes,' he said. 'Lie on your stomach.' Waiting until Marie had done as he asked, he added, 'Now prop yourself up on your elbows, chin in your hands. No, keep your elbows apart, darling, we want to be able to see your luscious breasts. Ah, that is so much better.'

Marie felt herself flush with embarrassment as he took a step back and appraised her. She was even more mortified when he stepped forward again and gripped each of her nipples lightly but firmly between his fingertips.

'Let's get these nice and hard,' he murmured to her, his fingers tweaking and tugging as he spoke. Then he called over his shoulder, 'Can we have some ice, please?'

A moment later the photographer's assistant, who was a young woman with long straight brown hair and a waiflike figure, produced a yellow plastic bowl containing ice cubes. Laurent nodded his thanks as he took the bowl. Then he selected one of the cubes and rubbed it across each of Marie's nipples.

They hardened instantly and she sucked in her breath. Knowing the ice would be cold was still no preparation for the touch of the glistening cube against her naked flesh. Her nipples burned from where Laurent had manipulated them and she fancied the ice would melt instantly under the fierce heat her body was generating.

At Laurent's instruction, the young woman handed ice cubes to the male models and they all attended to their own nipples. Now, Marie noticed, as she glanced from side to side, the models had removed their overalls and were completely naked. Their cocks – an interesting array of shapes and sizes – were flaccid, but once again the photographer's assistant was pressed into service.

'A little bit of fluffing, if you please, Michelle,' Laurent said. 'We don't want to disappoint our readers do we?'

Marie watched, feeling slightly awed, as the insipid-looking young woman took to her task with incredible enthusiasm. Working assiduously she stroked each of the model's cocks in turn until they just started to stiffen.

'Enough,' the photographer called out, clapping his hands yet again. 'Move out of the way, everybody, we haven't got all day.'

Once again the models sprawled around Marie and, as the motordrive began to whirr again, she felt a finger stroking between her slightly parted thighs. There was nothing she could do about it. If she wriggled or drew attention to the insolent caress the shots would be spoiled and they would have to start all over again. As shaming as it was to have an unknown finger exploring

176

her most private places, the last thing she wanted to do was prolong the photo shoot unnecessarily.

A moment later, another finger joined the first. This time the pressure was a little harder, the exploration lacking the finesse of the first, leading Marie to believe that this finger had a different owner. Smiling steadily at the camera she fought to contain her gasps as she felt her vagina and clitoris being stimulated simultaneously.

Glancing from side to side without moving her head, she realised there was no way she could tell who was touching her. The models were draped across her now and another finger was trailing the cleft between her buttocks. Wriggling impudently it began to probe her tight nether hole.

Controlling the urge to cry out, Marie concentrated on Lawrie's face. He was watching her with such an inscrutable expression that she found herself wondering if he could tell what was happening to her.

The finger inside her vagina slid in and out effortlessly on a stream of her own juices and was joined by a second finger and then a third. She felt herself being opened out wider and wider, with more fingers stroking the sensitive skin of her perineum and a couple rubbing either side of her rapidly swelling clitoris.

The duration of the photo shoot seemed interminable to Marie, who was rapidly losing all sense of reason. From time to time the models changed position but new fingers slipped between her legs and her buttocks instantly, resuming their hidden stimulation of her quietly simmering body. And every so often Laurent stepped forward and rubbed her nipples with the ice, giving her a valid reason to let out the gasps she was fighting so hard to contain.

Finally, after what seemed like an eternity of illicit pleasure, she was told to climb down from the car and instead had to recline on the driver's seat. The car door was open. A couple of the models were draped over it, while others squatted at her side and one lay full length across the roof.

'Open your legs for me please, miss,' the photographer said to her.

Marie shook her head. 'No, I – '

Laurent was in front of her in an instant. 'Amber, Amber,' he crooned, smiling engagingly at her, 'come on, we've nearly finished now. Just a few more shots.'

'I can't,' Marie hissed back at him. 'I don't want to.'

Although she wasn't normally ashamed of her body, she knew she would be unable to conceal the extent of her arousal if she opened her legs. Her clitoris was throbbing, her labia swollen around her streaming vagina. She couldn't let everyone see that, she just couldn't.

'Amber, please,' Laurent continued persuasively, 'don't be shy.'

Slowly, Marie inched her thighs apart, her hands instinctively fluttering over her pubis. She tried in vain to cover her blossoming sex but Laurent gently removed her hands. Glancing down and then back up at her face, he gave her a wolfish smile.

'So,' he said quietly, leaning forward and whispering so that only Marie could hear him, 'you have been a naughty girl.' He made a soft tut-tutting sound and his smile broadened. 'Oh, how I would love to take you away and play with your hungry little body properly. You need relief don't you, my darling? You need to have that little clitoris rubbed and licked and your hot little – '

'Laurent, please stop,' Marie begged him in a hoarse whisper. She felt faint with lust and despite her entreaty was almost tempted to say, 'Yes, let's go. Do what you want to me.'

She was so desperate to come – or at least, to have a little of her burning desire assuaged – she found herself wishing the entire studio would simply melt away. To be left alone with Laurent, or better still Lawrie, would be bliss right at that moment.

Glancing over Laurent's shoulder to the back of the studio where Lawrie sat, she caught his eye. And Lawrie returned her look with a gaze that seemed to convey everything she needed from him: understanding, compassion, lust and the promise of things to come.

'Let's just get this over with,' she said, throwing her head back and concentrating firmly on the roof lining of the car. 'I want to get out of here and carry on with my life.'

Without the probing fingers to distract her, Marie felt every second of the remainder of the photo shoot. But, finally, it was over. The photographer clapped his hands for the last time and then came over to thank Marie for being 'such a professional.' Marie smiled at him and nodded her thanks.

Then Lawrie was by her side, handing her the blue robe and whispering promises in her ear that she couldn't ignore.

'It's my last night with you before next weekend,' he reminded her as they walked back down the corridor to her dressing room. 'I want to make it a night to remember.'

And so it had been, Marie reflected as she lay in the huge bed and allowed her hand to play in the warm space Lawrie had only recently vacated. They had dined on oysters, doused each other in champagne and christened every room in the house. For two hours they had slept, entwined together as before, their bodies thoroughly satiated. Then it was time for Lawrie to leave for the airport.

His parting gifts to her had been a long kiss and a set of keys which he pressed into her hand.

'Use the house for the rest of the week, until you have to leave for Italy,' he said. Then he handed her a second set of keys. This time the key ring bore the distinctive Ferrari logo. 'And look after this for me,' he added. 'Drive it down to Monza and promise to meet me at the airport.'

Feeling stunned, Marie smiled up at him. 'Are you sure? I mean – '

He silenced her with a soft kiss. 'I'm sure,' he said, 'and I want you to enjoy yourself while I'm gone. I think you know what I'm talking about. No playing at Mother Theresa.'

Stunned into uncustomary silence, Marie nodded dumbly. She knew exactly what he meant. And the knowledge gave her all the more reason to think he was amazing. Lawrie was not just liberal with his possessions but also generous in spirit. After a moment during which they simply gazed at each other, she forced a pert smile, realising it was the response he would appreciate the most.

'You know me,' she said with a theatrical sigh. 'I'll do my best.'

Chapter Twelve

*A*t Marie's request, Carla joined her at the house and agreed to stay there rather than at the hotel.

'I know we were going to see a bit of Germany,' Marie said, looking contrite as she led her friend into the huge sitting room, 'but this place is fabulous and we'll be able to get some testing time in at the track while we're here.'

'Don't worry,' Carla assured her. 'I'm not bothered about shacking up in the motor home with the others and I've already seen enough of Germany to last me a lifetime.' She paused and gazed out of the window. 'Plus the fact Anders is staying on.'

Marie's cheeks dimpled as she grinned at her friend. 'Anders, is he the Swede you've been seeing?' she asked.

Carla nodded as she replied, 'Yes. The one and only.' Flopping down on to a large cream sofa, she sighed happily. 'God, he's a brilliant mechanic.'

Marie pulled a wry face. 'I'll bet you say that to all the boys,' she said. 'Can't you get your mind out from under the bonnet for five minutes? I want to hear the real lowdown on him.'

'That is the real lowdown,' Carla responded, looking surprised. Then she burst out laughing. 'OK. What can I say? He's got a fantastic body and he's dynamite in bed.'

'Ooh, you sweet talking thing, you.' Marie laughed

along with her friend. 'So, are you going to ask him to come and stay here with you or what?'

Carla glanced up, her surprise evident. 'Stay here?' she said. 'Are you sure you don't mind?'

'Of course not,' Marie insisted, 'I wouldn't have said it if I did.'

Privately, she wondered if she was being a bit rash. But then, wasn't that just like her? Thank goodness the walls of the house were thick enough to drown out all the moans and groans of pleasure that were bound to ensue from her invitation. Otherwise she didn't think she would be able to put up with just having her own hands for company.

Reflecting on this the following day, Marie realised she should have known her pleasure that week would not necessarily have to be self-induced. Knowing that Laurent had gone back to Holland with BB and the rest of the *Verval* team, she wasn't expecting any erotic liaisons with him. However, hers was not the only team that had decided to stay on in Hockenheim for testing.

'Hi there, it's Amber Barclay isn't it?'

Raising the arm that had been shielding her eyes, Marie squinted in the fierce sunlight. Hovering over her was a familiar figure, tall and extremely well built, with wavy nut-brown hair highlighted by natural golden blond streaks that framed a strong, square-jawed face. It was one of her main opponents, the American, Tony Bertorelli.

She was reclining on a padded chair in the unglamourous setting of the near-empty car park at the rear of the garages at Hockenheim. Determined to improve her suntan, she had chosen to wear a skimpy bikini in a brilliant shade of aquamarine. And now, as she gazed up at the burly American, she felt at a distinct disadvantage. Automatically, she felt her nipples stiffen beneath their inadequate covering as Tony's hazel eyes executed a very thorough appraisal of her body.

Replying to his question, she said, 'The one and only,' as lightly as she could manage.

Without waiting for an invitation, Tony sat down on the edge of the chair. He didn't take his eyes off her for a moment.

'I've been waiting for an excuse to talk to you properly,' he said in his distinctive Texas drawl, shifting his gaze to her face at last. 'You must surely be dedicated to be here on a day like this.'

Marie smiled. 'I could say the same about you.'

He shrugged, his massive shoulders lifting under the red T-shirt which he wore tucked into faded blue Levi's. 'Monza's important,' he responded. 'Hell, the car needs to be shit hot.'

'All the races are important,' Marie countered piously. She tried not to gaze in awe at his biceps, which bulged obscenely as he crossed his arms. 'But I know what you mean,' she added, smiling. Deliberately averting her gaze from him, she glanced at the garage behind her. 'We had a few little problems with the car that needed ironing out.'

'Such as?'

Marie thought he seemed a bit too interested for her liking and deliberately remained nonchalant as she answered, 'Oh, stuff like the timing,' before quickly adding, 'it's spot on now though,' just in case he thought he was in with a chance of winning the Championship. 'By the way, is it true you split your engine in half in the last race?'

'Yeah, it's true,' he said. 'You must have missed me going off the track. I went straight through the Armco, took a post and then hit a tree.' He grinned, showing off perfect teeth. 'But hell, something like that's only a hitch to a team like ours.' He shrugged again, uncrossed his arms and casually stroked a thick finger down her bare arm. 'You wanna win, don't you?'

Laughing lightly, Marie said, 'Of course I want to win – doesn't everybody?' She couldn't get over the fact that he could suffer so much damage to his car and still have something to smile about.

'Yeah, but you *really* want to win,' Tony persisted. 'I mean, like it's life or death to you, isn't it?'

'It's fairly important,' Marie said guardedly. 'I wouldn't say life or death.' If she could, she would have crossed her fingers. Shifting slightly on her seat, she added, 'I take it you're not all that serious about this Championship?'

His deep laugh startled her. 'Baby, I ain't never that serious about nothin'.'

His finger was still stroking her arm and Marie continued to stare at him. Her eyes searched his face for a clue to the agenda he was so obviously concealing.

'Is all this supposed to be leading somewhere?' she asked finally, fed up with playing games.

'I'm hoping it's leading to lunch,' he said to her surprise. 'A late lunch. Somewhere intimate, where we can talk properly.'

Oh, yes, *talk*. Marie almost laughed aloud. Despite her cynicism she found her body responding to him. Her sex was already moist and her clitoris had started its insistent throb that could sometimes be annoying when she was trying against all the odds to be level-headed.

'I wouldn't mind,' she said as lightly as she could manage, 'but I'll have to go and see what's happening with the car first. You never know, I might still be needed.' Shrugging his finger off her arm she made to get up.

To her surprise, Tony leapt to his feet, stooped forward and picked her up from the chair. Then he lowered her carefully until her feet touched the ground.

His sheer strength took Marie's breath away. His grip had been so sure and so tight she had felt a flicker of apprehension. It was easy to imagine that if he increased the pressure of his fingertips just slightly he could easily crush her bones.

The concrete was burning hot under her bare feet and so she slipped them quickly into her flat-soled sandals.

Standing upright, Tony towered over her. She barely reached his shoulder and felt extremely small and defenceless in comparison with his solid muscularity. He reminded her of an American football player, only without the need for padding.

'How on earth do you manage to fit inside a Porsche?' she found herself asking bluntly.

To her relief, he laughed. It was a deep, rumbling laugh that seemed to echo around the empty car park and shake the steel doors of the mostly empty garages behind them.

'It's not easy, babe,' he said, 'but as you can probably tell, I manage well enough.'

Marie realised he had left the way wide open for her to respond with something flattering about his driving skills but sheer devilment prevented her from commenting. Instead, she pretended to wave to someone in the distance. Then, turning abruptly on her heel, she walked into her garage and continued through it to emerge from the other side into the pits. As she walked, Tony stuck close by her side.

Out in the pits her car sat shimmering in a heat haze, its bonnet up and the front raised and supported by axle stands. Seeing it like that, she felt sharp fingers of apprehension clutch at her stomach.

'What's up?' she asked Carla as her friend's blonde head emerged from under the bonnet. She noticed Carla's face was streaked with perspiration and grease and the expression on her face conveyed that she was less than happy.

'Nothing much,' Carla said, straightening up. Giving Tony a curious glance, she picked up a rag and rubbed her hands vigorously on it. Then she walked over to Marie, grasped her by the top of the arm and led her away from the American driver. 'What does *he* want?' she hissed agitatedly, as soon as they were out of earshot.

'What the hell's got into you?' Marie said, shrugging off Carla's hand and examining her arm. 'He wants to take me to lunch that's all.' She rubbed at the greasy hand print Carla had left on her skin. It evoked memories of the photo session she had done for *Verval* a couple of days earlier.

'Something's wrong with the car that I can't fathom for the life of me,' Carla said with a quick glance around the pits. 'God, I wish Frank were here.'

'Why don't you ask Anders for some advice?' Marie suggested.

'What?' Carla stared at her in amazement. 'His team's in competition with us, I can't expect him to help us out.'

Unaccountably, Marie started to laugh. 'You're priceless, Carla, do you know that?' she said. 'How come it's okay to fuck the guy but it's not all right to ask him for his professional assistance?'

She noticed Carla looked suitably chastened. 'It sounds ridiculous when you put it like that,' she muttered.

'That's because it is ridiculous,' Marie asserted. Now it was her turn to glance around. As if on cue a flash of silver streaked past them. 'There you go,' she said, 'Reubens is out there testing. Why don't you ask him if he minds his chief mechanic taking a look at our car?'

'It's OK, there's no need for that,' Carla said quickly. 'I'll ask Anders. You're right, I'm sure he won't mind.'

Marie nodded and by silent agreement the two women turned around and began to saunter back in the direction they had come from.

'Tell me what you think my chances are of getting out in the car this afternoon?' Marie said.

Carla raised an inquisitive eyebrow. 'Other plans?'

Marie gave herself away by blushing. 'I'd like to take Tony up on his offer of lunch – I think.' She paused and glanced at the ground before looking back at her friend. 'I know this sounds crazy but I find him attractive, yet scary all at the same time.'

Pursing her lips, Carla said, 'What do you mean by scary?'

'Well – I can't really put my finger on it,' Marie

186

muttered. 'Perhaps it's just his size. He seems a bit overpowering and intense, if you catch my drift.'

Carla nodded. 'I get that feeling, too, but as far as I can tell from what other people have said about him, he's not someone to worry about. Everybody seems to think he's great.'

'*I* think he's great,' Marie said, 'otherwise I wouldn't even be considering it.' She paused and glanced around at the track and the banks of empty spectator stands. It seemed a far cry from a few days earlier when the place had been buzzing with activity – almost like a ghost town in comparison. 'Perhaps my reticence stems from my new relationship with Lawrie.' She laughed wryly. 'I think he's spoilt me for other men.'

'Christ, he must really be something to have that effect on you,' Carla said in amazement.

'Oh, yes,' Marie agreed softly, 'he is that all right.'

To Marie's relief, Anders agreed to have a look at the car straight away and Tony Bertorelli behaved like a perfect gentleman during lunch.

He chose a place which was out of town and surrounded by forest. And he made no off colour remarks about Marie's insistence that she should follow him in the Ferrari. In the back of her mind she thought it would be a good idea to have her own transport to hand, just in case she needed to make a quick getaway.

Looking like a very large log cabin, the restaurant was part of a traditional *Gasthof*. Halfway through a delicious meal of *wiener schnitzel* and green salad, washed down with a very potent Hock, Tony let it slip that he had provisionally booked them a room.

'That was a bit presumptuous of you, wasn't it?' Marie commented. She raised her glass to her lips and studied him keenly over its rim. Ridiculous as it seemed, she felt tempted to add, what kind of a girl do you take me for?

His smile was disarming. 'What can I say? I think you're one helluva woman, Amber,' he said, 'and I'd like to get you in the sack.' Picking up his own glass he touched the base of it to hers. 'It's a great bed by the way, one of those four poster things you English always seem to love.' His pupils dilated as he spoke, signifying to Amber that he was imagining the possibilities. His voice became low and seductive as he leaned across the table and added, 'I wouldn't mind tying you to it. Would you like that, Amber? Some of my girlfriends are really into that sort of thing. Bondage makes them hot for it. And, boy, am I hot for you. My dick is so hard just from thinking about the wild time we could have. If you let me, baby, I'm gonna show you just what I mean.'

Marie felt her resolve diminish in direct proportion to each outrageous comment. She wasn't sure whether her lightheadedness was due to the potency of the wine or his persuasive speech. Certainly, her body was responding to him. She could feel a lustful warmth in her pelvis and the moistness between her thighs was becoming difficult to ignore. Her arousal was like an itch that could easily be scratched if only she said yes.

She took another sip of wine and murmured, 'Yes, OK,' so quietly she wasn't sure if she had actually spoken aloud. From the slow, satisfied smile that spread across Tony's face, she realised her reply had been audible.

'Wow, honey, you've made my day!' he exclaimed with obvious delight. 'Now I'm gonna order us some champagne and something sweet and soft and sticky which we can take to the room. Then I'm gonna spread it all over you and lick it off.'

Marie's fingers gripped the edge of the table. She felt languid with desire. He was persuasive, there was no doubt about that, and she cursed herself briefly for being so weak when it came to sex. Life's too short, she told herself; must make the most of it while you can. Draining the last of her wine, she put her glass down decisively and pushed her chair back from the table.

'Come on,' she said, her heart hammering, 'let's go.'

The four-poster bed Tony had told her about was wonderful. Fashioned from wrought iron, it was wide and high and draped with swathes of chinzy fabric. The rest of the room was very simply decorated and furnished. Its rough timbered walls were hung with landscapes done in oils and the wooden floor was covered with brightly coloured rag rugs. Under a huge window, which overlooked lush green fields and the surrounding forest, sat a round pine table and two matching chairs with curved backs and arms.

Marie had slipped a short black and white striped dress over her bikini and, as she stood in front of the table gazing out of the window, she felt Tony's hands pushing the hem of her dress up over her hips. His fingers spanned her buttocks, squeezing them over the scant, satiny fabric of her bikini bottoms as he nuzzled the patch of bare skin between her shoulder blades. She rested her palms on the table top, feeling the smooth, warm wood beneath them as she leant forward, arching her back so that her bottom was thrust harder into his hands.

A long sigh escaped her lips. She could feel the heat of desire building rapidly inside her. The crotch of her bikini bottoms clung damply to her sex and she could detect the musky aroma of her own arousal. The air temperature was humid. Perspiration trickled between her breasts, the sensation tantalising her.

Her senses seemed heightened, she realised; her body feeling as light and ethereal as the wispy clouds that streaked the deep blue sky way off in the distance. She could smell so much: the fresh scent of the forest wafting through the open window; the smoky wood tones of Tony's aftershave, discreet yet inescapable. And added to these were the heady combination of her and Tony's personal aromas: perspiration, traces of lemony shampoo on freshly washed hair, and the irresistible muskiness of arousal.

The sense of touch also excited her. The firm, massaging grip of Tony's hands on her buttocks inflamed that part of her body, while her shoulders received the soft caress of his warm breath and the gentle pressure of his lips.

She had expected his actions to be rough, quick and decisive. Therefore she was pleasantly surprised by this gentler, more sensual side he displayed. In its own way, she found it incredibly erotic. The pleasure of slow discovery was hers for the taking, the long hours of the afternoon and evening stretching out tantalisingly before her. She would follow this blissful trail wherever it led, she decided, breathing deeply. Time and the future were not as important as the moment itself.

Feeling the pressure of his broad hand between her shoulder blades, she allowed him to push her face down across the table. Still with his hand in place, he ripped her bikini bottoms down to her knees. She gasped with surprise, her pleasure rocketing. So this was how he was going to play it, she thought as she felt her upper body melting into the warm wood – gentle one minute, then tempestuous the next.

She could feel the rough denim of his jeans against the backs of her thighs and the hardness of his erection nudging her buttocks. The sensation was exhilarating. She adored being naked, or semi naked, while her lover was still clothed. It made her feel wanton and slightly helpless.

When he removed his hand from her back she could still feel the echo of its pressure. A slight rustle of clothing told her that he was removing his T-shirt and then she felt him pulling down the zip on the back of her dress.

Helping him just a little, she allowed the dress to be pulled off over her head and in the next instant she felt the warmth of his bare skin as he pressed his broad chest against her back. She didn't bother to look at him over her shoulder. She didn't want to. With the side of her face resting on her folded arms and her eyes closed, she simply enjoyed the way her other senses took over. She could feel the soft springiness of chest hair against her naked skin. And his torso was hard, the muscles so well defined she could feel every bump and ridge.

His hands slid under her and pushed up her bikini top. For a moment her nipples came into contact with the hard table top and then she felt the softness of Tony's hands as they covered her breasts. They enclosed the small mounds easily and he rubbed his palms against her nipples, which quickly hardened into tight little buds.

Marie could hear herself whimpering and his breathing was short and hoarse in her ear. Presently, he slid his hands away from her breasts and began to knead her shoulders instead. The warmth in her lower body spread up her back and ended at the roots of her hair. His massage technique was good, easing the last traces of tension within her, and turning her bones to liquid. Using his thumbs, he followed the ridges of her spine, still kneading and massaging, working his way lower and lower.

At the base of her spine he changed his technique. Using the pads of his thumbs he began to describe small circles just above the swell of her buttocks. As he caressed her she could feel her sex swelling and moistening. She sensed her vagina gaping, longing to be filled, and her clitoris seemed to burn with the desire to be touched. She wouldn't ask him to touch her, she told herself; she would let him tease her and see who could last the longest.

All at once she imagined what Carla would have to say about her competitiveness – even in sex. The thought made her smile and in the next moment Tony was leaning over her and speaking softly in her ear.

'You like this, don't you, baby?' he murmured. 'You want me to touch that hot little pussy of yours.'

'Uh-huh,' Marie allowed herself to gasp out but no more.

To her delight she felt his fingers on her vulva, stroking and exploring, delving into the sticky wetness of her vagina, caressing the straining bud of her clitoris.

191

A tongue followed the path of his fingers, hard and wet. Probing like a tiny cock, it then licked, fluttered and slid tantalisingly over her swollen flesh. Within moments she felt her orgasm mounting, then crashing through her, holding her in its erotic grip before subsiding.

Once again he changed tactics, taking her by surprise. His strong arms lifted her, carrying her across the room. Instead of taking her to the bed, he turned her around and pressed her up against the wall, whispering to her to wrap her legs around him. Feeling as limp and as helpless as a rag doll, Marie complied. He was murmuring to her all the time: making small, salacious comments; filling her burning ears with shameful promises in that deep, accented voice of his.

She could feel her body gathering strength again. Passion surged anew within her. Still holding her, pressing her back against the wall, Tony unbuttoned his jeans. His cock immediately sprang free and she reached down, insinuating her hand between her open thighs and his stomach to encircle his glans. The tip of his helmet wept a tear which she smoothed over his flesh with the pad of her thumb. He was groaning, one hand stroking her vulva. A couple of fingers delved inside her, stroking her inner walls, sliding in and out easily, aided by a copious stream of her own juices.

Tightening her legs around his waist, she guided the tip of his cock, nudging his fingers out of the way until his glans just pressed lightly against the swollen flesh surrounding her vagina. There was a long pause, when time and their breathing seemed suspended. Then, with a deep groan, he was inside her, thrusting his hardness all the way up to the hilt. His hands encircled her waist, the pressure of them forcing her down, then up, then down again.

She felt hot and feverish as she heard him murmur, 'Oh, I'm going to do it hard, baby. I'm going to do you so good.'

'Don't stop,' she gasped, hardly noticing that the slatted wood behind her back was rough and splintered.

Her hands roamed his back and shoulders. She scraped his lightly furred skin with her nails, and pinched him. Bending her head forward she bit him, lightly, then again, not so gently.

'Bitch,' he growled thickly but with passion rather than rancour. 'Now I'm going to really fuck you good and hard.'

Marie gasped as she felt him slam into her, his cock going even deeper when she thought it was already as far inside her as possible. The base of her spine jarred against the wooden wall and she cried out, though not exactly in pain. The feelings suffusing her were too pleasurable to be painful. And anyway, she was past caring. Fulfilment and gratification were all that concerned her now.

When they came it was with such force Marie thought the wall behind her was going to come crashing down. Tony slammed his cock inside her hard: four; five; six times. Then he came with a loud groan and a shudder that ran right through her, precipitating her own orgasm.

'Jesus,' he said breathlessly, as they sank to the floor in a perspiring heap. 'Jesus H. Christ, you're one helluva woman!'

Another day dawned bright and clear. Outside the pit garage at the Hockenheim track Marie's car was all loaded on its trailer. Back in full working order, it nestled under its protective cover as Kevin, one of Marie's favourite mechanics, checked the straps that secured it.

'All ready for the off, Amber,' he declared, patting the car fondly.

Marie smiled. 'Thanks, Kev. Are you and Dave going to be OK? Have you got everything you need?'

Kevin and Dave were about to set off for Italy in the motor home, towing the trailer behind it. Carla's brothers, Frank and Simon, would be meeting them at Monza itself, while Marie and Carla would spend one more night in Germany before driving on to Northern Italy in the Ferrari.

'Yep,' Kevin said, nodding in reply to Marie's question, 'we've stocked up on plenty of beers and – '

'I was talking about spare parts,' Marie cut in with a wry grin. 'We can't afford risking anything at Monza. Things are getting too crucial now.'

Kevin placed a friendly hand on her shoulder. 'Stop fretting,' he said reassuringly. 'We've got two of everything and the car's in perfect shape. You're all set for a win, my girl.'

Excitement bubbled up inside Marie. 'I hope so,' she said.

With a cheeky wink, Kevin smoothed back his long, brown, slightly receding hair from his forehead, hitched up his jeans and turned to climb inside the motor home. 'I know so,' he replied firmly.

As the motor home and trailer became a mere speck in the distance, Carla, who had joined Marie to wave them off, suggested that she and Marie find somewhere for lunch and then return to the house to pack.

'What time is Lawrie supposed to be calling you?' Carla asked as they climbed inside the Ferrari.

'About six,' Marie said. Then she sighed and gazed dreamily out of the window. 'I know I had fun with Tony and everything but I can't wait to speak to Lawrie again. You wouldn't believe how much I've missed him.'

'I would,' Carla said, disagreeing with her. 'You've talked about nothing else. All Anders and I have heard this past week is Lawrie this and Lawrie that. Woman, you should be ashamed of yourself!'

Marie flashed her a surprised look. 'What for?'

'Wearing your heart on your sleeve,' Carla responded with an indulgent smile. 'It doesn't suit you – makes you seem far too human and we all know you're not.'

'Thanks a lot.' Marie took her friend's comment in the good-humoured spirit in which she knew it was intended. 'In that case, bitchface, I must remember to seduce Anders when you're not looking.'

Chapter Thirteen

*T*he first thing that struck Marie as she watched Lawrie walk through the Arrivals gate at three o'clock in the morning was how much more handsome he looked than she remembered him. Easy to pick out from the straggling crocodile of bleary-eyed travellers, he seemed enveloped in an unmistakable aura that combined wakefulness, vigour, success and overall charisma.

He was dressed in a pair of maroon trousers worn with a maroon and blue striped jacket that made him look as though he was planning to enter the Oxford and Cambridge boat race, rather than the penultimate leg of the Xtreme Oil Championship. All he needed was a straw boater, Marie mused, catching his eye and returning the broad smile that spread across his face. She watched him quicken his stride and then he was there, standing right in front of her.

'Hi, gorgeous,' he said, dropping the grey leather holdall he was carrying and wrapping his arms around her. 'You look beautiful – lovely and brown.' He took a step back and appraised her.

Marie glowed at his compliment. She knew she looked good but it was nice to receive confirmation, especially from someone like Lawrie. A frantic hour at the hotel in

Monza, which included booking in to the room, had resulted in her emerging from the building looking as though she had spent at least four times as long on herself.

Her hair – her real hair – had only taken a few minutes to wash and slick back away from her face with gel. The dress she was wearing was a simple white shift. Short and sleeveless, it showed off her slender limbs to perfection and provided a sublime contrast to her silky skin which, thanks to all the sunbathing she had been doing at Hockenheim, was now the colour of acorns. Her make-up she had kept simple: just a smudge of slate kohl around each eye and a single coat of black mascara. She had left her lips bare save for a slick of petroleum jelly to keep them nice and supple. All the better for kissing you with, Lawrie, she thought, grinning inside as she gazed at him.

Then, as though he had just read her mind, his arms were around her again, crushing her tightly against his lean, hard body, his mouth devouring hers in a passionate kiss that left her feeling weak and breathless when he finally pulled away.

'Did you come in the Ferrari?' he asked, stooping to pick up his bag.

Marie nodded. 'It's in the car park,' she said. 'I've really enjoyed using it this past week. Thank you.'

He smiled at her and said, 'No problem, I like making you happy,' as he took her hand and led her towards the exit.

They were halfway across the dimly lit car park when Marie pointed to the far corner where the sleek car was waiting for them like a slumbering beast. Although imposing, it looked less incongruous among the other Italian sports cars surrounding it than it had at Hockenheim. Apart from the two of them, the place was totally deserted which, Marie supposed, was only to be expected at that time of the morning. But despite the ungodly hour, the air surrounding them was still humid. Although it had been hot in Germany, the Italian temperatures were at least another ten degrees higher in the shade and didn't seem to drop all that much in the evening.

Marie felt her skin flush with warmth and then chill instantly. She recognised the feeling as the onset of desirous expectation. All the time she had been preparing herself to meet Lawrie, she had been formulating a plan. Now it was time to put it into action.

When they reached the car she reclined against it, resting her elbows on the roof. She watched as Lawrie, who had taken the key from her, opened the boot and flung his bag inside. He turned to look at her, his eyes making a deliberate journey up the length of her slim brown legs.

Marie thrilled to his appraisal of her, knowing that the hem of her dress had ridden right up to the tops of her thighs. Underneath her dress she was naked. Deliberately so. It was all part of her plan. Tearing her eyes away from Lawrie for a moment, she glanced around. The car park was still deserted and the corner in which she had chosen to park was barely illuminated. The only real light came from the silvery full moon which was draped seductively by the sable Italian sky.

'Come over here,' Marie said in a low throaty voice.

As Lawrie started to walk towards her, her fingers grappled surreptitiously with her dress. Her breath quickening with excitement, she raised it higher and higher until her hairless labia could be seen peeping out from under the hem.

Lawrie made a sound that was halfway between a curse and a growl of appreciation. His voice when he spoke was low and gutteral, suffused with passion.

'Tempting little thing,' he said, the corners of his mouth twitching as his eyes darkened. 'You had this planned didn't you?'

Smiling pertly back at him, Marie nodded. 'I didn't want to wait until we got back to the hotel,' she said. 'I knew I'd want you as soon as I saw you. And I do,' she added huskily, 'believe me, I do.'

With one swift movement she jumped up on to the front of the car and spread her legs wantonly. She glanced down between them, noticing how the folds of her sex glistened temptingly. Shifting her glance to the front of Lawrie's trousers she narrowed her eyes.

'Nice,' she said, referring to the obvious tumescence that strained at his fly.

'Wonderful,' Lawrie murmured in return, his eyes fixed to the delicate pink offering between her thighs. 'Bloody fantastic!'

In a flash he was all over her, easing her back against the bonnet of the Ferrari, pushing her dress further and further up her body until it was bunched up under her arms. Her exposed nipples hardened immediately as his hand brushed her breasts, the other skimming her belly and delving between her widespread legs.

For long, delicious moments he stroked her, his fingers caressing her swollen labia and rubbing her desperate clitoris until Marie gave an anguished groan.

She felt incoherent with lust. Pleasure swept over her in waves that left her feeling powerless under their onslaught. All week she had waited for this moment. And it was exactly as it should be. Wonderful. Exciting. Burningly exquisite.

Taking Marie by surprise, Lawrie grasped her by the hips. He dragged her acquiescent body across the bonnet until her bottom slightly overhung the edge of the wing. Then he was inside her, his stiff cock plunging straight into her grasping vagina.

'Yes – oh, God, yes!' Marie cried out, her fingers clutching at the smooth paintwork of the bonnet to stop herself from slipping off.

There was nothing to worry about, she realised quickly. Lawrie had her firmly in his grasp. His hands gripped her upper thighs, his thumbs pressing into her flesh as he held them and urged them back further towards her chest. She was as wide open as she possibly could be and yet she yearned for her body to open wider still. At that moment she fantasied about drawing Lawrie deeply inside her – not just his cock, but all of him. In a reversal of the birth process, she wanted to take him inside her and possess him completely.

As though he could read her mind, Lawrie gasped, 'Yes, my darling, you have me. Don't worry. You have me. I'm back where I belong.'

Marie felt her senses soar. Beyond the smut-stained concrete above her head. Beyond the black velvet drape of the night sky, shimmering with its sequins of stars. Anything was possible at that moment. Anything and everything. Even perfection. The most perfect orgasm she could ever wish for.

Bliss descended as surely as Lawrie's body on top of hers. Sliding smoothly over her to supplant the ebbing waves of her climax, it covered her body like a sheet of the finest silk. With trembling arms she encircled Lawrie's shoulders, her fingertips combing through his hair as she whispered her gratitude to him for giving her so much pleasure.

'You're thanking me?' Lawrie hadn't the strength to laugh. His words came out on a hiss of breath. Nor did he have the strength to shake his head in disbelief.

Here he was, he thought, his trousers around his ankles in a public car park and he couldn't care less. Only now he realised how truly wonderful it was to be collapsed over the bonnet of a hired Ferrari with his bare arse on display to anyone who happened to walk by. As long as it was this young woman who lay beneath him, everything was marvellous.

Lawrie was on the telephone when Marie walked back into his sky blue and peach hotel room. She was stark naked and feeling much better for having just emptied her bladder.

'Who was that?' she asked, plonking herself down beside him on the bed as he replaced the receiver.

'Room service,' he answered, glancing sideways at

her. 'I thought tiramisu and champagne might go down rather well at this point.'

Marie laughed. On the drive from the airport to the hotel she had told him all about her interlude with Tony Bertorelli. She had surprised herself, feeling no shame nor apprehension about regaling him with her exploits. Somehow she knew he would enjoy hearing all the details. And she was right.

Nor had it bothered her when he told her about a similar encounter he had enjoyed that week with one of his landscaping clients. What hadn't happened with Tony, she told him, was the promised fun and games with a sticky desert and champagne. Now it looked as though Lawrie was about to indulge her himself.

'We have to do the bondage part first,' he said to her, smiling wolfishly. Standing up, he walked to his leather holdall which stood open on a chair and rummaged inside it. He withdrew a couple of thin lengths of black fabric and dangled them in the air. 'Spare chinstraps,' he explained in answer to her questioning look. 'They should be long enough.'

Marie laughed. 'Well, what can I say?' she quipped. 'You've got a big head.'

In response, Lawrie lunged at her, pushing her playfully on to the bed.

'For that you get a good spanking first, young lady,' he growled with mock ferocity.

As he spoke, desire zapped through Marie at the speed of light, driving the breath away from her lungs and filling her head with a giddy sensation. It was nothing to what was going on inside her body. Passion tingled along every nerve, the aroma of her arousal oozing from every pore.

'No,' she gasped, half-laughing, half-moaning with lust as he flipped her over his knee and began to deliver a series of stinging but not too hard slaps to her bare bottom. She squirmed under the palm of his hand that kept her pinned to his knee. 'No, please.'

200

Inside her head she screamed, yes please. Yes. Yes. Yes!

'I'll teach you to mock me,' Lawrie's voice said. It entered her ears and swirled around inside her reeling head. 'You'll be begging me to stop.'

Marie wanted to laugh but she couldn't. She wanted to cry out but she couldn't. She wanted to beg him to fuck her but she couldn't. So she did the only thing she could manage at that moment – she orgasmed.

Lawrie held her on his lap, watching her changing expression, feeling the gentle squirming of her body. He stopped spanking her and simply looked at her, his fingers caressing her pouting sex lightly as he witnessed her in the throes of her sudden climax. He marvelled at it. Its intensity. Its immediacy. And he was amazed by her. By Marie. By her capacity for pleasure. It came from nowhere, sparking and raging instantly. It kept him in its grip as surely as it absorbed her. It held him spellbound.

Dangling limply over Lawrie's knees, Marie felt a series of sensations: her breathing, short and harsh as it slowly returned to normal; her breasts, full and aching, pressed into the soft material of his trousers and the hard muscle beneath; her bottom, hot and stinging – delighting to the sensation of the cool current of air coming from the air conditioning unit, and, most of all, the exposed, throbbing sensation of her sex.

'OK, sweetheart?' Lawrie asked, his voice solicitous as he stroked a fingertip lightly down her spine.

As he reached the cleft between her buttocks Marie felt her hips rising in an involuntary movement. Her glowing bottom begged for his caress. As he obliged her, his palm sweeping over her buttocks and across the tops of her thighs, her eyelids fluttered closed. He seemed to be deliberately avoiding her sex and Marie felt that part of her body yearning for him of its own accord. She wriggled her hips slightly, noticing how the cool breeze seemed to catch the moist flesh surrounding her vagina and linger there, drying her wetness and yet tantalising her all at the same time.

Lawrie slid an arm under her body, the soft flesh of the underside of his arm brushing the skin just beneath her breasts. Then he was lifting her up, turning her around and depositing her on the bed. Everything seemed to be happening in slow motion, Marie thought, as she struggled to raise her eyelids a fraction and watch his movements through the fringe of her lashes.

There was a knock at the outer door and she found herself curling into a ball on the blue cotton bed cover. Lawrie went to answer the door. She heard muted voices. Then he was back and she straightened out again, her face showing the relief she felt that Lawrie had only opened the door a little way and deliberately used his body to shield her nakedness from inquisitive eyes.

He held aloft a bottle of champagne, his expression as triumphant as though he had just won it in a race. In his other hand he carried a round silver tray, his splayed fingers supporting the bottom of it in true waiter fashion.

'Champagne and tiramisu for the lady,' he said, depositing the tray on top of the chest of drawers beside the bed.

Marie felt her body flush as he glanced down at her, his eyes transmitting so much promise that she sensed her vagina moistening afresh in response. He paused to uncork the champagne and pour some into two flute glasses. She nodded and murmured her thanks as she accepted one from him.

'A toast,' he declared, sitting down beside her on the bed and touching the rim of his glass to hers.

A small smile curved her lips. 'What to?'

'To victory,' he replied. 'May the best woman win.'

Marie felt her heart lift in excitement. Did he really believe she would win the Championship, or was he just being magnanimous?

'Or man?' she added.

He nodded. 'Or man. But I think I was right the first time.'

She couldn't help asking, 'Do you – do you really?'

'Why not?' he said, shrugging then sipping his champagne. 'You're only a couple of points down. We've got two races to go. Anything could happen.'

Marie kept her eyes smiling at him as she sipped her champagne. Yes, she thought, anything could happen. She only hoped it was going to happen the way she wanted it to.

Lawrie didn't give her much chance to ponder the possible outcome of the Championship. Taking her glass from her after she had enjoyed a few more sips of the effervescent liquid, he placed it on the tray, next to the tiramisu. Then he pressed her gently back against the bed and picked up the chinstraps, which lay at the foot of the bed like a couple of eels basking in shallow water.

'Aren't we going to eat our dessert?' she asked with a nervous giggle.

He took her left wrist and secured it to the bedpost. 'I am,' he said with a confident smile. 'Maybe I'll save some for you to have later.'

'You – you – ' Marie gasped, her breath shortening as he took her other wrist and wound the black chinstrap around it.

Desire flooded her. Feeling helpless was an unknown quality to her, but Lawrie had the knack of making her feel helpless without having to go to the trouble of binding her wrists to the bed. His sheer aura of sexuality did that. That and the exquisite way he made her feel when he touched her.

'Don't worry, I won't eat it all,' he said, picking up the bowl.

Marie smiled faintly at him. He was teasing her now but she didn't feel as though she had the strength to smile properly. All her energies were concentrated elsewhere: in her aching breasts; in her burning sex; in her quivering thighs as he parted them. She felt knotted up with lust as she watched how he concentrated his sultry gaze on the exposed folds of her sex while he undressed and then climbed on to the bed to kneel between her legs.

Her eyes glanced over his body. It gleamed like softly burnished gold, the hairs on his arms and legs so fair they were barely noticeable. Only his pubic hair was apparent, a white-blond nest surrounding the base of his semi-erect penis and barely obscuring the dark, wrinkled bags of his scrotum. She kept her eyes fixed to his groin, noticing how his balls dangled like a pair of plums as he moved. His cock slapped her hairless mound as he leant over her and she heard herself whimper.

Oh, God. The torment was too much to bear. His touch was light as his fingertips coated her naked body with the pale, sticky sweet. He dabbed it upon her nipples, ignoring the way they hardened and beckoned to him. He swirled it around her areolae and then smeared it across her breasts and throat. With her arms stretched wide she was only able to raise her head a little. But she watched him dip his fingers into the bowl again and smear the tiramisu over her stomach and belly. She felt her breath catch. His fingertips were brushing her mons, the gooey sweet melting into her warm flesh.

She watched him put the bowl down before continuing any further and felt a sharp stab of disappointment. She had so wanted to feel his fingers sliding over her labia, stroking the heated flesh between her thighs.

'Don't be so impatient,' he admonished her gently, as though he could read her thoughts. 'I need to lick all this off you first.'

His eyes swept her torso and continued up to her face. Their gazes locked and he moved to hover over her, his hands resting palm down on the bedspread to take his weight.

Marie felt as though she was sinking into the bed; her body contracting, shrinking in on itself. Then, just as quickly, it blossomed. At the first touch of his lips upon her breast she felt herself expanding outwards, every part of her yearning towards him.

He took his time licking her body clean, taking his tongue over every portion of her exposed flesh, nibbling and sucking at her until she was squirming with arousal and moaning incoherently. When he moved again she noticed that his cock had become rock hard. Obviously, she thought, with a thrill of delight, his enjoyment was just as great as hers.

'I know where I'm going to eat my share from,' she said, eyeing his hardness wickedly.

Lawrie's eyes seemed to gleam in the dimmed light as he smiled at her. 'Shut up, or I'll have to gag you,' he warned. 'Your pleasure comes first, then mine.'

'But it would be a pleasure for me,' Marie insisted, twisting her arms in retaliation to the straps that bound them. 'Really, I mean it.'

And she did. She couldn't wait to be free so that she could grasp his lovely hard cock between her hands, feed the ripe plum of his glans between her lips and gorge herself on it. Really, she mused as she gazed pleadingly at him, the addition of tiramisu was neither here nor there.

'Shut up,' Lawrie repeated. 'I won't tell you again. Do you want another spanking?'

Marie nodded feverishly.

'Well, too bad,' he responded, 'because all you're going to get right now, young lady, is this.'

Driving his fingers into the bowl he scooped up a huge dollop of the tiramisu and dropped it on to her mons. It landed with a soft plop and, at the same moment, Marie let out a harsh gasp of pleasure. The sweet oozed between her thighs and Lawrie aided it with his fingertips, smoothing it deftly over her outer labia as though he were anointing her body with the finest lotion.

'Now to feast,' he said, raising his head momentarily.

Marie's stomach clenched as she watched him bend over her, his head dropping between her thighs. The touch of his tongue on her sensitive flesh made her groan aloud. Then she was aboard that rollercoaster again, rising and dipping on the waves of pleasure that transported her from the bedroom into another realm.

How much pleasure could one person possibly take? she asked herself mindlessly as she soared towards yet another orgasm. For her, it seemed, the answer was simple. There were no limits. None whatsoever.

Heat as thick as a duvet hung over the Monza race track, encouraging its population to wear only the skimpiest of clothes. Lean brown limbs flashed everywhere, emerging from the hems of short shorts and the sleeves of cotton T-shirts. Breasts, barely constrained by midriff-baring tops and triangles of bikini tops, jiggled and gleamed under a thin film of perspiration. And masculine shoulders – some broad, some lean – were to be seen everywhere in the crowd. All toasted to varying shades of brown: some freckled; some covered with matted dark hair.

Marie couldn't stop herself from looking, her eyes darting everywhere as she leant against the pit wall. Opposite her, across the other side of the track, the stands were packed with spectators; their individuality merging into a constantly moving ocean of brightly coloured clothing. Music was blaring through the loudspeakers and everywhere was filled with the varying tones of excited chatter in a cosmopolitan melée of languages.

Exhilaration gripped her. There she was in Italy's famous 'Citadel of Speed'. Surrounded by acres of wooded parkland, yet only nine miles from the teeming city of Milan, it was one of the nicest tracks on the European circuit and the oldest. Marie considered herself extremely lucky to be competing there, to be following the straights and curves in the tyre tracks of the most famous names in motorsport: Andretti, Berger, Mansell, Alesi and, of course, the king of them all, the late Ayrton Senna. She thrilled to the knowledge and to her own tiny part in the track's history. It was race day. It was a wonderful day. Nothing was going to stop her from winning.

Studiously, she avoided the interested glances of a couple of young, bronzed Italians and their musical call of, 'Hey, *bella!*' She had been propositioned so many times already that day by sloe-eyed Latin Lotharios that it was beginning to get a bit tiresome. She realised that her attraction for them was not only her appearance but the fact that she was one of the drivers – the elite. It aroused their macho instincts to such an extent that they simply had to try their luck with her.

Ignoring the 'pretty boys', Marie glanced over her shoulder as Carla came to stand beside her. 'How's the car?' she asked.

Carla's finger and thumb formed an 'O'. 'Perfect,' Carla said, grinning, 'how's the driver?'

Marie smiled back. 'Perfect, too.'

'I'll second that,' a masculine voice said behind them.

The two women were startled by the arrival of Lawrie. He looked cool and, to Marie's eyes, unbearably handsome, in a pair of white cotton shorts and nothing else. His lean torso gleamed and, as she sniffed the air, Marie could just make out the faintest aroma of perspiration mixed with aftershave. She smiled broadly as he moved to stand at her other side. All three of them leant forward to rest their elbows on the white concrete wall.

From somewhere behind them came a cacophony of whistles and catcalls with a distinctly Italian flavour.

Marie didn't even bother to look around. Instead she said, 'Charmer,' to Lawrie, in response to his comment. Her eyes smiled as warmly as her mouth. 'What shape is your car in?' she added.

'Sorry to disappoint you but the answer's good,' he said.

'I'm not disappointed,' Marie responded, her lips pursing just slightly. 'I want you to come second.'

Lawrie grinned and patted her bottom as he made to move away. 'Ah, Amber,' he said, using her racing name as he promised he would, 'you've got no worries on that score. You know me; I always make sure you come first.'

Giggling, Marie watched him walk away, his loping stride carrying him into the crowd of journalists, mechanics and hangers-on that populated the pit area.

'You're totally hooked on him, aren't you?' Carla observed beside her a moment later.

Marie whirled her head around, her eyes wide as she gazed at her friend.

'I'd like to be able to deny that,' she said, 'but I can't. I am. Completely hooked. He's a fantastic guy in every way. He gives me pleasure, freedom, respect –'

'Wow!' Carla interrupted. 'Is there another Lawrie Samson going spare by any chance?'

Glancing at her friend, Marie said, 'Why, what's up with Anders?'

Carla gave a wry laugh. 'Nothing,' she said, 'just that he's only an ordinary man, not a saint.'

'I didn't say Lawrie was a saint,' Marie argued, wondering if Carla was trying to tell her something more.

'Well, he is compared with Anders, obviously,' Carla said. She remained silent for a moment, then added, 'The main problem with Anders is that he won't go down on me.'

'Get rid of him,' Marie responded quickly.

She noticed Carla's normally cheerful expression dropped a few fathoms.

'I have,' she said.

Marie wanted to continue the conversation but, as was absolutely typical, there was no time. Frank came striding across the pits to tell her to go and put her racing overalls on.

'Gosh, is it that time already?' Marie said, glancing at her watch.

Frank nodded. 'You've got about fifteen minutes before the warm-up.' Then he turned to Carla. 'Can you come back to the garage with me?' he said to her. 'I just want you to check the timing one last time to make sure it's absolutely spot on.'

Marie flashed Carla an apologetic smile and mumbled that they'd talk later. Then she accompanied her friend and Frank to the garage, leaving them there to attend to the car while she went out to the motor home to get changed.

Marie didn't think she had ever felt so hot. Strapped into the driver's seat of her Porsche, clad in layer after fireproof layer, she felt as though she was melting rapidly. She could smell her own perspiration, feel it running down her spine and between her breasts. Her helmet felt unbearably heavy and beneath that her Amber wig was making her head itch.

'Come on, come on,' she murmured agitatedly, drumming her fingers on the leather-covered steering wheel, 'let's just get on with it.'

Turning her head, she saw that both the spectator stands lining the track and the pits were crowded with people. Brightly coloured clothing mingled with tanned flesh, while bright spots of sunlight reflected off a thousand pairs of sunglasses and the chrome rails around each stand, sending out dazzling flashes.

The sultry air was filled with a heady concoction of aromas: sizzling hamburgers, sun tan lotion; melting tarmac; engine oil and petrol fumes. Marie inhaled deeply, then coughed. Her stomach growled as her nostrils caught the distinctive scent of fried onions. She had felt too nervous to eat lunch and now regretted it. What wouldn't she give to be holding a big juicy hamburger in her hands, dripping with cheese and mustard. No, she decided, on second thoughts, she'd rather be sitting down to a plate of delicate ribbon pasta, each melting mouthful coated with garlic, herbs and cream.

'Five minutes, Amber,' Frank said, pushing his head through the window on the passenger side.

Marie glanced at him across the empty seat well and gave him the thumbs up. She felt as though *she* were lunch – sealed inside an empty metal pot while heat flared all around her. One hour, she told herself consolingly, just one hour, or possibly less, and it would all be over. She'd be standing on the rostrum accepting her dues as the winner, spraying Lawrie and one other with champagne from the bottle she had won.

Having qualified in pole position, with Lawrie's car right behind hers, she had no more doubt about Lawrie coming second than she had about herself winning. All they had to do was hold the others off. But who would take third place? she wondered, thinking Darren was the most likely candidate. With Tony now out of the Championship – the damage his car had suffered at Hockenheim had turned out to be more extensive than he'd thought; far too much to repair in a week – only Darren and the Spaniard, Guillermo Castillos, were realistic contenders.

Carla walked up to the car, her head taking the place of Frank's.

'You can start the car now,' she said. 'That'll give you about two minutes to warm up the engine.' Glancing over her shoulder, she turned back and added, 'the track looks nice and sticky. You should win this one, no problem.'

Marie felt her stomach turn over. As actors suffered stage fright, she always experienced a panic attack just before the start of the race. As she turned the ignition key, the engine burst into life.

'Sounds good,' she said to Carla. Behind her ribs her heart was beating nineteen to the dozen but somehow she managed a smile. 'This is it. Keep your fingers crossed.' Her smile broadened as she heard Carla give a derisory snort.

'Cut the crap, Marie,' Carla said. 'Just get the car and your arse in gear and get out there and win.'

After Carla had moved to stand behind the pit wall, Marie found herself going over what her friend had just said. For the first time ever during a race meeting, Carla had called her Marie instead of Amber. She hoped it wasn't a bad omen.

Chapter Fourteen

Marie got off to a flying start from the grid, taking the tight *Variante Goodyear* chicane with ease. By sticking to a perfect racing line around *Curva Grande* and flooring the accelerator along the ensuing short straight, she managed to touch 130 mph by the time she reached *Curva di Lesmos* at the top end of the track. Along the next, much longer straight, she took the Porsche up to 140 mph and rounded the final *Curva Parabolica* a whole two cars' length ahead of Lawrie.

She knew this because Carla was constantly appraising her of her progress through the earpiece she wore, as well as letting her know what was happening with some of the other cars.

'Darren's just spun on *Rettifilo*,' Carla's disembodied voice said in her left ear. 'Oh, and Reubens is out, Konrad Slechter just forced him off into the tyre wall at *Parabolica*.'

Marie took all this in, feeling vaguely sorry for the drivers Carla had just mentioned while concentrating on *Lesmos* for a second time. Lawrie was right behind her again, nudging the back of her car as she gathered pace down the straight. The back of her car felt light and, knowing that Lawrie was trying to slipstream her – taking advantage of the fact that her car was suffering all the force of the air pressure, leaving him with a clear passage in which to gain speed – she had to decide whether she was going to fight him hard around the upcoming double curve, or give in gracefully and let him overtake her.

She was damned if was she going to give in, she decided in that instant. As a result, when she and Lawrie entered the decisive *Curva del Vialone* their cars were side by side. Her next course of action was to deliberately allow her car to drift sideways towards Lawrie's. He would either have to brake to avoid a collision, or drop back behind her again. To her horror she realised, too late, that he had no intention of doing either. She felt the side of her car brush his and risked a sideways glance. Lawrie was staring fixedly ahead, his gloved hands gripping the juddering steering wheel as she forced him to drive half on the kerb.

Damn him! The damage to her car was going to cost a packet. Where was all his talk about letting her come first now?

'Bastard!' she hissed, not realising she had spoken aloud.

'Let it go, Amber,' Carla's calm tone cautioned her through the earpiece. 'It's not worth it.'

It took Marie a few more seconds to finally concede defeat. Releasing the pressure of her foot on the accelerator slightly, she watched with disgust as Lawrie's Porsche gathered speed and eventually cut across in front of her to pick up the racing line. For the remaining eighteen laps she stuck doggedly to his bumper, occasionally slipstreaming him in return but unable to gain the same advantage around the various curves and chicanes that he had had over her.

At the end of the race she pulled into the pits and sat there for a few agonised minutes, trying hard to compose herself before getting out of the car and facing the barrage of TV cameras and reporters outside. Second place! She did some rapid calculations in her head. If she wasn't very much mistaken, she and Lawrie were going to compete in the final race of the Championship with equal points. Imola really was going to prove to be anybody's race.

Realising that she couldn't stay in her car forever, she took a deep breath and flung open the car door. Dragging off her helmet and then her gloves, she composed her demeanour into one of casual aplomb before turning to the journalists. Even before she started to smile and nod and answer their teeming questions, she knew the next half-hour or so was going to be one of the most difficult she had ever had to endure. Harder than any race.

She eventually managed to make her escape and met up with Lawrie at the foot of the rostrum.

'Congratulations,' she said to him through clenched teeth.

His beaming smile almost blinded her.

'No hard feelings,' he offered, holding out his hand.

Summoning up every last scrap of fortitude she took it, wishing she had a bit more strength so that she could crush it into tiny pieces. Sadly, her hand looked far too diminutive in comparison to his own. She tossed her head and smiled brightly at him, though only with her mouth.

'Of course not,' she said. 'A race is a race.'

There was no time to continue the conversation. The moment had come for them to climb on to the rostrum. Marie stared resolutely ahead and smiled at the cameras as Lawrie was awarded the winner's laurels and a bottle of champagne. It took every ounce of her willpower to pretend to enjoy being sprayed with the sticky liquid. Somehow, she thought wryly, being dumped on from a great height seemed horribly appropriate.

Even though she knew she was being churlish and totally unsporting, Marie couldn't bring herself to attend the victor's party that evening, nor accept Lawrie's bombardment of telephone calls.

'Just tell him I've got a terrible migraine and that I'll see him tomorrow,' she urged Carla.

Then, after her friend had left for the party, she took the phone off the hook, just to be on the safe side.

The following day she caught a taxi into Milan itself, leaving early before Carla or anyone else – especially Lawrie – was awake. The old city was one of her favourites and she found her tension gradually easing as she spent a pleasant morning strolling around its bright, clean streets, immersing herself in window shopping and enjoying the architecture.

At midday she decided to take a break and chose an enticing-looking trattoria which had an outside patio shaded by a vine-covered pergola. Choosing a table that overlooked the busy street, she picked up the menu.

It seemed she had hardly glanced at it when she heard, '*Ciao, bella!*' The cry was accompanied by a puttering sound.

Turning her head to look over the white painted brick wall beside her – in the top of which a profusion of highly scented flowers were planted – Marie noticed a couple of young Italian men seated astride a bright blue motor scooter. She smiled to herself. It was a common enough sight. Then she turned her smile outwards and directed it at them.

'Hello,' she said pleasantly, thinking: what the hell?

The two men climbed off the scooter, swinging black denim-clad legs over the padded seat. One of them, the passenger, walked up to her and leant his elbows on the top of the wall. He had longish, silky dark hair, sultry eyes and a petulant mouth. His skin was the colour of toffee and his biceps bulged enticingly under the sleeves of the white, round-necked T-shirt he wore.

Tearing her eyes away from his physique, Marie glanced up at his face, immediately finding herself dazzled by a brilliant smile.

'You lovely lady,' the young Italian said in broken English. 'You like to eat together?'

For some reason Marie's mind conjured a sudden, unwarranted vision of herself and this young man locked together in the classic sixty-nine position. Shaking her head fiercely to dispel the disturbing image, she watched his confident expression falter. Why not? she asked herself, feeling her body readying itself before her mind had decided.

But she already knew the answer. If the truth be known, she simply couldn't be bothered. She loathed herself for the thought, but she knew that if she consented now, the rest of the afternoon would consist of blatant flattery and attempts at persuasion. This guy, delectable though he was, wasn't just planning to share lunch with her. He wanted a whole lot more. Detecting the expectant look on his face, she found herself despairing of it.

'No, thank you,' she said politely as she silently urged her body to agree with her, 'I'm waiting for someone.'

'A girlfriend?' the young man enquired, looking even more hopeful. He glanced across the wide pavement to his friend, who was now resting his bottom on the seat of the motor scooter, his arms folded.

'No,' Marie lied, 'my boyfriend.' She glanced around. 'He should be here in a minute.'

'Oh.' The Italian looked crestfallen and Marie was almost tempted at that point to give in. He shrugged and gave her a rueful smile. 'Well, see you anyway, beautiful lady,' he said, straightening up. '*Ciao.*'

'Yeah, *ciao*,' Marie murmured.

With fresh resolve, she turned her attention back to the menu as he walked away, though she was aware of the couple of times he glanced back over his shoulder at her. Finally, she was relieved to hear the soft growl of the scooter's engine starting up, then the puttering sound again as it pulled away from the kerb.

As she ate her solitary lunch of spicy meatballs with linguine, washed down with a carafe of ice cold white Valpolicella, she found herself wondering why she felt so antagonistic towards men at the moment. Was it just the fact that Lawrie had beaten her at Monza? She didn't really think so. Or was it because men on the whole were always so available, so eager? Putting down her fork, she reclined in her chair and picked up her wine glass. She stared at the solitary meatball on her plate. Unwanted and destined to be thrown into the waste bin, it seemed to stare balefully back at her like an eyeball.

That could be you if you don't stop being so cynical, she warned herself. One day a time will come when men won't come flocking around you and then where will you be? She drained the last of the wine in her glass and put it down resolutely as she reached a decision. There was nothing else for it, she was going to have to go back to the hotel, find Lawrie and make her peace with him.

'So sorry, *signorina*, Mr Samson checked out,' the little dark haired man behind the reception desk said to Marie when she enquired after Lawrie's whereabouts, 'but he left you this.' Reaching under the counter, he pulled out a long white envelope and handed it to her.

Feeling sick with disappointment, Marie wandered over to one of the large, squashy couches that populated the reception area. The air was cool inside the hotel but she felt feverish. It hadn't occurred to her that Lawrie might not be there. She opened the envelope and unfolded the single sheet of hotel paper with trembling fingers.

'My lovely Marie,' the letter said, 'I'm sorry we didn't get a chance to say goodbye. I missed you at the party. It was no fun without you and I felt tempted to knock at your door when I got back as it was only just past midnight. Carla said you genuinely weren't feeling well, which was a relief in some ways because I thought you might be angry with me for taking the win yesterday. But you're not like that are you, Marie? You're a lovely, sexy, delicious young woman with a heart of gold. I can't wait to see you next weekend at Imola. We'll make up for lost time then, I promise you. I'm going to do so many things to you, give you so much pleasure . . .'

Feeling warmer than ever and hating the tears that pricked at the corners of her eyes, Marie dropped the letter on to her lap. She couldn't go on reading it. She couldn't bear to take in Lawrie's promises when she knew just what she had missed the previous night. Oh, God, she wailed inside, why am I such a stupid, stupid cow? She thumped her knee with her fist and was surprised to see Carla standing in front of her when she glanced up.

'There's a package waiting for you in your room,' Carla said, 'and a note. I don't know who it's from.'

Marie's heart leapt and then subsided. It couldn't be from Lawrie, she had his note here on her lap.

'I'll go up and look at it later,' she said disinterestedly as she made to get up. 'In the meantime, do you fancy getting drunk?'

The room was still spinning when Marie opened her eyes some hours later. Groaning she attempted to turn over on to her stomach and then gave it up as a bad job. Movement of any kind made her stomach heave alarmingly.

She wondered how late it was. Her hotel room was in darkness and she was all alone. No Carla. No Lawrie. No one at all. She felt so wretched that she began to cry. Mascara stung her eyes as tears of self-pity ran unchecked down her face. Thank goodness she *was* alone, she thought, grasping blindly for the box of tissues beside the bed, who would want to look at her in this state? She couldn't remember ever having felt so sorry for herself. No, she amended, her tears stopping as suddenly as they had started, she had felt much worse than this before. All she had to do was remember the days following Greg's untimely departure. God! She opened her stinging eyes and stared at the spinning ceiling; all that seemed like such a long time ago. She had made progress since then. She had.

She blew her nose and then stretched, easing the tension in her back and shoulders. Her foot touched something and for a moment she wondered what on earth it could be. Unable to bear the thought of trying to sit up, she wriggled her toes over the unseen object. Whatever it was it was long and wide and shallow. And covered with paper. Vaguely she recalled Carla saying something to her about a parcel.

Lawrie! Her heart leapt, her stomach following suit immediately afterwards. Swallowing deeply, she managed to calm her stomach and remembered that Lawrie had already left for England. But he hadn't left under a cloud, she reminded herself with a sigh of relief. As far as he was concerned, everything was still all right between them. Everything that had happened had only happened in her head. Go back to sleep, she told herself, and when you wake up in the morning, ring him. Ring him to tell him how much you're looking forward to seeing him at the weekend.

The next time Marie opened her eyes, the sun was streaming through the large picture window to her left, casting a golden glow over the modern ash veneered furnishings and cream carpet. Above her, the ceiling no longer spun and not even the slightest trace of a hangover lingered.

Gingerly, not trusting the resilience of her own body, Marie sat up. She pushed her hair back from her face and, in so doing, realised that she was still wearing her Amber wig. Yanking the wig off, she ruffled her natural hair and scratched her scalp. Then she noticed the package. Climbing on to her hands and knees, she crawled down to the end of the bed and hovered over it. It was a large box, a fairly shallow oblong, just as her feet had discovered the night before.

Well, open it then, she heard her mind prompting her. Picking it up, she scrambled to sit cross-legged on the bed and dragged the parcel on to her lap. It was covered in plain brown paper, and tied with string. Under the string lay an envelope, also brown. For a gift, she mused, it looked very businesslike and austere. She debated whether to open the envelope first, or the parcel. Finally, she decided on the envelope. At least then, when she discovered the contents of the package, she would know who it was from.

No such luck.

'Amber,' the typewritten message said, 'I urge you to follow the attached list of instructions to the letter. Do this and you will enjoy yourself, I promise you. Ignore it and you will miss out on a *lot* of pleasure.'

Before reading the instructions Marie glanced to the end of the letter. There was no name, which immediately set her mind whirling through the possibilities. It couldn't be from Lawrie. He was back in England and he wouldn't call her Amber in private. Who, then? Laurent was one possibility. So was Tony. If it came to that, so was anyone involved in the racing fraternity. It could even be from a journalist. She shook her head, trying to clear the fog inside it. Had she missed something – something that would give her a clue to the identity of the sender?

There was nothing for it but to carry on reading. As she scanned the list of instructions on the attached page, her heart began to gather pace. Whoever had thought this up was certainly inventive.

'You will be at the hotel for two more nights,' the message read. 'These instructions concern Tuesday night.' She paused for a moment. That was tonight. Who was aware that she intended to leave on Wednesday? 'Wear only what is inside the package,' the note continued, 'nothing more. Do not put your hands in the pockets. Prepare yourself for collection at eight o'clock. Do not question your guide. Do everything you are told. Failure to adhere to these simple instructions will result in immediate termination of your pleasure.'

Well! Marie thought as she sank back on to the bed, feeling mildly exhausted. That was short and sweet. Sitting up again, she picked up the parcel and began to undo the string. Her fingers were trembling now. Her stomach clenched tightly in anticipation. Wondering what she was going to find in the parcel was not the reason for her anxiety. Knowing that she was going to comply with the instructions – as bizarre as they seemed – was.

If she was expecting lingerie, or handcuffs and rubber, or any of the myriad possibilities that had shot through her mind, she was disappointed. All that lay inside the white, tissue-lined box was a stone coloured waterproof trench coat and a pair of matching stiletto-heeled shoes. On closer inspection, she found that the buttons had been removed from the coat. All that would fasten it was the broad, self-tie belt.

So, whoever had sent her the parcel expected her to prance around wearing just a long mac and stilettos, did they? OK, she told herself, no problem; I can handle that. The only niggling doubt she felt was what was going to happen to her from eight o'clock onwards? And, although she was loath to admit it because it made her feel hopelessly depraved, even her doubt was over-shadowed by excitement.

'You're mad,' she told herself later that evening as she regarded her reflection in the full-length mirror. 'Completely and utterly round the twist.' She knew it was just what Carla would have said to her if she knew, only Carla's language would have been a lot stronger. Which was precisely why she hadn't told her friend, she reminded herself, cinching the belt even more tightly around her waist.

She tucked the bottom edge of the coat closer around her body, her fingertips encountering her bare breast as she did so. She rubbed her nipple absently, feeling it harden. Further down, she felt her sex reacting to the message being transmitted by her nipple. In fact, she realised, her whole body felt aroused. All afternoon she had been preparing herself mentally and physically for sexual adventure: taking a long luxurious bath; oiling her deeply tanned body, and spraying perfume on all the places she was certain her undisclosed lover was going to see and touch.

It excited her to think that she was about to enter into

the erotic unknown, and her body was reacting to that excitement. The mac felt cool and smooth upon her bare skin. As she walked, the wrap-over front revealed intriguing flashes of her bare, tanned legs, and the neckline dipped quite low, showing the smoothness of her throat beneath her jutting collarbones. She had tested her outfit, such as it was, quite extensively in front of the mirror – walking, sitting, bending forward. It actually revealed very little of her body and for that she felt absurdly relieved. At least while she was in public no one could possibly guess that she was naked underneath, though it would seem a little eccentric of her to be wearing a coat on such a warm evening.

The telephone call, when it came at five minutes to eight, surprised her. Was it really that time already?

'Amber?' the voice at the other end of the line asked. The caller was definitely Italian, very feminine and attractively accented.

'Yes,' Marie replied, 'who is this?'

'That does not matter,' came the swift reply. 'Do not ask questions. Are you ready for your little adventure?' The woman laughed in a way that managed to sound both pretty and lascivious all at the same time.

'Yes, I'm ready,' Marie said, feeling her excitement begin to rise again. 'What do you want me to do?'

'I – or rather our master – would like you to go down to the hotel entrance. Outside you will find a black Mercedes limousine waiting for you. Before you get inside the car, take the item from your right pocket and put it on. Then we will be able to continue in person.' The woman's voice seemed to become huskier as she reached the end of her instructions. A moment later the line went dead.

Our master? Marie wondered. She stared at the receiver as though it were an alien being, thinking that whoever was behind this didn't know her very well after all. She was used to the rôle of mistress; she had no master. But it was of no consequence. She would soon be able to set the perpetrator of this strange encounter straight on a few facts. She laughed aloud, realising for the first time how assertive she had become since Greg's departure. Although everything about this situation conspired to put her at a disadvantage, she still felt oddly in control.

Unconsciously, she patted the right pocket of the coat, feeling that there was something flat and soft inside it. Her first instinct was to put her hand in the pocket to see what it was, but she remembered that the list of instructions expressly forbade it. Putting down the receiver, she stooped to the bed and picked up her shoulder bag. Her stomach was knotted tightly with anticipation as she slung her bag over her shoulder but she shrugged defiantly as she took one last glance in the mirror.

Her reflection, she noticed, was one of a young woman who looked completely calm and normal. Not of someone who was about to enter a strange new erotic realm. As she walked towards the door and grasped the handle she reached an instant decision. If she was going to play this game, she was going to make damn sure she played it to the hilt.

She noticed the limousine as soon as she approached the automatic glass doors at the hotel's entrance. The door slid back smoothly to allow her to pass through. Tripping lightly down the small flight of steps, her heels clattering on the rugged stone, she came to a halt on the pavement. Then she walked up to the rear passenger door of the car and stood there for a moment, trying in vain to peer through the car's tinted black windows. She put her hand in the right pocket of the coat, her fingers wrapping around something soft and silky. Drawing the object from the pocket she noticed it was a black eyemask, of the kind worn during long-haul flights.

Reaching up, she slipped it over her head, taking care not to dislodge her wig. Then she glanced up and down the street, making sure there was no one around to watch her as she pulled it down over her eyes.

Immediately, she was enveloped in blackness. The

state of blind helplessness made her self-confidence plummet. Depriving herself of one of her most vital senses, she realised, made her feel incredibly vulnerable. She heard a faint creak and assumed it was the car door opening. Then she felt a soft hand on her wrist and heard the same voice that had spoken to her on the telephone.

'Get in, Amber,' the voice said. 'That's it, lift your foot. Yes, now the other one.'

Tentatively, Marie climbed into the car. Her first impression was the smell of polished leather and the sensation of being enclosed as the door shut with a soft click behind her. Groping slightly, she found the seat and sat down. Her fingertips delighted for a moment in the texture of the butter-soft leather. Then she heard a low growl as the engine started up and felt a slight tug as the car pulled away. The engine was purring softly and she could hear two sets of breathing.

'You may call me Cherry,' the voice beside her said. 'Our master is seated opposite. He is looking at you. Now he nods his approval.'

Marie felt her stomach tense. Well bully for him, she thought, feeling slightly annoyed that this self-styled master should feel he had the right to approve or disapprove of her.

'I have no master,' she said defiantly, her fingers gripping the edge of the seat. She had not relaxed into the soft leather upholstery. Instead she sat bolt upright and assumed she looked as stiff and as wary of the situation as she felt.

'For the purposes of this evening you do,' Cherry corrected her. 'It is the master's express desire that you cooperate fully.'

'Fine, OK. I'll call him master if that's what he wants,' Marie responded with an attempt at a careless shrug, while all the time thinking, *but I don't have to feel it inside*.

Cherry spoke again. 'You are not relaxed, are you, Amber?' Marie heard the soft swish of clothing and sensed that Cherry was moving beside her. A moment later Cherry took her hand and she felt her fingers being wrapped around the stem of a glass. 'Here, drink this,' the woman added in an encouraging tone.

'What is it – am I being drugged?' Marie asked instantly, feeling foolish as she heard a burst of musical laughter.

'No, darling, of course not,' the other woman assured her, the laughter still in her voice. 'It is champagne. We are celebrating.'

Marie concentrated on carrying the glass to her lips, once again realising how difficult everything was now she was unable to see. She sipped the effervescent liquid and then sighed with pleasure. The champagne was deliciously chilled and dry.

'This is very good,' Marie commented, sipping again.

'Of course,' Cherry responded, 'the master always insists on the best. That is why you have been chosen.'

'Chosen?' Marie felt her eyebrows lift behind the mask, the short hairs catching on its bound edge.

'Chosen for the master's special brand of pleasure,' Cherry said. She paused and Marie heard the sound of muted whispers. 'The master would like you to finish your champagne,' the other woman continued, 'then he wishes me to open your coat and display your body to him.'

Marie felt her insides turn to water at the prospect and quickly gulped down the last of the champagne in her glass. Despite her determination to remain in control she felt her knees begin to tremble, the tremors continuing up her thighs. She shivered as she held up her empty glass. The glass was taken away from her. She heard a slight chink and assumed it had been put down next to another glass. For the first time in her life she wished she had more nerve – to demand another glass of champagne, or preferably the whole bottle. She didn't think she could continue with this charade without a lot more Dutch courage.

'Is the master called Laurent, by any chance?' she found herself asking. She realised she had inadvertently made a connection between Dutch courage and the man she had met in Holland.

'No questions,' Cherry admonished gently.

Marie had to bite her bottom lip to stop herself from apologising automatically. In the next moment she felt warm breath on her cheek, her nostrils picking up a delicate floral scent. Then fingers were plucking at the belt tied around her waist. As the belt was worked loose, Marie found herself holding her breath. Her stomach was contracting so hard she fancied it might touch her spine at any moment.

Soft fingertips brushed her skin as the edges of the coat were eased apart. She felt a rush of warm air caress her naked skin. The fingertips swept across her nipples as her breasts were bared, then her torso and thighs. A moment later she heard a soft hiss of satisfaction, though she was not sure whether it came from the woman beside her or the man who shared the back of the limousine.

'Where is he – the master?' she found herself asking in a tremulous voice. 'Where is he sitting?'

'Opposite us,' Cherry said, 'or rather, opposite you. He is looking at you. At your naked body. His expression tells me he is pleased by what he sees.'

Oh, God! Marie wailed inside her head. She had never felt so shamefully embarrassed, nor so helpless in the grip of her own emotions. Despite the strangeness of the situation – or perhaps because of it, she would reflect later – she felt hopelessly aroused. Even in the midst of her anxiety and shame her body seemed to be working independently, moistening and tingling insistently as, in her mind, she visualised the scene that was taking place. The one in which she appeared to be taking the starring rôle, though not the lead.

Cherry was leading her: guiding her body to arousal as surely as her fingertips stroked and explored her body. Feminine hands swept over her breasts, the fingertips plucking at Marie's nipples. Marie groaned as she felt her nipples harden and heard Cherry's whispered comments as her hands swept down her stomach and across her thighs.

The same hands parted her legs, gently but insistently spreading them apart so that she was completely displayed to her unseen audience.

'So lovely. So soft. Mm, so beautiful . . .' The words rolled off the woman's tongue and around Marie's head like a mantra as the fingertips began to dance lightly over her exposed sex.

Then another comment was added. One which made Marie whimper with desire.

'So wet.'

Chapter Fifteen

*T*hey seemed to have been driving for ages, the car gliding almost noiselessly along unseen streets to its unknown destination – unknown, at least, to Marie. Several times she felt moved to ask where they were headed but was admonished gently by Cherry.

'Do not ask questions,' she insisted. 'Trust us, myself and the master. Trust that you will be pleasantly surprised.'

Marie realised she had no option but to put her faith in them. Unless, of course, she wanted to end this strange yet erotic encounter. So there she sat, her bottom resting right on the edge of the seat with her thighs spread wide apart, as Cherry, diligently conveying the master's instructions, had told her to sit.

She didn't need to have her sight back to know how she must look. How wantonly and shamelessly displayed. The lips of her sex would be swollen, blossoming to reveal the moist pink folds of her inner labia. She could feel how her breasts yearned towards unseen hands and the way her vagina gaped and issued forth continuous trickles of her own juices.

Touch me, taste me, her mind implored.

'Ah, Amber, you look *bellissima*,' Cherry said, interrupting Marie's thoughts. Her hand swept almost carelessly up Marie's thigh and across her stomach, inciting a trail of goosepimples. 'The master agrees with me. He is nodding. His eyes are dark, Amber,' she went on remorselessly. 'Oh, if only you could see the way he is looking at you. It is pure lust, my darling. Complete, unadulterated desire.'

'Your English is very good,' Marie forced herself to gasp. She could feel her nerve-endings still tingling from Cherry's caress and didn't want to think about the master looking at her. Or rather she did, but she wanted him to do more than look. 'Why won't he touch me?' she found herself asking, glancing sideways in Cherry's direction. Then she turned her head and stared straight into the blackness that veiled her eyes, willing herself to be able to picture the man who sat opposite her. 'Why won't you touch me?'

Realising her voice held a plaintive note, Marie despaired of her own weakness. Almost unconsciously she found her hands drifting down her torso and between her thighs to cover her sex lightly. Beneath her fingertips she felt for herself how wide open she was and, as Cherry had described, how wet.

She drew in her breath sharply as her fingers began to explore her own body. They travelled down the fleshy slit between her swollen outer labia, caressing the sensitive petals of her inner flesh and exciting the hard bud of her clitoris. A groan of arousal escaped her lips as she circled the little bud with her fingertips.

'Excellent,' Cherry said softly in her ear, her hand cupping one of Marie's breasts. 'It is lovely to see you pleasuring yourself, Amber. Yes, the master agrees. He is smiling. Touch yourself some more, my darling. I think the Master and I would enjoy watching you make yourself come.'

Marie groaned again. It was an animal sound; lusty and full of wanting. Her fingertips moved more deftly, voyaging over familiar territory, caressing lightly and with deliberate restraint. Now she had the opportunity to bring about the release she craved she didn't want to rush it. Trying to pretend she was all alone, she urged herself to take things slowly. She slid a single finger inside her vagina, delighting in the velvety texture of its walls as she stroked the ridges and muscles of her most secret domain. Deftly she gathered some of her own juices and slid the finger out of her vagina. With bated breath she slicked the moisture over her straining clitoris.

'Ah!' She let out the cry on a long exhalation of breath.

She could feel her arousal gathering inside her like a ball of string. It seemed as though one end of the ball was attached to her clitoris and the other to the nipple that Cherry had just enclosed with her mouth.

The hushed interior of the car seemed to take on a new dimension as Marie's desire grew. All at once, it was filled with the heady scent of sex and an atmosphere of eroticism as tangible as the flesh that Marie felt beneath her fingertips. And then there were the sounds that caressed her ears; low jagged breathing – her own, she realised – and the soft, wet sucking sounds that Cherry made as she mouthed her nipple. Marie strained her ears for the third set of breathing, that of the master. But it seemed, even with her heightened sense of aural perception, she still could not detect anything about him at all. It was as if he didn't exist.

'What is the master doing now?' Marie asked hoarsely.

She felt the bereavement of Cherry's mouth leaving her breast.

'He is watching you,' the other woman said simply. She paused and Marie heard the muted sound of whispering again. 'He is wondering if you still want him to touch you.'

'Oh, yes, please.' Marie surprised herself with the vehemence of her reply. She felt her cheeks flame with mortification. Was she totally shameless? 'I – er – yes, I suppose so. If he wants to,' she amended.

Again came the sound of Cherry's musical laughter. 'He is moving forward,' she said a moment later. 'Now he kneels between your legs. He is looking closely at your sex and – yes, I think he is about to – '

Marie interrupted her with a gasp as she felt other, broader fingertips stroking the sensitive flesh on the insides of her thighs. His breath was warm on her skin. She could sense his mouth moving close to her. All at once she felt his tongue sliding along her inner thigh, stopping just a fraction away from her yearning sex. She felt him raise her leg and straighten it. His hands travelled the length of it: delicate yet capable hands, stroking her leg from the top of her thigh to her ankle, then up again.

She realised in that instant that no comment had been made about her shaven sex, which told her that it had come as no surprise to the two people in the car. Therefore the master, whoever he was, was more than a passing acquaintance of hers. Even so, that still left quite a number of possibilities.

She sighed deeply as the masculine hands took her other leg and began stroking and massaging it as they had done before. The hands slipped the shoe from her foot and she felt the master's tongue again. Stroking damply along her instep, it followed its high arch. The tongue dabbed at the sensitive flesh between her toes, sending little tingles of pleasure up her legs to her sex.

Marie moaned and wriggled her toes, feeling his mouth enclose them one by one. Hot and wet, his mouth sucked, drawing each toe in deeply, the tongue flickering around them, stroking the soft pads.

Unreasonably, it seemed, she found this form of stimulation more erotic than anything that had happened to her so far that evening. His touch was deft and arousing, and simply knowing that his eyes were able to glance along the length of each slender leg to alight on the pouting flesh of her most intimate parts was almost more than her tortured mind could bear.

The very thought tantalised her as much as his caresses. No longer tense, she felt as though she was floating. Cherry's hands were touching her breasts again and moving further down her body to stroke her swollen clitoris. Yes, Marie's mind screamed as she felt the ball of desire gather and knot inside her again. Oh, yes!

As she floated gently down from the pinnacle of pleasure she realised the car was similarly slowing and drawing to a halt. A new scent touched her nostrils, this time quite unpleasant. Marie recognised the smell as that of stagnant water.

Licking her dry lips she managed to gasp, 'Where are we?'

'At our destination,' Cherry said. 'That is all you need to know for now.'

Once again, Marie experienced the sense of helpless frustration that had gripped her earlier. She felt the shoes being slipped back on to her feet while the coat was wrapped and tied around her.

'Perfect,' Cherry said, with a note of satisfaction. 'Now, we leave.'

A blast of much cooler air hit Marie as the car door swung open. Then she felt herself being led from the seat. Stooping, she allowed herself to be guided from the car, Cherry telling her when to raise each foot and set it down. The surface Marie stepped out on to was uneven. Cobblestones, she realised, as she wobbled uncertainly. A strong hand grasped her elbow and she smiled gratefully as she glanced blindly sideways. At her other side she felt Cherry's much lighter grip.

'This way, please,' the other woman said and they started to walk slowly, first of all in a straight line and then turning right.

Around her Marie could hear different sounds: vague shouts in Italian coming from a distance, the peculiar sound of water flowing and lapping against something quite close. Then there was music drifting down from somewhere overhead – a piano concerto, delicate and harmonious in cadence.

Her heels made a clicking sound on the cobblestones as they continued to walk, tapping out a rhythm that seemed in consonance with the music. They turned right

231

again and then she became aware of high walls rising either side of her. The atmosphere was that of a more enclosed space, giving her reason to believe they were walking down a very narrow street lined with tall buildings.

'Almost there,' Cherry said after they had been walking for about ten minutes.

Marie breathed a sigh of relief. Her feet were starting to hurt and she kept wondering if anyone was watching the strange trio. How was it that this woman was walking along blindfolded in public? she imagined them asking themselves. She felt a light breeze catch the front of her coat and instinctively moved her hand to prevent too much from being revealed, but the hands under her elbows held her fast.

She blushed as the breeze swirled up her naked thighs and caressed her sex. Her clitoris still pulsed gently from the orgasm she had recently experienced and she could feel the wetness her own body had created drying on her inner thighs.

There was no opportunity to consider her embarrassment. They were turning left. Now Cherry was telling her they were standing at the foot of a flight of stairs. Marie raised her right foot and felt tentatively for the step.

'I am going to guide you,' Cherry said, squeezing past her, 'because the staircase is too narrow for more than one person. The master will be right behind you to catch you if you fall.' She chuckled softly and Marie imagined that the master had just given Cherry some sort of look of affirmation, perhaps a wink.

Putting out her hands to her sides Marie felt rough, damp stone under her flat palms. It was so cold that she felt the chill run right up her arms. She shivered. Then suddenly Cherry was telling her that they had reached the top of the staircase. There was a loud banging sound. A heavy knocker, Marie deduced, falling against solid wood. The knocker creaked as it was raised and thumped heavily as it hit the door. Once, twice, three times. Then there was a moment's silence, followed by a much louder creaking sound.

Warm air wafted over Marie as the door was opened. As she allowed herself to be guided through the door, she felt herself being enveloped by the warmth. The chill left her instantly, to be replaced by the soft prickling of perspiration oozing from her pores. All at once she felt fingers tugging at her belt again. Oh, no, she moaned inside her head. She could hear other voices surrounding them – male and female – and realised that her naked body was about to be revealed to a room full of strangers.

'Stop,' she said, wrapping her arms tightly around herself.

Cherry made a soft tutting sound. 'Do not be shy,' she said. 'You know you are beautiful. Why not share that beauty?'

'Because I don't know who any of you are,' Marie replied, still hugging the coat fiercely around herself. 'You could be a bunch of perverts for all I know.'

A small burst of laughter greeted Marie's words. She turned her head this way and that, trying in vain to estimate how many people might be surrounding her. She reached up, about to remove the mask, but a familiar voice stopped her hand in mid air.

'Please don't. Not yet.'

'Lawrie?' Marie said. There was no mistaking the gentle Scots burr.

His voice was filled with humour as he replied softly, 'Ah, you guessed, spoilsport.'

All at once Marie felt most of her tension dissolve. 'What's going on?' she asked, making no further attempt to remove the mask.

'A pleasurable encounter for you, my love,' Lawrie said. 'If you must know, we're in Venice, at the Villa da Vivacittà. It belongs to a couple of distant relatives of mine, the Count and Countess Sansone.'

'How grand,' Marie murmured. 'You didn't tell me you were related to royalty.'

She felt Lawrie's warm breath on her ear as he whispered, 'I'm not, they paid for the title.'

Marie laughed then. Partly out of amusement but mostly out of relief.

'Can I take this blindfold off now?' she asked, adding in a sardonic tone, 'master.'

'What, and spoil the rest of your fun?' Lawrie said. 'I think not, young lady.'

Feeling much more lighthearted now, Marie allowed him to guide her to a sofa where she sat and accepted a glass of champagne. She still insisted on keeping her coat on but was happy to remove her shoes and rub the sore soles of her feet on the deep pile carpet.

'I think you need another foot massage,' Lawrie said and in the next moment Marie felt her left foot being grasped by his capable hands.

His thumbs massaged the balls of her feet and Marie relaxed back into the soft upholstery, sighing luxuriously as she sipped her champagne.

'This is the life,' she commented as he started on her other foot.

'This is nothing,' Lawrie said. 'You've got a lot more pleasure to come yet.'

Around them, it sounded as though a party was in full swing. There were many voices chattering incomprehensibly in Italian, the soft tinkle of piano music and the slightly louder chinking of crystal. As far as Marie was concerned, she and Lawrie might as well have been cast away on a desert island. All that existed for her right at that moment was the oasis of pure joy she felt at being with him again and the pleasurable sensation of his hands caressing her feet.

Several glasses of champagne and a thorough foot massage later, Marie was feeling more relaxed than she had felt for ages. Just for a moment she wondered how late it was. Although time seemed largely meaningless, she realised, to someone who was cloaked in blackness and had all responsibility removed.

'Carla,' she murmured, slurring her words slightly. 'Imola.'

'Don't worry about any of that,' Lawrie assured her, his voice close to her ear. 'Carla knows you're here with me. We're going to Imola sometime tomorrow. She's already agreed to go on ahead with her brother.'

Feeling relieved, Marie sighed and allowed her head to drop back, resting it on Lawrie's arm.

'Don't get too comfortable,' he warned her lightly, 'we're going to move in a minute.'

Marie glanced blindly sideways. 'Where to?' she asked.

'Another room,' Lawrie replied, sounding a little mysterious. 'You don't think I'm going to let your pleasure end yet, do you? This is just a wee interval.'

'You sound so Scottish,' she murmured, giggling, 'I like that.'

'I like you, Amber,' he said, stressing her pseudonym. 'Well, you never know who might be listening,' he said in answer to her unasked question. 'Even walls have ears, especially old Italian ones.'

Wallowing in happiness and champagne, all she could manage in response was a lopsided smile.

'All right, come on, sweetheart,' Lawrie said firmly. He moved forward and grabbed her hand, pulling her to her feet. 'That's enough chat,' he added.

Marie sensed that the people populating the room were clearing a path for them as Lawrie led her. The sound of footsteps behind them as they took a winding route that eventually led them down some more stone steps told her that a number of the crowd were following them. She tried to estimate how many but gave up. She heard the creaking of another door and then there were more steps leading down.

For a moment she thought they were outside again but the constant air temperature told her differently. It was too warm. Far too warm for comfort, really. This time when Lawrie untied her coat and began to slip it from her shoulders she didn't try to stop him. Around her she heard a few murmurs of approval. '*Bella,*' some of them said, one female voice adding, '*Rasato, que attraente!*'

'That's my cousin, Alexia,' Lawrie supplied for her. 'She was just admiring your shaven cunt.'

Marie gasped. Even though Lawrie's comment had been whispered, that one lewd word seemed to echo around her. She swayed, feeling faint as a wave of lust washed over her.

Lawrie's hands gripped her waist. 'Come on now, my love,' he said gently.

She allowed him to lead her, his arm around her waist. The floor beneath her bare feet was of flagstones and she sensed from the acoustics that the walls were also made of bare stone.

'Are we in a cellar?' she asked.

'At one time it was a cellar,' Lawrie said. 'Now my cousin Alexa puts it to much better use.'

As Marie felt Lawrie drawing her arms up above her head and enclosing her wrists with leather cuffs, she realised that they were in some sort of dungeon.

'I'm not submissive,' she protested, hearing the familiar sound of leather cutting the air beside her. 'Is that a tawse?'

'You are and it is,' Lawrie affirmed.

Marie shook her head vehemently. 'No, I'm not. I'm – ' She broke off, gasping as the tawse whistled through the air and slapped against her bare buttocks.

It took a few moments for the sting to register but before she could protest, the tawse smacked against the backs of her thighs. In the next instant a hand seemed to come out of nowhere and slap her breasts. Marie gasped, straining against the wrist cuffs and against the realisation that she was starting to enjoy the treatment she was receiving. Giving in to the situation she gradually became aware that a rhythm seemed to form of its own accord: smack, slap, smack, slap.

She turned her head this way and that, wondering who was chastising her. Her breasts, buttocks and thighs felt as though they were on fire – burning, stinging, glowing so warmly that the heat quickly spread through the rest of her body. Her nipples felt swollen and her bottom incredibly sore. Yet the desire that flooded her was like nothing she had ever experienced. It was mesmerising: a purple haze of pure lasciviousness. Nothing could stem the flow of her need for carnal gratification.

'*Stupendos senos!*' the voice that Marie had now come to recognise as Alexa's exclaimed.

In the next moment a pair of slender hands covered her breasts. Marie gasped, the fingers wore many rings, which she could feel pressing into her flesh. Her nipples seemed to scream silently with physical craving as the fingertips toyed with them, stroking then pinching firmly.

'No,' she moaned, feeling helpless in the grip of her own lust. Heat swept through her again, filling her pelvis and melting her insides so that moisture began to run from her vagina in a steady trickle.

'No?' Lawrie's tone was questioning as one of his hands stroked her stinging buttocks and the other hand snaked around her hip and between her legs. His fingers began to stroke her vulva. 'No?' he asked again.

For once Marie was grateful that her arms were suspended. Her body seemed to sag under the weight of her desire. Lawrie's fingers were stroking her clitoris deftly, sliding its little cowl of skin back and forth across the sensitive tip. Marie felt her legs trembling. Her whole body felt liquid, as though her bones had dissolved.

Somewhere along the line it had ceased to matter to her that she had an audience. If anything, the knowledge only served to magnify the erotic charge she felt as her body wantonly responded to the indecent caresses it received. In the next moment she came with a force that surprised even herself. She churned her hips frantically, grinding her sex lewdly against Lawrie's fingertips, while all the time Alexa's fingers played with the distended buds of her nipples. As she groaned and gave a final shudder a small ripple of applause ran around the cavernous room, echoing off the walls.

Marie let her head fall forward limply. It might have looked as though she felt shamed by what she had experienced but inside Marie felt only elation and profound relief.

'É il mio turno,' Alexa declared a moment later, as the final delicious waves of Marie's orgasm ebbed away.

Her fingertips released their grip on Marie's nipples and she stroked her hands across Marie's breasts and over her shoulders, giving them a brief squeeze, as though of approval.

'My cousin wants her turn,' Lawrie said to Marie.

She nodded and felt him soothe her sore nipples for a moment with his tongue before sliding his hands up her left arm and releasing her wrist from its restraint. After he had unfastened the other cuff, Marie found herself automatically rubbing her wrists, although the leather had been soft on the inside and had not chafed her skin at all.

'May I take the blindfold off now?' she asked him. 'I would really like to watch.' She sensed Lawrie smiling.

'Of course,' he said.

In a moment the bond was released from around her eyes and she shut them quickly. Then she opened them gradually, blinking rapidly, allowing her eyes to become accustomed to the light again. Thankfully the lighting inside the low-ceilinged room was dim. The lighting that did exist was supplied by a single row of downlighters set into the suspended ceiling and a few groups of flickering beeswax candles here and there.

Glancing quickly around, Marie realised that her earlier assumption had been correct. Her surroundings were very similar to Chantal's dungeon, though not nearly as professionally equipped. Only a set of stocks and the cuffs suspended by thick silver chains which hung from a pipe that ran across the width of the stone-walled room furnished it. Otherwise it was bare save for four wide divan couches which sat in each corner. These were covered with gold velvet and were occupied by half a dozen couples, all in evening dress. Marie sank down gratefully on to the end of one of the divans, next to a swarthy man with thick, black hair that was just greying at the temples.

Marie noticed he gave her an interested glance as she sat down but she ignored him, glancing across him instead to his companion. On the other side of him sat a woman in a red taffeta evening gown. She had dark hair shot through with red which was drawn back in an elegant chignon. Her features were pointed, her bone structure almost birdlike in its delicacy. And she wore diamonds around her slender neck, her left wrist and in each earlobe. Marie thought every one present looked a little incongruous to be seated in a dungeon. But she still felt somewhat shell-shocked by her recent experience and was far too interested in watching Alexa being secured by the wrist cuffs to make any comment.

In contrast to the woman in red, Lawrie's cousin Alexa was a statuesque woman. Shamelessly naked, she had smooth olive toned skin and was ever so slightly over-weight. Her breasts were pendulous – the areolae reminding Marie of large chocolate buttons – and her hips were generously rounded. At the apex of her thighs a thick bush of black hair concealed her sex and the same dark hair sprouted from her armpits. The hair on her head was a few shades lighter – more dark brown than black – and hung around her shoulders in rippling waves. Marie estimated her age at somewhere in her mid to late thirties.

As Lawrie fastened the wrist cuffs a much smaller woman dressed in leather trousers and a fine mesh top, all in black, stood beside him. Marie guessed she was about a decade younger than Alexa but the two women were very similar facially. Suddenly the young woman said something to Lawrie in Italian and Marie realised that she must be Cherry. She recognised the voice instantly; if she needed any further confirmation, the musical laugh that followed Lawrie's reply was enough.

As soon as Alexa was firmly restrained, the man and woman seated beside Marie stood up. The man walked over to the wall on which hung a rack of whips, canes and tawses. He picked up a cane and began slapping it upon his outstretched palm, his expression remaining implacable as the bamboo connected with his flesh. The woman in the red dress reached out and selected a pair of nipple clamps which were joined by a thin gold chain.

Marie gasped. Nipple clamps hurt. She knew that, not just from personal experience but from the comments she had received from her own slaves while she was Portia.

'My cousin is used to a lot of pain,' Lawrie said to Marie, as he sat down on the divan. He pulled her against him, cradling her naked body in his arms. 'Now it's our turn to rest and simply enjoy the show.'

'OK,' Marie agreed relaxing against him. She watched Cherry, who still stood beside Alexa. 'Is Cherry a relative of yours as well?' she asked.

Lawrie nodded. 'Another cousin. Alexa's younger sister, in fact.' He paused to drop a kiss on her bare shoulder. 'Now shush,' he said, 'there'll be plenty of time for talking later. For now just watch.'

Glancing up at his handsome face for just a moment, Marie smiled at him, then turned her head to watch the entertainment.

The woman in red was just fixing the nipple clamps to Alexa and Marie couldn't help noticing that Alexa uttered not a sound. Nor did she allow her enigmatic expression to falter when the man began to strike her buttocks and thighs with the cane. Cherry's rôle, Marie observed, seemed to be that of voyeur cum aide. She watched intently then inspected the lines that criss-crossed Alexa's flesh when the man stopped beating her for a moment.

Everyone in the room remained totally silent. Marie glanced around. They seemed totally absorbed in the scene taking place in front of them, though some were stroking themselves quite shamelessly through their clothes. Eventually, after the man had swapped the cane for a crop and delivered six hard swipes to Alexa's quivering bottom, there was a brief pause. The whole room seemed to be holding its breath, wondering what was going to happen next. Cherry inspected her sister's flesh once again and then nodded. As far as Marie could tell, it seemed to be a cue. All at once the woman in the red dress dropped to her knees and burrowed her face into Alexa's bush.

Only then did the older woman make a sound. It was somewhere between a wail and a whimper. With her crimson dress billowing around her, the kneeling woman reached out. Her fingers stroked Alexa's thighs for a moment then slid inwards to part her labia. As she did so she sat back a little, allowing the small audience a glimpse of moist red flesh, her fingertips parting the swollen folds even more. Glancing up at her companion who stood motionless beside Alexa, she licked her lips deliberately. He nodded, and in the next moment she stuck out her tongue and waggled it lewdly. A ripple of delighted laughter ran around the room.

Marie gripped Lawrie's knee, realising what was going to happen next. She felt her stomach contract as the woman in red moved forward again and began to lathe Alexa's exposed inner labia with long, assured strokes. Marie realised she was holding her own breath as she watched the erotic scene taking place in front of her. Her stomach was knotted once again with desire as she imagined herself in Alexa's place. She saw Alexa throw her head back, her voluptuous body writhing as the other woman continued to stimulate her with her tongue.

'Oh, God!' Marie gasped as Alexa began to moan.

Her eyes flickered between the dark head working diligently between Alexa's thighs and the ecstatic expression on the older woman's face. She could feel the warmth of arousal sweeping over her again and, only half aware of what she was doing, slipped a hand between her thighs, seeking out the pulsating bud of her own clitoris. She rubbed as she watched, feeling the delicious waves of eroticism overtake her again.

Lawrie sat perfectly still, though when Marie glanced sideways at him through heavy-lidded eyes, she noticed he had unzipped his trousers and was rubbing his cock.

Leaning over him, she nudged his hand out of the way and took his hardness in her mouth. She welcomed the rod of throbbing flesh between her lips as though it were the greatest delicacy. And, to her, it was. Delicious, fabulous, the most wonderful cock she had ever tasted. Rimming the plum-like glans with her lips, she allowed her tongue to flutter back and forth like a butterfly's wings down the length of his stem.

Lawrie groaned and clutched at the back of her head, urging his penis deeper into her mouth. Relaxing her throat, Marie took as much of him as she could, all the time mouthing him while one hand burrowed into his trousers to cup his balls. Within moments she could feel that he was about to come.

To her surprise he pulled her head back, masturbating himself furiously until he ejaculated over her naked breasts.

Smiling with satisfaction, Marie massaged his pleasure gift into her straining orbs. Then she flicked out her tongue and lapped at a tiny drop of fluid which still lingered on the tip of his cock.

Later, she would reflect that this was one of the best evenings she had ever spent with Lawrie – if not the best. Then she realised, with a wry laugh, that the same thought seemed to occur to her every time. With Lawrie it just seemed to get better and better.

Chapter Sixteen

*T*he view from the third floor balcony of the Villa
Vivacittà was magical. Marie turned her head this
way and that to take in the crenellated vista of tightly
packed buildings whose dilapidated, lichen-stained
walls seemed to be virtually toppling into the broad
canals below. On the murky green water of the canal
that flowed below the balcony two gondolas passed each
other. Their occupants – one a business suited male and
the other a smartly dressed female in a broad-brimmed
hat – turned their heads and nodded politely to each
other as they floated past in ancient splendour.

Suddenly, a motor launch disturbed the tranquil scene.
In comparison to the stately gondolas it seemed like a
drunken young hooligan as it wove from side to side,
the prow leaping clear of the water. As it cut between
the gondolas it sprayed the occupants, causing one of
the gondoliers, who was traditionally clad in black
trousers and a black and white striped top, to shake his
fist angrily. Marie smiled to herself; road hogs were
everywhere it seemed, even on the canals of Venice.

Turning away from the scene she leant back against
the wall of the balcony and allowed her gaze to travel
instead through the narrow French doors which opened
out on to it. In the stark white bedroom beyond, on a

canopied four-poster swathed with cobwebs of fine muslin, Lawrie still slept.

Marie smiled softly as she noticed how his blond head made a profound dent in the mound of snowy white pillows beneath it. His lean body was partially covered by a thin white sheet – the temperature was too high for even the lightest blanket – and she could easily trace the exquisite lines of his body through the fine linen that lay draped over it. The top half of his chest was uncovered, his arms flung carelessly over his head, and one tanned leg escaped the sheet. Bent at the knee, it seemed to gleam under the shaft of golden sunlight cast over it through the open French windows.

As her glance skipped over Lawrie's lightly muscled thigh, Marie couldn't help allowing her gaze to come to rest on the intriguing mound at its apex. Through the thin sheet she could clearly see the outline of his penis. It was erect, she noticed. Shifting her glance to his face she saw the way his lips curved slightly and wondered if he was enjoying an erotic dream.

Certainly the night before had held a dreamlike quality. After several more of Alexa's guests had been chastised, they had all drunk some more champagne and a few of the guests had gone on to take their pleasure further in the cellar. Marie and Lawrie, however, had opted to escape to the privacy of their own room where they had made rapturous love until the small hours. As always, Marie had felt overcome with lust for Lawrie. And he for her, he had admitted several times during the sex-soaked night.

He told her he had started planning that evening's entertainment while they were still in Germany. When he left Monza he had not gone back to England at all but had made straight for Venice where he had enlisted the help of his cousins. They relished sexual adventure, he told her. So much so that Alexa and her husband, Guido – the man in the dress suit – had been eager to offer the use of their limousine and, furthermore, to organise the impromptu party on Lawrie's behalf.

'Oh, so *he* is Alexa's husband,' Marie had said, amazed. 'I thought he was with the woman in the red dress. They looked like a couple to me.'

Lawrie had laughed then. 'Well, they are in a way,' he said. 'She is his mistress. Another countess, no less.'

'And Alexa doesn't mind?' Marie was even more amazed.

'No,' Lawrie said, shaking his head, 'they don't believe in monogamy. Alexa has several lovers of her own.'

'Well!' Marie had flopped back on to the bed, suddenly feeling exhausted. 'Your relatives certainly know how to live.'

'I'll say,' Lawrie murmured, covering her with his hard, naked body. 'If you'll allow me, young lady, I'd like to demonstrate some of the things I've picked up over the years.'

And so they had gone on to make love, each taking it in turns to take on the more dominant rôle, sharing their erotic skills in unselfish abandonment.

Now, just the recollection made Marie's flesh tingle. That and the beguiling sight of Lawrie, enjoying the sleep of the not so innocent.

Coming in from the balcony, she padded back over the cool marble floor to climb on to the bed. As she drew back the sheet she allowed her eyes to feast on the glory of Lawrie's naked body for a moment before climbing astride him. Then she felt for his cock, and with a gentle sigh of satisfaction, slipped it inside her.

They finally left the Villa by early evening. This time Alexa and Guido had not only insisted Lawrie and Marie use their limousine to drive to the airport but had also arranged for their private jet to fly them down the coast to Imola.

'God, this is more luxury than I ever thought possible,' Marie said as she gazed down through the tiny window of the aircraft at the blanket of fluffy white cloud beneath them. She sipped from a flute of champagne and glanced sideways at Lawrie. 'I'm scared I might get used to all this. Then it'll be back to boring old reality.'

'By the sound of things, your life is far from boring,' Lawrie commented. 'What with all your different characters dodging creditors and playing the dominatrix, then racing a Porsche in your spare time.'

Marie laughed. 'No, all right, maybe not boring exactly,' she conceded, 'but there's nothing luxurious about it. It's mostly hard work.'

Lawrie reclined back against the padded white leather seat and draped his arm around her shoulders. 'If you win the Championship your money worries will be over.'

'*If* I win,' Marie said, sounding glum all of a sudden. 'There are no guarantees.'

'Nothing in life is guaranteed,' Lawrie pointed out sagely, 'not even life itself.'

Marie turned her head to look at him, her lips curving into a smile. 'You wise old thing, you,' she said.

'Less of the old, thank you very much,' Lawrie countered.

All at once he took her by surprise, taking the glass from her hand, setting it down and then lunging at her. Feeling for the sensitive spot beneath her ribs, he began to tickle her. The tickles turned to caresses and the caresses to something way beyond Marie's expectations for the flight. By the time they landed at a private airfield about ten miles from the race track, she and Lawrie had joined the Mile High Club three times over.

The track at Imola, which is just outside Bologna in Northern Italy, is just over three miles long and follows a sinuous course of fast straights punctuated by deceptively dangerous chicanes and a couple of tight corners. Marie had only raced there once before and remembered that at the time she had likened it to a rollercoaster ride – reckless curves which called for hard braking, followed by hair-raising plunges down the straights.

Now, as she carried out her customary recce of the track, she found her stomach knotting with dread.

Lawrie could so easily take her on any of these bends, she found herself thinking. As far as she could tell, even though her car was in prime condition, there was nothing at all to stop Lawrie taking the win.

'Hey, what's the glum face for?' Carla greeted her as she finally wandered back into the pits. Unlike Marie, Carla looked as though she was bursting with optimistic enthusiasm.

'I'm worried that Lawrie's going to win this championship,' she admitted bluntly, running her hand over the wing of her car.

'That's balls!' Carla said in a vehement tone, 'Why should he win when you've got everything going for you?'

'Everything apart from a brand new car,' Marie pointed out.

Carla shook her head and patted the bonnet of the Porsche. 'This car is like brand new,' she said. 'Every part on it is pristine.'

'Even so, Lawrie managed to beat me last time,' Marie insisted stubbornly. She paused to glance over the pit wall at the track. 'Look at all those curves,' she said, waving her arm expansively. 'I'm never going to be able to hold him off for twenty laps.'

'Rubbish!' Her friend exclaimed with a look of disbelief. 'I can't believe I'm hearing this. You've won practically every other race. What is the matter with you?'

Marie glanced down at the ground and said in a small voice, 'This is so important, Carla. If I don't win – '

'Right, that's enough,' Carla interrupted her and held up her hand. 'Stop right there. Do you think the boys and I have slogged our guts out all season to hear you whingeing on like this? Get a grip, woman, for Christ's sake.'

Pursing her lips, Marie raised her eyes to meet Carla's implacable gaze and gradually her face softened into a sheepish grin.

'OK,' she conceded, 'I'll consider my wrists well and truly slapped.' She paused and rubbed her hands together, glancing at the car. 'Now I think it's time I went and got changed, then took this little beauty out for a test drive.'

By the time Marie drove into the pits an hour or so later, she was ready to admit that the Porsche really was running extremely well. Always good at hugging the corners, even at high speeds, it seemed determined not to let her down no matter what treatment she gave it. And the track was nice and dry and sticky. Perfect conditions for a winning drive.

Later that afternoon, after she had qualified in pole position with a good thirty second advantage over the next fastest car, which was Lawrie's, Marie decided to call it a day and relax instead in the press lounge. With only ten minutes of the qualifying session left to go, she was seated directly behind the glass wall which overlooked the pits and the track beyond, watching some of the other drivers trying in vain to improve on her time. She had her feet up on the steel tubing that ran across the bottom of the glass in front of her and kept shifting her gaze from the track itself to the monitor above her head. Everyone seemed to be doing fairly well but she had noticed that, during the last couple of laps, Lawrie's car had been losing speed.

'I'd say he's losing compression,' Carla said as she took the seat beside Marie.

They watched as Lawrie's car seemed to struggle around a particularly sharp bend known as *Tosa* and then hardly looked to pick up any speed at all along the ensuing straight. In the bottom left hand corner of the monitor the timing display showed his speed to be down to 76 miles per hour.

'That's dreadful,' Marie observed, sounding concerned rather than elated. 'A tractor could overtake him now.'

The two young women knew Marie's statement was something of an exaggeration but the situation did look dire. As they kept their eyes glued to the red figures displayed on the corner of the screen they watched Lawrie's speed drop consistently lower and lower. He snaked slowly around *Acque Minerale* and then curved *Rivazza* at a speed that made him look as though he was driving a milk float. This was followed by a snail's pace drive along the final straight.

When he finally pulled off the track into the pits a couple of minutes later Carla and Marie leant forward to watch the purple Porsche draw to a halt beneath them. As Lawrie emerged from his car they could tell by his sagging shoulders and the way he shook his head that he was hopelessly disappointed.

About half an hour later, when the final placings for the following day's race had been announced, he joined Marie and Carla in the press lounge. Without asking if they wanted anything, he got three cups of coffee from the vending machine and then beckoned them over to a table.

As she sat down Marie patted his hand consolingly. She noticed his usual relaxed expression looked tight and drawn, his blond eyebrows knotting in frustration.

'I just don't understand it,' he said. 'There doesn't seem to be any rhyme or reason why the car should start playing up now.'

'What did your crew have to say?' Carla asked.

Lawrie shrugged. 'They haven't given me a diagnosis yet.' Suddenly he slapped his palm on the table, startling both Carla and Marie and spilling some of their coffee in the process. 'I sometimes wonder if I'd be better off employing a bunch of chimpanzees to take care of my car.'

Marie and Carla exchanged wary glances.

'It's probably just something stupid,' Marie said placatingly. 'You know how these things go. One minute the car's running perfectly and the next – '

'The next it's a crock of shit,' Lawrie cut in. Uncharacteristically, he swore quietly under his breath, then put his head in his hands. A moment later he raised his head and gazed sorrowfully at Marie. 'Looks like you've already won the Championship,' he said.

Instead of elation, Marie felt her heart go out to him.

Only another racer could understand the way Lawrie must have been feeling right at that moment.

'Let Carla have a look at your car,' she suggested, surprising herself. She glanced at her friend, noting her look of amazement. Marie nodded to her silently, then added, 'Would you mind, Carla? It couldn't hurt.'

Carla shrugged and gave Marie a look as if to say, 'Are you sure?'

Again Marie nodded. She glanced at Lawrie. 'Do you think your crew would mind?'

'Too bloody bad if they do,' he said. For a long moment he stared hard at Marie, then his expression softened. He reached out and took her hand. Raising it to his lips he kissed the back of it. 'You don't have to do this, you know,' he murmured. 'I realise how much winning the Championship means to you. With me out of the running you'd be practically home and dry.'

'I know,' Marie said, smiling softly.

Her eyes locked with his and at that moment she knew that winning the Championship by default would be no win at all.

They were interrupted by Carla pointedly clearing her throat.

'Look,' she said as she pushed back her chair and stood up, 'if you two don't mind, I'll go and look at Lawrie's car now. I'm going out tonight so I want to get back to the hotel and get changed out of these.' She pulled disparagingly at the front of her overalls.

'Of course,' Lawrie said, dropping Marie's hand and also standing up. 'I'll take you down there and introduce you to my crew chief.' He glanced at Marie. 'Are you coming?'

Marie shook her head. 'No, not unless you particularly want me there. I thought I'd go back to the hotel and take a nap. These past few days have been quite exhausting one way and another.' She cast a knowing look at Lawrie who winked at her.

'No problem,' he said. 'Tell you what.' He paused and glanced at his watch. 'Whether Carla manages to diagnose the problem or not, how about I meet you in the hotel bar at nine?'

Marie smiled. 'OK,' she said, 'I'll look forward to it.' Then as Lawrie glanced away she turned to Carla and gave her friend a pat on the shoulder and muttered, 'Thanks.'

Carla smiled at Marie and gave another of her renowned shrugs.

'What are friends for?' she said before adding, 'You know I'll do my best with his car. I only hope you don't regret it afterwards if I manage to solve the problem.'

'I won't,' Marie assured her, hoping it was true.

As she watched her friend and lover walk off together she found herself marvelling at the sudden change in her thinking. It was more than a question of being sporting and doing the right thing. She wanted to compete against Lawrie on equal terms. Then, if she still won the Championship, she would know beyond a shadow of a doubt that Porsche racing would be the way she wanted to spend – if not the rest of her life – at least the foreseeable future.

The other option hung in mid air. As far as Marie was concerned there wasn't an option. Tomorrow she had to win. That was all there was to it.

They met in the bar at nine as agreed. Marie could see instantly by the expression on Lawrie's face and the way he had resumed his usual confident gait that Carla had proved once again what a brilliant mechanic she was.

'Your friend is amazing,' Lawrie said the moment he sat down. 'I have never met a mechanic like her.'

Marie smiled inwardly. Most men would have said they had never met a *woman* like Carla. It just went to show, she thought, how Lawrie could never be considered most men.

'What was the problem?' she asked.

Lawrie shook his head as he picked up his drink. 'I've no idea,' he said. 'Something to do with the head, I think

251

she said. I'm no mechanic but, whatever it was, she had the right parts and the knowhow to fix it.'

'So you're all set for tomorrow, then?'

Marie kept her voice light but inside she felt a knot of pre-race anxiety and anticipation tighten. She swallowed her drink hastily, her gaze downcast. Her fingers were wrapped around the tumbler of scotch and soda and were gripping the glass far more tightly than she realised. When she glanced up she noticed Lawrie was studying her closely.

'What?' she asked, staring him straight in the eye. She watched as a warm smile spread across his face.

Then he reached out, prised her fingers away from the glass and held her hands lightly in his own. He raised each hand to his lips, his tongue lightly travelling across the knuckles.

'There's no need to be nervous,' he said, his gaze holding hers.

She tried to shrug. His hands still grasped hers lightly but firmly and she felt herself similarly in the grip of his keen grey-eyed gaze.

'Don't try and tell me you're not,' he went on, 'I know you well enough by now – '

'I hope you're not planning to let me win,' Marie interrupted forcefully.

The moment the words had left her mouth she was aghast. Why was it that the thing which was uppermost on her mind should burst out verbally when she least wanted it to?

Relaxing back in his chair slightly, Lawrie laughed. His grip on her hands relaxed. Seizing her chance, Marie snatched her hands away and curled them into fists in her lap. For once his easy-going manner annoyed her and she had to remind herself that it had been her idea for Carla to fix his car, thereby putting him firmly back in competition with her.

'There is absolutely no chance of me letting you win,' Lawrie said, shaking his head. His eyes sparkled with amusement and creased up at the corners where his smile travelled up from his mouth to meet them. 'I might like you a whole damn lot. I might fancy the knickers off you. I might even think you're the greatest fuck I've ever had. But I would never, not under any circumstances, dream of letting you beat me. When we get out there on that track tomorrow it'll be every man – ' he paused to nod at her, ' – or woman, for themselves.'

Marie sat for a moment absorbing his words. Gradually she felt the tension leave her body and she uncurled her fingers. Raising one hand to her Amber wig she played lightly with a few strands of hair, rubbing them between her fingers.

'Am I really the greatest fuck you've ever had?' she said eventually.

She noticed Lawrie's smile grow broader and felt her body shift gear. Now she was back in seductress mode. She licked her lips and cocked her head, waiting for his reply.

'You are,' he said simply, 'although I suppose I shouldn't have told you that because now you'll take advantage of me.'

Marie felt her lips curve and her breasts swell beneath the black silk blouse she was wearing. 'Oh, you can count on that,' she said huskily. 'In fact, I intend to take advantage of you right now.' She stood up and held out her hand to him. 'Come on, let's go up to your room and I'll prove just how ruthless I can be.'

The next day dawned bright and clear. Although it was only seven in the morning the temperature was already nudging the eighties. Marie didn't need to be at the track until midday but nevertheless had been in two minds about whether to go there early, or stay at the hotel. In the end Carla and Lawrie ganged up on her, persuading her that she would feel much more relaxed if she spent the morning swimming and sunbathing rather than mooching around the pits.

'I'm staying here at any rate,' Carla insisted, popping a piece of *pain au chocolat* into her mouth and munching on it. 'If I go to the track, I'll only start fiddling around with the car and it doesn't need it.'

'Nor does mine, thanks to you,' Lawrie said, flashing Carla a warm smile.

Marie licked a few flakes of golden pastry from her fingers and glanced from one to the other. It made her feel glad inside to know that she was going to compete with Lawrie on equal terms. If Carla hadn't been able to fix his car, she thought, she would have always looked back on this day with a tinge of regret. As it was, she was looking forward to the final of the Championship.

Tony Bertorelli stopped by their table, which sat on the patio outside the hotel restaurant, and gave Marie an encouraging hug. His huge arm wrapped around her shoulders and almost squeezed the breath out of her lungs.

'Just wanna wish you good luck, honey,' he drawled. 'I hope you won't feel too badly if I win.'

'*If* you win,' Marie said, giving him a sardonic smile. 'I wouldn't bank on it.' She winced as Carla gave her a sharp kick under the table. 'Sorry,' she added, 'I suppose I just get a bit uptight before a race.'

'Sure, don't we all, honey,' Tony said, grinning broadly. 'Well, as I said, good luck.'

Marie smiled back at him. 'Yes, good luck yourself.' She continued to smile as she watched him walk away. Then she turned to Carla and responded to the kick with, 'That bloody well hurt, you bitch.'

Carla looked unabashed.

Lawrie glanced from one to the other, trying not to laugh at the way they conducted their friendship. Women! he thought in his head.

Aloud he said, 'Well, if you don't mind, ladies, I'm going to go and finish packing.' Using his hands on the arms of his chair he pushed himself up. Then he stooped to plant a kiss on the top of Marie's head and asked, 'Shall I meet you by the pool?'

She looked up at him and pulled the ends of her hair ruefully. Because the hotel was swarming with racers and journalists she had no option but to wear her Amber wig at all times in public.

'I daren't swim in this,' she said. 'I don't know if it would stay on.'

'How about a cap?' Carla suggested. 'I noticed they sell them in the hotel shop.'

Marie thought about it for a moment, then nodded, her ready smile brightening her face. 'OK, I'll go and get one now,' she said. 'Are you coming, Carla?' She glanced at her friend.

'You bet,' Carla replied. 'I've been looking forward to getting into that pool ever since I arrived.'

The water in the round pool glistened a deep, inviting blue. It was edged by white paving stones which in turn were encircled by a small sun trap garden. About a dozen or so blue and white striped sunloungers were dotted about. Marie pulled three of them close to the edge of the pool, then put her towel and sunglasses down on one of them. Turning around she walked to the edge of the pool and simply stood there, watching the way the sun glinted enticingly off the surface for a moment before diving in.

The shock as she hit the water almost took her breath away. In contrast to the blasting heat of the air temperature, the water was icy cold. Striking out for the opposite end of the pool, Marie executed a fast crawl. She turned, swum back, and had completed ten lengths by the time Carla and Lawrie appeared. Swimming lazily over to the edge of the pool, she rested her forearms on the flagstones and grinned up at them.

'Come on in, the water's lovely,' she said.

The wicked imp that dwelt inside her encouraged her to smile, while forcing her not to give anything away by shivering. She noticed, with an inner flicker of glee, that her friends took her invitation at face value. The shock that registered on their faces as they surfaced from the water made it all worthwhile.

'You bitch!' Carla yelled, her teeth chattering. 'This water's bloody freezing.'

Marie smiled sweetly back. 'You'll get used to it,' she said.

All at once she gasped as she felt strong hands gripping her shins. They dragged her down further and further until she was fully submerged. Twisting in their grasp, Marie noticed that it was Lawrie who held her fast. She kicked out wildly and, as he let go of her legs, rose quickly to the surface spluttering and gasping for breath.

He rose too, grinning at her. 'Serves you right,' he joked. 'I ought to give you a good spanking for tricking us like that.'

Straight away, Marie felt her body become warm despite the water's temperature.

'Bastard,' she murmured, allowing her body to float towards him.

She stopped in the circle of his arms. A certain familiar hardness pressed into her belly and she wrapped her legs around his hips, deliberately grinding herself against him.

'Oi, stop that. Frustrated woman present!' Carla called out to them.

Marie and Lawrie turned their heads simultaneously and grinned at Carla as she rose dripping from the pool. She was wearing a white one-piece costume that showed off her golden tan and curvaceous figure to perfection. Glancing back at Lawrie, Marie couldn't help noticing the look of interest on his face.

'Back off, buster,' she muttered to him. 'Don't you go trying to poach my crew chief.'

'As if I would,' he said, giving Marie a look of wide-eyed innocence. Rubbing his hard cock against her mons, he glanced over her shoulder. 'Hey, Carla,' he shouted, 'fancy a threesome?' He let out a gasp of surprise as Marie punched him none too lightly in the stomach. 'Sorry,' he said, 'I couldn't resist it.'

Marie raised one eyebrow archly. 'Well, see if you can

resist this then,' she said. With that she reached down, pulled the crotch of her bikini bottoms to one side and ground herself down on his cock.

As Lawrie started to move his hips instinctively, thrusting gently inside her, Marie turned her head. With relief she noticed that Carla had totally ignored Lawrie's suggestion and appeared to be dozing on one of the loungers. As they were as good as alone, Marie started to move her own hips, meeting Lawrie's thrusts with equal enthusiasm.

It wasn't easy, making love in the pool. Lawrie's feet kept slipping on the bottom and they had to gradually work themselves over to the side of the pool for support. Eventually though, Marie felt Lawrie's cock growing inside her and heard his breathing change to short, sharp gasps of pleasure. A few heroic thrusts later she felt him explode inside her, the warmth of his semen flooding her vagina.

'My poor darling,' he said a moment later as he slipped out of her, 'you didn't come.'

Marie shook her head, assuring him that it didn't matter, although in reality she felt desperate for release.

Lawrie gave her a long hard look. 'Do you think I would leave you high and dry?' he said. In the next moment he grasped her around the waist and lifted her easily, depositing her on the edge of the pool. Then he pulled down her bikini bottoms before she had chance to protest. 'Spread your legs,' he murmured, licking his lips suggestively.

With only the briefest glance round the tiny garden to make sure that no one apart from the sleeping Carla was around, Marie reclined back on her elbows and opened her legs wide enough for Lawrie's head to nestle between them. As she felt his tongue dabbing softly at her labia and insinuating between them to find the excited bud of her clitoris, she allowed her head to drop back. The warmth from the hot sun on her throat was as delicious as the fire between her legs. And Lawrie's tongue quickly stoked that fire, sending her mind and body spiralling into the black hole of erotic bliss.

Marie cried out as she came, her whole body shuddering. She hadn't realised she had been quite that tense. As she opened her eyes and raised her head, she noticed, with a flush of shame, that Carla was watching them openly. Thankfully, Marie thought as she pretended she hadn't seen Carla looking at them, her friend hadn't decided to take Lawrie up on his offer. Sharing her friend with Lawrie as a mechanic was one thing, sharing her as a sexual partner was something else. It was something she couldn't contemplate seriously, not even for a moment.

Later, as Marie and Lawrie enjoyed a warm shower together, Marie said, 'I hope Carla manages to find herself a horny guy tonight.'

As usual, a party was planned for after the race. This time it was going to be held at the track itself, in a huge marquee that was being especially erected for the event.

Lawrie murmured his agreement as he soaped Marie's shoulders. By the time he had reached the bottom of her spine he had made a decision. Tipping a little more shower gel on to his palm, he worked it into a creamy lather and began to soap Marie's bottom. He had to try extremely hard to restrain himself as his slippery hand swept around and around her taut, glistening buttocks.

'I've got an idea,' he confided in her, 'but it means we'll have to cut this shower short.

Marie pouted as she glanced over her shoulder at him. 'Why?' she asked him.

'Because I've got to make a telephone call,' he said. 'I think I know just the person to help Carla out in her moment of need. If she can't come up with the right horny guy for your friend I don't know who can.'

Smiling, Marie asked, 'Alexa?'

Lawrie grinned at her as he nodded. 'Alexa,' he said.

Chapter Seventeen

Marie stood by the pit wall, her eyes shielded from the glare of the sun by a pair of Gucci sunglasses. Before they had left the hotel, Lawrie had given her and Carla a pair each, by way of 'a wee thank you.' Now she was desperately trying to take her mind off the blinding heat by concentrating instead on her surroundings.

The vista looked like a work of art. Beyond the perimeter of the track, thickly wooded hills rose to meet white streaks of cloud which looked as though they had been daubed by a child's hand on to the startling blue backdrop of sky. Tall square houses with tobacco coloured roofs, their walls either cream or salmon pink, clustered together on the hillsides, forming the small town of Imola. Closer to the track, tall firs and spreading oaks pressed themselves against the wire netting that formed the official boundary, their foliage a palette of varied shades of green.

Inside the track the scene was more colourful still. Thousands of spectators filled the stands that lined the start straight. Everyone was dressed in bright colours, and those who were strolling around shielded themselves from the sun with huge technicolour umbrellas.

Within the hallowed area of the pits, anxious media people jostled with mechanics – each in the distictive livery of their respective teams – and the drivers themselves. Without exception the drivers were nervous. All wondered if their cars would be okay and if they could really last to the end of the race without suffering a breakage or, worse still, an accident of some kind. Many of the smokers among them produced a pack of cigarettes at this stage and all, without exception, longed for a stiff drink.

Added to the bright spectrum of colour was a cacophony of sound: cheerful shouts of greeting, or anxiously issued instructions; the latest in popular Italian music blaring from the track's sound system, and, of course, the omnipresent roar of powerful two point seven litre engines.

Despite her own trepidation Marie loved it all. As at every race meeting she felt suffused by sensation: the sights; the sounds; the way the air thrummed with expectancy; and, best of all, the combined aromas of petrol and engine oil – to her the most delicious concoction ever invented.

Feeling overpowered by the all-pervading heat, she pulled at the neckline of her racing overalls and the fireproof vest beneath and blew a thin stream of warm breath over her perspiring chest. She was so concerned about feeling hot that at first she didn't notice the dark head trying to peer down her cleavage.

'Laurent!' she exclaimed when she glanced up.

His dark eyes twinkled back at her mischievously. '*Buon giorno, cara,*' he said in an enviably good Italian accent. '*Come sta?*'

'*Molto bene, grazie,*' she replied, knowing she still sounded horribly English. She added with a smile, 'Is BB here?'

'In the VIP lounge downing Dom Perignon by the bucketful,' he said, tucking her hand into the crook of his arm. 'Why don't you come and join us?'

Marie shook her head. 'I'd love to but I'm driving,' she joked.

Then she sighed. There was nothing she would have

enjoyed more right at that moment than a glass of cold champagne. Instead, she invited Laurent to join her in her motor home for a glass of iced orange juice.

His petulant lips made a slight moue. 'I suppose I could always imagine it is a Buck's Fizz,' he said.

Ten minutes later, just as Marie and Laurent had sat down, tumblers in hand, Carla appeared through the doorway. A moment later Lawrie turned up.

'How are you feeling, sweetheart?' he said, sitting down next to Marie and taking her hand.

She turned her head and smiled at him. 'OK,' she answered, 'if you can call nervous as hell OK.'

'You'll be fine,' he assured her, raising her hand to his lips.

Apparently ignoring the presence of Laurent and Carla, he smoothed his thumbs over her knuckles, splaying her fingers. Then he lightly kissed the gaps in between them.

Marie felt a shiver of desire run from the sensitive web of skin at the base of each finger, the delicious sensation continuing up her arm and down her body to tantalise her sex. She saw the way Lawrie looked at her, his grey eyes knowing, and felt a couple of fresh streams of perspiration trickle down her cleavage and between her shoulder blades. This time the heat she was experiencing had nothing to do with the midday sun.

'How are *you* feeling?' she asked, trying to ignore her overwhelming desire to get rid of Carla and Laurent, rip off her constricting clothing and throw herself on top of Lawrie.

He pulled a wry face. 'Like you, OK,' he said, adding after a moment's hesitation, 'a bit nervous as well I suppose. But then that's only to be expected.'

Marie nodded and for the umpteenth time asked herself why she consistently put herself through this: the anxiety; the tension; the sheer terror.

Because she loved it, she answered herself. Because she felt as passionate about racing as she did about sex in general and almost as passionate as sex with Lawrie.

Stop it! Her mind urged. It was too bad that her body was starting to get ideas which were simply not practical right at that moment. Turning to face Lawrie properly, she wrapped her arms around his neck, her fingers delving into his hair as she pulled his face close to hers.

'Good luck,' she murmured as she kissed his brow, then his eyelids and the tip of his nose: 'may the best person win. And I really mean that,' she added forcibly before kissing him full on the mouth.

After Lawrie and the others had gone, giving her a few minutes alone to compose herself before she went out to her car, Marie realised she had meant what she said. She really did want the best person to win — whoever it might be.

Back in the pits a short while later, Marie was trying to kill the last frustrating quarter of an hour until she could get in her car. An exasperated Carla had shooed her away from the car, reminding her that the crew were perfectly able to check the tyre pressures without her help, thank you very much. With a petulant frown, Marie had wandered back over to the pit wall to resume her visual recce of the surroundings.

'Marie Gifford?'

The authority in the questioning voice made Marie jump. All her instincts told her this was not good. Feeling as though she were moving in slow motion, she turned. Behind her stood a man in a brown suit which looked ridiculously inappropriate, considering the surroundings and the heat. He was holding out a sheet of paper to her. Marie gazed blankly at him. He looked familiar but she couldn't place him. Then her gaze was drawn to the two uniformed *polizia* standing behind him.

'Marie Gifford?' The man said again. 'Or should I say Amber Barclay, or even Portia Lombardi?'

Marie felt herself reeling. Each name was an accusation. As much as the contemptuous expression in his eyes and the sneer on his lips.

'What? I – ' she stammered, uncharacteristically lost for words.

'Repossession order,' the brown-suited man continued mercilessly, thrusting the piece of paper into her hands. 'It's all in order. I just got it from the local magistrate this morning.'

Marie's eyes quickly scanned the sheet of paper. All the wording was in Italian but there was no mistaking the meaning of the word *RIAPPROPRIAZIONE* in bold capitals across the top, nor the registration number of her Porsche.

'No!' she cried.

Feeling her heart begin to pound, Marie crumpled the piece of paper in her hand and threw it on the ground. She was just about to stamp on it when she felt a restraining hand on her arm.

'Is there a problem here, Amber?'

Sounding more Scottish than ever, Lawrie spoke, his eyes narrowing as he glanced at the man who Marie now recognised. He was the one who had come to the flat when she had pretended to be Hippy Jane.

'They want to repossess my car,' she said, her voice hardly more than a strangled whisper.

'Is that so?' Lawrie glanced at the man again and one of the *polizia* spoke over the repossession agent's shoulder to Lawrie.

Despite her blind panic, Marie couldn't help feeling impressed by the calmly assured way Lawrie answered the police officer in his native tongue.

'They say you owe your bank a large amount of money and that they've been trying to track down this car for ages,' Lawrie explained to Marie.

'I know that,' she hissed back in an undertone. 'I told you all about it ages ago, remember?'

'Don't start getting het up with me,' Lawrie said firmly, 'I'm only telling you what's what. Now – ' he added, effectively shutting Marie up with a pointed look, 'you can't wriggle out of this one. They want you to either pay up or they take the car.'

'I can't. They can't – ' Marie began. Oh, God! she wailed inside her head. This was all like some terrible nightmare come to life. 'They are *not* taking the car,' she said stubbornly, 'at least not until I've had chance to win this race.'

'Forget it,' the man in the brown suit said, 'you've given us the run around long enough. Either hand over payment in full, or we take the car now. We at the bank don't take too kindly to people who play games with us. Did you really think for one moment we'd be fooled by a few cheap wigs and a silly accent?'

You were for almost a year, Marie wanted to retort. Instead, she said, as calmly as she could under the circumstances, 'How did you know I was here?'

To her annoyance the man gave a thin little laugh that was barely more than a wheeze.

'Some say there is no such thing as bad publicity,' he began, clearly enjoying being centre stage, 'but not in your case, Miss Gifford.'

The contemptuous way he stressed her name made Marie want to grasp him round his scraggy little neck and throttle him until his eyes popped.

'Go on,' she said through clenched teeth. Her hands formed fists by her sides.

'Well,' he continued, 'there was some piece in the sports pages about a Dutch magazine which had just signed up a British lady racing driver. They showed a photograph of you and the car. The registration number was clearly visible.'

Please God, just let it have been a head and shoulders shot, Marie prayed silently, remembering the studio shoot.

'What newspaper was it?' she asked aloud.

The man looked momentarily nonplused, then said, '*The Times*, I think. One of the broadsheets anyway.'

The relief Marie felt must have shown on her face because Lawrie drew her to one side.

'No nudie shots in *The Times*,' he said with only the

merest hint of humour. 'Now, Marie, what are you going to do about this?'

'Die,' she replied dramatically. Feeling wretched, she turned her face up to his and looked him squarely in the eye. 'I'll sort this out,' she said, 'you'd better get going.'

He gave her an apologetic smile. 'OK,' he murmured, stroking her hair gently. He looked torn by indecision, Marie noticed. 'Will you be all right?'

Thrusting out her chin defiantly, Marie nodded. 'I'll be fine,' she insisted. 'You go out there and win.'

As she watched Lawrie stride briskly away she immediately felt the loss of his support. All at once the fight seemed to drain out of her.

'Just give me a minute while I go and get my handbag,' she said to the repossession agent.

'Don't bother thinking you can write us a cheque,' he commented, with a further sneer. 'I know the state of your bank account, remember.' He paused to say something to one of the police officers, then turned his attention back to her. 'We'll be waiting by your car. Don't be too long; I daresay you'll be wanting to wave it goodbye.'

Bastard! Marie fumed as she stumbled blindly across the pits in the direction of her motor home. Tears of frustration and disappointment were running freely down her cheeks by this time but she hadn't wanted to give him the satisfaction of seeing her cry. For a few long minutes she sat in the motor home and wept as if her heart would break. There was no way out this time, no other place she could run and hide and no disguise which would save her.

Time to go and face up to it, Marie, she told herself. Standing up, she grabbed a wad of tissues from the box on the kitchen counter and blew her nose. Then she walked outside into the blistering heat. The repossession agent was right about one thing, the slimy little toad, she couldn't let her car go without seeing it for one last time.

* * *

The pit board showed that there were five minutes to go before the start of the race. Lawrie was there on the grid in third place, with Tony Bertorelli – his car all back in one piece again – in second. Moments later, the pole position car pulled into place beside and just in front of him.

'I'd love to be able to wish Lawrie good luck again,' Marie said to Carla.

'Don't panic, I'll see the message is passed on.' The assuring voice crackled as it came over the radio. 'How are you feeling?'

Marie laughed into the microphone. 'Nervous. Excited. God, I'll never be able to thank him enough. Do you think I should let him win?'

The expletives that Carla uttered in response could have turned the inside of Marie's car blue.

Glancing up to the mirror, Marie noticed that she was still grinning. And she couldn't help wondering how long it would take her to stop grinning, if at all. At that moment she felt as though she loved the whole world, even the horrible little man from the bank. But most especially Lawrie. Thank God he had bailed her out.

She recalled how less than ten minutes earlier, she had returned to the pits prepared to kiss goodbye to her beloved Porsche and her future in one fell swoop, only to find Lawrie handing the repossession agent a cheque.

'Pay me back when you can,' he had said to her, waving away her feeble protests.

It took her a while to recover from the shock.

'I could pay you in kind,' she had offered cheekily, her old spirit re-emerging. But Lawrie had just given her a wry grin and kissed her on the top of the head.

'Cash will do just fine,' he said, 'but I wouldn't say no to a spot of interest every now and then.'

Their shared laughter had been interrupted by the five-minute call for competitors to take their places on the grid.

Now, here she sat in the coveted pole position, watching the row of start lights intently and wondering if she could actually make the most of this chance she had been given. Lawrie had warned her not to give him any leeway, reminding her that if she won he would get the money she owed back in his bank account all the more quickly.

A moment later the lights changed to green. Pressing her foot down hard on the accelerator, Marie shot forward, putting herself firmly in front of Tony Bertorelli's car as she started the first of twenty laps – the rapid climb to the *Tambourella* chicane.

After all the panic and heartache of the season, the final race of the Championship was something of an anticlimax. Marie stuck to the racing line the whole time, fighting Tony off each time they drove up to the *Villeneuve* chicane and eventually, on the twelfth lap, losing him on the tight left-handed *Piratella* curve.

She heard Carla's unsporting cheer as his car went off and instantly became aware of Lawrie's car closing the gap. The purple and white car stuck to her bumper around the next three laps and, with only five more to go, seemed to increase the pressure.

Good old Lawrie, she thought, her smile concealed by her helmet; he was going to give her a good race after all.

Down to *Rivazza* they shot like bats out of hell, both braking hard as they took the left-hander and then even harder for the second ninety-degree curve. Marie could feel her heart thumping behind her ribs, the adrenalin pumping through her veins.

She almost lost her concentration on the climb to *Viarante Alta*. Veering from the racing line a little, she felt the car judder as it drove over the white rumble strips that edged the track. Forcing herself to remain calm, she quickly righted the car in time for the hellish *Rivazza* again.

Although it was clear to everyone watching, and Marie, that Lawrie was putting up an excellent fight, there was no way he could get past her. Marie was going all out to win and no one, not even the man she cared for most in the whole world, was going to stop her.

The victor's party that night was the best Marie had ever been to. It helped that she had been able to hand a cheque straight over to Lawrie. Though he made a bit of a fuss about all the 'interest' he would be losing out on and tried to persuade her to, 'spread the repayments.'

'No way,' she said, laughing as she gave him a playful punch in the ribs, 'I never want to be in debt to anyone again. Not even you. But,' she added with a lascivious twinkle in her eye, 'I wouldn't mind giving you a taste of what you could have had.'

'What's this – who's tasting who?' Carla asked, coming up behind them. In her hand she held a glass of champagne and she had a very delicious looking Latin in tow, Marie noticed.

The other thing she noticed was how happy and relaxed her friend looked. And how prettily she smiled at her new companion.

Lawrie's cousin Alexa had come up trumps yet again. The man she had sent for Carla was absolutely perfect. Tall, dark and handsome, and a saxophonist, no less.

'You know what that means,' Marie said to Carla when they excused themselves to go to the lavatory.

Carla shook her head. 'I don't really care about his musical ability, Marco is gorgeous and he hasn't stopped flattering me all evening.'

'Well, I'll tell you anyway,' Marie said, pausing to slick a fresh coat of lipstick over her full mouth. She smacked her lips together, then stuck out her tongue and waggled it lewdly at Carla's reflection in the mirror. 'Saxophonists have to have a very flexible one of these,' she said, touching her finger to the tip of her tongue. 'According to everything I've read, they have to practise their mouth exercises every day, for hours and hours . . .'

The way she rolled her eyes suggestively made Carla laugh. 'OK, I get the picture,' she said. 'Lucky me.'

Marie smiled. 'Yes, lucky you. And if anyone deserves

it you do. You've been fabulous. I couldn't have won the Championship without you, or Frank, or any of the others for that matter.'

'Get away with you,' Carla said gruffly as she grabbed her bag and slung it over her shoulder. 'You know I can't stand all that sloppy stuff.'

They rejoined Lawrie and Marco with smiles on their faces.

'Marco suggested we go and stay at his villa for a few days,' Lawrie said, slipping his arm around Marie's waist. 'I don't know if you and Carla would –'

'We'd love to,' Marie cut in quickly. 'Don't take any notice of Carla if she tries to say no.'

'I wasn't going to,' her friend protested, flashing a mock glare at Marie.

Throwing her head back, Marie laughed. She didn't know if it was the prospect of a hedonistic few days with Lawrie at a luxurious villa. Or the fact that she had won the Championship. Or even having the financial burden lifted from her – not to mention the mental strain of having to keep changing her appearance and personality. There was no need to change her identity ever again. Marie was who she was, her true persona, encompassing Amber's strength of purpose and Portia's limitless eroticism. From now on she would dress herself up and put on a wig for no other reason than to have fun.

The relief she felt was overwhelming and tinged with anticipation. For once, the future seemed to stretch out in front of her like a glistening path strewn with bundles of promise. Glancing down at her hands, she realised that in them she held the power to succeed at whatever she wanted to do. The only difficult part would be choosing which direction to follow.

'Are you ready to leave, or would you rather remain in the limelight a little longer?' Lawrie asked her.

She gazed at him, feeling all the warmth of desire, affection and friendship she held for him rise up inside her. As he skimmed his hand provocatively over her hip to rest tantalisingly on the taut curve of her bottom, she felt the warmth turn to raging fire.

'Leave,' she said, making the first decision of her new life, 'and I hope this villa's not too far away. I don't know if I can control myself for very long.'

BLACK LACE NEW BOOKS

Published in January

NADYA'S QUEST
Lisette Allen

Nadya's personal quest leads her to St Petersburg in the summer of 1788. The beautiful city is in a rapturous state of decadence and its Empress, well known for her lascivious appetite, is hungry for a new lover who must be young, handsome and virile. When Nadya brings a Swedish seafarer, the magnificently-proportioned Axel, to the Imperial court, he is soon made the Empress's favourite. Nadya, determined to keep Axel for herself, is drawn into an intrigue of treachery and sedition as hostilities develop between Russia and Sweden.

ISBN 0 352 33135 6

DESIRE UNDER CAPRICORN
Louisa Francis

A shipwreck rips Dita Jones from the polite society of Sydney in the 1870s and throws her into an untamed world where Matt Warrender, a fellow castaway, develops a passion for her he will never forget. Separated after their eventual rescue, Dita is taken back into civilised life where a wealthy stud farmer, Jas McGrady, claims her for his bride. Taken to the rugged terrain of outback Australia, and a new life as Mrs McGrady, Dita realises her husband has a dark secret.

ISBN 0 352 33136 4

Published in February

PULLING POWER
Cheryl Mildenhall

Amber Barclay is a top motor racing driver whose career is sponsored by Portia Lombardi, a professional dominatrix with a taste for control as forceful as Amber's driving. In the run-up to an important race, competition is fierce as Marie Gifford, Portia's financial dependent, sparks a passionate sexual liaison with the dashing Lawrie Samson, Amber's only rival. But what will happen when Lawrie discovers an astonishing link between the three women?

ISBN 0 352 33139 9

THE MASTER OF SHILDEN
Lucinda Carrington

Trapped in a web of sexual and emotional entanglement, interior designer, Elise St John, grabs at the chance to redecorate a remote castle. As she sets about creating rooms in which guests will be able to realise their most erotic fantasies, her own dreams and desires ripen. Caught between Max Lannsen, the dark, broody Master of Shilden, and Blair Devlin, the sexy, debonair riding instructor, Elise realises that her dreams are becoming reality and that the future of these two men suddenly depends on a decision she will be forced to make.

ISBN 0 352 33140 2

MODERN LOVE
An Anthology of Erotic Writings by Women
Edited by Kerri Sharp

For nearly four years Black Lace has dominated the erotic fiction market in the UK and revolutionised the way people think about and write erotica. Black Lace is now a generic term for erotic fiction by and for women. Following the success of *Pandora's Box*, the first Black Lace anthology, *Modern Love* is a collection of extracts from our bestselling contemporary novels. Seduction and mystery and darkly sensual behaviour are the key words to this unique collection of erotic writings from the female imagination.

ISBN 0 352 33158 5

To be published in March

SILKEN CHAINS
Jodi Nicol

Fleeing her scheming guardian and an arranged marriage, Abbie, an innocent young Victorian woman, is thrown from her horse. She awakens in a lavish interior filled with heavenly perfumes to find that Leon Villiers, the wealthy and attractive master of the house, has virtually imprisoned her with sensual pleasures. Using his knowledge of Eastern philosophy and tantric arts, he introduces her to experiences beyond her imagination. But will her guardian's unerring search for her ruin this taste of liberty?

ISBN 0 352 33143 7

THE HAND OF AMUN
Juliet Hastings

Marked from birth, Naunakhte – daughter of a humble scribe – must enter a life of dark eroticism as the servant of the Egyptian god Amun. She becomes the favourite of the high priestess but is accused of an act of lascivious sacrilege and is forced to flee the temple for the murky labyrinth of the city. There she meets Khonsu, a prince of the underworld, but fate draws her back to the temple and she is forced to choose between two lovers – one mortal and the other a god.

ISBN 0 352 33144 5

If you would like a complete list of plot summaries of Black Lace titles, please fill out the questionnaire overleaf or send a stamped addressed envelope to:-

Black Lace, 332 Ladbroke Grove, London W10 5AH

BLACK LACE BACKLIST

All books are priced £4.99 unless another price is given.

------ ✂ --------------------------------

Please send me the books I have ticked above.

Name   ....

Address   ....

                  ....

                  ....

           .... Post Code   ....

Send to: Cash Sales, Black Lace Books, 332 Ladbroke Grove, London W10 5AH.

Please enclose a cheque or postal order, made payable to **Virgin Publishing Ltd**, to the value of the books you have ordered plus postage and packing costs as follows:

UK and BFPO – £1.00 for the first book, 50p for each subsequent book.

Overseas (including Republic of Ireland) – £2.00 for the first book, £1.00 each subsequent book.

If you would prefer to pay by VISA or ACCESS/ MASTERCARD, please write your card number and expiry date here:

....

Please allow up to 28 days for delivery.

Signature   ....

------ ✂ --------------------------------

BLACK
lace

WE NEED YOUR HELP . . .
to plan the future of women's erotic fiction –

– and no stamp required!

Yours are the only opinions that matter.

Black Lace is the first series of books devoted to erotic fiction by women for women.

We intend to keep providing the best-written, sexiest books you can buy. And we'd appreciate your help and valued opinion of the books so far. Tell us what you want to read.

THE BLACK LACE QUESTIONNAIRE

SECTION ONE: ABOUT YOU

1.1 Sex (*we presume you are female, but so as not to discriminate*)
    Are you?
    Male   ☐
    Female   ☐

1.2 Age
    under 21   ☐   21–30   ☐
    31–40   ☐   41–50   ☐
    51–60   ☐   over 60   ☐

1.3 At what age did you leave full-time education?
    still in education   ☐   16 or younger   ☐
    17–19   ☐   20 or older   ☐

1.4 Occupation _____

1.5   Annual household income
          under £10,000   ☐   £10–£20,000   ☐
          £20–£30,000   ☐   £30–£40,000   ☐
          over £40,000   ☐

1.6   We are perfectly happy for you to remain anonymous;
      but if you would like to receive information on other
      publications available, please insert your name and
      address

      _____

      _____

      _____

      _____

SECTION TWO: ABOUT BUYING BLACK LACE BOOKS

2.1   How did you acquire this copy of *Pulling Power*?
          I bought it myself   ☐   My partner bought it   ☐
          I borrowed/found it   ☐

2.2   How did you find out about Black Lace books?
          I saw them in a shop   ☐
          I saw them advertised in a magazine   ☐
          I saw the London Underground posters   ☐
          I read about them in _____
          Other _____

2.3   Please tick the following statements you agree with:
          I would be less embarrassed about buying Black
          Lace books if the cover pictures were less explicit   ☐
          I think that in general the pictures on Black
          Lace books are about right   ☐
          I think Black Lace cover pictures should be as
          explicit as possible   ☐

2.4   Would you read a Black Lace book in a public place – on
      a train for instance?
          Yes   ☐   No   ☐

SECTION THREE: ABOUT THIS BLACK LACE BOOK

3.1 Do you think the sex content in this book is:

Too much ☐ About right ☐

Not enough ☐

3.2 Do you think the writing style in this book is:

Too unreal/escapist ☐ About right ☐

Too down to earth ☐

3.3 Do you think the story in this book is:

Too complicated ☐ About right ☐

Too boring/simple ☐

3.4 Do you think the cover of this book is:

Too explicit ☐ About right ☐

Not explicit enough ☐

Here's a space for any other comments:

SECTION FOUR: ABOUT OTHER BLACK LACE BOOKS

4.1 How many Black Lace books have you read? ☐

4.2 If more than one, which one did you prefer?

4.3 Why?

SECTION FIVE: ABOUT YOUR IDEAL EROTIC NOVEL

We want to publish the books you want to read – so this is your chance to tell us exactly what your ideal erotic novel would be like.

5.1 Using a scale of 1 to 5 (1 = no interest at all, 5 = your ideal), please rate the following possible settings for an erotic novel:

Medieval/barbarian/sword 'n' sorcery ☐
Renaissance/Elizabethan/Restoration ☐
Victorian/Edwardian ☐
1920s & 1930s – the Jazz Age ☐
Present day ☐
Future/Science Fiction ☐

5.2 Using the same scale of 1 to 5, please rate the following themes you may find in an erotic novel:

Submissive male/dominant female ☐
Submissive female/dominant male ☐
Lesbianism ☐
Bondage/fetishism ☐
Romantic love ☐
Experimental sex e.g. anal/watersports/sex toys ☐
Gay male sex ☐
Group sex ☐

Using the same scale of 1 to 5, please rate the following styles in which an erotic novel could be written:

Realistic, down to earth, set in real life ☐
Escapist fantasy, but just about believable ☐
Completely unreal, impressionistic, dreamlike ☐

5.3 Would you prefer your ideal erotic novel to be written from the viewpoint of the main male characters or the main female characters?

Male ☐ Female ☐
Both ☐

5.4 What would your ideal Black Lace heroine be like? Tick as many as you like:

Dominant	☐	Glamorous	☐
Extroverted	☐	Contemporary	☐
Independent	☐	Bisexual	☐
Adventurous	☐	Naïve	☐
Intellectual	☐	Introverted	☐
Professional	☐	Kinky	☐
Submissive	☐	Anything else?	☐
Ordinary	☐	_____	

5.5 What would your ideal male lead character be like? Again, tick as many as you like:

Rugged	☐		
Athletic	☐	Caring	☐
Sophisticated	☐	Cruel	☐
Retiring	☐	Debonair	☐
Outdoor-type	☐	Naïve	☐
Executive-type	☐	Intellectual	☐
Ordinary	☐	Professional	☐
Kinky	☐	Romantic	☐
Hunky	☐		
Sexually dominant	☐	Anything else?	☐
Sexually submissive	☐	_____	

5.6 Is there one particular setting or subject matter that your ideal erotic novel would contain?

_____

SECTION SIX: LAST WORDS

6.1 What do you like best about Black Lace books?

_____

6.2 What do you most dislike about Black Lace books?

_____

6.3 In what way, if any, would you like to change Black Lace covers?

_____

6.4   Here's a space for any other comments:

_____
_____
_____
_____

_____

Thank you for completing this questionnaire. Now tear it out of the book – carefully! – put it in an envelope and send it to:

Black Lace
FREEPOST
London
W10 5BR

No stamp is required if you are resident in the U.K.